THE
HUNGARIAN
GAME

THE HUNGARIAN GAME

Roy Hayes

Secker & Warburg · London

First published in England 1973 by
Martin Secker & Warburg Limited
14 Carlisle Street, London W1V 6NN

Copyright © 1973 by Roy Hayes

436 19135 0

Printed offset litho and bound in Great Britain
by Cox & Wyman Ltd,
London, Fakenham and Reading

For Armineh and Helene

ACKNOWLEDGMENTS

My thanks to the Agency for encouraging me to write this fictionalized documentary. In these days when intelligence groups are so easily attacked—and so utterly without defense because of the sensitive nature of our work—it is a distinct pleasure to put this Project Report into the public's hands. I hope that it will bring about a better understanding of our Agency and the people who make it go.

Very special thanks indeed to my Field Officer, Mr. ———* (the F. O.), for his assistance in editing out certain Q Clearance details that are neither germane to this report nor safe for you to know.

*Edited, F. O., SoCal SubSection

Homo homini aut deus aut lupus.
(Man is to man either a god or a wolf.)
Desiderius Erasmus

In chess, the winner is the one
who makes the next-to-last mistake.
Savelii Grigorevich Tartakover

N.B.   Like plumbing, TV repair, dentistry and other trades, intelligence work has a sometimes confusing argot. When in doubt about terminology, or about political institutions and personalities mentioned herein, please refer to the Glossary that begins on page 339.

THE
HUNGARIAN
GAME

1

Q: Will you explain to the Committee, sir, the qualifications for employment by your agency?

A: Yes, sir. Ahn . . . dedication. *Profound* dedication.

Q: And that, sir, is the extent of it?

A: Dedication, sir, and . . . ahn . . . sincerity.

Minutes of the Hearings,
Subcommittee on National Security Affairs
Volume VII
Page 59

I have never worn a cloak, nor have I ever used a dagger.
My suits are all off-the-rack and the Smith & Wesson .38 Police Special that I keep in a night stand by my bed is for home protection only. I bought the revolver with my own money. It's not even tax deductible.

Although I've been through Unarmed Combat Training at the Agency's school in Virginia, I'd only had to use that knowledge once prior to the Routenfield affair. And that wasn't during my overseas duty but in one of those button-down bars just off Wilshire Boulevard. I had struck up a conversation with the wrong girl. Her friend was a particularly aggressive advertising body; an account executive whose head was filled with booze instead of discretion. When I heard the bone snap in his wrist I wondered if I'd been overtrained for my job.

The Agency I work for, like most intelligence groups (yet

unlike those I've read about), is strictly an information-gathering service. While some of our counterintelligence people lead rather exciting lives shooting up enemy operatives in exotic cities, my own life was relatively undisturbed until Routenfield. Before that I was the Student Rad Project Officer in our SoCal SubSection. I spent most of my time reading and forwarding reports from our university informants.

When I tired of correcting their grammar I plotted to put the skids under my secretary Harriet.

My pay was fairly decent; with that—along with whatever I could pad onto the expense account and overtime slips—I'd managed to stay about fifteen pounds overweight and had even purchased a 1932 Mann Egerton 3.5 Bentley Sport Saloon that verged on complete restoration and total collapse.

Marion's alimony and the child support payments are automatically deducted from my pay. My Civil Service pension plan is comfortable enough. And there is some chance that I might live to collect it.

While basically dull (and who can deny the mind-numbing boredom of monitoring a stranger's phone calls? ["How's the weather down there darling?" "Wonderful. It's just wonderful. How's the weather at home?" "Wet. Jesus, it's been raining like hell. Three sparrows drowned in the birdbath." "Here, Robby wants to say hello." "Wuwho dada." "How's daddy's little man you little rascal you?" "Wuwho dada."]), my work is occasionally interesting.

Like a seismograph printout of Southern California, my work graph's hohum index buzzes along nicely for a time when—*whoops!*—the needle bangs off the chart and something odd happens.

For every *whoops*, though, there are endless phone taps to yawn over, reports to muddle, memoranda to ignore and expense accounts to pad. And most often the *whoopses* turn out to be nothing more than a female embassy staffer caught *flagrante delicto* with a bearded Russian or, and it happens with embarrassing frequency, a male embassy staffer caught *flagrante delicto* with a bearded Russian.

The Routenfield affair began with a *whoops* when I saw Gyula Jakaz, like Lazarus, risen from his grave.

2

Johnny the Contractor checked into the Beverly Wildwood shortly before noon. He hunched over the register and wrote "Richard T. Hagopian" in neat script.

His luggage was travel-scarred and punctuated with customs tags from England, France and Germany; countries he had never seen. Although he had been in Los Angeles for nearly a week, time enough to have checked himself into another hotel under another name, Hagopian arrived at the Wildwood in the hotel's airport limousine.

Details.

Details were the key to success and Hagopian worried about them. Details. He felt a twinge in his stomach. That glass of warm milk at the airport hadn't done much for his gut. *Christ.* It was almost impossible to steal prescription pads nowadays. Just one bottle of Probanthine, he thought. Just one.

The bellman unlocked the door to Bungalow 14 and Hagopian stepped through to inspect it. An incredibly tasteless collection of Regency and Salon furniture in the drawing room. Hotel furnishings in the bedroom. But a terrific little gas stove in the kitchenette. And the air conditioning drew fresh air from the outside rather than recirculating the stale air within the bungalow. Beautiful. That would help spend whatever odors his work might create.

The bellman rolled Hagopian's three suitcases into the bungalow on a cart and began settling them on a stand next to the small desk. Lifting the final and largest case he grunted with the effort. Cords rose from his neck.

"Samples," Hagopian said. "I should have warned you."

18

He looked through the sliding glass door onto his private patio, then over the patio wall to the green and rolling grounds beyond. "Okay to jog in the morning?"

"Guess so," the bellman said. "Those Russians stayed here once. Ran around the place every morning."

"Russians?"

"Yes, sir. Cosmonauts."

Class, Hagopian thought. Flash and class. "How about the squash courts and the pool. What time do they open in the morning?" Hagopian pressed a finger to his graying mustache as though wondering if it was still there.

"You'll find that in your directory, sir. In the desk. Tells you about the hours for all the facilities. There's a steam room, too, if you want to use it."

Hagopian grinned; unattractive teeth under an irregular, pock-scarred nose. Any other guy would have been holed up in a dump or some abandoned building. Not me pal, he thought. Steam rooms and squash courts; that's what you get when you're the cream.

"I don't know anyone in town," he said. "What're the chances of getting up a game?"

The bellman said, "Shouldn't be any problem. We're the only hotel in Los Angeles with squash courts, so a lot of Easterners who've moved out here will drop by looking for a partner."

"Terrific," Hagopian said.

"Is there anything more, sir?"

"Not now. I want to sleep a while."

"Thank you, sir." The bellman held his folded bill in one hand while draping a Do Not Disturb over the doorknob. "Shall I tell the switchboard to hold your calls?"

Hagopian nodded. "Thank you." There would be no calls for Hagopian: He didn't exist.

"Thank you, sir."

"Thank you."

The bellman stopped his retreat through the closing door, popping his head back into the room. "Thank you."

He'd had the last word.

Alone, Hagopian pulled on a pair of light cotton gloves, bolted the front door and unlocked the large heavy case. He removed a layer of knitted shirts and revealed a locked panel. This case, this handmade love of his life, perfect even to the "American Tourister" label that was riveted under its reinforced handle, was far too valuable to travel with him by air. Hagopian couldn't risk landing in Los Angeles while the case was on its way to Seattle. He had crated the case in Detroit and shipped it REA. Slower, but much more reliable.

He slipped a key into the panel's double-tumbler lock and eased it open. The panel turned back on its hinges to show the tools of Hagopian's trade. Each item was cradled in plush-lined Styrofoam that had been cut and neatly shaped. Nothing could rattle. Nothing could scratch. Nothing could bend.

Hagopian's tools ranged from a Louisville Slugger bat to a rare M1944/16 SIG-Neuhausen 9 mm. Parabellum with three extra clips, each loaded with sixteen live rounds. From a Minox 8 mm. camera to a police band radio. There was enough electronic equipment in the case to wire a moderately large house.

Hagopian smiled, baring his large ugly teeth.

The word was out about Johnny the Contractor's tool kit. One guy in Newark had even put out a contract of ten big ones just to get the tools. But no one, not the other guys in the business or the sharp dudes who employed them, knew who Johnny the Contractor was or what he looked like. Hell, even his agent Bernie had never seen his face. Hagopian thought, you mothers miss the details.

He was the cream; the contractor's contractor. While the others banged around with their faces hanging out like old

Murder Inc. guys he was hitting impossible targets for unbelievable retainers. Imagination, preparedness, attention to details and the proper tools, Hagopian thought. That's what made him the cream; that and the intelligence and cool that helped him blend into almost any situation. The cream. Though Bernie tried to get him to work more often—and why not? Hagopian thought; his agent got ten percent of the action—he accepted only four jobs a year.

Hagopian refocused on his case. Between the makeup kit and a collection of credit-card blanks there were two crudely finished black boxes the size and shape of transistor radios. Hagopian lifted them out and, after flipping on the toggle switch, pressed a button marked "BC" on the first box. A red glow illuminated the button. Releasing it, he checked the batteries on the second box. They both were ready.

He began in the bedroom, paying particular attention to wall plugs, light switches, telephone and lamps. Punching the tone button, he twisted the dial beneath it to demodulate the sound across the radio frequency spectrum to see if there was a mike in the room that was live and transmitting. Hagopian checked out the power lines with his second black box; this one would pick up baby-sitter bugs. It took fifteen minutes to cover the room. It took a half hour more to double check.

The bedroom was clean.

The bathroom, kitchenette and patio were clean. And, electronically, the drawing room seemed clean.

An unbroken coat of paint covered one air conditioning duct plate. But on the other a hairline crack violated the paint between plate and wall. And the screw heads were marred with scratches.

He turned the thermostat down to 55° and walked back to the plate. A rumbling noise came from the ceiling, then settled into a steady whine. Hagopian held his hand in front of

21

the plate. No draft. He walked to the other duct plate and held up his hand. It was cold. He moved the Honeywell back up to COMFORT RANGE and started working.

Hagopian used a knife from the kitchenette to unscrew and lift away the plate. He dropped it on the couch. Inside the duct, gently bedded in a polyfoam cushion, was an Elradyne CM 1406–1r ceramic microphone. It was an older model, large enough to cover a dime. The wire leading from it followed the duct, elbowing up toward the roof.

It was hell trying to move his arm beyond the duct's elbow. Tonight though was soon enough. Tonight he could inspect the roof and learn where the microphone wire might lead him.

As he replaced the duct plate Hagopian remembered the first time he'd found a bug. It had been wedged into a wooden lamp base, sealed over with green felt on the bottom, and Hagopian had ripped out the mike and smashed it before showing it to his older partner Tony the Teacher.

"What are you, kid, some kind of stupid?" Tony had said in a low voice. "Now they know we're here, hunh?" His tone had carried an undisguised edge of contempt. "They know that we know about 'em, see. So the next thing you wanna do is—you wanna go over to their hotel and tell 'em 'Hey, buddy, there's a coupla guys are gonna try and hit on yous.'" Tony had spat on the crushed mike in Johnny's hand and now, thinking back on it, Hagopian cringed with self-loathing. Oh Christ, he thought, oh Christ. *Hate*.

Details. Remember the details.

When they'd cornered their man, getting him into the front seat of Tony's old Chevy, it was Hagopian who burned him. He took the guy out with a two-foot length of picture wire and sweet *Jesus* it was great; almost like being with a woman but even better in the sense that it erased his stupid mistake with the bug. "You've got a touch for it, kid," Tony said. "You sure got the touch."

22

Still looking at the air conditioning duct, Hagopian stepped from the couch.

Had someone tagged him? Hagopian stretched out on the couch. Who was "someone"? His client? Impossible. The target? Impossible.

Few knew of Johnny the Contractor. And no one knew he was in Los Angeles. Hagopian, certainly, was in Los Angeles. He had just checked into the Beverly Wildwood. Richardson was in L.A. too. He'd used that name to check into the Hollywood Executive House a week ago. But *he*, Johnny the Contractor—the man who accepted the job—*he* was supposed to be in Detroit; not due until tomorrow. Not even Bernie could have known he was here.

And hell, the only guy who could have tied Hagopian's naked face with Johnny the Contractor was his old partner. But the Teacher was dead—long dead. Hagopian remembered the heft and texture of his staghorn-grip switchblade. The knife had a tempered, eight-inch blade with a blood groove running the length of it. Whenever he pressed the button on that mother, flashing the blade open, the thing nearly jumped out of his hand. Tony was long, long, long dead. It had been a sort of graduation exercise.

Hagopian lit a True Menthol. Possibly it was an old tap. God knew, the Elradyne was a classic. It had looked as archaic as an ear trumpet. He dragged deeply on the cigarette. Possibly it was an old tap.

Possibly.

Item: 12 lbs. potatoes (Idaho) $2.47

Death became Gyula Jakaz. He was a vigorous, ruddy-cheeked corpse when I saw him at Mammoth Lakes Airport.

I had spent the weekend skiing Mammoth with a girl whose name I never quite caught. What I remember of her was the comfortable roundness of her body; soft warm curves that were a pound or so beyond pleasing plumpness. Our two-day romp had been enjoyable but not sensational; no bad spills or twisted joints, though more than the usual snuggling together for warmth, among other things, in the ill-heated cabin. Although she skied like a sack of grapefruit that had been flung into the snow, my chubby bunny was first-rate for warmth.

We had confirmed our reservations and were waiting for the last flight of the day when he walked into the crowded airport office. Except for his wedge of a face he was hardly noticeable in the room. A cubic yard or so of fresh, chill air followed him and died a horrible death in our atmosphere of ski sweat and cigarette smoke.

"I know him from somewhere," my plump bunny said. She pouted quizzically at the counter. "Aspen I think."

The man with the wedge of a face waited anxiously behind a standby who was oozing charm all over the ticketing girl. The standby's white teeth flashed as he spoke to the girl. "You know me, honey." He smiled; bright pearls of teeth in a snow-

24

burned face. "And I really have to get back to L.A. this afternoon. I mean really."

"Gee, I'm sorry," the girl said. Her arm was in a cast on which ASK ME NEXT SEASON was crudely printed in Day-Glo red. "Can't you wait another five minutes for the ticketed passenger to show or no-show?"

The crowd shifted like a sleeping animal and my already limited view of wedge-face and the standby was blocked. "He sure isn't the kind of guy you forget," the bunny said with a sigh. I looked at her and thought there's no accounting for personal taste. Wedge-face was a distinctive looking type, but hardly the sort to raise a sigh from the bunny who was with me in spite of my very average, unheroic appearance.

I heard the standby murmur something to the girl. Only ". . . an extra ten for you . . ." came through.

"I'm sorry. I really must wait another five minutes for Mr. Kay to show up."

"I am here. Milos Kay. I have a ticket."

The crowd shifted again and I watched wedge-face elbow in front of the standby with a look of mild irritation as though the other had made an impolite noise in public. "Is Milos Kay familiar?" I asked the bunny.

"Not him," she said. "*Him.*" She pointed a plump finger at the bronzed blond standby. "I think he's a ski instructor."

I looked from the standby to Kay. What I could see of the man's face grated like sandpaper at the rough edges of my memory. Who did I know with a Balkan accent? Was it Serbo-Croat? Or Slovene? Turn around, I thought. Let's get a good look at your face.

"Are you Mr. Kay?" the girl asked.

"Yes, yes. Milos Kay." He looked at the reservations sheet as she checked off his name. "I purchased a round-trip ticket from Los Angeles." His accent wasn't Balkan but Magyar;

25

he'd lived in Hungary a long time before he learned English. "I am confirmed on this flight?"

"Yes sir," the girl said. As she tore off a portion of his ticket she said, "Sorry," to the standby.

"You can always tell a fabulous skier," the bunny said. She looked pointedly from my bright new clothes to the standby's shapeless parka and faded stretch pants. "A super-good skier has old clothes and new equipment." My skis and boots were going on five years.

Turn around, I thought as I watched Milos Kay. He responded as though I'd spoken out loud. His face was sharp enough to split logs. An extreme widow's peak of hair gave his head an aerodynamic look; he might have been born in a wind tunnel. What caught the attention, though, was his nose. It cleaved the air before him like the blade of an ax. Despite his unforgettable features I couldn't place him.

Closing my eyes I riffed a mental thumb across my memory's filing cards. His face should have been younger, fifteen years younger at least. I was in college then. Professor Kay? I drew a blank. There was something wrong with his face, something basically different about its color and texture and animation. I opened my eyes and looked at him again and when the memory came to me it landed like the wakening aftershock of a nightmare.

Gyula Jakaz.

"Someone walk on your grave?" asked my plump little bunny. "You look ghastly."

"I've got to go back to the cabin," I said. "I forgot my watch."

"No you haven't. It's right there on your wrist."

"My pocket watch," I said. "My Waltham stem-winder." I hadn't recognized him because I'd never seen him like this— not in three-dimensional living color. "It's in that night stand

26

by the bed." The face I remembered was not only younger, it was grainy black and white; a two-by-two-inch photograph taped to the front page of a slim dossier that had landed on my desk in Budapest five years ago. "I didn't pack it," I said. "I'm sure I didn't." When I saw it, the dossier was already ten years old. It had DECEASED stamped across its cover.

"You *can't* go back," she said.

"Got to. That was my grandfather's watch," I lied. I'd bought the Waltham from a pawnshop. Right now it was packed in a rolled-up pair of sweat socks in my overnighter. "Been in the family since 1880."

"What about me?"

"You're adorable but you've only been in the family since Friday, pussycat. Wait here and I'll fix you a ride from L.A. International." I patted her generous bottom. "It can't be helped. I've got to miss that plane."

"You're really *something!*"

"I know, lover." I patted her bottom again, more for my own pleasure than for her reassurance. "Don't fret, I'll sell my ticket to your friend from Aspen." Her face brightened. "I'm sure he'll give you a lift from the airport in L.A." I patted her once more. It was possibly the last I would see of that comfortable derrière. "After all, it's for the memory of Gran'pa."

I didn't tell her it was for the memory of Gyula Jakaz; a sort of memorial service some fifteen years after the curious fact of his death.

I waved goodbye to my plump girl as the plane taxied away, but she didn't notice. She was laughing brightly at something the fabulous skier from Aspen had said. I watched them lift off and wondered if I would ever see her again. Very likely not. *Sic transit gloria* Sunday.

27

"Jeez, babe, it's Sunday," Basset said. "Don't you ever take a day off?"

I hunkered into the less than private area created by two soundproofing panels that flanked the pay phone. With a hand cupped around the telephone mouthpiece I said quietly, "Things could be worse. You could be stranded here at Mammoth. I gave up my seat on the last flight out . . . and my date left with the plane."

"So how come you didn't follow him?"

"With what, the Bentley?" I closed my eyes and rubbed my eyebrows in frustration. "That's what I'd be using after we landed at LAX. The Bentley. I'd be less noticeable in a hook and ladder. This one is for you, pal," I said.

"You've gotta understand. My wife's parents are coming over for dinner."

"So much the better. You've got an excuse to skip out."

"But I *like* my wife's folks. Her dad is putting me into a choice real estate deal out in the desert. Ground floor stuff, babe. It's a real sleeper . . . recreational land."

I had visions of Basset's wife's father's "sleeper." For those who fancied lizard shooting it could be terrific recreational property. "Pleasure before business, Frank. You'll remember what our boy looks like?"

"Gray hair, widow's peak, big schnozz, red ski parka and no luggage."

"And phone the old man when you get to LAX. Tell him I'm going to sniff around Mammoth for a couple of days. I'll give him a call tomorrow."

"Okay, sure." Basset was silent for a moment. "Look, there're over a hundred guys in the SoCal SubSection. Why don't . . ."

28

"This isn't a clear line, pal."

"What if I lose the guy? What if he slips me?"

What if you don't go to the airport, I thought, and tell me later that he slipped you? "I'll write Mrs. Basset a lovely letter," I said. "And I'm sure the old man will send flowers."

No one sent flowers when Colonel Gyula Jakaz was killed in '56 during an assault on the AVH barracks overlooking the Danube and St. Stephen's Boulevard. Everyone agreed that Colonel Jakaz was better off dead: students, workers, the Red Army—everyone. As a devout Stalinist of the former Rákosi Mátyás regime, he was out of favor with Nagy Imre's liberal new government and with Nagy's shoe-thumping antagonist in the Kremlin.

(For that matter, few were sure who was in favor with whom. Chairman and First Secretary Khrushchev had unwittingly set up Hungary [and, before that, Poland] for ethnocentric bloodletting with his de-Stalinization policies of early '56. After all, the pro-Moscow backbone of Hungary was equally pro-Stalinist. Had Nikita Sergeyevich not de-clawed the Stalinists—Rákosi, Gerö Ernö and Gyula Jakaz, among others—there is doubt within the Agency that Hungary would have blown apart on October 23rd. While throwing out the bath water—the Stalinists—Khrushchev managed a spectacular infanticide.)

At any rate; Colonel Jakaz, like all men, was born to die on the day his number was drawn. Student members of Petöfi Circle drew his number with a vengeance, blowing out bricks, chairs, typewriters, desks and anonymous shards of human flesh and bone from the AVH building. He was better off dead.

Some ten years after his death I read the Agency's dossier on

Gyula Jakaz during my tour of duty in Budapest. Reading old documents was part of the Dulles syllogism: If you know where they've been and can see where they are, you therefore might conclude where they're going.

The Jakaz dossier was vague about his origins and confusing about his function. He was born in Pest or Györ or Miskolc or possibly not in Hungary at all. He functioned as an AVH hatchet man in Budapest or as Soviet liaison at the AVH prison and training center in Nyiregyháza. Although the only solid data we had on him were the name of his dog and the degree of obvious clout that he carried with the former government, it was generally agreed that Gyula Jakaz was a dangerous body. Where the Petöfi Circle students hated him, Rákosi's functionaries were terrified of him.

I neither hated Jakaz nor feared him. I simply wondered why he was alive—and who had sent him to SoCal SubSection. AVH? Or KGB?

The Agency's dossier on Colonel Jakaz was never completed. It had been initiated in June of '56 and its subject had been scattered like so much birdseed over the Danube and St. Stephen's Boulevard in October of the same year. Since the Agency was busy squirreling local friends into the new government that Kádár János was trying to piece together from the torn fabric of his country, we never completed Jakaz' dossier. Gyula Jakaz was both dead and a dead issue when I read of him in '66.

When I saw him at the Mammoth Lakes Airport five years later he became a live issue indeed.

The room had emptied with the departure of the plane. Nearly a dozen standbys had taken the stage back to Mammoth village. I was alone with the ticketing girl. I looked at the cast on her arm and wondered what I was expected to ask

30

her next season. What I had in mind didn't require the full use of two arms. "I'm stranded," I said. "Can someone give me a lift back to the village?"

"I'll be leaving in an hour," she said. "Can you wait?"

"Yes," I said.

"You shouldn't have let him buy your ticket. He's notorious with women, you know."

"Ah well," I said. "I feel I got the better of the trade. What are you doing for dinner tonight?"

I smiled sincerely when she looked up. She smiled back with even greater sincerity. "If we can get a sitter, my husband is taking me to the Rafters."

Hohum.

Gyula Jakaz left no more impression on Mammoth Lakes than a pebble in a stream. Whatever ripples he made went almost unnoticed in the press of winter visitors. And I was limited in the ripples I could safely make while searching out his trail. That is: a covert investigation becomes immediately overt when every innkeeper and gas station attendant in town knows that a bureaucratic body is nosing around for a man named Milos Kay or, worse, for a man named Gyula Jakaz. My job is not without its frustrations.

Since hunger is the lowest common denominator, I started with the grocers and provisioners in the village. Although my Magyar was a little rusty from years of disuse, I affected a Hungarian accent and went shopping. After buying eleven pounds of potatoes from as many stores I picked up a thread on Jakaz/Kay.

As the twelfth clerk weighed my twelfth pound of spuds I sighed and said, "Very beautiful place for a vacation, but also a very lonely place for a foreigner."

He paused with his fingers hovering over the cash register

31

keys and gave me a sidelong glance as though wondering if I would leap the counter and do something familiar with him.

"Oh plenty of girls here," I said. "But back home in Budapest I could play chess and drink a toast . . . *'Egészsegedre!'* when winter nights grew long."

"Oh, Budapest," the clerk said. "Bulgarian, are you?"

"Magyar," I said. "Hungarian. Plenty of Hungarians in Los Angeles. Not any up here."

"There's a guy talks like you. He stays up on Pine Vale Drive I think. Nice guy . . . quiet, you know. Looks kind of Indian, like on the old nickels." The clerk laughed. "This guy's got a face, you could chop firewood with it."

"Nothing," I said into the phone. "He stays somewhere on Pine Vale Drive . . . maybe. I checked the county property tax rolls over at Bridgeport, but there's nothing remotely like Kay or Jakaz for Pine Vale. How are things at your end?"

"Basset did well," the F. O. said. His voice was crisp and clear on the phone, as though he had taken a special diction course from Pacific Tel. "He followed the party to a prune ranch in . . ."

"A *prune* ranch!"

". . . in the Palmdale area. His car is registered under the name Kay, but the ranch is owned by a party named Steven Routenfield. Does that ring a bell?"

"A *prune* ranch?"

"Come come. I'm not interested in your sophomoric sense of humor. What does 'Routenfield' mean to you?"

I struggled to control the laughter. "Two things," I said. "Before he dropped out of public life he was involved in political activities somewhat to the right of Alaric the Visigoth. And, two, he is listed on the Mono County tax rolls as a property owner on Pine Vale Drive."

32

"You are quite sure?" the F. O. asked.

"He's not just any old landholder . . . he owns nearly forty acres that reach from Pine Vale Drive into the wilderness. And with Routenfield's money, it's not the kind of name you miss. I'm sure, yes."

The F. O. said nothing. I knew what he was waiting for. I'd worked with him for a year in Eastern Europe and almost three years in SoCal SubSection. We had gotten to a point in our communications where certain forms were observed like the predictable gestures of Kabuki drama.

"The next logical step is to get a backgrounder," I said. "Will you telex Virginia for me to see what they've got on our party?"

"I have and they don't," the F. O. said. "They know what you know; that slim file you read some years ago is the extent of our information. But not the extent of our sources of information. I'll set up a lunch for you with Beebee."

"You're not damn selective in your business associates," I said.

The F. O. laughed once, "Ha!" like the bark of a taciturn dog. "One look at my staff would tell you that," he said. "And frankly I would do business with Kim Philby if the price were right and the data sufficiently interesting."

"The next logical step after that," I said, ignoring his thrust, "is a safe house. I'll get Basset going on it."

Generally speaking a safe house is used for clandestine meetings in not-overly-friendly countries. In this case, however, obscurity was our motive: The investigation of Gyula Jakaz might call for certain extralegal tactics on our part—and we would set up the place to obscure our ties with the Agency's downtown offices. (A former Project Officer, in the course of a similar investigation, had kidnapped—there is no other word for it; we are not empowered to arrest anyone, only investigate them—had once kidnapped a KGB agent and dragged him

33

downtown. He was unfortunately followed by a reporter from the L.A. *Times*. In the ensuing mess the F. O. was nearly unseated from SoCal SubSection. He was not amused.)

"I've already spoken with him," the F. O. said. He was silent again and I wondered what I'd forgotten. Finally he said, "Much nicer up there midweek, is it?"

"I hadn't noticed," I said. "I've spent most of my time arguing the price of potatoes."

"Potatoes?"

"It's hard to explain," I said. "What I mean to say is, I've been busy working on this thing and hadn't noticed and, yes, you're right; it's better midweek because you can get on the mountain and ski instead of waiting in line all day."

"Take another day or so up there," the F. O. said. "You're getting soft. The exercise will do you good."

He was pleased that I had spotted Gyula Jakaz. It was the closest he could come to saying "thank you."

4

Lovely vu home, cls in, 15 min to B.H., 10 min to Vly, 4 bed, 3 bth, lots of entrtmnt area, ideal for lrg fmly, safe fr smll chldrn.

Los Angeles sprawls in a large flat soup plate that our Air Pollution Control District calls "the basin." From east to west the basin is divided physically and culturally by a ridge of mountains: the Santa Monicas. And winding along the crest of the Santa Monica Mountains like a piece of limp string is Mulholland Drive. From its beginning at the Pacific Ocean to its terminus near the Hollywood Reservoir, Mulholland claws its way across the mountain ridges and leaves a forty-mile scar of narrow twisting asphalt.

The pale yellow house on Mulholland was in a sparsely populated area between Laurel and Coldwater canyons. There were no other houses for two miles on either side. And the yellow house was cantilevered out over a four-hundred-foot drop. It was a very expensive piece of real estate that Basset had found.

As I wedged open the electric gate latch with my American Express card I made a mental note that its easily raped mechanism would be among the first items on our list of repairs and conversions.

I nursed the Bentley and my hangover through the gate and parked in front of a four-car garage, making another note in my head; we would need remote-control door openers for quick access to the garages. A drive full of cars or an abundance of activity in broad daylight would attract attention. And even in this nearly desolate area our comings and goings to a private residence all but guaranteed an inquiry from the Los Angeles Police Department. The F. O. did not like inquiries from local law agencies.

I walked through the vacant old house, listening to my footsteps echo in its hollow rooms as I inspected them, and was leaning on the terrace railing when I heard a car crunch across the gravel drive. Pulling myself away from the view I returned through the house in time to open the front door before he could knock.

I said, "We can't go on meeting like this."

"Nice place Basset picked," the F. O. said. His face was without shadow, almost two-dimensional in the whitewashed room.

"It's okay," I said. "It won't take much to make it secure. Let me show you around."

"In a moment. First let's have a look at Basset's famous view." With a confidence that seemed born of knowledge he took the shortest route from front door to terrace. Curious man. I wondered if he'd been there before or if his clinically logical mind had told him that there could be only one path to the terrace.

We were both leaning against the terrace rail, puffing at our cigars and absorbing the view. The city spread out before us for miles in all directions backdropped by superb mountains that rose majestically from the noonday smog.

"When Haring sells you the package, we'll take it," the F. O. said. "It's a hair over budget but it's exactly the kind of place I like. Very secure." He grinned wolfishly at the surrounding land and sighted down his cigar, going "bang bang bang" at the sage and wild mustard. "One man could hold back a battalion from here."

36

"If he sells me the package, I'll sign the lease today," I said.

"When," the F. O. corrected. "Not 'if.' When. When he sells you the package." He handed me an envelope heavy with cash.

"Whose name shall I use?"

"Your own."

"Which one?"

"Charles R. Remly," the F. O. said. "I'll arrange your credit references for the lease. Just call Documents when you need them."

If you met him on the street you'd think the F. O. was a successful little banker or the administrator of a conglomerate. Whatever the business activity you would know that he was a tiger in his field. What he wanted he got. And he used the shortest line to get it, pushing and kicking aside anything that might stand in his path. Years ago, when I first started working for him, the F. O. admitted that his small and very slight stature had made his childhood years the most miserable experience imaginable. But as he grew older he was happy that his final, adult height was just under five foot three. "It gave me a sense of uniqueness," he said. "It wasn't a Napoleonic feeling, not at all. I felt that I was developing my own sense of megalomania and my own will to succeed."

He was in perfect condition, far better shape than I, with not an extra pound on his small frame which he clothed in handmade suits. He tended toward banker's stripes and rich wool fabrics and such tailored details as sleeve cuff buttons that actually buttoned, a special pocket inside the jacket so his cigar case would not bulge, and inverted box pleats instead of a vent in the back.

"What if Haring won't sell?" I asked.

The F. O. offered me a tight little smile and rubbed the manicure on his left hand with the fingertips of his right.

"Let's not discuss that. Not even as a hypothetical point, hmm?"

I puffed at the cigar and gauged the determination in his face. I said, "Why pay for Haring's information? It might knock a few months off the project, but it compromises us to the extent that Haring knows we're interested in the package he's selling. What if he's after Gyula Jakaz too? What if he knows something about the Hungarian end of it that he's not willing to sell us?"

"It's a risk," the F. O. said. "But it's going to shorten the project by more than a few months. I want this whole investigation tied up and on the DDI's desk within thirty days."

"No way."

"*Thirty days, I said. Not a day over.*"

"Who's leaning on you?"

The F. O. rubbed his thumb against his middle and index fingers as though he was feeling the texture of a fine fabric. "Budget," he said. "It always comes down to that, doesn't it? They're talking about consolidating all of the regional Sub-Sections into one big windowless office in the ———* building. Without some measurable proof that we are indispensable, SoCal SubSection may not exist after next month."

He was silent for a moment.

"It won't be so bad for you," he said. "They'll give you a nice broom closet at the Federal Building here in L.A. But I despise the idiot, bureaucratic games they play at ———*. I've been with the Agency since it existed. Before that, even. I don't intend to spend my last years regimenting piles of paper on some anonymous desk."

I shaved a quarter-inch ash from my cigar and watched it plummet over the railing. An errant breeze carried it back and forth as it dropped to the hillside below.

* Edited, *F. O. SoCal SubSection*

38

"Careful with that," the F. O. snapped. "This is a fire zone." He contemplated his own cigar for a moment, then shifted it to his left hand and turned to face me. "Some other things you must be careful of." He reached up and punched a finger against my chest. "Haring's not what he seems to be."

"He never was," I said.

"Come now?"

"I'm just a slack-jawed Project Officer," I said. "I'm not supposed to know that Beebee's a freelance body from Rhodesia. My God. What does Virginia take us for? Every time they want to run a security check they dust off old Beebee Haring and send him around as a kind of crypto-Colonel Blimp from London who just wants to 'buy a few nonsensitive tots of gossip, old man.' Jesus, what a farce. No wonder you don't look forward to going back to a desk surrounded by those lumps. They couldn't pass their own kidney stones, let alone a Postal Service exam, so they wind up at the Agency."

The F. O. raised and lowered himself brightly on his toes and smiled like the father of an eight year old who just knocked one over the fence. "I must remember that," he said, "next time I have lunch with the Secretary."

With his luck, I thought, the Postmaster General would be lunching with them when he repeated it.

"Look," I said and pointed. Two hawks were gliding in circles, buoyed by a warm updraft from the canyon below. They floated effortlessly as their wing-tip feathers rippled in the breeze. "Beautiful. Right in the heart of the city."

"Hawks survive," the F. O. said. "The canyons are full of predators. Hawks, hunting owls, coyotes, raccoons, opossum."

"And rats," I said. The hawks circled and circled; there was no rush, they were the hunters. "I'll need an extended personnel authorization; the more bodies I have, the less time it'll take."

The F. O. pulled a thin doeskin-bound notebook and a gold ballpoint pen from his jacket. Holding the pen above a virgin sheet of paper he cocked an eyebrow at me. "How many?" he asked.

"As many as I can get." The hawks circled with cool assurance; they could hunt at leisure since they had no budget worries. "As many as it takes to find out what a dead man's been up to these past fifteen years."

The F. O. drew back the corners of his mouth to form a fine, dry line. "Anything else you need?" His pen still hovered over the paper.

"A new secretary," I said. "Harriet's getting harder to take with every new day."

The notebook snapped shut. "Bring this one in for me and I'll get you a new secretary. Any particular model?"

"Large breasts," I said. "Large breasts and a willing disposition."

"I'm not interested in your sexual fantasies." He pushed away from the balcony and walked back into the house with neat little steps. "Show me around."

But he was already ahead of me, walking briskly through the house with a firm, almost proprietary gait. His footsteps cracked with the authority of pistol shots on the bare, hardwood floors. "Nice," he said of the kitchen. His words reverberated in the empty room like an echo in a cave. "You and your people can bring in groceries. Avoid long restaurant lunches, eh?"

"You mean keep the expense account down," I said.

"That too." He ran one of his immaculate hands across the inside surface of the ventilating hood over the stove. His fingertips came back with a coating of grease. He stared at his hand as though a dog had relieved itself there. "Well now." He shook his head. "Well now. At least it's a secure house.

I'll say that for it." He found a drawer filled with paper sacks and used one of them to wipe his fingers.

I heard a scream from outside; the cry of a cat. Our hawks had scored their lunch.

The F. O. strode to the dining room. "*This* is a revelation," he shouted. His voice bounced crazily: he might have been calling from purgatory. "Have you seen this?"

"Yes, I have." The dining room was elevated about three feet above the level of the living room floor. "It's almost like a stage, isn't it?" I walked into the dining room and watched him pace it off.

"I could give quite a show here," the F. O. said. "Put a few folding chairs out there in the living room and set up all my equipment right here. Use the kitchen door for entrances." He looked around with almost childlike glee. "With a stage like this . . . why I could saw a lady in half."

"I'll volunteer Harriet for the act."

"Use this for a conference room," he said. "You can put your blackboard and projection screen up here and hold progress briefings."

"You're doing it again."

"Hmmm?"

"First you tell me to assume responsibility and after I get you to agree that responsibility requires an equal amount of authority, you turn around and start dictating again."

"I do have a penchant for that, don't I? I hope you don't resent it."

"I don't resent much of anything. It was just an observation."

"But you do think I'm a paternalistic son of a bitch, right?"

"I don't mind. You just keep on verifying my expense chits and I'll play Chingachgook to your Natty Bumppo."

"Not Chingachgook, not you." The F. O. peered at me.

41

"Though you might pass for Indian John. Let's see the rest of it," he said, bustling through the house.

"What about phone lines?" I asked. "We can microwave the scrambler to your office, but all those answering service lines for my university contacts will be a headache. They'll attract attention."

"Don't worry. You get Haring's package, I'll give the university assignment to a new man. Get his feet wet. You concentrate on that package and Jakaz and leave the other to me."

"So we'll need just a three- or four-line rotary from Pacific Tel."

"Fine. Fine. Here! *What's this?*" he cried from the master bath. "*Great God. How did Basset find this place?*"

I ran to the bathroom to see him turning a valve on the bidet. It splashed like something in the gardens of Versailles. "What do you have planned for this place?" asked the F. O. "And look there; a sunken bathtub. There's room enough in that for your entire crew!"

5

Hagopian punched a dime into the phone and dialed.

"Courteous Telephone Secretary," a girl said in his ear.

"You handle messages for Mr. Bernard from Detroit?"

"Who's calling please?"

"Johnny."

"This is not a ring-through service, sir. If you wish to leave a message . . ." She let the implication dangle.

"He's got a message for me. Check it, will ya?"

A Sony low-impedance pickup coil clung to the telephone handset with a suction cup. The coil was plugged to a Norelco Model 85 cassette recorder in his shirt pocket. Hagopian's thumb hovered over the Record button.

Although Bernie picked up the tab on this telephone message service, the assignment would come directly from the client. That way his agent would know nothing about the job beyond the fact that it was in Los Angeles. And the less Bernie knew, the safer Hagopian felt.

"I found it, sir . . . but you're not due until tomorrow."

Hagopian looked down the aisle, past Men's Toiletries and Household Goods, to where a group of wilted secretaries chewed on Thrifty sandwiches.

"I'm here today."

The voice in his ear turned petulant. "But I can't *possibly* give you anything today, sir."

The smoke in the booth was killing him. Hagopian ground out his cigarette and coughed. "Lissen, gawdammit, I'm here today and I want the fuckin' message."

"Sir!" The girl's voice trembled.

"Gimme the message or forget it."

"But sir, I'm not authorized . . ."

"Okay. You tell your boss you canceled a big deal for a customer. Okay?"

"But, I just work here. If you'll give me your number I'll have my supervisor call you when she gets in."

"Nuts. You tell your super you canceled a customer's deal. G'bye."

"No, wait. Let me think."

"What's to think? You got two choices, lady. You're gonna give me the message. Or you're gonna tell your super you screwed a client's deal."

"Just, please, just hold the line a second. I have to get the message from the file."

One of the secretaries left a dime and a nickel on the counter. Hagopian knew it was a dime and nickel tip because he had seen, even at this distance, a quarter in her hand. She had looked at the quarter, then at the check, then put the quarter back in her purse and withdrew two other coins, one smaller than the other and both smaller than the quarter. The girl walked away from the counter while her companion, lingering behind, swept up the fifteen cents and followed her out.

"Are you ready for the message?"

"Shoot."

Hagopian pressed the record and play buttons.

A shrill electronic squall assaulted his ear. He jerked the handset away from his face and waited for the noise to end.

The waitress who cleaned up after the secretaries was thin almost to the point of caricature. Her Aztec face dropped a bit when she saw that the secretaries had left no tip. But she stoically cleaned up their plates and cups.

44

The message took slightly more than thirty seconds. When it was over Hagopian hung up the phone without verifying that he'd received it. And without saying goodbye.

On his way out of the drugstore he passed by the lunch counter. He dropped two quarters on the counter where the olive-skinned waitress was cleaning up.

"What's that for?"

Hagopian shrugged. "*Por nada.*"

"Thanks." She smiled. Very expensive teeth, Hagopian thought. A little out of sync with the drab black hair and forgettable face. "Thanks a lot."

6

EXPENSES

Item: Lunch	$15.83
Tip	$2,000.00

Boys! Earn $ in spare time!
Sell papers! Good route!
Plenty of customers!

Bernard Brooks Haring was the most charming of men.

He had a talent for making you feel like a favored guest —even in your own home.

"My dear Charles," he said, holding both hands before him like the Pope in benediction. "I'm so happy to see you." He clasped my offered hand in both of his and held it with a cordial squeeze. "So glad indeed."

Beebee hadn't bought a new piece of clothing for ten years. Everything he wore had once been perfect; first-rate fabrics and immaculate tailoring. But Beebee had gained thirty more pounds in the ensuing years and the buttons, zippers, belts, shoulders and seams strained to confine his body. He looked like the fat employee of a thin country squire who wore only the boss's hand-me-downs. If one of those buttons popped it could be lethal.

There was an extra bulge in his jacket. I knew that Beebee didn't smoke. And I doubted that he was armed. It had to be the package. Beebee was ready to sell.

"It's good seeing you Beebee," I said.

We were lunching at a new place in Hollywood. It was expensive but I intended sticking Beebee with the tab. My own expense account was just three dollars short of its monthly limit. And once Beebee sold me the package he'd be richer than when he entered the restaurant.

"Cocktail before you order?" the waiter asked. He spoke as though he were reading lines from a telephone book.

I knew that Beebee was game; Beebee was always game for a drink. I ordered a Coors. "Hair of the dog," I said.

"I shall have one of those superb Mexican drinks. The one with tequila and salt on the rim."

"One Coors, one Margarita," the waiter said.

"Hangover?" Beebee asked when he left. I nodded. "Take Alka-Seltzer before breakfast. Absolutely cures it."

I said, "A bit less grape the night before. Absolutely prevents it."

"Marvelous beverage," Beebee said when the drinks came. He sipped at his Margarita and made noises like a vacuum cleaner in a bathtub. Salt crusted his fat mustache from the rim of the glass. "Just the other week I was saying to Hymes in London that U.S. duty has some rather nice compensations." He swirled the drink in his glass and then threw it back like water. "Can't get these at home, you know."

"How is Hymes?" I asked.

"Same old Hymes. Still pottering about in that old supercharged Fraser-Nash."

Beebee hadn't been in London "the other week" because Major Lloyd Hymes wasn't pottering about in his F-N; or in anything else for that matter. Hymes had injudiciously stepped in front of a London bus at least a month ago and his widow was trying to unload the F-N for six thousand pounds sterling.

47

Beebee said, "Another?" as the waiter passed our table. I shook my head, the glass before me was still half full of beer. "Just for me, if you please, then," said Beebee. The waiter nodded without looking at him. Beebee was well into his fourth Magarita when we ordered lunch.

Over the antipasto I got to the point. "Everything's been cleared at my end. I've got two thousand for you in fifties."

"What would that be in real money?"

"Eight hundred sterling," I said. "Something like."

Beebee squinted his eyes and looked through me. "Seven hundred, seventy-three . . . plus thirteen shillings and rather few pennies. Not enough."

"That's all it's worth to us," I lied. "I had to fight like hell just to get this much for you." Beebee's boozy face measured the innocence within mine; the old liar versus the younger liar. I smiled blandly.

Beebee seemed as though he was trying to guess my weight. "You wouldn't consider exchanging a bit of news, would you now, Charles? I'm more than a little curious about this colonel of yours."

"My lips are sealed," I said.

"That price might be lowered a bit, should you wish. I somehow doubt you'll be asked whether you gave me two thousand dollars—or one."

I shook my head. "It's a cash deal, Beebee. No allowances for trade-ins." We watched each other silently while Haring destroyed three olives.

Beebee nodded and smiled. I had won. "All in good time," he said, indicating the hand in my jacket. "All in good time." He dabbed oil and vinegar away from his fat mustache with a napkin as large as a towel. "Perhaps you might help me with another matter. A tot of gossip about one of your local groups of fanatics."

48

"You're not into religion now, are you Beebee?" I speared a piece of prosciutto. It was thin enough to see Haring smiling at me through it.

"No. I'm still working for the old firm." He looked at me with calm, unblinking assurance. "And I thought you might know something about your student radical groups with red European connections."

"There're a lot of groups in Los Angeles," I said. "I've got some Anglophiles under the microscope."

"What a vivid imagination!" A lump of half-chewed prosciutto and olives shifted in his mouth at he spoke. He wrapped an anchovy with a slice of Genoa sausage and crammed it under his mustache. "Vivid indeed."

"Seriously. Agitprop types. They're going to picket the mayor's Bastille Day speech."

"Now now now now Charles." The Scampi Villa Sassi had arrived. We arranged the plates on our table to accommodate it.

Beebee dug into his lunch. In the English style he held the fork upside down in his left hand. It was covered with a collage of scampi, rice and zucchini that he'd pressed onto it with his knife. For a moment Beebee held the fork midair as he thought. I wondered if he was preparing a balancing act for my amazement. A bit of zucchini dripped from the fork and left a stain of sauce on his tie.

"One is quite serious," he said. "We hope to learn if there is a common ground between our bomb throwers and yours. Should you but help, I would certainly reply in kind. A bit of mutual backscratching, you see."

"I'm matching you scratch for scratch, Beebee. My envelope for your envelope."

Beebee covered his embarrassment and his mouth with the napkin. "Yes, well then." He scrubbed at his mustache and

49

seemed to grow plumper within the confines of his suit, like a chicken fluffing out its feathers. "I'm so pleased that it is you who've come with the offer. Quite pleased." He dug once more into his scampi. "Have you finished the Bentley yet?"

"Just about," I said. "I had the body painted and was starting on the interior when one of the pistons collapsed."

"What a *terrible* pity. Must cost a fortune to replace it; specially cast part from the works, I would imagine, on a model as old as yours."

"No, I junked the engine. Got a hell of a deal on a GMC pickup mill at a wrecking yard."

Beebee's eyes bulged. Food stuck in his throat and he was convulsed with a spasm of coughing. "A pickup truck motor in a Mann Egerton Bentley," he wheezed. "It's rather like asking the Royal Family to endorse a brand of soap flakes."

"It works," I said. "What else is there?"

"But, do you see? that is exactly the point, Charles. Had you wanted a *reliable* motorcar, you would have better chosen a new Rolls; possibly even a new Mercedes." Beebee paused to sop up the sauce from his plate with yeasty slices of bread which he sieved through his mustache. "You are seeking some sort of pragmatist's nirvana and you will settle for nothing less than everything. But your goal is like a two-car garage in which you can fit neither car because you are storing a fiber-glass boat for the winter. Your objectives are mutually exclusive . . . thoroughly contradictory."

The envelope was growing heavy in my pocket. "Life itself is a contradiction, Beebee."

He rattled his head. "Ah, Charles. Far better had you sent for that new piston from the works. Less practical, perhaps; but much better form, you see. Much better."

Something landed in my lap, hidden by the tablecloth. I reached under the table and felt a fat envelope. I passed my own money-bulging envelope to him and looked at the stain on his tie as he grasped the other end of it.

"Don't pull at it, Beebee. Bad form, yes?"

7

Hagopian leaned forward on the living-room couch. His lip curled slightly as smoke from a freshly lit True Menthol brought tears to one eye. His Norelco Model 85 miniature cassette recorder was patch-corded into a Sony 800B 4-speed. Tony the Teacher hadn't taught him this; most of the mothers in the business wouldn't understand the subtlety of it: Hagopian was having a dubdown session.

He dubbed the message from cassette to tape with the Sony set at 7½ ips. He played it back into a fresh cassette at 1⅞ ips, effectively quartering the speed.

Dubbing back to the tape recorder again at 7½, he reduced the speed by a quarter again so the message could almost be recognized. It was normally paced speech—normal if you understand Geek, he thought. Hagopian flipped the reels over to run the tape backwards, then relaxed on the couch as he listened to a wavering voice, sometimes a hair too fast, sometimes a hair too slow, spell out his assignment.

"His name is Steven, that's S-T-E-V-E-N, Routenfield."

Hagopian stopped the tape and ran it again from the beginning. Routenfield, he thought. Steven-with-a-V Routenfield. Why was that name familiar? It wasn't a mob name; no, there was some other kind of connection in his mind. And the name smelled of money.

"His name is Steven, that's S-T-E-V-E-N, Routenfield. Address is four fifty-two Oakview Terrace, Bel Air. Routenfield is of middle height and very thin. He has thick white hair, blue eyes, fair complexion. Age is seventy-two or about. We can give you no better description; we leave it to you to find the man and properly identify him. Although he still has some business interests . . ."

He stopped the tape and backed it up again. Business interests. Bel Air. The more he heard, the more it sounded like a big money hit.

". . . tify him. Although he still has some business interests Routenfield seldom leaves his home in Bel Air. He is widowed and his nearest relative, an adopted daughter, lives away from him.

"Within the next two weeks, Steven Routenfield will spend some time at the lodge he owns in Mammoth Lakes, a Southern California mountain resort."

Mammoth Lakes, Hagopian thought. First Bel Air, and now Mammoth Lakes. This wasn't a simple ten-yards hit. For that kind of money he'd take out a mob guy; maybe some small-time politician. But a guy who owned property where the dirt alone went for close to six figures—that was a whole different contract.

". . . lifornia mountain resort. Whether you complete the job in Los Angeles or in Mammoth Lakes, it is important that it looks like an accident. A suicide, perhaps, or a traffic accident. But not murder."

If he could find out more about the guy, if he could really learn something about him, maybe there was a bigger payoff for the job.

"Remember; an accident. No violence. Nothing suspicious. An accident. You have one week. Erase all tape."

Hagopian erased all but the original cassette which he would mail to John Sertashian in Fielding Hills, Michigan.

"Beverly Hills City Hall."
"Library, please."
"The lines are busy. Will you wait?"

"Yeah," Hagopian said. "Sure."

It was a short wait. He had time to clean only one fingernail with his lower eyetooth when the voice said, "I can ring now. Thank you for waiting."

After a click another voice said, "Beverly Hills Library."

"Reference, please."

"Hold on."

To what? he wondered. He cleaned two more nails with his teeth and was pinching the soft dirt away when the voice clicked on and asked, "Are you waiting for reference?"

Hagopian said, "Yop."

"Oh. Hold on."

There was an abrupt series of electronic noises and a tired woman said, "Reference," in his ear.

"In the *Reader's Guide* for Steven Routenfield," Hagopian said.

The same waitress was there, making setups for the coffee-break traffic. Her sweat stains had dried, leaving slightly off-colored rings under her arms and beneath her small breasts where the uniform clung tightly to her ribs.

The librarian was back on the line, delivering her information in a bored monotone. Then she hung up. Hagopian dialed again.

"Popper's Periodicals."

"I'm looking for a July 9, 1964 copy of *Forbes*."

"That's going to be rough to find. It goes back a long time."

"Could you check it?"

"Well, that's a pretty old copy, mister," the man said.

"Look, it's worth five bucks to me. See if you've got one, okay?"

"Sure. Sure."

Hagopian's view was blocked. A fat, red-faced man studied the colognes in Men's Toiletries. Casually well dressed and seemingly energetic, he shifted his weight from foot to foot as he peered at the colognes.

Take the Jade East, Hagopian thought.

"I don't have *Forbes*. How about *Business Week*. I'll let you have the whole month of July sixty-four for five bucks."

"Harry's used magazines. If we ain't got it, it ain't worth readin'."

"I'm looking for an issue of *Forbes*. The July . . ."

"It ain't worth readin'."

Hagopian had shucked his jacket and loosened his necktie. The closed phone booth was beginning to take on the smell of his body and breath. His feet hurt; they felt swollen within his shoes. But Hagopian couldn't sit on the palm-sized triangular bench because a large dirty lump of chewing gum had beaten him to it.

"Hello, Berlick's Books and Magazines," said a perky little voice into his ear.

"I'm trying to find a back issue of *Forbes* magazine," Hagopian began.

"Just a moment, please," the young girl said before he could continue. "I'll give you a salesman in Business Periodicals."

The big man settled on a bottle of Agua Lavanda Puig. He looked down the aisle in both directions, pocketed the bottle and walked coolly toward the lunch counter.

"Business Periodicals." The voice cracked, unsure of the octave in which it would speak. Hagopian could almost hear the acne growing.

55

"July 9, 1964 for *Forbes*. Do you have . . ."

"Half a second, sir. It's all computer carded." During the brief pause Hagopian heard a sound like an adding machine in a poker game. "Yes sir. We have exactly one copy."

"Look, could you hold it for me until maybe an hour from now? My name is . . ." Hagopian stumbled mentally, then recovered ". . . Mr. Johnson."

"I'm sorry, Mr. Johnson, but we cannot hold periodicals without a deposit."

"Okay, great. How much does the damn thing cost?"

"It's listed at a dollar fifty, sir."

"I'll tell you what. Have you ever . . . Hey, I don't know your name."

"Phil."

"Okay Phil, I've got a proposition for you. Pull that *Forbes* from the stacks and I'll give you ten bucks for it. A buck fifty for the store, eight fifty for you."

"But I can't hold the periodical without a deposit, Mr. Johnson."

Hagopian stared blindly out of the phone booth. "Let me put it this way, Phil. What I'm trying to do is bribe you. But it's a gamble on your end. If I show up before you close today, you get eight and a half dollars. If I don't show up, you're out a buck fifty."

"But I can't take the magazine out without a . . ."

"Fuck it," Hagopian said and smashed the phone's handset into its cradle. He ripped out the listing from the Yellow Pages and slammed his way from the booth. The thin waitress looked up, startled, as he passed her section of the lunch counter.

"Hi!" she called.

Hagopian slowed his pace. "How's it going, kid?" He tried to smile.

"You're my lucky guy. I had a real good day."

"Great. Keep your chin up, hunh?" He continued into the street to look for a cab. Her lucky guy, he thought. What could she make in a day? Five bucks in side money? Mama made less than that and she paid for every cent of it with varicose veins and arthritic feet. Waitresses. Mexican waitresses. Armenian cooks. It was like betting on an inside straight.

8

The following is not for the idle hobbyist, but for the sincere, profoundly dedicated student who wishes to excel in the art of deception.

Preface to *The Cyclopædic Dictionary of Magic*

Our downtown offices were in the Federal Building on Hope Street. Once in the building I took a public elevator to the forty-fifth floor, exited, walked across the hall to the bank of private elevators, unlocked one with my key and stepped in.

The private elevators had two doors; one facing the public hallway and one facing the other direction. I descended to the thirty-third floor and used another key to let myself through the door opposite the one I'd entered.

And stepped directly into Glenda's office.

Without looking up from her IBM 3270, Glenda said, "You'll have to wait a moment. He's talking to Berlin."

The F. O.'s new secretary had a strange, almost homely beauty. Her light red hair strayed in wisps away from her coiffure. Her nose was a touch too narrow with a slightly prominent bridge. From her lean small-breasted body I guessed she hadn't gained a pound since midpuberty. And from the delicate look of her freckled white skin I also guessed that she would have you shave quite closely before joining her in bed: that sort of complexion bruises easily.

I slumped in Glenda's visitors' chair and watched her work at the terminal. She punched a code on the keyboard and green characters flashed on a screen behind it. Glenda checked the message to verify its accuracy then pressed a keyboard button marked ENTER. This would send the message to a computer, either here or in Virginia depending on the data she required. Even before she could release the button she got her answer. It made a fresh pattern of green characters on the screen.

"You're so efficient; a demon of proficiency, Glenda. Wouldn't you like to work with me at our new safe house on Mulholland?"

Her attention was fixed on the screen. After reading the reply she pressed a button marked TRANS and activated the data storage tape. This magnetic tape would hold the message for retrieval and transcription at a later date.

"Wrong girl," she said. "I don't have big tits."

" 'Large breasts,' " I corrected.

"One way or the other, I don't fit your sexual fantasies."

Glenda had been with us for only two weeks. As with any new body, gossip flittered around her like gnats on an August evening. From different sources I'd heard that she was nymphomaniacal or homosexual or frigid or, according to my secretary Harriet, all three simultaneously. The F. O. didn't seem to give a damn about the gossip. He said she was the most efficient Agency staffer in SoCal SubSection.

"Since sex is out, how about dinner tonight?"

"You say 'sex' so easily, like other people say 'lunch' or 'tree' or something equally mundane." Her tone was mocking. "Doesn't 'love' ever cross your mind?" She didn't look at me but flipped a page on her steno pad and began pecking a new question into the terminal.

"I've been crossed by love," I said. "Given a choice I'll take sex . . . or even dinner."

Glenda looked up from her work and nailed me with two

impersonal green eyes. "I'm sure you'd know what to do with dinner," she said. Glenda studied me from hairline to shoeshine then returned to her IBM console.

Almost simultaneously a light flashed on Glenda's desk and the F. O.'s door swung open. I stepped toward the door. Without looking up from her work Glenda said, "Not tonight. Ask me again, maybe."

"How was lunch with Haring?" the F. O. asked as the door closed behind me with a hydraulic *whooosh*. The office fit him as impressively as his handmade suits. All leather and rough-textured fabrics and mahogany, it might have housed a captain of industry. The F. O. had somehow gotten an expense authorization and called in Pollock & Greene to do the place.

"Superb. I've found a new place on Cahuenga that really knows how to make *Scampi Villa Sassi*."

"I'm not in the least interested in your gastronomical fantasies," the F. O. said. "Tell me what you got from Haring."

"Empty beer cans," I said. "Old shoes. Smoke. And the package. I signed the lease for our safe house on my way over."

"Any hint of what he's doing here?"

"You probably know more about that than I." I waited for a response, but if the F. O. had an opinion he was keeping it to himself for the moment. He tilted back slightly in his chair and, though I couldn't see them, I knew his feet were well away from the floor. In order to come to working terms with his desk the F. O. had to crank his chair up to the absolute top limit: He was the only man I knew who didn't sit *down*.

The F. O. was still waiting.

"Beebee doesn't know from anything about Routenfield," I said. "But he's hot for Gyula Jakaz."

"What did he ask?"

"Damn little. It's what he didn't ask that interests me. He's been out of circulation for a long time; didn't know that Hymes was done by a London bus." I fumbled inside the

F. O.'s humidor for a Havana. (Access to immune diplomatic pouches is one of the fringe benefits of working for the Agency.) "If Beebee was familiar with Routenfield he wouldn't have sold. He's on a fishing expedition. He wants to find out where Gyula is holed up and he thought he could wedge some dope out of me."

"So, how much did he get out of you?"

"Your confidence in me is almost crippling," I said as I warmed the end of the Havana. "Beebee's growing old. He doesn't hold the booze the way he used to. After a clumsy bribe and a gambit about student rads he pulled in his pieces."

The F. O. said, "But nothing about Gyula, eh?"

"Nothing. We talked cars."

"Clever. You pumped him like a master I imagine." The F. O.'s smile was like a sunburst. "What would I accomplish without you, hmmm? You had him boozed a touch, and you didn't pump him for data. Have you considered basket weaving as a trade?"

"I got what I went for. Here's the baby," I said and plopped Beebee's fat envelope down on his desk. "I had to pick up the tab on our lunch. Can you get me an extension on my expense account for extraordinary items?" Even though Beebee had paid for lunch, I managed to slip the small tear-away receipt from the bill.

He weighed the envelope like a fish in the flat of his hand. "It depends on how extraordinary," he said.

"I've read it," I said. "On the way over. It's worth twice what we paid for it . . . worth the extraordinary extension and a travel per diem."

"Another vacation?"

"Belgrade," I said. "Beebee's package points to Belgrade and Budapest; unless we have an embassy in Tirana that I haven't heard about."

He stared blankly at me for a moment then said, "I wonder

61

why he would sell it to us." He fondled the envelope with his immaculate little hands. "Two thousand dollars. Not much to a thief like Haring. I wonder why he sold it. Jakaz. He wants Gyula Jakaz, does he? Did he follow you here?"

I shook my head. "Beebee knows where I work."

"He also knows more than he's selling. I wonder *what* he knows." As the F. O. slipped the document from its envelope a Ping-Pong ball rolled out of his sleeve and bounced across his desk into my lap. Without blinking he said, "Hold that for a moment," and thumbed through the papers.

Beebee's memorandum was a Xeroxed copy of a Xeroxed copy.

A front piece had been added which said in effect that the memorandum had been lifted from an SIS pouch by a friend of ours in London. It identified neither Xenophon nor Eremites.

"Xenophon," the F. O. said. "Have our Eastern Europe people identified Xenophon yet?"

"Not yet," I said.

"You wouldn't have run into him, would you?"

"Not me," I lied. I'd run into Xenophon and would again; he was one of the magnets drawing me to Belgrade.

He returned to the memorandum. "Haring's covered himself nicely," the F. O. said. "If anything leaks back to Whitehall, it will seem that we stole the thing years ago."

"Soft job," I said. "Picking their pockets and pointing at us."

"You could learn from him," the F. O. said.

12 JANUARY 1968

FROM XENOPHON VIA IMMUNE POUCH TO ERE-MITES

NO STAT M.I.5, NO STAT YARD SPEC. BRANCH, DI-RECT TO FILES ONLY, NO RECEIPT REQUIRED, NO

MINISTERIAL CONFIRMATION, NO DEPARTMENTAL CROSS FILING, EREMITES & FILES EYES ONLY

You were absolutely correct, my dear fellow. These are a very unusual group indeed. In '56, while most were dashing across the border to Austria, nearly 10 or so scurried south from Budapest, crossing near Subotica in the Voivodina sector of Yugoslavia.

I've managed to trace them to Albania, right to Tirana itself. Dr. Tibor Kovács seems to have been the reason for the group. He was, at any rate, the honey around which the other bees swarmed in Budapest. Yet he did not travel to Tirana with the others. He seems to have gone underground in Austria for a bit, then turned up in Los Angeles where your man saw him 5 years ago.

One chap, Gyula Jakaz, held the 10 together since Kovács' disappearance—then himself disappeared last year. Rumour has it that Jakaz was a KGB informer in Nyiregyháza, using AVH Personnel Section as a cover.

All 10 seem to be unreconstructed Stalinists, somewhat to the fanatical left of both Rákosi and Gerö. They consider themselves an Hungarian government-in-exile. While the Hoxha government exercise some tenuous control over the group, the relationship is delicate at best. They are tolerated by Albania because they bring two very distinct benefits with them:

First, they have established a propaganda cadre in Hungary. By spreading pro-Mao, anti-Moscow propaganda amongst Magyar nationalists, they serve Albania in her courtship of Peking.

Second, they seem recently to have acquired a not-irregular source of money and are quite self-sustaining. Although their funds are almost exclusively U.S. dollars, I have no information regarding the point of origin. It may be safe to assume that the dollars come from our cousins across the sea. (You will remember that Kovács slipped through your fingers in Los Angeles . . . *of all places!*)

It is equally safe to assume that they are sprinkled liberally with old boys of the AVH. After the revolutionary fires were banked sometime in '57, Kádár János invited the contingent of 10 to return home to Budapest. The 10 apparently had information missing from AVH files, and the Kádár government wanted it quite desperately. They also wanted this fellow Gyula Jakaz who was becoming an embarrassment because of his pro-Stalinist attitude during the rather un-Stalinish years of First Secretary Khrushchev. But by now the group have other loyalties and divers connections.

KGB are trying to infiltrate them, but have so far failed. What I find most curious is their attempt at infiltration rather than extermination. With very little hardship, KGB could destroy the entire group. Yet they chose, instead, to court trouble by attempting to place a counterintelligence person within this obviously closed society. One wonders why KGB are interested in this little clan. What could USSR possibly hope to obtain from them?

Should you be interested, I suppose one could further investigate the group of 10. It is my feeling, however, that such enquiries will yield precious little of genuine value.

"Curiouser and curiouser." The F. O. put the memorandum down on his desk and smoothed it with his hands. "What was it? 'A not irregular source of money' did it say?"

"That would be Routenfield," I said. "God knows, Jakaz isn't going to support his friends on the other side with profits from a prune ranch."

"Do you think Routenfield knows where his money's going?" he asked. "Could it be we've misjudged him?"

"Not on your life," I said.

"I suppose you're right." The F. O. made a cathedral of his tiny fingers and peered over them like the Eyes of God. "It would take a mind like mine . . . or even yours . . . to enter into such double dealings. But what a joke, just the same; this sword bearer of high finance and low politics stuffing dollar bills into a rump group of the AVH, eh?"

He tapped his fingertips together and said, "When he was still a cinder in the public eye, Routenfield was caricatured as a madman . . . but he's not. He's simply *too* sane. If you define sanity as the ability to adjust to your environment, Routenfield has adjusted to an almost grotesque degree. What he needs . . . what we all need . . . is a new definition of sanity."

I said, "If you ever find that new definition, please don't tell me. I'm a functioning neurotic . . ."

"Paranoid."

". . . and I hope to stay this way."

"I wouldn't change you for the world." When the F. O. smiled there were few who could hold a candle to him.

"Outside of the fact that he's as sane as a hatter, we know something else about Routenfield." I tapped the SIS memo on the F. O.'s desk. "His money is going to a group of people he'd like to see shot. That means someone has suckered him into believing that left is right."

"Jakaz?"

"Who else."

"Then it was worth it," he said. He snapped on the intercom. "Glenda, bring in an extraordinary expenses form. Make it out to Charles Remly, five hundred dollars, this month only."

That was a break. I needed at least a hundred and fifty to have the Bentley's wire wheels tuned, sandblasted and painted.

The F. O. said, "The questions are seemingly endless," and tapped delicately at the SIS report with his finger. "Who is this Kovács . . . a leader of the group?"

"No," I said. "He's the '. . . honey around which the others swarmed in Budapest . . .' or something like that. That would make him a reason, not a leader."

"Why did they swarm? What is his significance?" he wrinkled his nose as though he might be able to sniff out Kovács' significance from Beebee's stolen report. "Jakaz was holding the group together in sixty-three. Why did *he* leave for Los Angeles? To work with Kovács? To look for Kovács? Fund raising?"

"Maybe," I said. "The report was written something like four years after Jakaz disappeared. Maybe he came here looking for money."

"No no. There is something here . . . something about L.A. or something *in* L.A. that has attracted first Kovács, then Jakaz." He licked his finger and shuffled through the pages. "Perhaps the mysterious files . . . yes?"

"Yes," I said. "The Mysterious Files: From the movie by the same name, produced by Alexander Korda."

Ignoring me he snapped on the intercom again. "Glenda . . ."

"Coming," she interrupted. "I've got the form in my hand."

The F. O. said, "If you will listen rather than speak you might discover why I buzzed you."

"Oops. Sorry."

"Before you bring that expense form in, put Tibor Kovács through the 3270. I would like to know what the electronic gnomes in Virginia have to say about him."

"Tibor Kovács?"

He spelled it for her. "There is an acute accent over the final vowel . . . and a 'Doctor' precedes the name."

"That propaganda item is a laugh," I said when he took his demanding hand from the intercom. "Can you see ten hot rods from AVH trying to convince themselves that *politiprop* work doesn't put them to sleep?"

We puffed quietly at our cigars until the F. O. pointed at the Ping-Pong ball in my hand and said, "Roll that back to me." He showed me his new trick while we waited for Glenda.

"They're just shells," I said as the last Ping-Pong ball disappeared from his hand.

"You were holding one for a good ten minutes."

"That was a blind," I said. "It's fundamental in the art of deception."

He repeated the trick, spotting four of the white plastic spheres between his fingers and, with a twist of his little hand, sending them to limbo one at a time.

"Can you do it with your cuff rolled back?" Glenda asked from the doorway. She had my expense form and a blue folder in her hand. Dropping the quadruplicate form on the F. O.'s desk, she watched as he sent his Ping-Pong balls into nothingness for the third time.

"They're hollow shells," Glenda said.

"Not at all." I shook my head. "I bounced them on his desk."

Glenda raised an eyebrow at me. "At any rate, Tibor Kovács is a hollow shell. Virginia has nothing on him."

"Nothing?" I said.

"Sorry."

"I expected as much." The F. O. rolled down his sleeve, replaced his cufflink and buttoned the cuff of his jacket. "You know where to sign this thing and where to initial it," he said.

I began spreading ink on the form. "That's it. I'll have Basset assemble a team and some furniture for the new office on Mulholland. Then I've got to see Documents and Travel about my vacation in beautiful Belgrade."

"You're forgetting something," the F. O. said.

I suppose I looked blank.

"The girl," Glenda said. "You forgot the girl."

"Strange," the F. O. said. "He seldom forgets girls."

I completed the expense authorization, detached my carbon copy and waited to see who would speak next.

After a brief pause the F. O. said, "Routenfield's adopted daughter. Surely you remember the stink it caused at the time, an old widower adopting a little girl.''

"Yes. Now I remember," I said. "He got this foster child
. . . a ward or whatever. Around fifty-six, fifty-seven."

"Bit old for a foster child," the F. O. said.

"*Nineteen* fifty-six." I turned to Glenda and said, "Can you
run a make on her?"

Closing her eyes and facing heavenward Glenda spoke in a
flat monotonous voice: "Mary Louise Paál. (There's an acute
accent over the second A.) Twenty-three years old. Working
on her Master's in psychology at UCLA. Lives in an apartment
near the campus in Westwood. Outside of that there's nothing
on her."

A very blank life, I thought. "No traffic tickets? Nothing?"

"Nothing." Glenda smiled her mocking smile at me. It was
the merest compression of her lips, that smile, with a grudging
dimple that appeared on her left cheek. "A dull girl."

"That is simply a once-over," the F. O. said. "The rest you'll
have to get for yourself."

"You'll enjoy that," Glenda said. "Let me know if she has
big . . . um . . ."

I asked, "What does her immigration folder say?"

"Born in Budapest to János and Mary Anna Paál," Glenda
said, reading from the blue folder. "Both parents died in a car
accident in fifty-five. That would make her . . ." Glenda
counted in her head.

"Six when her parents died, seven when she came over the
wall," I said. "Who sponsored her, Routenfield?"

"No; some church group. Quakers, I think."

"Any way she might be connected to Gyula Jakaz?"

"When you find the answer to that, remember to tell me,"
the F. O. said. "As I recall, that is how you earn your salary."

I smiled wanly at him and asked Glenda, "Any way Routenfield could have chosen her specifically?"

"I don't understand."

"Could he have laid a path from Budapest to Los Angeles for this one particular girl? Or was it just chance that she ended up here instead of someplace like Detroit."

"Oh, yes," Glenda said. "It was all random. You put in your name if you wanted one of the Hungarian kids and the sponsoring agency just pulled one out of the hat."

The F. O. and I puffed on our cigars while Glenda fanned herself with the immigration folder. It might have been a precinct office in Chicago, or a meeting of the Cuban Revolutionary Council, for all the smoke we created. "They close down SoCal SubSection," I said, "we can always fumigate houses." The F. O. didn't smile. Glenda was silent. I stared out the window. "I'm leaving at noon tomorrow," I said.

"Travel diplomatic," the F. O. said. "I'm running low on cigars."

9

The store was fluorescently brilliant; a supermarket of literacy. Hagopian hated it. He elbowed his way through the patchwork crowd of browsers and wished he was back at the Wildwood with his feet in a tub of scalding water.

To the clerk at business periodicals he said, "You Phil?"

"Phil's on his break. May I help you?"

"*Forbes*, July 9, 1964."

As the clerk ducked through a door marked STACKS EMPLOYEES ONLY, Hagopian surveyed the crowded store. What a glossy dump. In his heightened stage of fatigue the lights seemed blinding. He remembered the bookstores of his childhood; dim and cluttered places where the books that he wanted were almost impossible to find but, once found, simplicity itself to steal.

"That's a dollar fifty, sir. You pay at the main cashier." The clerk sealed the magazine in a bright orange sack on which he marked the price. "Will there be anything else?"

"Yeah. When Phil gets back, tell him he dropped eight dollars and fifty cents."

wire (wïr), n., adj., v., slender, flexible metal, usually circular in section.
shad·ow (shăd'ō), n., dark figure cast by a body intercepting light.

When I emerged from the elevator again, this time on the thirty-first floor, I walked directly into Harriet's office. The furnishings were identical to Glenda's—Government Gray that would never show dust—but lacked a 3270. Not that she needed one, since we always had access to Glenda's, but Harriet believed the Agency owed her a bright electronic terminal as a gesture of gratitude for her twenty or so years of grim service.

One other thing the office lacked when I entered: Harriet.

I walked to her desk and poked curiously about in the clutter of unfulfilled requests that covered it. On top of one mound of paper was a note to me. She had scribbled it that day but neglected to slip it under my door. As I read it I rubbed my eyebrows.

> Farewell lunchion today for Gladys at Dominique restaraunt on Las Feliz. Might be back late. Dont forget sign authorozations safe house. If you leave before I get back from lunch will you PLEASE call in before day over.

I wondered if they were accepting transfers from the Agency to the Bureau of Land Management. At the moment managing land sounded very attractive.

I tried Basset's door but it was locked. He's out shooting

lizards, I thought, and planning for the future with his parcel of recreational sand. Weaver's door was also locked. Something at least was going right. Weaver was wiring Gyula Jakaz for sound.

Unlocking my own door I paused before stepping through. A note was on the carpet just beyond my threshold.

I gave old Weaver compassionate leave for the day, babe. His Siamese is having her first litter and they're afraid it might have to be Caesarean Section. If they all pull through, he's promised you pick of the litter. Think you'll have time for that wiring job? I'm running a little late myself. I'll be back this afternoon.

Basset

I'm not sure if it was Basset's assumption that he could give anyone compassionate leave, or Harriet's unbelievable brass and even worse spelling, or Weaver's cat's Caesarean Section, or the prospect of driving an hour out and an hour back to wire a prune ranch, but I was in a foul mood when I walked into Documents.

"Make it damn fast," I told our startled forgers. "I've got to get up to Electronics for a wire."

"Okay, fine, we'll priority it," said the pale young clerk. An embryonic mustache hovered uncertainly between his nose and his nervous smile. "I'll just take your prints and we can fill out the other stuff while you're upstairs."

"Balls." I helped myself to a pen from his desk and scrawled "Charles Remington Remly" on a scrap of paper. "Here's the signature. Use someone else's prints."

"But we . . ."

"You've got at least ten guys in here. That's eighty fingers and twenty thumbs. Use 'em. When you've done the stuff, send it down to Basset. He'll get it to me later."

Wiring a house is not as difficult as you might imagine. It takes only an infinity transmitter, a low-impedance compatibility disc and an ———,* none of which is available at your local hi-fi shop and all of which can be grouped on a dime.

The only danger I faced was the threat of minutes running out. Though I had screened the house and surrounding orchards for stray bodies, the constant tick of seconds played at my nerves. The longer I stayed the greater the risk became.

My tool kit was simple enough: a stubby little screwdriver. I used it to undress the phone and insert the infinity transmitter. That plugged Jakaz' phone into an unlisted line that we'd already co-axed to his present number. All that Basset, Weaver or I had to do now was dial the unlisted number from any direct dial phone and sound a two-tone signal into the mouthpiece of our originating phone before his instrument rang. (The unlisted line and two-tone signal are critical. Had we plugged into his existing line, it would have tied up the phone during those periods when our wire was active. And a one-tone signal could have been tripped by the harmonic chaff that's unavoidable in today's telephone systems.) Even when his phone was still cradled we would hear every sound in the room.

The compatibility disc interfaced all transmissions into our SoCal SubSection scrambling cable. In the event that fate played tricks with our wire and plugged the unlisted line into some bystander's phone (it had happened once before that I know of), our scrambler guaranteed that nothing intelligible came through; except, of course, to authorized phones on the scrambling cable.

Finally I installed the ———,* which would warn us of

* Edited, F. O. SoCal SubSection

73

any de-bugging hardware within the wired phone's perimeter of effectiveness.

The entire job, not counting the previous coaxial work, took just under four minutes. When I was done Gyula Jakaz had provided us with a source of information at the expense of his constitutionally guaranteed right of privacy.

Hohum.

Sixty seconds, I told myself. I'll take just a minute more and see what the colonel might have lying about.

The rooms of his little stucco cottage were forgettable, as though furnished by three generations of strangers. Every vertical surface inside was wallpapered with one of those asymmetric medallion patterns that seems to sweat brown no matter what the season. You could smell the dust.

I scavenged the wastebaskets first and it's well that I did. The living room basket yielded nothing. But when my watch showed that fifty of my sixty seconds were gone I dug an empty envelope addressed to Milos Kay from the large plastic bin in the kitchen. It was the only piece of mail, the only personal item in fact, among a stew of old newspapers, animal bones and fermenting cabbage leaves. There was no return address but the postmark said *Miami Fla* and was dated just last week. I jammed the envelope back into its grave and fled. My watch told me that I'd used nearly seventy seconds—and time was my immediate enemy. If Jakaz discovered me I'd have been at a loss for words, among other things.

The interior of the Bentley resembled the exterior of Beebee Haring; genteel disrepair. The leather was worn and discolored and patched in the areas of heaviest wear. And the mahogany woodwork on the dash and window frames needed a good varnish. But it smelled nicely of saddlesoap and wax. I always felt at home within the Bentley, like a squirrel in its nest.

Although the car was a four-door saloon it had the long low lines of a sportster with its exaggerated hood and long, flowing fenders. Mann Egerton had a penchant for that: designing lean, hungry-looking Bentley and Royce sedans.

I had driven ten miles from Gyula Jakaz' orchards when I noticed the Buick Riviera on my tail. The Riviera would have escaped my eye if I hadn't shaved a yellow light that was turning red. After clearing the light I heard a scream of brakes and tires behind me. In my rear-view mirror the black Riviera had just made the cross street while a Porsche 911 was turning around in insane circles, passing through the intersection from left to right across my mirror. The Riviera had run a red light.

Since desert intersections between Palmdale and Lancaster are separated by miles of barren wind-whipped highway, it's not unusual to shave or even run the signals. If you get caught at one of them you lose the feeling of pace that you've developed over the last few miles. I guessed the Riviera was breaking the speed limit right along with me and not prepared to sit out the dull, two-minute wait at each signal.

Following his wild maneuver at the intersection I kept a close eye on the mirror . . . not because I thought he was tagging me, but for Highway Patrol cars that he might have attracted. The only car that stayed with me was the black Riviera. He was on my tail all the way to Newhall where the road begins climbing through the San Gabriel Mountains. Halfway up the San Gabriels my engine shut out. As I put the Bentley into neutral and turned off the ignition I checked the oil temp. water temp. and gasoline gauges. Everything was normal. The car was just dead. I eased onto the gravel roadside once my speed got down to 25 mph. The black Buick Riviera passed me like a rocket loaded with bricks.

I popped open the Bentley's hood, unsnapped the carburetor air filter and jerked on the throttle linkage a couple of times. Nothing happened. No gas squirted from the jets. Vapor lock. Out of the five hundred that the F. O. had authorized for extraordinary expenses I would have to spend a few dollars for an electric fuel pump. When you have an electric pump back at the tank, it pushes gasoline to the engine. The standard engine-mounted pump tries to suck fuel from the tank. It often fails.

It was a good fifteen minutes before the Bentley came alive. I had to carry fuel from the tank via a bottom end drain plug with the collapsible drinking cup that I stored in my shaving kit in the glove box. By the time I primed the carburetor my hands stank of gasoline and the plastic cup was beginning to dissolve into sculptured lumps. I buttoned down the hood, cranked over the Bentley's GMC engine and started through the pass. Shortly after I crossed the summit a black Buick Riviera loomed in my rear-view mirror.

It was supposed to have been a routine job, the wiring of Gyula Jakaz. I wondered if the Riviera was part of the routine. There was one way to find out.

Directly over the pass there is a combination gas station, liquor store, souvenir shop and café. I pulled into the lot and walked toward the place. When the Riviera passed I didn't turn to look.

Once in the café I ordered a container of tea to take out and took it out to the men's room. The telephone was just behind the door. As I dialed the office I read some local graffiti. Besides the usual sort of thing there were two that I'd never seen before. One was "Hic erat Kilrox" and the other said "Andy Wyath (sic) is a neoclassicist." Culture had come to the desert.

76

"Agricultural Bureau," Harriet said after the fifth ring.

"Is Basset still there?" I asked.

"Who's calling please." Harriet's voice was as charming as the writing on the wall before me.

"Harriet . . ." I slumped against the wall and wearily rubbed my eyebrows ". . . Harriet, after three wonderful months together don't you recognize my voice?"

"This is the Agricultural Bureau," she said through her nose. "Who's calling please."

"This is your boss; your *numero uno*, you lovely thing you. Put Frank Basset on the phone."

"Can you identify yourself?"

I closed my eyes and breathed slowly. "Harry Houdini is Erich Weiss," I said. It was the F. O.'s clearance code for the week. I had pushed for "Bishop to knight five," but the F. O. had overruled me. "Now let me talk to Basset."

"I thought that was you," Harriet said. "I've been waiting for you all day. I should have locked up a half hour ago. When are you coming to the office? We need your authorization for some expenditures on that stupid house. Where are you? Will you be in after I close up the office? I'm only human, you know."

"Subhuman, Harriet."

"I can't do everything by myself while you're out driving around in that fancy car of yours." She stopped only to inhale and quickly uttered an all-indicting, "Well?"

I was absorbed with the news item I was scrawling on the wall. I wrote with my left hand to give it the appearance of moronic script. The news, untrue of course, involved the rather bizarre sexual and scatological practices of someone named Harriet. I said, "Put Frank Basset on the phone," and asked myself if it was wise to include her phone number.

"You can't expect me to run this office and . . ."

"Harriet, you little teacup you, I imagine that you can run

77

the office and balance our budget with equal facility on the end of your ugly nose. Let me talk to Basset."

"I don't think you understand . . ."

I hung up the phone, dropped some more coins in the slot and redialed.

"Horticulture."

"Glenda, this is Charley."

"Can you give me the word of the day?"

"Harry Houdini was Erich Weiss . . . but he wished he was the F. O.," I said. "Punch me through to Frank Basset. I'm having difficulty with our regular line."

"No trouble," Glenda said. "Are you in some kind of a bind?"

"Some kind of."

"Caught in bed with someone's wife?"

"Not at this time of day. I'm working right now."

"I'll let that pass. Here's Frank."

"Basset," Basset said.

"I'm having car problems," I said.

"Zat a fact?"

"A black Buick Riviera. California plates, VSH 000."

"Vshooo?"

"Right," I said.

"Gesundheit!"

"Ha-ha. Meet me at The Point."

"Gotcha."

11

". . . $32 million . . ."
The phrase caught his eye and he read the words that surrounded it.

> . . . just completed negotiations that will bring him $32 mil-
> lion for his share of Mrs. R's Fried Chicken stock. Buyer
> Harvey Fulton Harvey, mega-conglomerator (see *Forbes*, Jan-
> uary 4, 1961), will pay cash for Routenfield's food franchise.
> He had originally offered $45 million in stock and debentures
> which Routenfield turned down as "wallpaper," saying at
> the time of debentures that they were ". . . as worthless as
> the government's word . . ." and ". . . almost as useless
> as the dollar."

Hagopian glanced again at Routenfield's picture. An un-
likable looking old bastard, he might have been sucking a
lemon before the shutter snapped. His stiff white hair was
clipped short and almost shaved above the ears. "Why waste
you?" Hagopian said aloud. "You're going to get hit on soon
by the old guy with the scythe."
He scanned to the last paragraph of the article.

> Asked about his future plans, Routenfield stated that he
> would be announcing the formation of a new corporation
> within the next six months. The firm will supply security
> guards to business, and burglar prevention devices to both
> business and public. "This is where the country's going," he
> said. "We're at a point where local government can't handle

law enforcement or protection of property. Hell, the federal government can't even run its espionage establishment. It is the responsibility of private enterprise to fill this need."

Hagopian glanced without smiling at the Weber cartoon of a large, plump chicken dressed with badge and gun like a security guard. He looked away from the cartoon back to Steven Routenfield's picture.

An accident. Someone wanted him to give the old bastard a fatal accident. "It's okay by me," Hagopian said as he studied Routenfield's face. "But it's going to cost more than a lousy ten yards."

"But that was the contract; ten thousand bucks. How d'ya expect me to get more, Johnny?"

"Tough," Hagopian said. "*Get* it."

"No can do, baby. I don't even know who the customer is."

Hagopian stared idly from his phone booth to the abandoned gas station in which it sat. Only one of the vandalized pumps still had its hose attached. It looked like a short robot cleaning its ear with one finger. "Tough," Hagopian said. "The guy who takes delivery on the package is loaded. He picked up thirty-two million bucks a few years ago. With that kinda scratch, Bernie, he ain't going out for any ten yards." Hagopian sucked on the True Menthol and blew smoke into the mouthpiece as though trying to asphyxiate it. "I want thirty."

"Jesus! Who's the guy?"

"Nope," Hagopian said. "You don't get to know that."

"Look, what d'ya want from me, John-baby? I dunno who the customer is, I dunno who the contract is . . . how'm I gonna get another twenty yards for you?"

Hagopian smoked and thought about it.

80

"Tell me who the contract is," Bernie said. "Just let me know that much and I'll try and get the extra scratch. Okay?"

"Routenfield," Hagopian said. "Steven Routenfield. You think he's worth thirty?"

Bernie whistled softly into the phone. "Yeah; worth it and more. But I'm gonna have a rough time finding the other twenty. Can you call me tomorrow?"

"Sure."

"Say around noon?"

"Make it later," Hagopian said. "I'm getting in a few sets of squash after lunch."

12

And I see but shadows around me,
Illusion in everything.

The Hindu King's Reply to the Missionary
SIR ALFRED COMYN LYALL

She giggled like a chipmunk and wrinkled her nose.

"I've seen you in here before," she said. "You're always pick-ing girls up."

It was a slow night at The Point and she was the only body available. I wondered where they all had gone, those hungry little office girls. Maybe they were regrouping; taking a night away from the game so they could freshen up for tomorrow's crowd. Tomorrow might produce Mr. Right who would sail them to Catalina for the weekend. Or something equally glamorous.

"Is that the way?" she asked. "Is it 'picking girls up,' or is it 'picking up girls'?"

"Either way," I said. "As long as it works."

"That's John Dewey. 'That which works is right.' Right?"

"Absolutely."

"So how do you do it? How do you pick all these girls up?"

"Trade secrets," I said.

I ate up every dark corner of the bar with my eyes but there were no other unattached girls. There were a few couples and, hunched over his Coors at the end of the bar, the redoubtable Basset. But no loose female bodies. The chipmunk was it.

Either that or I could go home alone and scrape varnish from the Bentley's dashboard.

Basset and I had ignored each other from the moment I walked in and saw him nursing his Coors in the gloom. It was a waiting game now. We would wait to see if Buick Riviera's curiosity was strong enough to spur him into The Point.

"C'mon," she said. "Just for practice. Try and pick me up."

"This is my night off."

"Aw, c'mon."

"Okay," I said. "First I'd buy you a drink."

"You did that."

"Then I'd say, 'I don't think you've met me. My name is Charles Remly.' And you'd say, 'Pleased to meetcha. I'm . . .'" I looked deep into her eyes to see if there was intelligent life on earth.

"I'm Shirley."

"Shirley," I said. "Ah, Shirley, you little chipmunk you. How would you like to have dinner, a midnight snack and breakfast with me?"

"And they *fall* for *that?*"

"I make one hell of an eggs benedict. I use Worcestershire sauce in the hollandaise."

She giggled again and I worried that her nose would come unglued as it writhed about on her face. "I've met some pretty smooth guys, but that's really a bad line Charley. Really."

"Sometimes the magic works. Sometimes it doesn't."

"That's Chief Dan George," she said.

A very average, very neat-looking man in a forgettable brown suit walked in, glanced without interest at me and settled himself at the bar midway between where I sat with the chipmunk and where Basset hunched over his Coors. The newcomer ordered a beer; they seemed to be having a run on it that night. Basset got up and moved toward a hallway that led to the

83

men's room, leaving his pack of cigarettes and a handful of change on the bar. But he wasn't going to the john.

"If I thought you were the type I'd invite you to take in *Bohème* at the Music Center. We can just make the curtain if we leave right away."

"*Bohème.* That's an opera, right?"

"Right."

"Bleagh," the chipmunk said.

"Or blues." I was reaching for anything by then. "I've got everything that Billie Holiday and Dinah Washington ever cut. We could drink champagne and have a good cry while Lady Day sings."

"Who?"

"Okay. Who do you like?"

"Tom Jones is okay I guess. But I wouldn't go to a guy's place just to listen to Tom Jones records."

"Nor would I," Glenda said. "Though I might take you up on Billie Holiday." She had slipped through the dark interior of the bar and was sitting on the stool to my left. "Champagne and tears, that's a pretty combination."

I swiveled from the chipmunk to Glenda. "You come here often?"

"First time." She peered around the dim bar. "Last time, too."

"Say, do you know her?"

"Never saw her before in my life," I said to Shirley.

"Buy me a drink," Glenda said.

The chipmunk leaned back on her bar stool and took the measure of Glenda's slim body. She priced Glenda's simple dress and the shoes on her large feet. Finally she sniffed at Glenda's wispy pink hair.

I said, "What are you drinking, stranger?"

"Spies always drink beer. It keeps the tongue from getting loose."

84

I drained the glass before me and ordered two Coors. Shirley had barely touched her banana daiquiri.

"I can't drink beer." Shirley pulled her shoulders back and the development gap between the two women was immediately obvious. "It all goes to my bosom."

"How very interesting," Glenda said. "Some sort of plumbing problem I would imagine." She took a couple of large gulps from her glass. When she smiled at Shirley there was a line of foam on her upper lip.

Shirley's eyes widened. She hadn't met anyone like Glenda before. I hadn't either.

"Fella who drove me here is interested in cars," Glenda said. "Are you interested in cars?" She knocked back an enormous mouthful of beer.

"Sometimes," I said. "It depends whether the car has a following."

Basset emerged from the rest-room hallway and sat down to his beer. If I walked into The Point just then, not knowing Basset or Glenda or brown suit or myself, I would have guessed it was the dullest bar in Los Angeles. Even the jukebox was dead.

"I knew a man who collected cars in Nice," Glenda said.

"That's on the Riviera, right?" Shirley said to no one in particular.

"But you know how those rich Europeans are. Blasé. He just lost interest in his collection." Glenda drained the last of her beer and gave a ladylike little belch. "He said that after a while, everything goes flat for him."

"Time for me to leave," I said. "Can I give you a lift?"

"Which way are you heading?"

"I'll follow your lead, stranger."

Glenda gathered up her purse and slipped from the stool.

I patted the chipmunk's knee. "Sometimes the magic works."

13

The wire led to two clipped ends at the edge of the roof. From what he could see in the light of his pen flash, the wire was old; had been there for years.

The air-conditioning duct had been punched through and stuffed with newspaper. He pulled out a crisp, fading wad of it and played the pen flash on the upper-right-hand corner of a crumbling page. "Los Angeles *Mirror-News* October 23, 1964 page 2."

Forget it, Hagopian. It's not a client tap. It's not a target tap. It's nothing. Forget it, he thought.

He moved slowly across the roof, feeling carefully with his sneakered feet. At the edge he gripped the rain gutter first with one, then the other gloved hand. He kicked off and dropped lightly to the patio deck.

Inside he broke the federal tax stamp on a bottle of Jack Daniel's and poured a straight shot. It was time to disturb Richardson's room at the Hollywood Executive House.

Now that he'd registered as Hagopian at the Beverly Wildwood, this would become his nightly ritual:

Hagopian peeled the scar from his chin, then the graying mustache and the two hair pieces on each side of his widow's peak. Dipping a comb into dark brown lotion he combed out both the premature gray and the part in his hair, accentuating the length of his homely face.

Padding about Bungalow 14 in his bare feet, Hagopian collected cigarette butts in a "New—the Top Locks—Just Right for Sandwiches" Glad Bag. He would take these to his Richardson room at the Executive House where he would distribute them in ash trays. He would wrinkle the bed, steam the bathroom, sop up water in at least one of the bath towels, pour a spot of Jack Daniel's into a glass, then flush four shots of the sour mash down the toilet in order to bring down the level of whiskey in the bottle.

Although his methods would not mislead an educated investigator they would convince the hotel that Richardson had not checked out; that Richardson was still using the room. And as a result Hagopian would have his secondary shelter should it be necessary.

The telephone rang.

"Mr. Hagopian?"

"Yes."

"Check out, Mr. Hagopian." The voice spoke quietly. There was no threat in it, just courteous reason. "And take Johnny the Contractor with you. There is no need for your services, Mr. Hagopian. No reason for you to stay in Los Angeles."

What a very reassuring voice, Hagopian thought. How did the mother find me? How could he know about Johnny the Contractor? Cradling the handset between shoulder and ear he opened the Jack Daniel's and poured himself another shot.

"We are willing to match your retainer, Mr. Hagopian. Check out of the Beverly Wildwood."

"I've already been paid. I don't welsh on deals."

"Check out of the Wildwood. A messenger will deliver ten thousand dollars, small bills, and you may consider your services terminated."

That's twenty thousand for not doing the job, he thought. And another twenty from Bernie would make it an easy forty yards. But there were other considerations. "I've got a client relationship to think about," he said.

"Mr. Hagopian." The voice sighed. "Ah, Mr. Hagopian. I

am trying to find in my heart some convincing argument that will make you understand the wisdom of my advice." Hagopian sipped some of the Jack Daniel's. "To begin with, your clients do not have the manpower to cause violence. If they had, your services would hardly be necessary. It therefore follows, quite logically I think, that they cannot harm you if you do not complete your work. Then there is a matter of efficiency. We are more efficient than your client. We know what they are doing. We know what you are doing. We have even breached your client's organization to the extent that we know the amount you charge for your services. Yet, you do not know what we are doing, nor does your client know what we are doing." There was a smile in the man's voice. "Do you follow me, so far?"

Civilized, Hagopian thought, lighting a True Menthol. We are quite civilized. "I follow you."

"Marvelous. Now, let us consider the alternatives. First, you can leave and keep a whole skin . . . and be paid another ten thousand dollars. As conscience dictates, you may even return the ten thousand retainer to your clients. On the other hand, you can stay and be killed, absolutely dead, by eight o'clock tomorrow morning."

"No other options?"

"None."

Hate.

A spasm racked him, doubling him over, nearly dropping him from the couch. Hagopian spilled his drink on the carpet.

"Mr. Hagopian, I'm waiting for your answer."

He forced himself to relax. He opened his eyes and leaned back on the couch. He placed his empty glass on the end table.

"Go fuck yourself." His voice was low and intense. Consonants popped in every word.

"Mr. Hagopian, that's hardly . . ."

"Go . . . *fuck* . . . yourself. You send any of your mothers after me, I'll waste them." He was breathing heavily. The adrenalin of hate and fear was pouring into his system. His heart pounded.

Stupid.

Yes, he knew that. But he had lost control.

"Is that your final word?"

"I'm better than you are."

"Oh, I'm well aware of that, Mr. Hagopian. Individually, in your line of work, you are far better than I. But my company is rather large, and our resources are much vaster than yours. Our representatives will call on you sometime between now and eight o'clock tomorrow morning . . . unless, of course, you should have a change of heart. In which case your ten thousand will be delivered to you sometime between the time you check out of the Beverly Wildwood and the time you board your airplane."

Hagopian smashed the handset into its cradle. His reaction had been stupid. *Stupid.* But still, he could not control the flashes. Pouring another Jack Daniel's, he rose and paced the drawing room. Slow down, he thought. Slow down. He breathed deeply.

Were they really trying to get him out of town? Or were they trying merely to rattle him? Any other guy in the business would be wetting his pants by now because when they tag you they're a step ahead of you. But not ahead of me, Hagopian thought.

Despite what the voice on the phone had told him there were four choices. Not two.

First, he could cancel the job and leave town. But there was no guarantee that the opposition would let him live. They could as easily cut him down on the way to the airport, saving themselves ten thousand dollars.

He could leave now for his room at the Executive House. But if they were as good as the voice implied, he had no more chance there than here. They would find him.

He could find some other shelter for the night. But, again, their efficiency might as easily take him out at the new shelter.

Finally, of course, he could stay the night in his comfortable bungalow. Whether or not they could nail him by eight in the morning was a moot point. Hagopian dragged at his True Menthol, sipped his sour mash, and slowly paced off the drawing room. If they scare me once and get away with it, he thought, they'll keep after me. But if I can take out one of their people, that'll slow the bastards down.

Screw 'em, he thought. They threw money around like it was meaningless; but if he blew just one job, *this* one, the word would get out. No more sweet jobs at ten yards a pop. No more forty thousand tax-free dollars every year.

"Screw 'em," he said aloud. And emptied his glass of Jack Daniel's.

14

If you don't eat your vegetables, you'll go to bed without dessert.

Familiar Refrain

Glenda plopped a plastic bag into the pot of boiling water. I lifted a torn package from the large paper sack that she used as a garbage can. A few seconds ago the package had contained the plastic bag that was to be part of my dinner. I read the ingredients: "Garden Fresh Tender Baby Peas 'n' Sweet Little French Onions in a Gourmet Sauce of flour, margarine, hydrogenated coconut oil, hydrogenated palm kernel oil, sugar, dehydrated onions, cornstarch, wheat starch, chicken fat, dextrose, hydrolyzed vegetable protein, monosodium glutamate, whey, nonfat dry milk, artificial flavoring and coloring, disodium inosinate and disodium guanylate."

"Do we eat this stuff?" I asked. "Or do we rub it on our skin to relieve psoriasis?"

"Get out of my kitchen."

I looked around at the clutter. A week's collection of dirty dishes, glasses, pots and pans was piled in her sink. Spots of crusted food clung to the counter. And a large black patch on the ceiling told of a frying pan fire that must have been a three-alarmer. "I'll cook next time."

"If there *is* a next time," Glenda said. She opened the broiler door and prodded our steaks with a long fork. "All I know about you is rumor." The steaks bled as she turned them.

I unwired a bottle of Korbel and eased out the cork. "Any clean glasses around here?" Glenda shook her head. I washed two glasses and poured some wine.

"You are the object of a lot of talk around the office," Glenda said. She sprinkled the steaks with a yellow-hued pre-seasoned salt. "I wonder sometimes about your notorious promiscuity: Are you running *to*? Or are you running *from*?"

"Usually," I said, "I walk."

Glenda turned on her mocking smile. "C'mon. Serioso, now. What makes you run?"

"Shut up and drink your champagne."

"If you can't make polite conversation," Glenda said, "go shave your bristly face. There's a razor in the bathroom."

Needlepoints of water splashed off my back as I shielded Glenda from the shower head. A thick lather covered her shoulders and back where I had soaped her. I stepped aside to let the spray rinse away the soap. Little rivers of it ran down her narrow, freckled back. Looking at her slender little body I felt like I was bathing a young child.

"I grew up in a factory town near Mojave," Glenda was saying, "where all the girls were teasers. At the high school gym dances they would give the boys a good rub while they danced. Then they all got together in the girls' locker room where they'd argue about the relative hardness of George as compared with Paul."

I wiped the last traces of soap from her shoulders. "Turn around."

"It didn't make a lot of sense to me. I figured, why order a fudge sundae if you don't intend to enjoy it." Her pink-lashed green eyes were cool in their appraisal of me.

"Lift your chin." I soaped her fragile neck and upper chest.

"*God* but I was happy to get away from Johnstown. Everything was owned by the chemical plant; the stores, the movie show, the schools . . ."

"Really?"

"No," Glenda said. She reached out and held my wrists. "Please, don't stop. That's a nice man."

I was soaping her small breasts. They were like soft, shallow mounds on her chest.

Her nails dug painfully into my wrists. "That's beautiful. That's really beautiful. I never understood why men drool over large . . . umm . . . unless it's the 'mother' thing."

"Johnstown sounds as paternalistic as the Agency," I said.

Glenda reached through the shower curtain and lifted a bottle of Korbel from the sink. It was our second bottle, already half empty. Glenda emptied it some more. When she spoke again her voice had a dreamy sound that was out of context with her words. "They had this hospital that the company built. It was a typical small-town hospital except it had a cardiologist and a respiratory specialist because heart and lung disease were the two side effects of working for the company."

She drank again from the bottle of Korbel, handed it to me and wrapped herself around me as I drank. "I guess that dinner wasn't so good," she said. "But how did you like the dessert?" She rubbed her budding breasts against my rib cage.

"Loved it," I said, trying at the same time to drink from the bottle and hold her writhing, slippery little body. "But next time, I'll cook."

"Oh no," Glenda said. "No no no. Next time is right now."

"Be realistic," I said. "I'm not up to it."

Glenda tilted her head back and fixed me with an ironic smile. A stray wisp of damp pink hair bisected her cheek like a welt of pale blood. "Don't worry darling. I *get* you up to it."

93

I was cramped in Glenda's twin-size bed. Like a pullover sweater that was a size too small it was not so uncomfortable that I wanted to climb out of it, yet not comfortable enough to relax in.

Her whole apartment was like that, inexpensive and small, as though she had furnished it from an aggressively merchandised drugstore.

I rekindled my dead cigar and said, "That sounds like it was a hell of a place, that Johnstown."

"It was murder. I got into a little trouble, but of course that was Before Pill. The company took it as a matter of morals, not medicine, when I got an abortion. My father was fired." Glenda dragged fiercely on her cigarette. "That was exactly two weeks after my fourteenth birthday."

Her face was lively now, more animated than before. Even during our love play she was in control of her features. There hadn't been passion or ecstasy or pleasure in her look; just dreamy amusement and a craftsman's simple interest in the quality of the job she performed.

I climbed from Glenda's confining little bed and started gathering up my clothes. They lay in an irregular line from the bed to the door.

"Hey, don't go."

"No more," I said. "I need the sleep."

"Yes," she said. "More."

"I've got to go," I said. "Basset may be waiting for me at my place."

"Phone him."

"I can't remember the number; I call myself so seldom."

While I climbed into my wrinkled suit Glenda watched as though I was a music-hall act that she might be booking.

94

"Now I know your secret," she said. "You *do* get into your pants one leg at a time."

"Next time, I'll cook dinner."

"Okay." Glenda smiled like a pussycat. "I'll fix dessert."

15

The figure in the bed breathed regularly and heavily.

It coughed once when a thin blade snicked open the window lock. The two figures outside stopped their work. They started once more when the breathing became smooth again.

After slipping inside one stayed by the window while the other moved carefully to the bed. He glided across the floor, not lifting his feet but sliding them forward. At the edge of the bed he touched a Jack Daniel's bottle with his left foot. In his hand he had another sort of bottle, a soft plastic bottle, and a pad of gauze.

Uncapping the bottle he poured some liquid from it into the gauze pad. The liquid had a pleasant odor, sweet and relaxing. He recapped the bottle and dropped it into his jacket pocket. When his hand returned from the pocket it held a pen flash.

HATE.

Hagopian moved violently from the closet, his gloved hands clutching a 27-inch Louisville Slugger extruded aluminum baseball bat weighted with shot to a total of eight pounds. When he struck he followed through so absolutely that the wart-faced little guy at the window lost both his life and the entire left side of his bald head. The bat was going 185 mph at the last critical second and struck with a force of 9,156.8 foot-pounds. Hagopian felt the impact up to his elbows as the bat crushed the man's head, sending splinters of bone through his brain and into the right side of his skull.

Blood and bits of liquefied cerebral tissue splashed onto Hagopian's cashmere sweater.

Before the man collapsed to the floor Hagopian had already begun swinging in the opposite direction.

Even so, he was too late.

The mother at the bed dropped under the blow, holding up his left arm, the one bearing the gauze pad, to protect his face.

Hagopian cut short his follow-through as he felt the bat whistling in empty air.

Hate.

As the man dropped Hagopian started a perfect kick. He jerked his knee up, like a drum major, then swiveled his foot outward, hinging from the knee. The object of the kick was to aim his toe at a point some six to twelve inches *behind* the target. This assured follow-through.

The adrenalin was flowing beautifully. In quick succession he heard the figure behind him, the lump of bloody meat, hit the floor; he felt his toe dig into the other man's abdomen just below the solar plexus, moving his guts outward from the point of impact and line of follow through; then he finally stopped the swing of his baseball bat.

Bastards.

Hagopian brought the bat lightly down on the man's head. Enough to put him out. Perhaps enough to cause a concussion that would give the guy a lifetime of headaches and memory lapses, or cause vascular damage at the optic thalamus—damage that was sure to blind him. But not enough to kill him.

He worked quickly. A large Glad Wrap freezer bag over the dead, gushing skull, tied and sealed with dental floss. It was too late to save the rug, but he hoped to keep it from getting so thick with blood that it squished under his feet.

And now, with the bedside lamp on, Hagopian nearly vomited at the sight of the Glad Wrap freezer bag filling with blood. He covered the thing with his stained sweater.

The lumpy figure in the bed coughed again and settled back to its heavy breathing.

At the sight of the other man, the one he'd kicked and tapped, Hagopian grinned; lips drawing back over big teeth. The man looked happy, sleeping like a child. Hagopian placed the ether-soaked gauze pad over his slack mouth. Lullaby, Hagopian thought. And good night.

Reaching into the mess of pillows and blankets in the bed, he turned off the Sony 800B. He had rigged a continuous loop of tape on an open-topped reel and plugged the thing into an AC outlet through a transformer; the snoring, coughing, breathing machine would have played forever.

Back again in the closet Hagopian began dismantling his defense system. First the earplug that led to a switching system. The system had two Lucite indicators, one red the other green.

The red light led to a solenoid that was attached to the telephone. If power in the phone was shut off the solenoid would lose its magnetic field, snap shut and cause the light to glow while a quiet buzzer sounded in the earplug.

The red light had glowed fifteen minutes before the attack, and Hagopian knew that his phone had been cut.

The green Lucite was wired to the air conditioning microphone. Here the solenoid was just the opposite of the first: a surge of electricity in the line would activate a magnetic field, causing the green light to glow and the buzzer to buzz.

The green light had not glowed at all. But one out of two wasn't bad, Hagopian thought.

The voice on the phone had lied to him. They didn't want to waste him, not with that ether-soaked gauze pad. So why had the guy called? To make it easier to snatch him? Sure, it had to be a snatch. These punks weren't contract guys; hell, they couldn't hit on a bed case at an old folks home. But why a snatch?

Figure it later, Hagopian thought. Right now, let's get rolling.

His cases were packed and waiting on the far side of the bed. He lifted the large tool case, unlocked the safety panel and stowed his electronic gear. After wiping down his Louisville Slugger on the sheets he packed it away. Sleeping Beauty had a set of keys in his pocket. Thank God. Hagopian wasn't sure he had the stomach to frisk the corpse.

He carried his cases one at a time through the sliding glass door to the patio and lowered them gently over the low patio wall. Moving through Bungalow 14's rooms and spending a quiet minute in each, he cased them visually and reflectively. He remembered every room and every action that he'd taken in it. Clean; absolutely clean.

He fingered the keys in his pocket. Passing over the miscellaneous door and padlock stuff Hagopian identified the car keys by touch. Details. His deft fingers rejected the trunk key and explored the ignition key's contours. It was FoMoCo: It was a—sure, sure; now to find a two-year-old Merc parked somewhere around the Beverly Wildwood.

16

Q: You have used the expression "dirty tricks" a number of times, sir. Will you define that for the Committee?

A: They are practical jokes that you play on the other side, sir.

Q: And you indulge in practical jokes on Government time, sir?

A: Ahn . . . I should add, sir, that they are practical jokes with a point.

Minutes of the Hearings,
Subcommittee on National Security Affairs
Volume LVI
Page 374

Frank Basset had a Mona Lisa smile and the heart of Niccolò Machiavelli.

He was sitting in the rocking chair in my living room, smoking one of my few Berings and talking on my phone. If it had been anyone but Basset I would have resented his free use of my rocking chair. I had found the chair at a junk shop in the farmlands of Central California, paid three dollars for it and refinished it to its original 1930s ugliness. But ugly as it was the chair was also comfortable, secure and sturdy. It had to be, to support Basset's weight.

As for the cigar and the phone I could expect nothing less from Basset. And nothing more for that matter.

Basset winked as I entered and continued his conversation: ". . . five hundred acres?! Jeez! My Uncle George can get *twice* the cash crop yield on *two* hundred acres." He was shouting as though he hoped to talk to his party without benefit of electronics.

I settled myself at the upright piano, folded down the keyboard cover and slid open the panel above it. That was my bar. During that run through the farmlands I had found the piano for twelve dollars. After stripping out the guts—and that had taken over a month of weekends, pouring boiling water on the old casein-glued joints and attacking the strings and soundboard with a blowtorch—I installed shelves and a single-tap sink in the upper part and a small, secondhand bar–fridge underneath.

As I measured out a neat shot of Christian Brothers brandy Basset's eyes glowed. Still talking, he flashed a shy smile and held out his big hand.

". . . I don't give a flying fuck about the blight. If you don't come up with a profit this year, I'll shove every last pineapple on the place into your personal nose."

I nearly dropped the brandy. "Who're you talking to? Hawaii?"

Basset covered the mouthpiece with his huge paw. "Don't worry. It's on my Agency credit card."

"But it's from *my number!*"

"Look," he said into the phone. "Call me tomorrow. And no more excuses or I'll fly out there and pull off your fingers one at a time."

"Hello Basset," I said as he cradled the phone.

"Hi babe," Basset said. "How'd you like to get into a good deal? I can put you into high-yield pineapple acreage in Hawaii."

"I heard," I said. "My money's all tied up in debts."

"It's a beautiful shot."

"I'll remember that when I testify at your bankruptcy hearing." I sipped at the brandy and dug around in the piano's humidor for a cigar. "How did you get in? This place is tighter than the National Archives."

"Weaver's been showing me a few tricks." He waggled his blunt fingers in the air. "There's no such thing as a pick-proof lock, stud." Basset heaved his large body out of the rocking chair and walked toward the bar like a grazing elephant. "You drive Glenda home?" he asked not quite innocently.

I said, "How come you took her there? It made for complications."

Basset poured twelve fingers of brandy into an iced-tea tumbler. "She wanted to see an operation; said she'd never seen one before." He drank the brandy as though it was water. In Basset's huge frame it would take the alcohol at least a week to reach his brain.

"Never again," I said.

"What could hurt? Hell, it was only a little operation. Glenda's been cleared for Q level stuff."

"You've got pineapples on the brain." I shaved off a bit of cigar ash and dipped the other end into my brandy. "What if we screwed up the job? With Glenda there, the word gets back to the F. O. Without her we could fake it a little on our report. Are you listening?"

"Yeah, well, she's pretty hard to say no to." Basset prodded my shoulder. "Right?"

"Okay, so what happened? Glenda said you gave the guy a flat, but he followed me almost a mile after we left The Point."

"I tried a new kind of shot on the guy. Muriatic acid."

I closed my eyes and massaged my eyebrows; I knew what was coming. Basset was a great fan of espionage thrillers. "You've got to stop reading those damn books," I said. "Now tell me about the muriatic acid."

102

"Nothing to it. You get a couple of 10 cc. glass vials and fill 'em with muriatic and seal off the tops. Then you wedge them against the guy's right rear tire, one in front and one in back. The guy doesn't see them because the right rear is against the curb, right?"

"Right as rain," I said. "But much more complex."

"It's simple," Basset said. "It doesn't matter whether the guy drives straight out or backs out, he's going to run over one of the vials and smear his tire with acid. He drives nearly a mile and *BOOM!* Flat. You get away and I follow him back to his little nest."

"What about the street?"

"Okay," Basset said. "What about the street?"

"The street where the guy ran over the acid. Muriatic acid is used commercially for cleaning concrete off of tile. It eats through concrete, Basset. *Eats* through it. There's going to be one hell of a big hole in the street in front of The Point."

"Yeah," Basset drained his brandy. "Jeez, that's a bad side effect sure enough. I've got to work on that one."

"And what about the other vial? The next guy that drives into that parking spot is going to be one surprised *hombre* when he stumbles out of The Point. I mean, let's face it: it's not every day your tire melts while you're having a drink."

"Maybe I can fix it," said Basset as he poured more brandy.

"Going to mix up a batch of concrete at this time of morning?"

"Hell no," Basset said. He looked at me as though I was speaking Greek. "Not the street; *Glenda*. I'll call her first thing at the office and tell her that we don't always operate that way and maybe she shouldn't tell the F. O. about the muriatic acid."

"Never again," I said again.

"Yeah, well, she's pretty hard to put off. She sure has a hot

103

wheel for you, stud." Basset's innocent face was wreathed in happy lines. Although the smile made him look a bit dull-witted, it was the closest he could come to leering. "All the way to The Point she kept pumping me for stuff on you. 'How come he's divorced? What was his wife like?' Stuff like that."

"It's late and I'm tired, pal. Just tell me about the black Riviera and let me get some sleep."

"Black Riviera?" Basset snapped his fingers; it sounded like two raw steaks landing together. "Oh, sure, the Riviera. He fixed his flat and drove to the downtown Statler." He pulled the cigar out of his face and knocked back the rest of his brandy.

"You find out who he was?"

"Oh sure. Just a guy, like you and me."

"A guy like us?"

"Sure. He's with that Russian Cultural Delegation," Basset said. "I guess he's KGB."

17

One of the Marines was kicking his head in.

Two others held Mama, naked Mama, while the fourth unlocked his shining brass belt buckle and dropped his blue pants.

"I'll kill you! I'll kill you."

Crunch.

The cordovan boot smashed his nose sideways and took out a tooth. Little Juanito tasted fresh blood. He pushed his tongue into the empty spot where the tooth used to be.

"Cabrones. Dirty bastards."

Crunch. Another tooth came loose.

"Mamacita," he called.

Mama screamed.

Crunch.

Hagopian screamed. He opened his eyes.

Hagopian was soaked through. He had nearly sweated off one of his hair pieces. I'll kill you, he thought, touching the hair into place.

On his feet and stretching, he walked to the shattered window and looked out. Two blocks of junked and weary buildings were fenced off around his abandoned hotel. What a lousy night, trying to sleep in this filthy place. But if the bastards had nailed his Executive House rooms—better here than there.

Urban redevelopment, they called it. He snorted. Some redevelopment. Downtown Los Angeles, from where he stood, looked like the topside of hell. They were smashing the place flat.

105

Puffs of silt crowded up from each step as he moved from the window to his tool kit.

Crunch.

The building shook and rattled. Hagopian looked around the room in disbelief: they were demolishing *this* building. Christ. A plate-sized patch of plaster dropped from the ceiling onto his tool kit. Let's get out of here, he thought. But how? The building would be surrounded by demolition and construction guys. Let's see where they are. At the window again he saw that his abandoned hotel was cordoned off with vivid yellow rope. There was no one on his side of the building; the action was all to his left. That was where the wrecking ball was gathering momentum again. The crane operator and a handful of guys watched.

Crunch.

Something gave way in the building's structure. The floor tilted beneath him and Hagopian scampered after his tool kit as it began an unhurried slide toward the door. Grabbing the kit, heaving it up with a groan, he felt as though he was trapped in a new and even more horrifying nightmare. What if the stairwells were gone? It was time to run. Leave the clothes; leave the other two cases. Get out. He could think about it later.

The stairwell was okay. Christ. Thank you Mother Mary. He grabbed the banister with one hand and held his heavy tool kit in the other as he skittered down the steps. What was it, seven flights to the bottom? Or was it eight?

Crunch.

When he hit the second-floor landing he thought the world was coming to an end. An entire section of wall gave way, spitting plaster and shards of timber like shrapnel from a fragmentation grenade.

Hagopian's heart nearly stopped as a four-ton wrecking ball

106

plowed through the wall and hovered before him. It was close enough to touch. The thing looked like a huge, black iron pear, chipped and scarred and bruised from so many years of assault against Los Angeles.

He could hear the ceiling timbers giving way above him and he choked on the dust that suddenly shook loose from walls and floor and ceiling. *Unreal*, Hagopian thought. A six-by-six joist swung from the plaster overhead with a weird popping sound; it had snapped as easily as a toothpick. What now? *What now?* The scarred ball began its pendulum backstroke, moving lethargically through the disaster it had created.

He heard bricks falling and framing joists breaking away from their nails.

The floor began to sink beneath him. To his left, opposite the gaping hole that the wrecking ball had created, a narrow window exploded.

Sweet bleeding Jesus Christ. The whole fucking building is coming down on my fucking head.

He threw his case out the yawning window.

With his thumb Hagopian touched a hasty cross on his forehead. And jumped.

He couldn't stop trembling. He sat up and stuffed his bleeding hands under his armpits, but they shook like some kind of crazy vibrating machine. His vision was blurred and his cheek burned where it had plowed into the dirt. I'm still here, Hagopian thought. He'd lost both shoes. Good sweet mother of Christ I'm still here.

Focusing on his stockinged feet he said, "Every week, a candle. I promise. A candle every week. And after I get this bastard Routenfield, no more jobs. This I swear, dear Virgin . . . no more jobs."

"On your feet Mex."

Hagopian looked toward the voice and saw a pair of legs

107

wrapped in gray whipcord cloth. His eyes traveled up, taking in the pink hand on the holstered gun, the phony looking badge and the bored face. Rent-a-cop, he thought.

"C'mon. Get up, bean head."

Rolling painfully to knees and left hand, Hagopian dipped his right hand into his trouser pocket. "Yes sir," he mumbled. His face was numb. "Gi' me . . . give me a li'l time." Hagopian inhaled and exhaled, inhaled and exhaled. He'd need oxygen if his muscles were to function. "Please . . . gettin' right up." He pulled his hand from his pocket and placed a closed right fist against the dirt to take the pressure from his left hand and arm.

Then he saw the guard's boots. Blood-rich cordovan boots.

When Hagopian moved it was not with a series of separate acts of separate groups of muscles. It was more like the fluid motion of a striking snake. He pushed off with both hands to throw his weight back onto the balls of his feet. Pulling his torso into a squatting position, knees bent, he whipped his closed right fist back to a point behind and beside his right buttock. Once his hand was at the apex of its backswing he flexed the muscles of his thighs and calves, pressed his thumb against the switchblade's release button and arced his arm upward. The snap of the knife's heavy eight-inch blade threw his hand slightly to the right, but he had already compensated for that by aiming just a hair to the left of his target. The force of his thrusting arm was more than doubled by the uncoiling of his legs.

The guard snatched at his holstered gun. But the sighting nib on the tip of the barrel never got beyond his holster's leather rim.

Hagopian's blade carried such violence and follow-through that it not only punched into the rent-a-cop's throat, it severed the vertebrae just below the base of his skull. Before he could stop the force of his skewering blow, Hagopian's thumb had entered the other's neck, piercing the larynx.

Hagopian rolled away from the falling body, fearful of the gusher of blood. His switchblade pulled clear with difficulty from the other's neck bones.

It was clean, he told himself. No noise.

The sour taste of dinner came up in his throat. Hagopian put his head between his knees to keep from losing what was left in his stomach. Dear Virgin Mother, I promise . . .

18

Q: Would you repeat, sir, your qualifications for the sort of
   work you are engaged in?
A: Yes, sir. I have a nasty suspicious mind.

Minutes of the Hearings,
Subcommittee on National Security Affairs
Volume XCIV
Page 81

Days break in my neighborhood with the open-throated
roar of a motorcycle three buildings uphill from my apartment.
Every weekday before my alarm goes off the big Norton ex-
plodes like a pound of *plastique* and rattles shutters outside
my bedroom window.

I live in a sprawling apartment in the Little Morocco section of Hollywood. It's a rolling area forested with white
stucco walls and red tile roofs. Little balconies look down on
narrow, winding streets. Because of the steep slope on which
it was constructed over thirty years ago, my place sprawls not
only out, but up and down; no two rooms are on the same
level. It's a pleasant place to live in and its furnishing, like the
restoration of the Bentley, seems always to verge on comple-
tion.

When the unmuffled bike woke me I walked downstairs for
an Alka-Seltzer and breakfast.

Like the champagne that was working painfully in my head,
thoughts of Glenda were eating away at the corners of my

mind. I watched the two tablets dissolve into carbonated salvation and wondered if she was also nursing herself with morning-after nostrums.

I held a paper filter under the spout of my junkshop coffee grinder and filled it with fresh, aromatic grounds. I had settled the filter in its hourglass pot and was pouring almost-boiling water into it when the phone rang. The shock of the telephone to my hangover was such that I carefully poured a full eight ounces of scalding water on my left hand.

Blowing on the tender skin I silently cursed my way to the living room and lifted the phone's handset from its cradle. In my ear Glenda said, "Basset get his man?"

"This isn't a clear line. How's your head? You have a hangover?"

"Nothing I won't live through. I took some Vitamin B^{12} so it should clear up by the time I get to my bus stop."

"Does that really help?" I picked up the phone and walked toward the living room balcony, nudged open the door and sat in one of the ice cream chairs that I'd picked up only last week at a swap meet.

Glenda said, "Like a charm. Why, do you feel bad?"

"Nothing that coffee and breakfast won't cure."

"You should have stayed. I'd fix you eggs benedict."

"No thanks." I remembered the Gourmet Sauce. It wasn't that I disapproved of prefab food. But Marion had fed me a diet of cardboard and plastic every night during the two years we were married. I felt that I'd eaten my share of disodium guanylate.

Glenda said, "You owe me a dinner when you get back. What will you fix for me?"

The street was filled with long morning shadows that threw Mondrian patterns on whitewashed stucco walls where they curved away and out of sight as the street wound its way up

111

the hill. Patches of the walls that were touched by the sun seemed to glow in pink reflection.

"Look, let's not plan anything that far ahead. I might get enough data over there to keep me busy day and night."

"Or you might find something interesting at The Point," Glenda said with a sardonic edge to her voice.

"Promiscuity pays," I said.

"Ha ha," Glenda said. "You've already made a reputation as a bad boy; there's no reason to talk about it."

An ugly piebald cat was lounging across the street in a narrow patch of morning sunlight. He was the king of the street: I'd once seen him chase off a large mongrel.

"I'll phone you one way or the other when I get back."

"You'd better. Bad boys go to bed without their dessert."

After choking down the flat Alka-Seltzer, I carried a mug of coffee to the tampered phone upstairs.

The phone at my bedside looked like an average instrument from Pacific Tel and Tel. It had the shape and color and weight of every other phone in the system. If you took it apart you would find the same components that are in the phone for which you're overcharged in your own home. Only a well-schooled technician could find the three microminiature products of electronic wizardry within it; even then he would be hard put to explain just what they did.

I dialed a seven-digit number, waited for exactly thirty-five seconds and dialed another seven-digit combination. The code put me into phase with our SoCal SubSection scrambling system. A series of clicks told me that a line was available and I dialed Virginia. When my party got on the line I said, "This is ———,* Q Clearance authorization number ———,* with a request for a Q level security review."

* Edited, F. O. SoCal SubSection

112

"Just a moment," the voice said.

I looked out my bedroom window to the whitewashed apartment across the way. Someone had scattered bread crumbs in his doorway and a lone house sparrow was pecking mechanically at them. Behind the sparrow and separated from it by a six-inch-high concrete gutter rim was the ugly piebald cat who crawled with infinite patience. When the sparrow hopped forward to a fresh patch of crumbs the cat froze.

"Sorry for keeping you," the voice said. "I had to check something with my Operations Officer. The Op. says you'll have to go through regular channels to get a Q level security review."

Following the path of bread crumbs the bird was now within wing-tip distance of the concrete gutter rim. On the far side of the rim the cat crouched and bared its teeth.

"Did you hear me? You'll have to get that review cleared through your Field Officer's secretary."

The cat pounced. Feathers flew as the cat gripped its dying prey.

"That might prove embarrassing," I said. "She's the subject of the review."

19

R.E. INVESTMENT

R-1 residence, 2 acres of viewsite land (can subdivide),
good leverage

"This project's bound to last for years," Basset said. "Years."
The house on Mulholland was crawling with security men
who tapped the walls for ominous noises and were rigging an
elaborate electronic alarm system.

"I've figured it down to the penny." As he paced the floor
he looked like a mechanical bear from Disneyland. "The first
trust deed comes to five hundred and eighty a month. Taxes,
fire insurance, homeowner's insurance and water bond are
another three hundred; say even three-fifty. That makes . . ."
the security crew foreman entered while Basset counted in his
head ". . . nine hundred, thirty dollars a month."

The security foreman was standing behind Basset, shifting
his weight from one foot to the other.

"Something?" I said.

"The microwave transmitter's in," he said. "Where do you
want the scrambler?"

"That will go into my office," Harriet said as she entered
the kitchen followed by a scent of stale powder. "The little
bedroom next to the service porch."

I looked at Harriet, then blinked my eyes against the sight
of her. She even looked disagreeable; neckless, as though she
had been carrying a safe on her head for the last forty years.

114

The security foreman was turning to leave when I said, "Master bedroom. It's that big room in the back with a view."

He stopped and looked from Harriet to me and back again to Harriet. He worked almost exclusively for the F. O. No one had told him who the senior officer was at our safe house.

"Bring me this morning's *Times*," I said to Harriet. "Then make us a fresh pot of coffee."

"There are much more important things to be done," Harriet said. She rubbed the back of what might have been her neck if she'd had one.

I felt my face relax. I kept on watching Harriet. She returned my stare without a trace of discomfort, but she had gotten the message; part of it at any rate.

"Follow me," Harriet said to the security foreman. "I'll show you Mr. Remly's office."

"The newspaper, Harriet. I want the *Times*. And fresh coffee."

"After I've shown him your office," Harriet sniffed as she walked away.

When they left the room Basset said, "What do you think? It's a clear profit of two hundred seventy dollars a month and we end up owning the property."

"You've overlooked the two basic principles of cheating," I said. "First, always cheat in a small way. Second, always assume that the F. O. knows that you are cheating."

"But this one could make us rich, babe. This Routenfield project has got to last for at least a year."

"Thirty days," I said. "What are you using for ears?"

"Balls," Basset said. "DAAD has been on his back before this. And the little guy always handles them."

"It's not DAAD. It's the Agency. We've got thirty days."

"Balls," Basset said. "At *least* a year. That's around three thousand bucks profit which we can use to pay off the note for

115

a few months until we sell the place. And we write off the insurance and interest against our taxes. Everybody wins."

"The F. O. would never go for it," I said.

"He'll never have to know. We can handle it through my father-in-law, see, and who's going to find out?"

"The F. O.," I said. "He'll find out."

"Okay, babe. So what? They've got to rent the house from someone; why not us?"

He was out of his mind. Completely out of his mind. But still, it was a chance to make a profit. "Okay. Let's suppose we can get away with it. How about the down payment? How will you and I raise twenty-four thousand dollars, plus escrow costs?"

"That's nothing." Basset smiled his innocent smile. "I just wanted to know if you would go along. I'll figure out the down payment."

"Twenty-four thousand dollars?!"

Basset rubbed his huge hands together. They looked like two enormous loaves of bread. "I'll figure it out."

"While you're figuring, get moving on this Routenfield thing." I filled the kettle and put it on a front burner. Our bottled water stand hadn't arrived, so I used the chlorine dilute that came from the tap. "What's Weaver on?" I asked. "Is he back from the maternity ward?"

"He's wiring Routenfield for sound," Basset said. "Both houses, his office, and a transmitter in his Fleetwood."

"That house in Mammoth . . . who's going to monitor it?"

"I got authorization to connect Mammoth with our L.A. to Vegas trunk line. Weaver can tape everything right here at the safe house."

"When he's finished with Routenfield have him wire the girl," I said. "Mary Louise."

Basset patted his trouser pockets and pulled out a wadded

pack of Winstons. The cigarette that he lit looked antic in his mouth, bending sharply in three different places like a broken toothpick.

"Downtown gave me zilch on her," I said. "Try to fill in the blanks while I'm in Europe."

Basset said, "The wire oughta be enough."

"No. More than that. Her background story stinks. That orphan line just doesn't balance in the credit column. If she was a seven-year-old girl, how did she get over the wall? How come there's no information about adults who brought her over the thing?" I smiled without humor. "The only orphan that tough has blank eyeballs and a dog that goes 'Arf arf.' Let's get something more."

Harriet entered the kitchen just as the kettle began to whistle. "You'd better leave me your key," she said. "If you're going to be fooling around in Europe while we're here working, you won't be able to answer the scrambler or get to the Q files."

The kettle screamed madly, ignored by Harriet who thrust her open hand at me. I felt my face relax. If the F. O. would not authorize a new secretary after this project, I would compromise Harriet. A Confidential file in her apartment. Maybe a bearded Russian. "The water's boiling," I said.

Harriet remained firm, her outstretched palm a demand, not a request. I studied her face. The eyes seemed sure, self-confident, as though she was accustomed to dealing with idiots and children. Although the whine of the kettle grated against my nerves, Harriet seemed not to mind it. "If you please," she said.

I moved the bubbling, whistling kettle from the burner and settled it next to a can of ground coffee on the sink. Basset watched us with his implacable face. Harriet took a half step toward me as I took the kettle from the stove.

"Harriet, you've got to understand something," I said as I

117

measured coffee into the pot's paper filter. "In the three months that you've been almost working on my team, I have been driven to a simple conclusion: the F. O. assigned you to me for my sins. Right?"

Her hand faltered, then formed a little fist, fingers clutching her thumb like an infant, and dropped to her side. "I'm just doing my job," she said.

"Not at all. You're trying to do my job and letting your own work go to hell." I poured water over the coffee. "And because of that, you force me and Basset and Weaver to handle most of your work. Including the coffee detail. *Now where is that damn newspaper?*"

"A little rough," Basset said after she left.

"Civil Service," I muttered and poured more water over the coffee.

Basset contemplated his wrinkled cigarette, then puffed on it a few times. He spoke without looking at me. "You're a great son of a bitch for getting information. But what you know about human nature you could write on the head of a pin."

"How do you read her?"

"Same as you. The thing is, I'd *handle* her differently. After all, she's not so stupid." Basset doused his cigarette in a stream of tap water. "If you handle her right, she'll crank out work like some kind of fanatic."

I lifted the paper filter and dropped it into the sink. The coffee smelled of chlorine. I poured a cup and added a half teaspoon of sugar. Basset helped himself to the coffee and drank it straight.

"Okay, you've got the assignment. You handle Harriet."

"Right-oh, babe."

As though on cue Harriet stuffed her head through the kitchen door, said, "Your cab for the airport is here," sniffed once for the effect of it and disappeared.

118

I was at the door when a sickening noise stopped me. It sounded like a tub of raw bread dough that had been slapped against the wall. When I turned to look, Basset's beefy hand was still where it had landed on his forehead.

"I could sell my pineapple futures," he said.

"What?"

"I could sell my pineapple futures. That's a clear four thousand; maybe even five. So all we need is twenty thousand more for the down payment."

20

The dunker shop was filled with flies and losers.

Hagopian breathed the blending smell of fresh coffee and donuts, dunked his puffed, glazed circle of carbohydrates and chewed absently at the thing while he read the morning paper. He'd made the front page.

"That's some kinda nut, hey?" the counter man asked.

"Who's that?" Hagopian said. "The president?" The top story on page one was about the current Middle East crisis.

"Naw, not him. The killer. The 'Bludgeon Murder' guy. He's gotta be outa his mind, hey?"

"A real screwball," Hagopian said, keeping his face neutral. He hadn't had a chance to look at himself yet; he didn't particularly want to. If he looked as bad as he hurt, he resembled an ambulatory corpse.

Routenfield, though—that was a different matter. The old guy wasn't going to be anything close to ambulatory once he was hit. And it sure as *hell* wasn't going to be an accident, not after last night.

That still left the problem of how to do the job. Hagopian finished his donut and licked a few glazed chips of sugar from his fingers. Can't use the SIG-Neuhausen, he thought. Too much noise. If only there was some nice quiet way of doing the bastard in; some kind of silenced weapon.

Hagopian glanced at the clock. It would be two o'clock in Detroit. He wondered if Bernie had raised the dough.

"You got some kind of pay phone around here?" he asked.

"Naw," the fat counter man said. "Nearest phone is down to the Greyhound."

"Thanks." Hagopian dropped a two-bit tip next to his empty mug and slipped off the stool. It didn't matter. He had to go back to the Greyhound station anyway; his tool kit was in a pay locker.

"I got it," Bernie said. "Twenty thousand fish."
Hagopian felt his lips drawing back in a grin and fought the instinct. It was like touching a burning match to his cheek. "Hold it for me. I'll have a guy pick it up when I get back to town."

21

EXPENSES

Item: 1 clock   6,000 dinar

From the air Belgrade resembles a bastard child spawned by Los Angeles out of the Vatican.

In the old city in the center of town you can see remnants and rubble of Byzantine, Bulgar and Magyar architecture. Since the end of Serbia and the beginning of Yugoslavia they've been tearing down the old gypsy slums that once ringed the city. In their place new concrete and glass slums have been rising.

The church of St. Vlah was in the gypsy quarter, and Uncle Stosh worked in one of the sanitary new rabbit warrens.

The Church of St. Vlah hid its face behind crumbling monastic walls on Avenue Koca Popović. As I picked my way through the weeds that separated wall and church I wondered if its boarded windows had contributed to the rumor of God's death: No one had worshiped here for a decade or more.

The old woman in the nave wasn't worshiping. She was holding a 7.63 mm Mauser M1932 machine pistol in her delicately veined hand.

I said, "Cyrus the Younger is dead."

The Mauser's little eye stared hypnotically at my stomach. "Artaxerxes Memnon is vengeful," she said.

122

"Aren't we all," I said. "Where is he?"

She moved her hand in a graceful arc and the Mauser peered at the second confessional from the door. I walked into it and said, "ForgivemefatherforIhavesinned," without kneeling.

"I'm sure you have," said a voice on the other side of the grill. "And you will sin again, no doubt."

"Willingly," I said. "It's the nature of my work." I sucked on my lip and studied the confessional grill. Each of its bars was a long, thin cross with a stunted transverse arm. They looked like a row of daggers. "I have a trade for you."

"I'd like to hear it."

"No way," I said. "I went first last time."

Xenophon said, "So you did, so you did. What would you like to hear from me?"

"You have an interesting group of Hungarians in Tirana," I said. "You referred to them as the 'Group of Ten' in a memorandum to Eremites."

"Oh my," said Xenophon on a declining scale of notes from *fa* to *do*. "Oh my my my. That cannot be discussed." His prim voice was as Victorian as a bustle. "That is out of the question; absolutely out."

Xenophon had traveled a precarious underground route from Tirana to keep this appointment. "Nothing is out of the question," I said. I doubted that the Group of Ten could not be discussed. "But everything is subject to price."

Xenophon was silent.

"I can tell you where your pipes leak. Give me enough information and I'll help you patch them."

Xenophon was still silent, as though the confessional had been profaned.

I said, "Goodbye," and stepped toward the door of the penitent's box.

"A moment," Xenophon said. "There can be no leaks . . . it's impossible. My pipeline is inviolate."

"I read the memo to Eremites," I said. "You don't suppose that *he* gave it to me . . ."

I waited quietly while he thought. He said, "What do you know of the Group of Ten?"

"All I know is what I read in the daily memoranda."

Xenophon said, "I know precious little more than that myself. They seem to have begun running covert operations throughout Eastern Europe . . . and they would appear to have developed some ties with Ustachi. I have no specifics because Whitehall lost interest and I am kept busy enough, thank you, within the Hoxha government." He paused, then said, "About that leak."

"Bernard Brooks . . ." I began.

". . . Haring," Xenophon said. "And to plug the leak?"

"Tell me more," I said.

"There is nothing more to tell."

"What about Kovács? And Jakaz . . . how come he didn't die when he died? And what sort of files, if any, did the group take from Hungary?"

Xenophon said, "I frankly haven't the faintest."

"Rumor, gossip, anything," I said. "This thing is so embryonic with us that I'm not looking for answers. I'm still trying to learn the right questions to ask: Like, what are these people up to?"

When he said, "You'll never penetrate them, you know," I accepted it without replying. "They are a closed society, and to try to learn their inner workings would be like trying to learn what makes a cat: you would never be able to reassemble the thing properly because you'd have had to kill it in the process."

"Yes," I said. "About these rumors now . . ."

"There appears to be some dissension within the group. One faction is after the mysterious Kovács and the other wants

124

to become a fully operational C and D unit. But this is rumor, of course."

"Of course," I said.

"The *chercher* Kovács faction is very much in control, it would seem." Xenophon stopped talking as though he was a badly spliced magnetic tape; articulate one moment and mute the next. He had finished.

I said, "Where do you want Beebee?"

"Can you get him for me? I thought he was rather a friend of yours."

"Everyone is rather a friend of mine," I said. "Where do you want him?"

"I imagine our Embassy in Washington will do."

As I stepped from the penitent's box Xenophon called after me, "If it's not too much bother, we would prefer him alive."

I entered the store under a blanket of noise, the sound of hundreds of ticking clocks. Uncle Stosh's cluttered shop had only a stool and a chair to sit on. He was already sitting on the stool.

There was room for little else in the place because everything, every vertical and horizontal surface, was covered with aging mechanical clocks. On a counter full of oak-cased provincials and chimers that showed their works through glass panes, a good French planetarium reproduction caught my eye. Although the gilt had worn thin on its pea-sized planets, it seemed to be in good working order; the moon nearing perigee with earth.

"Hello, Uncle Stosh," I said.

Stosh was on his stool at the work table dissecting a lavishly ornate cartel clock. "Say it again," he ordered.

125

"Hello, Uncle Stosh."

"William!" Uncle Stosh said. "I thought they pulled your visa." He jabbed a hand at me. He missed the mark by less than three inches. I compensated with my own hand and we shook.

Uncle Stosh was my own age; possibly younger. His constant smile was not a smile at all. It was an indication that he was relaxed and that his face was in repose.

"They pulled a lot of visas after that assignment," I said. "Those of us who weren't compromised were given soft berths back in the states. My name is Charles, now."

"It's a bad business," Stosh said. "New names. New identities." He spoke to a point over my right shoulder. "Some day you will forget who you are and they will pull more than your visa. It is a very bad business, my friend."

Stosh rocked back and forth on the stool, his narrow little body resembling a stick figure that darted from his *Münchin* chimer to strike the hour.

"It's an okay business," I said. "The fringe benefits are good. No one's taken a shot at me; I've got no broken bones. When something goes wrong they can always give me a new name. It's a hell of a lot less precarious than the game you used to play in Budapest, Stosh: They dumped you into the big brick building where St. Stephen's meets the Danube, and you didn't get out until someone blasted a hole in the place in fifty-six. If anything goes wrong with you now, you'll have no organization to support you. No one to give you a new name."

"Here is where you do not understand," Stosh said. "You act in terms of winning and losing. You see information as a part of the gear train that produces a certain day and hour and minute and second—like the works of a clock. But I see information as a hobby, not as the process that achieves results." Stosh continued smiling. For him it was just another conversa-

126

tion; nothing to take to heart. "One day your information will misfire in your hand and you will no longer worry about visas or names or identities because then you will know *surely* who you are."

"And yourself?" I asked. "What happens if you step beyond Josip Tito's threshold of tolerance?"

"It is not possible. Tomorrow they will come to me and ask 'Stosh, what is the news?' And I will say to them 'You have come at an interesting time. Only yesterday I spoke with William whose visa you revoked. He has a new name and a new visa and he asked me this and that.' They are most forbearing with me. They know they can rely on my information, just as you rely on it."

A small boy, hardly more than eight, entered the dim shop. He spoke to Stosh in Slovene rather than Serbo-Croat and I followed their conversation with difficulty. "Is it time to wind the clocks Uncle Stosh?"

"How many would you wind?" Stosh asked in reply.

"Three. But I do not know how to fit the keys."

"Come back later."

"Yes Uncle Stosh."

Stosh waited for the boy to leave, then said, "There are three men outside. They are not KOS . . . not the men who will come to me tomorrow and ask for the news of you; my young friend does not recognize them. Perhaps you have forgotten who you are. Or perhaps someone else has remembered."

"It's nothing important," I said.

"As you wish," Stosh said easily. "What would you know?"

"If I was an AVH body named Tibor Kovács, why would I run in fifty-six?"

Stosh smiled genuinely this time. "Oh, I can answer that. That one is simple. What can you pay me?"

"Are you in the market for U.K. personnel changes?"

"Not especially," Stosh said. "The English are too good at this game. They are like fleas on the back of a sleeping dog. I find more entertainment in your country's activities. You are like fleas on a scratching dog. You jump around and lose your visas."

"I don't know what else to offer," I said. "Would you like something juicy about the movie stars in Hollywood?"

"No no. No interest. Give me the English information."

"Lloyd Hymes is gone. Kaput. Sir Robert Champion has assumed his desk in Whitehall."

"Interesting," Stosh said. "My friend at M.I.8 said that Logsden-Beal had taken over."

I said, "Champion. I got it straight from Virginia."

"Interesting," he said again. "I wonder why my friend wanted to confuse me."

It was totally dark within the shop. I had a plane to catch, among other matters of a more pressing nature. "I don't like to rush you, Uncle Stosh, but there are three men outside who may or may not be looking for me. I'd hate to keep them waiting."

"Yes yes. If you were a body named Kovács, as you say, you would not be strictly speaking under AVH control. You would be loyal to Gyula Jakaz. Kovács left Péter Pazmány University to work for Jakaz on something of the mind, something psychological, but reports of his work never reached the upper levels of AVH. He was being run by Jakaz."

"There was a report that Jakaz bought one during the first attack on AVH headquarters," I said. "Do you know what happened?"

Stosh reached to his workbench and slapped a hand down within a quarter inch of his pack of cigarettes. He moved his hand slightly and shook a cigarette loose. "I have heard from

128

a friend in Tirana that Jakaz threw his wallet and watch into the mess of bodies and bricks on St. Stephen's Boulevard. He wanted them to think he was no more with them."

Stosh lit the cigarette by touch. He said, "He wanted to disappear so he could continue running Kovács. But Tibor Kovács disappeared. He had something valuable, some files, and he disappeared. He was doing something with the mind. He was researching . . . you call it *mnesis* . . . yes?"

"*Mnesis*?"

"Yes. What is that in American?"

"*Mnesis*," I said. *Mnesis*; of the mind. Of memory. Of course: "Mnemonics," I said. "Memory. The ability to remember. The science of remembrance."

"That is it," Stosh said. "This Kovács was researching the memory. Gyula Jakaz was running him like a Projects Officer runs agents."

"That doesn't make sense," I said. "Everything I've heard about Jakaz makes him out to be a hatchet man or a KGB face. Why would he give a damn about research?"

"I am not sure what Jakaz was, Charles," Stosh said. "All I know for sure is this Tibor Kovács. He was having people remember things."

"Why Albania?" I said.

Stosh's cigarette glowed in the dark. "Some have said that Jakaz is in business like I am in business . . . but seriously."

"A private C and D org?"

"It would seem. Albania is a logical place for it . . . they need a professional."

"And then Kovács disappeared," I said. "Where did he go?"

Stosh shrugged his shoulders.

"No idea?" I asked.

Stosh said, "No idea." In the dimness I could see Stosh rocking easily on his stool, hands wrapped around one uplifted knee and a cigarette in his mouth. The polished tools behind him gleamed dully in their rack.

"Okay," I said. "How did you get the poop on Kovács? Were you there?"

"I was there, Charley," Stosh said. "It was when they first attacked the AVH building, before Nagy emptied all the prisons. They let me mop floors and I was glad to do it; much better than sitting in a cell. I heard Kovács tell someone to bring him the files when Petőfi's first bomb tore at the building. Then there were shots, gunfire within the building, and he shouted something about getting his children out."

"Children?" I asked.

"He had two boys. He wanted them out of the building where he had quarters."

"Okay," I said. "So Kovács took off with some files. What files? What was in them?"

Stosh drew on his cigarette and replied through a cloud of smoke. "Just files, William. Just files of some sort." Stosh rocked silently for a moment. "That is all I can tell you."

I said, "Were they the details and results of his research project?"

"Perhaps," Stosh said. "They seemed very valuable, whatever they were."

Stosh heard me rising from my chair. He said, "I will see you again soon, William or Charles?"

"Maybe, Uncle Stosh," I said. "Maybe."

"If no one lifts your visa, or worse, you must come for a chat instead of business. Perhaps you would even care to buy the planetarium."

"Oh really?" As I scanned the street through his shop window I slipped the wallet from my pocket.

"I heard you stop to inspect it. Certainly it was the planetarium because the others on that table are not worth your interest. And it is a good purchase. In your capitalist cities, where fortunes are made on antiques, it would bring no less than . . ." Stosh paused to convert dinar into Western values in his head ". . . nothing less than a hundred and sixty-five pounds sterling."

Some fortune, I thought. "What's that in real money, Uncle Stosh?"

"Real money?"

"You know, dinar," I said.

"Six thousand, eight hundred and twenty-four," Stosh said. "But for you, six thousand."

Although it was cheap at the price it would nearly blow my extraordinary expenses. I said, "You've got a deal." The Bentley's wire wheels would have to wait. Stosh held his hand under my chin as though he expected me to bite it. I bobbed my head aside and counted off the bills for him.

Stosh made the bills into a neat roll, turning from me as he did so. He leaned forward on the stool and opened one of the hundreds of drawers in his jeweler's cabinet. As he stuffed the roll into the drawer he said, "Goodbye William."

As simple as that.

A street lamp flickered to life, creating sharp silhouettes of the timepieces in Stosh's shop window. Beyond the window and across the street a figure in a black fur coat moved from the doorway in which he'd been standing. He walked without haste to another doorway three buildings away. Earlier the setting sun had given him shadow in his doorway, but he hadn't considered the different angle of light that the street lamp would throw.

"Goodbye William," Stosh had said. "Goodbye," and nothing more. In his world "espionage" was only a word. He knew that someone was waiting for me outside but his ideas about what they had planned for me were purely mental exercises.

I didn't take it personally. Stosh's indifference was not directed solely at me. He couldn't empathize with any of us, the frail fallible bodies who played this odd game. Yet I had to admit, he was quite fond of his clocks.

They let me get as far as the sidewalk bar two blocks away. The one in the black fur coat kept pace with me on the other side of the randomly lit street, walking with an aimless gait and stopping often to peer into shop windows along the way. In spite of his various digressions he managed to keep abreast of me. At the crossing he beat me to the opposite curb.

I picked up number two as I walked by him in front of a corset shop in the middle of the second block. Even in Los Angeles he would have been arrested for the way he leered at a tremendous, melon-cupped maternity bra. He was dressed in one of those shapeless suits that seem to be a trademark of East European countries; the lingering element of Soviet non-style. The suit was dark blue and had been tailored by the local sack maker out of good, hard-worsted wool.

Sack suit followed me just a hair too eagerly. I stopped. Behind me sack suit's clicking feet stopped. I stamped out a clumsy "shave and a haircut two bits" with both feet, but he seemed to have lost the tempo of our teamwork.

Number three was waiting for us at the bar. He looked first at me, then across the street at fur coat, then behind me at sack suit, then back to me again. He nodded encouragement to me like a doting father at his baby's first steps. He took half a pace forward to catch me in case I should fall.

A light sprinkling of neighborhood people had turned out for their evening constitutionals. Besides myself and my three would-be companions there were less than a dozen bodies on the street. A few of the shirt-sleeved neighbors had ducked into the bar to buy glasses of *travarica* and *lozovaca* which they

132

brought to the sidewalk tables outside. The rest were content to stroll and bump into friends they hadn't seen since the night before.

As I approached number three he smiled encouragement and jerked his chin at the bar.

I went in, followed by number three. Ordering a shot of travarica I ducked outside again to find a table. Number three followed. He sat two tables away, caging me between himself and sack suit who was standing on the sidewalk.

Fur coat, the one I had originally seen in the doorway across from Stosh's shop, crossed the street and walked into the bar. As he passed my table I saw that his coat was not fur. It was a dull black suede, good pigskin suede that the Yugoslavs manufacture primarily for export. The coat had a tall collar and enough buttons and straps on its double-breasted front to seal out a hurricane. Inside the coat, where the topmost buttons were undone, I caught a glimpse of the Bakelite grips and blue metal frame of a pistol butt.

When he reappeared in the shop doorway he was doing a balancing act with three shot glasses and three demitasse coffee cups. His friends didn't offer to help so he walked alone to my table, clittering and clattering cups and saucers and glasses all the way. There was a dicey moment when he settled his things on the table. His topmost cup of demitasse teetered precariously, nearly falling on my planetarium. I reached out to steady it and he said, "Spasibo." * Straight from Moscow.

Without responding I gave myself over to the pleasures of travarica. My hangover had disappeared somewhere in the middle of a latish lunch and I prayed that my stomach was ready for the aromatic, grass-flavored vodka before me. As I sipped at it I watched sack suit and number three amble to my table.

Black suede and I were playing kneesies under the little

* "Thanks."

133

table. I had picked a romantic table for two and there was hardly enough room beneath it for both of us. I wondered what kind of a *ménage à quatre* the four of us would make as sack suit and number three sat down.

"I'm so happy to see you, Charles," number three said. "So glad that you could join us."

"Hello Beebee," I said.

22

A feast is made for laughter, and wine maketh merry: but money answereth all *things*.

Ecclesiastes: 10:19

"What brings you to Belgrade, Beebee?" I took a sip of *travarica* and grinned hugely. The stuff burned like drain cleaner on its way down my throat and landed in my stomach with a sensation that resembled scalding grease. I grinned even more brightly, hoping that I didn't look too much the idiot. "Are you here for the convention?"

"Convention?" Haring asked. He emptied his shot glass, straining *travarica* through his mustache.

"International spy convention, Beebee. Just this morning we resolved to form a public relations arm."

"My dear Charles, what a marvelous sense of humor you have."

"I'm serious. We're going to call it the Censored in the Interests of National Defense Anti-Defamation League." I sniffed cautiously at the *travarica* but decided that I'd had enough. "Now you know my secret. I'm here for the convention because I'm really a joiner at heart. A regular Rotarian, Beebee. But tell me, what brings you to Belgrade?"

Beebee's plump face burst into a smile. "To be quite candid, I followed you here. I've a proposition, one I rather think might interest you."

"What are you selling this time, contingency plans for the invasion of Battersea?"

135

"Not at all," Beebee said. "In fact I'm not here to sell but to buy."

"You've come to the wrong source. The Agency doesn't sell stuff, Beebee."

"Ah, of course. I thought this might be a personal arrangement between the two of us," Beebee said. "I've done some investigating of your private finances, Charles. You seem to have a somewhat difficult time keeping body and soul together."

"I live well enough," I said.

"You live rather *too* well. You've a penchant for simply pissing your salary away; what's left of it after alimony and child support. Why, your food bills alone would feed a family of four."

"I have educated taste buds," I said.

A Citroën DS-19 pulled to the curb just eight or so yards away from our table. The driver killed the ignition and the car's hydraulic suspension system relaxed, settling the DS-19 like a wounded animal.

"Yes," Beebee said. "Then surely you would not turn down a handsome offer, one that would allow you to indulge your superb taste without having to look at the price tag on everything that catches your fancy."

"Flattery will get you everywhere," I said. "But keep talking. I could use a few extra bucks right now."

"Exactly," Beebee said. "How does fifty thousand sound to you?"

I gave a low whistle.

"I rather hoped you would say that," Beebee said. "And you need do quite little work to earn it."

All four doors of the Citroën opened and a large body unlimbered from each of them. They were dressed like sack suit; lumpily inelegant as though they had slept in their clothing. Glancing casually at them I told Beebee, "I'll be go-to-hell if

I could tell you how much work is involved in 'quite little work.' "

Beebee chuckled and fluffed himself, his plumpness straining against his clothes. After priming his vocal cords with another shot of *travarica* he said, "It's quite little work indeed. Should you ever run across a fellow named Kovács, I would like you to arrange an introduction for me. A *private* introduction, in a place of my choosing."

I closed my eyes and massaged my eyebrows. I said, "You're incredible, Beebee. Incredible. I've never met the man."

"The chances are excellent that you will, however," said Beebee. "Kovács disappeared in your area . . . in what your people refer to as your *SubSection*."

"And you think I'll find him?"

Haring said, "I have no end of faith in you, Charles." When he smiled his cheeks blossomed like ripe peaches. He said, "Fifty thousand dollars." I was quiet and he said it again: "Fifty thousand dollars."

"I suppose it could be arranged," I said. "But I have a feeling that it's worth a lot more than fifty thou to you."

"Those will be tax-free dollars, my dear fellow. Obviously you could not report them."

"Just a meeting with Kovács?"

"That's the extent of it. A private meeting and a few hours of uninterrupted conversation."

"You said a place of your choosing. Where would you want him delivered, Beebee?"

"Mexico," Haring said. "Nothing elaborate, just a little place I can arrange for in Baja, two or three hours south of San Diego."

"How about payment? Not that I don't trust you, pal, but these things should be worked out completely beforehand."

"I've thought of that." Beebee tilted his head back and I watched his larynx bobble in his fat neck as the *travarica* coursed down his throat. He sent a mouthful of demitasse after the vodka. "I shall be happy to trust you with ten thousand dollars before and forty thousand upon delivery. Your second forty thousand, however, would be in torn bills."

"That's against the law," I said, "defacing Federal Reserve notes."

"But it creates absolute trust. Neither your halves nor mine will be worth so much as a string of glass beads; one needs at least two-thirds of a note to redeem it. You are guaranteed that I will not renege on our agreement because, should I *not* deliver the other halves to you when you bring me Kovács, I will have gained nothing. Do you see?"

"It sounds tempting," I admitted. "Fifty thousand would certainly take the edge off of my money problems."

Beebee smiled. "I was quite sure you were my man, Charles."

"You know, Beebee, I lead a very dull life. I try to keep it that way . . . uncomplex . . . without making too many enemies or too many friends. But I'm really happy that you've given me this chance to say 'fuck you,' my dear fellow." I knocked back the rest of my drink, gagged slightly and stood up, reaching into my jacket for a cigar.

"It would not be wise to reach for that," Beebee said. Black suede's hand was inside his coat and coming out fast.

With my left hand I unbuttoned the jacket and slowly opened it to show that I was only holding one of the Havanas I'd bought for the F. O. "You know I never carry those things," I said. "They make me nervous." I unwrapped the cigar. "If we were back in the States, Beebee, I'd kick your ass until it turned blue for making an offer like that."

"But, Charles," he said, emptying the last of his grass vodka, "we are not in your country, nor have I offered anything so awkward."

138

I said, "I'm not what you would call chauvinistic. I mean, I don't go about my work wrapped in a flag. But I'm not a hypocrite, Beebee. I wouldn't work for the Agency if I thought it would be to my advantage to sabotage the Agency's efforts." I struck a match and held it to the end of my cigar. "And you just invited me to be a hypocrite. I resent that."

"You are hardly in a position to resent anything," Beebee said. "This is my field, dear boy." He nodded at black suede whose hand was still inside his coat. "And I'm the batsman."

The end of the cigar was glowing now and I puffed on it. After my first puff the four bodies from the DS-19 walked toward our table. "Wrong again," I said. "I told you I lead a dull life. I intend to keep it that way. If you ever show up in the States again, Beebee, I'll have you trussed up like a butchered hog and turned over to the British embassy. And tell the hot rod there," I jerked my chin at black suede, "to get his goddam hand out of his coat."

My four Agency heavies stood quietly around the table, making the odds five to three. The big guy behind black suede placed a friendly hand on his shoulder. With a foot behind the chair leg he pulled gently back, tilting him precariously.

"You were wrong. Dead wrong. It's not your field, Beebee. It's Josip Tito's field and we are all just visiting teams." I picked up my planetarium.

"What'll we do with the fat man?" asked the body who was tilting black suede's chair. He nodded casually at Beebee Haring.

"Ignore him," I said. "He's impotent."

"They've got ordnance."

"Let 'em keep it. They're all impotent: They use guns to relieve their sexual identity crises."

Beebee smiled gallantly throughout our exchange, his fat

mustache curving up like a scimitar. "Tsk tsk tsk," he said. "Ah, Charles Charles Charles. You take things so seriously, dear boy. I wanted only to chat you up a bit."

"I enjoyed it, Beebee. Sincerely, I'm very glad we had this little talk."

Beebee helped himself to sack suit's drink and threw it back. His hand was steady.

"I am also sincere about turning you over to the British," I said as I turned to leave. "Just this morning Xenophon said he'd like to have you. 'Preferably alive,' he said. But he didn't make it an absolute condition."

When I heard the shot glass drop from his hand and shatter on the cobbled sidewalk I didn't look back.

23

Q: The previous witness stated that contacts are more vital
to your work, sir, than knowledge or skill.
A: With all due respect, sir, he was out of his mind.

Minutes of the Hearings,
Subcommittee on National Security Affairs
Volume CXXIV
Page 5

"Mnemonics," Stosh had said. "Something of the mind."
He had pointed me like an arrow to Kisvárda.

If you were lucky you got to Kisvárda by car after flying JAT
Yugoslav Airlines from Belgrade to Budapest and *Malév* Hungarian Airlines from Budapest to Nyiregyháza.

The flying part was easy. Getting a car was not. I couldn't
hire one for love or money.

In Hungary the forint was as much a joke as the dollar is
becoming here; and love, of course, is held in universal disregard. But the barter system was another story.

I found a farmer in Nyiregyháza who was going to visit his
cousin in Kisvárda. In order to travel with him I had to cough
up some of the goods I'd brought in my diplomatic pouch; a
carton of Benson & Hedges Menthol 100s and two rolls of
Baggies.

"Done," I said. "Where's the car?"

"Car?" he said and gestured around his little stall in the
open vegetable market. "Cars are bought with profits from
this?" He was an incredibly old man, his face like a map that

showed no principal cities; just a maze of back roads that meandered aimlessly from birth to death.

"Don't tell me," I said. "You have a horse."

"Horse? What horse?" He snorted a laugh, setting all the lines and crags of his face into startling motion. "I have a very fine mule and a magnificent wagon. Why, I once hauled over five hundred kilos of manure from here to Miskolc in that very wagon. Why, not once did my mule complain. Let me tell you something about mules," he said. "No comparison with a horse. None at all. Why, I'll tell you something about my adventures with a wagonload of manure from here to Miskolc. . . ."

All the way to Kisvárda he assaulted my senses with his adventures in the wagonload of manure. By the time we got there I could hardly breathe.

"Hello, Teresá," I said.

The woman who stood before me seemed to have aged twenty years in the last five. She wore a gray blouse and a gray skirt and an expression that was grayer than both. Standing in the doorway of Number Four, Bela Kun Street, she looked like a fixture of the time-beaten house; like one of the bricks that showed through where the plaster had fallen away.

She shielded her eyes with a large-knuckled hand and squinted at me as I stood in the light, spongy snow. "You have the advantage I believe," she said.

"I'm William," I said. "Mityas and I once played chess on occasional Saturdays."

"You."

I nodded.

"You cannot see him. Go away. You cannot."

"I've come a long way, Teresá. Let me say hello at least."

142

She took my measure, seeming to devour my lightweight California suit, the leather overcoat I'd borrowed from one of our chancellery people at the Embassy, and my lingering tan. After studying me Teresá looked down at her own gray woolen clothes and her chapped, red hands. When she met my eyes again I felt as though I was standing before a tribunal.

"It couldn't be helped," I said. "He chose to stay when the others were compromised." It was painful looking into her eyes. Teresá's expression was flat, noncommittal; neither hate nor forgiveness showed there. "You could have both gotten out. It was his choice."

Teresá said nothing.

"I didn't have to come here," I lied. "I just wanted to say hello to Mityas while I was in this part of the world." I took a step away from the gray look of her. "Tell him I stopped by; that I just happened to be passing through."

"No, wait," she said. "I have decided. Please. Come inside. You have traveled a long distance to see Mityas. Let me take your coat."

She hung the chancellery body's leather coat on a peg in the dim hallway. The heavy hem of the thing knocked over a telephone and I picked it up. It was a country phone; no dial, just an instrument and handset. I returned the phone to its place on a three-legged stool.

"This way."

She led me to a huge, plaster-worn room at the end of the hall. It was not the kind of room you'd expect in a house but more like a miniature rug factory. There were seven large wooden tubs against one wall, their insides brilliant with dye. A rug-weaver's rack dominated the center of the room. The half-started tapestry on it showed dogs and horses' hooves. Pinned to the wooden side of the rack was a colored illustration of some ancient Magyar nobility riding the hunt.

143

Teresá said, "I do not teach music any more." She glanced at her hands. "Nor do I play." She stared coolly at the weaver's rack and said, "This is how I earn our potatoes."

The room was cold, colder than Teresá, and gloomy enough to start a mushroom farm. I tried to warm my feet by curling and uncurling my toes within my shoes. There were worse ways of earning potatoes, I thought. Rolling back on her round little heels, for example, with half the faculty of Péter Pazmány University in order to smooth the way for Mityas' revolutionary theories in psychology.

"You should have come over the wall with the others," I said. "Mityas' work in narcohypnotics has been justified by the results of Barnay's research at the University of Toronto." I tried to read her face but it was worse than a blank page; she looked like she'd been trying to erase everything that had ever been written there.

"I could not talk to him," she said. "Your people had groomed him too well . . . he believed there was no threat of exposure. None at all." When she smiled it wasn't a smile but a thin, dry line that cleaved her face. "Even as the AVH took him to Nyiregyháza he believed that he had not been compromised."

It would have ended differently if I had been running Mityas: I liked my agents touchy—worried—slightly paranoid. It kept them on their toes.

She read my expression. "But do not look so troubled; we all came to a happy ending. Mityas and I are happy to have gotten the five hundred U.S. dollars. AVH was happy to get Mityas. And your people were happy to get the university's reserve officer training roster, even though it became dated in less than three months. So you see, everyone is happy."

"Ecstatic," I said.

"Wait, please," Teresá said. "I will tell Mityas that you have come to see him."

While waiting for Teresá and Mityas I looked at the tapestry she'd begun. It was going to be worse than the illustration she was copying, much worse. Just from the bottom part, the horses' hooves and the dogs, you could see that she had no eye for perspective.

I curled and uncurled my toes and reached into my jacket for a cigar. After unwrapping it I returned it unlit to my pocket and stuffed the cellophane in with it. Mityas didn't need to see that; the capitalist spy puffing on his cigar.

There were sources in the U.S. (or Barnay in Canada) that might have some background on Kovács' work in mnemonics, but Mityas was the simplest and most obvious choice: He had been a student at Péter Pazmány University in the early '50s and must have had some psych courses from Dr. Kovács.

Our Agency body at the embassy had assured me that neither AVH nor KGB had a watch on Mityas' house. He'd become such a non-person that not even they worried about whom he saw or what he did.

After a few minutes I decided that Mityas was in no particular rush to see me. A few minutes more and I wondered what he and Teresá were doing upstairs. Then the door opened.

When she wheeled him in I knew why no one was watching Mityas.

I said, "How long did they have him?"

"Eight months. One in Budapest, seven at Nyiregyháza prison," she said as she smoothed back a sweaty hank of hair from his forehead. His head lolled back with the stroke of her hand. "Eight months. He doesn't think, he doesn't speak; I clean him twice a day." She bent close to his ear. "Look, Mityas. Look who has come to see you. Your very dear friend has come to play chess."

I pushed myself away from it, closing my mind to both Mityas and Teresá. "Goodbye," I said. "I can get out by myself."

"But please, stay and talk with Mityas. Did you bring him some work? Money is scarce, very hard to come by."

Just as I had pushed away from it mentally I walked away from it in fact, grabbing my borrowed leather coat on the way out.

They were waiting for me at the curb in what looked like a '47 DeSoto. It wasn't. It was a brand-new four-door, 53-horsepower Pobieda M-72 (from *Zavod Imieni Molotova* in Gorki) with four-wheel drive. It was not the sort of car the Soviets could successfully export to the west. However—they are working on a new 58 hp model.

They wore blue uniforms with red lapels; very Russian— very AVH. They hadn't changed their style, they were still copying the big boys from the east.

One of them opened the rear door and climbed languidly from the car. He said, "Get in." No question of papers or who are you? or do you have a pass for this sector? or anything as banal as that. Just, "Get in."

As they drove me back to Nyiregyháza I experienced a wave of nostalgia: I missed the old farmer's droning story about his five hundred kilos of manure.

24

"You!" said the caterpillar contemptuously. "Who are you?"
Alice's Adventures in Wonderland
LEWIS CARROLL

He said, "*Ülj le egyenesen*," * so I slumped a little more in the chair and smiled vaguely at him. "Does anyone around here speak English?" I asked.

The AVH major looked like he should be filing papers in some dusty back room. But the room in which we sat was barren and without papers to file. We watched each other across a Spartan desk.

He was a pallid man with eyes that were weirdly distorted by trifocals. The thick glasses might have been a couple of milk-bottle bottoms that he had wired to his nose.

"Look, someone around here's got to speak English," I said. My words were slower and louder than normal, as though I was speaking to a deaf cretin.

"You are a very persistent man, Mr. . . ." he peered at my passport ". . . Remly, is it?" As he spoke he ran a file absentmindedly across his fingernails with the sort of unassuming conceit that the very plain affect. His red-lapeled, blue uniform was tailored well enough to show that he cared, yet ill-fitting enough to defer to modesty.

"Had me nervous there," I said. "I thought you didn't speak English."

* "*Sit up straight.*"

147

"Isn't that a coincidence. I thought you spoke Magyar."

"Magyar?"

"The language of Hungary." He tapped my passport against his forehead then used it to scratch himself behind the ear. I had a feeling that he didn't think much of it. "After all, Mr., ah . . ." he looked inside the passport again ". . . Remly, if I were sent to your country to gather intelligence, I would certainly brush up on my English. Does that make sense?"

I shrugged. "I'm just a diplomatic courier. All I know about spies is what I see in the movies."

"Then you must surely know that the next step is to torture you until you break, Mr. ah . . ." he played the passport game again ". . . Remly." The major studied his fingernails and found no fault with their perfect crescent tips. He turned to my passport and used the nail file to pick small divots of emulsion from my photo. "Isn't that how it happens in your movies?"

"I've been watching the wrong films," I said. "I'm just a guy who got lost. If you'll call our embassy in Budapest, they'll confirm that for you."

"There's no rush," he said. "I think first I shall talk to the farmer about your language gap."

"The farmer?"

"Your chauffeur to Kisvárda. You seem to have spoken Magyar quite clearly to him."

"Oh. *That* farmer. You know, I was trying to hitch a ride when he picked me up. I thought he was taking me back to Nyiregyháza." It was all very unconvincing. I wondered if he was serious about torturing me. That, I thought, would cure my hohums.

"This is not a time for games, Mr. . . ." divots again from my passport face ". . . Remly. You visited old friends in Kisvárda; friends with a telephone. Why? If you do not tell me *why* you have returned to Hungary after a five-year absence

I will have you taken to a cell." My face was disappearing beneath the point of his nail file.

"Oh." I looked around the barren room. Except for the wooden table that separated us, and the stiff wooden chairs in which we sat, the place was like the inside of a stone box. Even the light bulb seemed to be carved from rock. "I thought *this* was the cell."

He almost snapped to attention as he rose from his chair, tipping it over as he did so. I thought, well I've done it now. This must be the major's office.

Before taking me below they stripped me totally and gave me an enema to flush out any microfilm capsules I might have swallowed. After taking an emetic and losing my breakfast I choked down a double dose of laxative. Either they weren't taking any chances or this was a hint of what the major had in mind when he said "torture."

Standing in front of my new home I was naked and cold and more than a little embarrassed.

"In prison administration, as in every other important area of modern civilization, personnel is the largest single expense. It eats unrelentingly at our budget." He spoke as though he was passing bits of bureaucratic Clausewitz.

The major flashed his light around inside my cell. He might have been a guest speaker at an architectural convention. "Notice that the cell is roughly one and three-quarter meters high; you cannot stand to your full height." He flashed the light horizontally across the floor. "The bottom of the cell is one and a quarter by one and a quarter meters which prevents you from lying down in comfort. So you see, we have eliminated the personnel costs." He scuffed at the cell with his boot and said, "In here, you will torment yourself."

There was nothing in the cell. No light, no chair, no cot, no

149

blanket. Nothing. One corner had a hole in the floor for waste.

"Your food comes in here," the major said, indicating a slot at the bottom of the planked door. "Please notice the light trap. We do not wish to disturb your meditation; not with light or sound."

"Meditation," I said. "That's not my strong point."

The major smiled owlishly, big distorted eyeballs behind thick lenses. "You will have much to think about. For the most part you will reflect on your aloneness. I am told it is good for the soul," he said. "In the eleventh century King Stephen the Holy meditated with quite astounding results."

"Yes," I said. "He enforced serfdom for the greater glory of God and his treasury, but not necessarily in that order. He might have become your patron saint if Péter Gábor had converted back to Catholicism."

"With our methods, comrade, we would have converted him." He gestured toward the yawning cell. "When you grow weary of meditation and wish to speak to me of espionage, tell the walls. They will hear you."

150

25

Man holds an inward talk with himself alone, which it behoves
him to regulate well.

BLAISE PASCAL

> 1 P—K4   P—K4
> 2 N—KB3   P—Q3
> 3 P—Q4   N—KB3
> 4 N—B3   . . .

Mityas was a thinker. He broke in eight months. But I am
not an introspective person and, what the hell, I had always
wanted some privacy to concentrate on my chess game.

After a couple of years I might be ready for Bobby Fischer.

> 4 . . .   QN—Q2

It is a peculiarity of the Queen's Knight in Philidor's Defense, I thought, that it sometimes blocks both the Queen
and the King's Bishop; leaving the Bishop with little recourse
beyond direct appeal to Rome. After White's Bishop move:

> 5 B—QB4   . . .

Black could move:

> 5 . . .   B—K2

But it would have been wiser to move to the American Embassy—and that's when it occurred to me: *Nuts! Don't play
into his hands with:*

5 . . .   B—K2.

Much wiser to play:

5 . . .   B—American Embassy!

In all the years of chess, I exulted—in all these what? thousands of years they've been playing chess, I thought in the darkness—with what? millions of bodies playing the game?—with all that convoluted *bullshit*—it took *ME* to answer White's:

5 B—QB4   . . .

with:

5 . . .   B—American Embassy!

My God, it was so simple. *Simple!* It was so simple I laughed. Even Capablanca, the great invincible "Capa," José Raúl Capablanca Y Graupera, had never thought of it. Alekhine hadn't thought of it. Fischer, mighty Fischer, had not the first breath of an idea about the move.

I would call it the Nyiregyháza Defense. Not the Remly Defense, no no no no no no. That would compromise me. But the Nyiregyháza Defense. What *logic!* I would quit the Agency and become an international grandmaster. Chess would become my life. A brilliant move! I laughed so hard, with such violence, I found it hard to concentrate on the game. But what the hell, White had no answer to my profound Bishop move. How could he reply?

6 Kovács—Los Angeles?   . . .

Bad move. Questionable. Very very very very questionable. Chess is a game of logic. *LOGIC!* I will play

152

My laughter bounced around the little cell and gave me comfort in the darkness. I had them beaten. Whipped. I would last them out and become the finest grandmaster ever to belly up to a chessboard. *I had beaten them at their own game!*

Mityas was a thinker, but I was not an introspective person.

7 Jakaz—Los Angeles?   F. O.—Virginia
8 Routenfield—Mammoth   Glenda—bed!

26

Hagopian stepped from the cab and passed a bill to the driver. "That'll hold you?" He took his package from the back seat and shoved the door closed with his knee.

"For a couple of days," the driver said.

"Ten minutes," Hagopian said. "I might be back, okay?"

"Sure."

The Executive House was a commercial hotel; flash and class, Hagopian thought as he stepped through its electric glass door. Flash and class.

His pupils contracted slightly in the lobby's aluminum and vinyl glare. The place was done in vivid shades of red and heliotrope. Glass spheres dropped from the ceiling like celestial edicts and threw brilliant, almost unbearable light on the scene.

His upper lip felt naked without the mustache. Maybe I'll grow a real one, he thought.

Hagopian's hands and face were killing him. He shifted his awkward bundle and smiled at the day clerk as he passed the desk. Jesus, smiling was like trying to crack nuts with his teeth. You'd think the skin would heal after two days, he thought. The clerk nodded back without seeing the Max Factor Dark Egyptian Pan Stick that covered his face. His right cheek was darker than the left; it had taken a second coat of the stuff to smooth out the abraded skin.

At the elevator he shifted his package again and touched a small panel. It glowed under his fingers. With sensual insinuation a speaker over the panel said, "Your elevator is at the brrzz third floor and will be here soon. Thank you."

"Thank you," Hagopian replied and wondered how many others responded to the taped voice.

Glancing around the lobby Hagopian indulged himself a smug, painful grin. Flash and class. Their taste was lousy but their money was good. The place stank of dough. He bared his teeth to the room and thought about the other guys in the business, those thick-witted mothers who holed up in rat traps that had WEEKLY & MONTHLY RATES signs clinging desperately above their doors. Kiss off, Hagopian thought. He was to them what a Sheraton was to a folding card table; head and shoulders above the bastards.

Most of them were simpleminded dudes. They not only moved their lips when they read, some of them moved their lips when they watched TV. Like Deaf George, Hagopian thought. The jerk had gotten a contract to hit on some securities dealer in Chicago—but the gimmick was that he had to waste the guy in his office on La Salle Street.

"Ground floor," the velvet voice said behind him.

Deaf George had decided to use a silencer on the job, but no one had told him about silencers; it was supposed to be common knowledge that the things only worked with subsonic cartridges in autoloading pistols. You'd never use one on a magnum revolver—or even a standard-load, standard-bore revolver—because the things only silenced the expanding gases that escaped through the gun's muzzle. With a standard or magnum load the noise of the bullet breaking the sound barrier would still be there. And though you could silence its muzzle noise, a subsonic revolver still had all that slop between cylinder and barrel.

Hagopian could have used a silencer on the SIG-Neuhausen. But hell, he thought. The thing'd be more lethal as a *club* once it was loaded with those damn subsonic cartridges.

The elevator doors whooshed. "Lobby, coffee shop and the fabulous 'Board Room' lounge where Happy Hour drinks are now only seventy-five cents." Hagopian turned. The thing was empty and talking to itself.

As Hagopian entered the elevator the package slipped from his hands. He touched his floor button and leaned down to retrieve it. Before closing its doors the elevator said, "Going up, please." Hagopian smiled and said, "What time do you get off tonight, honey? I'd like to buy you a shot of hydraulic fluid." The package said, APEX SPORTING GOODS—TEN BIG LOCATIONS TO SERVE YOU.

At the door of his room Hagopian settled the long sporting goods package on end, leaning it against the wall. Squatting until his head was beneath the level of the doorknob, he checked the strip of two-sided transparent tape that he'd stuck to the knob before leaving on his shopping trip. There was a fingerprint on the tape; someone had tried his doorknob.

Hagopian unlocked the door and rattled it. The thing wouldn't open. Good. At least the bolt was still holding.

Good old Deaf George, Hagopian thought as he dug two carbon-iron wafers from his pocket. What he was doing now would have perplexed Deaf George beyond words.

The two metal wafers clung to each other as though they'd been glued. Wedging a thumbnail between them Hagopian separated the magnetic sandwich. After casing the hallway with a quick snap of his eyes and finding it empty, he pressed the + pole of one wafer against a faint pencil mark on the door just inches away from the jamb. At a second mark, three fingers to the left of the first, he pressed the + pole of the other magnetic wafer. Hagopian scraped the left-hand wafer across the door and away from the jamb. When he heard a click he tried the doorknob again. His door swung open.

Once he got the package in, he closed the door and untaped his bar magnet from the door's bolt. The + pole of the bar had been taped to the bolt's little locking knob—when he pressed the first wafer against the door, the inside + pole had been repelled and swiveled the knob up from its locked position. After that it was simple work to attract the — pole of the magnet and slide the bolt back.

A red light glared at him from the phone by his bed. Beneath the light a label said MESSAGES—DIAL 7. Hagopian dialed 7 and chuckled in spite of the stabbing pain it brought to his cheek. Deaf George had blown his whole wad when he jury rigged a Parker-Hale silencer onto the business end of a .357 magnum Colt Police Python.

"Messages," said a voice in his ear.

"Mr. Richardson," Hagopian said. "Room 439."

"Yes sir. Just a moment."

Deaf George was hiding in the securities broker's closet when the guy opened his office in the morning. George had figured it beautifully—perfectly in fact, given his forty-point handicap for stupidity. He'd practiced lining up the shot all night with the closet door open and could make a perfect bead on the target's swivel chair even with his eyes closed.

"Yes, Mr. Richardson . . . the maid tried to get into your room to clean it earlier, but you were apparently asleep. Is there a more convenient time for you?"

Nice, he thought. I won't need the cab. Hagopian said, "Send her up in thirty minutes or so. I'll let her in, okay?"

"Thank you, sir."

"Thank you."

"Thank you."

Hagopian cradled the handset and turned to the large package from Apex Sporting Goods. Old Deaf George, he thought and shook his head. When George heard the guy's swivel chair squeak he pulled the trigger and sent a 158 grain .357 magnum slug down the barrel at something over eleven hundred feet per second.

Silencer! Christ, the thing had acted like a plug on the muzzle of his gun. The securities dealer nearly peed in his pants when he heard the thing. He'd looked up to see a ragged piece of plywood, about the size of a dinner plate, flying from his closet door—pushed by the six-inch silencer that had blown off of Deaf George's Police Python.

Inside the closet George was earning his nickname. The concussion within the confining area had irreparably torn the delicate tympanic membranes in his ears.

Silent weapons? Deaf George could tell you about silent weapons, Hagopian thought as he lifted the cardboard cover from the box and admired his new crossbow.

27

. . . but a good cigar is a smoke.
The Betrothed
RUDYARD KIPLING

I dragged my feet when they dragged my body from the cubby and threw a gray woolen robe around my shoulders. The light was shocking, like an assault on my eyeballs, though I remembered that it had seemed dim months ago when they'd locked me into the cell.

After struggling into the robe's rough sleeves and cinching its cord around my middle I squinted carefully at the three vague figures around me. It was the major and two AVH monsters. But this time they seemed apologetic rather than ominous.

"We must hurry," the major said. "You are expected upstairs in no more than five minutes."

I looked dumbly from the major to the monsters.

"No time to think," he said. "The colonel expects you."

After a period of disuse the optic nerves go soft and the eyeballs cannot focus properly. "Patience," I said. "A little time. I can't see anything too clearly." I felt my stomach and my arms. I hadn't lost any weight and the muscle tone was still there. "I need a hot shower. I stink." It was true. Within the coarse robe I smelled like the inside of an old tennis shoe.

"No time," the major said as his two monsters grabbed me.

I looked back at the cell, then at the major. "I was just getting settled," I said.

It had to be their equivalent of a dirty trick because the Soviet colonel was like something out of an erotic movie.

Her pneumatic breasts gave lie to her Soviet Issue unisex blouse. She rose solicitously when the AVH giants hustled me into the room. "Gentle with him," she said, as though I was a Dresden vase that she had just bought. "Put him there. Careful. Careful."

They settled me into a plump chair. I thought, she's right. I am made of ceramic. When they let go of me I collapsed weakly into the chair.

"Leave him," she said. Although I couldn't see the monsters, I imagined that they hesitated because she said, "Do not worry. He is no threat."

After searching for an ego-salving reply and finding none I let her comment pass. Probably she was right; I was in no condition to insult her, let alone threaten. I decided, instead, to absorb her with my eyes. They needed the exercise.

The colonel was the most three-dimensional woman I had ever seen. She looked like she tended toward plumpness—but dieted with a will to keep her waist trim. The dieting, however, had not diminished her breasts or her hips which hourglassed out from her slender middle. Her hair was black, her eyes blue, and her skin was as fair as a bowl of cream.

"I was told you had lost your mind," she said. "But not completely, hah?" I was suddenly aware that she had been watching me as I measured her.

"Not completely," I said. "I've got a room downstairs if you'd care to join me. Nothing lavish, mind you, but you might enjoy spending a year or so with me while I'm in Hungary."

When she laughed and showed her molars I realized that

160

the colonel, like all of us, had feet of clay. Unfortunately hers were in her mouth, a showcase of socialist dentistry; uncapped and glaring fillings that looked as though they'd been wrought from some bright metal—chromium, say, or anodized aluminum. There was something very charming, very open about that laugh of hers. Before she closed her mouth I remembered that I was never to trust the Russians when they laughed.

She sat down again behind her neat oak desk. I guessed that this was a borrowed office. It was more completely furnished than the major's sparse sanctuary but the photos on her desk were of a woman and children instead of a man and children. That meant she was a ringer unless Soviet science had unlocked a genetic key that allowed women to procreate without benefit of—but no, even in my residual delirium that was too unreal to consider.

She said, "This was all so unnecessary. A mistake, you see, because you would not tell Major Laszlo why you are here in *Magyar Népköztársaság.*" *

The next step was obvious: My sexy inquisitress would charm me into telling her why indeed I was here. I didn't reply but watched her rich, sculptured lips and wondered what she would say next.

"If only you had told Laszlo that you were seeking information about this fellow Haring, I am sure he would have sent you back to Budapest with good wishes."

I smiled back at her and reached instinctively for a cigar. But the rough wool robe yielded nothing. "You wouldn't happen to have a cigar," I said. "I've left mine in my room downstairs."

"No, Remly, do not joke at me."

I shrugged. I told myself that I didn't need one; I could cover my thoughts without that comforting screen of smoke.

* "Hungarian People's Republic."

161

"Yes, of course, Haring," I said like dialogue from a '30s movie. "So you're on to him too."

"Not at all," she said. "He is your problem. Yours and the English." As she leaned across the desk I found it difficult to look her in the eye; the second and third buttons of her blouse had defected. "Tell me frankly now, what did you hope to learn of Haring in Kisvárda?" The question was a trap, her warm, wet-lipped smile the bait.

"The usual thing," I said.

"And what would that be?" she asked. "The usual thing?"

"I understand he had an appendix transplant. I came to Kisvárda to verify the news."

She laughed again, a great shaking of breasts and flashing of dental work. When she calmed a bit the colonel pulled some papers from one of the desk drawers. Among them I recognized my passport and a file folder with ————* typed across the top. Beneath my name was a two-by-two-inch photo of me, taken five years ago. She mushed through the papers and set aside my passport and visa. "This you may have," she said, pushing the passport to me with her finger. "The visa I shall keep. You have forty-eight hours to leave *Magyar Népköztársaság.*"

I glanced at the visa. It didn't matter what she did with it since it had been issued for only a two-week stay. "I couldn't use it anyway," I said. "It's expired."

Raising her eyebrows she opened the visa and looked carefully through it. "No, it is still good. You have been in Hungary only two days; twelve hours here at the detention center."

"Twelve hours?"

She gave me a sympathetic look. "Do not take it as a matter of pride, Remly. You did well to go so far in twelve hours."

"Go so far?"

* Edited, *F. O. SoCal SubSection*

162

"Chess problems. In your head chess problems, but you spoke as you thought." Tapping her ear, she said, "The walls were listening."

I nodded and said, "How far did I go?" and wondered who they'd brought in to analyze my game. No one rational, I hoped.

"Giuoco Piano to the seventh move. I am surprised that you did not let it turn into a Hungarian Game."

"Hungarian's a weak defense," I said.

"Not if you know how to exploit your pawns. It is an opening that we use well in Russia."

28

When it rains in Chicago, people get wet. When it rains in Los Angeles, people get killed.

Old Saying

It was raining when we landed at LAX. The 707 skipped once as its wheels hydroplaned on the wet runway.

"Hello, sweet tooth," said Glenda as I stepped from the accordion ramp into TWA's Customs Lounge.

Swinging my handcuffed pouch in one hand and an overnighter in the other I asked, "Where's Basset?"

"Sitting curbside in the car. I've cleared you for dip."

"Thanks." I smiled and wondered what she was doing there. Basset was to have picked me up and briefed me on the Routenfield tap on our way from the airport.

Glenda said, "You smell fishy."

"It's a surprise," I said.

Flashing my diplomatic authorization I stepped through the door without slowing. Glenda followed and slipped her arm through mine as we waited for the elevator. "Did you have fun?"

"It was a swell trip," I said.

"Clearly defined, you met a girl with big tits."

"Did I ever," I said. "Chromium teeth, too."

Basset was waiting in his Country Squire. The thing sagged on its left side from his weight. I put Glenda into the front

seat then threw my single overnighter into the rear and followed it. Unlocking the dip case's handcuff I massaged my
wrist.

"Hiya, babe."

"Did you bring the transcript?" I said.

He handed me a nine-by-twelve envelope that was covered
with pink seals like a case of smallpox. As I broke the seals and
ripped open the flap he flicked on his lights and pulled from
the curb.

"There's a light next to the ash tray," Basset said. "On the
back of the front seat. See it?"

"I see a panel here," I said. "What do I do with it?"

"Pull it out at the bottom," he said, "and you get a nice
light."

He was right. The panel moved away from the vinyl upholstery like a wedge of cheese. It glowed on the papers in my
hand without lighting up the whole back of the station wagon.

Weaver had added a preface to the transcript:

I know it sounds crazy, but these guys are playing for serious.
The one called "Strauss" runs a private security force that
Routenfield has some dough in. The "Smith" character is
just a hired hand.

If you want to read eight hours of dull stuff, the complete
transcript is downtown in Stenography. They've got an overload of work so I told them not to bother typing out the whole
thing unless they got a verify from you. This thing is a digest
of the highlights that Frank and Harriet and I picked out.
There's a juicy tape from his bedroom but I didn't send it
downtown because it's mostly noises and the girls in Steno
couldn't get it typed right. If you want to hear it, let me know.
It's a riot ha ha. I didn't know old guys in their 70s could even
get it up anymore.

W.

165

P.S. Thanks for letting me use the Bentley. I got the door opener in and I think it works OK. You ought to get your wire wheels tuned because it looses traction on fast curves and yoyos a little bit over 90 on the straights.

It's not the wheels, I thought, it's the suspension that sets up that high-speed wobble. If he wanted a real thrill he should have tried it at one-twenty.

Flipping Weaver's note to the back of the transcript I began reading the private life of Steven Routenfield:

Q CLEARANCE

Nodis Nodis Nodis Nodis Nodis Nodis Nodis Nodis Nodis Nodis

LIBRARY (Srvl. #SCss 738-it5z4)

RTNFLD: Did Kay give you the report?

STRAUSS: He wasn't in when I went there. The report's not important, Steve.

RTNFLD: What's important is the report. It was part of our agreement. He's getting real sloppy about the agreement. Where'n hell is he?

STRAUSS: I don't know, Steve. He wasn't at the ranch and he's not in Mammoth.

RTNFLD: The man is not conscientious. Not conscientious, no sir. He is not fit to sling guts to a bear. I can understand how these fellas keep losing to the Ruskies; they're all basically lazy . . . self-indulgent. They don't know the meaning of hard work and accomplishment.

STRAUSS: Steve, look, about this meeting . . .

RTNFLD: That report was due *last week*. They expect me to support their efforts, I want to see results. How many AVH people have they discredited? How many factories have they demoralized? How far've they penetrated Z.2? Have they cut back production so that quotas aren't met?

STRAUSS: I'll get the report, Steve. I'll stay on him. But this meeting; isn't it premature?

166

RTNFLD: Last decent thing they did for us was getting rid of Ranković in '66.

"This is unbelievable," I said.

"Yeah," Basset said. "It's a pretty wild wire. Old Routenfield really thinks he's got himself a private C and D organization."

An Imperial swerved in front of us as Basset approached the San Diego Freeway on-ramp at Century Boulevard. Basset leaned on the horn and shook a clenched fist at the Imperial.

"Chances are, he *has* got himself a private C and D org," I said. "But Ranković; that's incredible."

Glenda turned to look at me. "Ranković?"

"He was the number-two body under Tito. Through Jakaz, Routenfield may have been responsible for having Ranković dumped."

"That Ranković stuff isn't so incredible," Basset said as he raced the Imperial around a high-banked curve of the on-ramp. "You ought to hear some of the bedroom tapes. He gets two, three broads from the Strip and has them grease him up before . . ."

"Later, Frank, okay?"

Basset said, "It's wild stuff."

"I'll take your word for it," I said. "This guy Strauss; who's that?"

"We've got him nailed like a coffin; he's Routenfield's right-hand guy. I got a Title 19 and balanced his bank account for him. Strauss has got over a hundred thousand in small bills stuffed into safe deposit boxes all over town."

"Declared income?" I asked.

"Nope. We'll turn him over to IRS when this thing's finished."

Pellets of rain spattered against the windshield as we approached the National off-ramp.

167

"Get in the right lane," I said. "The Santa Monica's the fastest way to my place."

Under a sign that said NATIONAL NEXT, SANTA MONICA F'WAY ¼ MI, Basset levered the station wagon abruptly to the right. An XKE 2+2 blared its horn at us as Basset forced him out of his lane. "Up yours!" Basset shouted automatically. "Strauss started pulling in money when he sold controlling shares of Strauss Security Systems to Routenfield. The old man doubled his salary and gives him fat bonuses every Christmas."

"When was that?"

"Sometime in early sixty-five," Basset said. "About the time the old guy sold his chicken business."

I said, "And that's when Strauss started salting money away in safe deposit boxes?"

"No. Strauss didn't start the undeclared income until early sixty-seven. Right after Jakaz split from Tirana."

Basset rammed the Country Squire onto the Santa Monica Freeway as though he was fighting a deadline. Ignoring the MERGING TRAFFIC sign he shot from the access ramp to the fast lane with a short diagonal burst. Glenda cringed in her seat; her head almost disappeared as the wagon gathered speed.

KITCHEN (Srvl. #SCss 738-it5z9)

STRAUSS: This man is a professional; a *professional*. What in the hell did you have in mind when you phoned him?

SMITH: You said to get rid of him. What did you have in mind? Violence?

STRAUSS: Yes. I wanted you to break his leg for him, not bend his fucking ear.

SMITH: I hoped to shake him up first. (*Pause—sound, ice and unidentified liquid in glass container*) When these people get rattled they make mistakes.

STRAUSS: You call the Wildwood mess a mistake on his part? You think you rattled him enough?

SMITH: Does the old man know anything?

STRAUSS: Good Lord no. (*Pause—sound, drinking, unidentified liquid*) We've got to get this guy and pay him off.

SMITH: You seem a tremendous fan of violence: Why not corner him and smash his ugly brains out?

STRAUSS: That's murder, damn it. Murder. Let's get him and pay him off. (*Pause—sound, drinking, unidentified liquid*) But first, you've got to catch him.

SMITH: So how do we catch the gentleman?

STRAUSS: I've set up airtight security around the old man. If he tries to get through, we'll catch him.

SMITH: What if he doesn't try?

STRAUSS: That's your department. You put us on the front page of the *Times* and you can damn well clean up the mess you made.

SMITH: I'm going to need help.

STRAUSS: You'll get it. But if you don't have him before the meeting, you're going to need more than help.

"What's this 'Wildwood mess' that Strauss talks about?" I asked the back of Basset's head.

"Got me, babe. It sounds like they're trying to snatch someone."

"Have you checked the hotel?"

"Ahn . . . not yet," Basset said.

Glenda peeked over the back of her seat. "Wildwood mess?"

"Strauss mentions it; something that got on the front page of the newspapers," I said.

Glenda said, "There was a murder a couple of days back. Someone had his head crushed . . . very bloody thing. The killer tied a plastic hood over the corpse's head." Glenda smiled crookedly. "The hotel's hopping mad because the suspect used a phony credit card to identify himself and ran up a tremendous clothing bill at their men's shop."

"Frank," I said and scrubbed at my temples, "if you've got

169

time, why don't you check with the Beverly Hills police on this."

BREAKFAST ROOM (Srvl. #SCss 738-it5z13)

STRAUSS: I've got the report from Kay.
RTNFLD: What has he done to earn his keep?
STRAUSS: Not much. He says they've subverted some people within the Albanian government and expect results in a few months.
RTNFLD: Albania, eh? That will be a tough nut to crack.

How right you are, I thought. Although Albania was in the Stone Age compared with the industrial capacity of the Hungarians, Poles and Czechs, their internal security police structure was even tighter than Beria's was in the fifties.

STRAUSS: He told me they'll be ready for the conference by next week. Friday at the latest.
RTNFLD: Will the Hungarian liaison be there?
STRAUSS: He guaranteed it. Absolutely guaranteed.

We stopped at the Highland Avenue, Hollywood Boulevard signal. The Christmas decorations were up; plastic and anodized aluminum that turned Hollywood Boulevard into "Christmas Tree Lane" and totally obscured all street signs.

"So we've got a meeting in Mammoth next week," I said. "So who's the Hungarian liaison?"

"I guess we'll find out at the meeting," Basset said. The light turned green and Basset's station wagon leaped across the intersection. "The Jakaz wire is about as useful as tits on a chicken, babe. Either he knows we're watching him or his old AVH instincts are still functioning. I'm trying to get a Title 43 authorization to do his mail."

"Maybe KGB scared him off," I said. "They picked me up at Jakaz' place, so they've been watching him."

170

"No," Glenda said. "The Russian Delegation for Culture and Heavy Machinery has left town."

"Then they've got someone else out there; they've got to," I said.

"Vanished completely," Basset said. "I put a couple of guys on the place and a couple of other guys on the first two. No one's watching them. And no one's watching the place except us."

"Something smells," I said. "Something smells very bad."

TELEPHONE (Srvl. #SCss 738-it5z1)

BERNIE: Hello, Strauss?

"Who's this?" I said. "This Bernie character?"

Basset said, "Long distance from Detroit. We couldn't get a make on it."

"Terrific," I said.

STRAUSS: Yes.
BERNIE: This is Bernie the Booker. Was I right? Did you find your hotel with the squash courts?
STRAUSS: Yes, you were right. My people made him.
BERNIE: Okay. Beautiful. You owe me twenty yards.
STRAUSS: We don't have him yet.
BERNIE: That don't mean shit, pal. The deal was, I tell you about the guy and if I'm right you owe me twenty yards. If you can't catch him, that's your trouble.
STRAUSS: Yeah. (Pause—sound, drinking, unidentified liquid) Okay. How do I get the money to you?
BERNIE: Don't worry; I'll send a guy.

I said, "This looks like chaff. How did it get into the folder?"

"It was a weird conversation," Basset said. "We thought you'd want to see it."

171

"Thanks." I massaged my eyebrows and wondered if the pressure was only temporary.

"The Wildwood's got squash courts," he said as an afterthought.

Basset turned left just short of Hollywood Bowl. We were in my neighborhood now; narrow, winding streets and whitewashed stucco walls that had turned sepia in the rain.

I said, "Turn here, I'm halfway up the street," and stuffed the transcript back into its pink-pocked manila envelope. I could read the rest of it later.

As he turned right, smashing on his brakes to avoid the cars on my narrow street, Basset said, "Got nothing on the girl."

"The girl?" I said.

Glenda asked, "Have you forgotten again?"

"Mary Louise Paál," I said. "That's who we're talking about?"

Basset said, "Nothing."

"Don't worry about it. I'll get something on her."

"Be a good boy," Glenda said.

Basset parked across from the Bentley and I climbed out of his wagon.

"Will you give me a lift home?" Glenda asked.

"Glad to," Basset said.

"Not you." Glenda turned her thin little face to me and said, "You."

"I just love it," Glenda said when I flicked on the lights. "Where did you find all this marvelous old junk?"

"All over," I said. "Swap meets, farms, junkshops, you name it."

"It's incredible. I thought you'd have some kind of a 'Playboy Pad.' But *this* is really you." She turned her mocking smile on me. "Junk and leftovers."

"What did you get from our sister agencies on Jakaz and Kovács?" I said.

"Nothing. Absolutely nothing."

"This is some investigation," I said. "It's like trying to swim in a bowl full of Jell-O."

But Glenda wasn't listening. By the time she reached the living room, she was down to her pantyhose.

29

Hagopian parked his rented car, killed its headlights and peered through the rain at Bel Air. The ill-lighted street was above Routenfield's place on Oakview Terrace. Sliding across the seat and opening the passenger door he wondered where the oaks had gone; he could see only pine trees on the slope that dropped abruptly from the curb. Dim moonlight filtered through the pines and dropped little splashes of silver on the hillside, like a school of suddenly beached fish.

The new crossbow was rewrapped and locked away in his room at the Executive House. This wasn't a hit, not tonight; he wanted a closer look at his working area first.

Hagopian stepped from the car and closed its door with a gentle touch. He double-checked the street. Empty.

A platoon of trees marched with Oriental asymmetry down the slope and Hagopian moved through them until he was stopped by a fence.

He could almost smell the money.

Routenfield's security system was one of the best he'd seen at a private residence. The chain-link fence alone was worth a fortune: It was alarm wired at each fencepost stretcher so that no significant disturbance would go unnoticed. A chipmunk could bump it, perhaps, but the weight of a man would set the thing off.

Beautiful, Hagopian thought. He ran his pen light across the alarm wires. Really beautiful. Each six-foot section of fence was wired separately; they would have a control board inside that would tell them exactly where an intruder was trying to climb the fence. And this—he brought the light closer and squinted in the rain—this would be an anti-tamper wire. Try to shortcut the system and the power drop would set off the alarm as though he'd tried to climb the fence.

Snapping off the flash, he trudged uphill and shook his head at the private forest; the thing was a product of landscaping, not nature. Money, he thought. Lots of money; lots of fried-chicken money.

Twenty feet up the hill he stopped and turned to contemplate the house. The fence wasn't much of an obstacle; like locking a car, it would only keep the amateurs out. One of the pines was within five feet of the fence. Although its lower branches had been trimmed to avoid any overhang on the Routenfield property, he could tie a length of nylon line to one of the higher ones and swing over the chain link.

No, it wasn't the fence that worried him; it was what might be on the far side. If they'd set up a system that elaborate to keep out the amateurs, they must have put together a lulu for the pros.

Hagopian blinked his eyes to squeeze the water away. He resisted the urge to wipe his face and take off a fistful of rain and Max Factor.

It was a shame about that security system. Hell, it was more than a shame—it was a stinking pity. This kind of weather was designed for a hit. No one liked to leave his comfort to go out in the rain, not private cops or public cops or even contractors. Of all the guys in the business, he was the only one who worked in this kind of weather by choice.

Screw it, Hagopian thought. If Routenfield's Bel Air house wasn't right for the hit, maybe that lodge in Mammoth would be easier.

Slogging up to the car he said, "Maybe I could have some fun in the snow."

175

30

Q: If your computer system has all the answers, how do you justify your existence, sir?

A: Ahn . . . yes, sir. Umm . . . the computer doesn't know which questions to ask.

Minutes of the Hearings,
Subcommittee on National Security Affairs
Volume CXCIII
Page 385

"*It stank,*" I said, slapping my open hand against the F. O.'s desk. A gaggle of perfectly sharpened pencils rattled like spears in their leather canister.

"I'm not at all amused by your display of temper," said the F. O. He wrapped his little face around one of the tremendous Havanas I'd brought back in my immune dip pouch. After a few contented puffs he removed the cigar and said, "If you will contain yourself I am willing to sit through the rest of your report."

It was not fun and games this time; no Ping-Pong balls, no magic tricks. I had shot six days of my thirty-day deadline. And though I'd awakened with the exploding motorcycle up the hill, I had gotten Glenda to the F. O.'s office an hour late —and in yesterday's dress.

"Okay, it stank," I said quietly. "Belgrade wasn't so bad; I got some interesting news from our friend Stosh regarding Tibor Kovács . . . and a few choice words about what Jakaz' group *might* be up to in Tirana." I unwrapped one of my own cheap cigars after the F. O. scowled at my hand as I reached for his humidor. "Then Beebee Haring gave me something even more interesting: He offered me fifty thousand dollars to set up a privy conference with Kovács."

"And that's significant?" He swiveled about in his chair, not looking at me but not looking away either.

"It's significant in at least three respects," I said. "Beebee assumes that I can . . . or that I might be *able* to . . . put my hands on Kovács. That's number one; and that puts Dr. Kovács somewhere in Los Angeles or in the States. Then there's the money thing. If Beebee's willing to pop fifty thousand dollars for such a meeting it means there's at least *twenty* times that amount in it for him. Beebee's one of the great tightwads of the western world, you know."

"I know. Just as you are one of its great wastrels."

I ignored him. "So if Beebee is willing to spend money to pick Kovács' brain, he thinks those missing files contain something that's worth a lot on the open market; something more than just security matters." The cigar tip was glowing and I puffed at it, wishing that I'd brought back a few Havanas for myself. "Stosh talked about Kovács doing some research in mnemonics, but it has to be something more impressive than that. These files are worth quite a few multiples of fifty thousand skins."

"Twenty times fifty thousand," the F. O. said. "That's a million dollars." He hummed softly. "And number three?"

"Obvious," I said. "Beebee's desperate. Either that, or he's more of a clot than he appears because I'm not what you'd call a logical target for bribery."

A large flake of ash fell on his jacket and the F. O. flashed up a hand to brush it away. Inspecting his lapel to see if it was burned he said, "That's not necessarily so. Even the most cursory balance of your income against your spending habits would make you a very logical bribee indeed."

"Then we can rule out number three. Beebee's not desperate."

"That is not what I meant. I believe that Haring may also suspect, just as I know as a certainty that you haven't the *imagination* to accept a bribe of those proportions. No, fifty thousand isn't your style; nickel and dime cheating on your expense account's more like it."

"So we don't rule out number three. But why is Beebee desperate?"

"Why indeed?" the F. O. said.

The view from the F. O.'s window was one of the ugliest I'd ever seen. Although the rain clouds were clearing, there was still the city itself. Los Angeles was in the throes of nightmarish growth, a civic delusion of progress, and looked as though it had been bombed. Great clumsy machines wambled through the central city gouging up sacrilegious amounts of earth and smashing blindly against every upright thing in their paths.

I stared at the Hogarthian view and said, "So that's what we've learned from Beebee; that this project's worth our time and expense. But as for the rest of it . . ." I worked to control my voice ". . . it stank. Here, I've got a list for you." I dug the folded, green-lined yellow sheet of paper from my jacket and tried to smooth out its wrinkles by drawing it across the sharp edge of his desk.

As I turned again to glower at the view, the F. O. glanced at the note I'd written to myself.

When the F. O. said, "This is quite a piece of work," I turned to see him sniffing my list. "According to what little I can read of this, the more you learn the more confused you become."

178

I said, "I put a lot of hours into that thing."

"And a considerable amount of brandy. It reeks of the stuff," he said, sniffing it again. "Had I the time I would send this thing to Ft. Meade for decrypting. As things stand, I haven't the time . . . do you think you might explain this unintelligible scrawl?"

"Yes," I said. "To begin with . . ."

"Not from the beginning, damn it. I'm not quite ready for Genesis through Revelation. Just give me some highlights."

"Kovács," I said. "He was doing something for Jakaz in mnemonics. He disappeared for a few years. He reappeared in Los Angeles. And somewhere along the line he picked up the mysterious files. If we can find out what Jakaz' function was, we'll be able to put a lot of the Kovács puzzle together."

The F. O. squinted at my memorandum. "Yes, here," he said. "I can make that out."

I said, "If I come to a blank wall on Jakaz, I'll go to Canada and talk to Barnay about Kovács' work in mnemonics. It's a carom shot . . . but it's better than nothing."

Stabbing the memo with a neatly manicured finger he said, "About this 'Fifteen, who M.L.—REALLY?' Who M.L. indeed?"

"That girl, the Hungarian girl Routenfield adopted. While Jakaz and Kovács are prisms that refract a glut of semiconnected information, Mary Louise Paál comes out a total blank."

The F. O. said, "And this item regarding KGB? It was my impression that you were detained by AVH."

"Detained by AVH, sprung by KGB," I said. "That *zoftig* colonel wasn't a colonel at all. I checked her out in Budapest with some of our Agency bodies before I left. She's a Delilah type; some kind of a nobody in KGB infrastructure."

"Then she hadn't the authority to spring you, eh?"

179

"She didn't have the authority to scratch her butt without specific approval in triplicate from Moscow. They used her to front the job so I wouldn't see any important noses."

"Yet you were sprung."

"Like a pogo stick," I said. "Though there was no real reason to keep me at Nyiregyháza, there was even less reason to let me go; especially with a cock and bull story about how they understood that I was investigating Beebee. So we can assume it was a Pre-Summit Gambit. They want something from us and I just got lucky with my timing."

"No, we cannot assume that. Nothing's come down from State about a meeting with them. Nothing at all." He looked from me to the window and back again. "What is out there that fascinates you so?"

"That construction machinery," I said. "They're like dinosaurs, except that they are making us extinct."

"No. They are preparing us for the future." He puffed at his cigar, waiting for me to get on with it.

"I left word with our people in Budapest to follow through on the Jakaz/Kovács thing, but I'm negative about what they'll dig up. There is one other approach, though, if you'll lend me Glenda and her magic 3270."

"I can imagine what you have in mind for Glenda," the F. O. said. "But why you want the 3270 is beyond me."

"So far I've been working it the hard way. You had Glenda run Jakaz and Kovács through the data banks in Virginia and we got zilch for an answer. Then I tried running down the information by myself; that was the hardest way of all."

"I didn't realize there was an easy way."

"So easy that we missed it," I said. "We've been feeding the wrong questions into the computer. We don't want data about Jakaz or Kovács."

Slapping my open hand again on his desk I ignored his

clouded look and said, "What we need are data regarding our own Agency personnel. I think it's damn likely that one of our people has an answer or two."

He sat and puffed and watched me in silence. He was wearing a new tie, his usual gray but covered with small blue polka dots. Sitting in his richly appointed office and looking at his well-tailored suit I felt as though I was negotiating a loan from my banker.

"Look," I said. "We've got something like fifteen thousand people on the payroll."

"Where did you hear that?" he snapped.

"L.A. *Herald-Examiner*. They did a feature on us; fifteen to sixteen thousand people on the Agency's payroll, and maybe another fifteen thousand people who do odd jobs for us on a regular basis—but who aren't eligible for group insurance or the pension fund. Now, we know that there has been a bottleneck in Data Processing because we scrounge up too damn much information. It has always been impossible to program every datum that we dig up. And it's next to impossible to coordinate what we've got and draw halfway illuminating conclusions. So Jakaz is 'dead' according to Data Processing. And Kovács was never important enough to get programmed. Yes?"

"Yes," the F. O. said. "We should hire another fifteen thousand people just to feed what we've got into the machines. Yes. It's quite likely that someone within the Agency knows of them."

"And that his knowledge never got programmed," I said. "So I'll need Glenda and her IBM console to search out bodies . . . any bodies that were assigned to Budapest until nineteen fifty-seven. If we can find out what Jakaz and Kovács were up to, we might get a picture of their million-dollar files. Make sense?"

"Very good sense," the F. O. said. "I'll assign Glenda to you, but only after my office hours. Let's see what the two of you can dig up."

I said, "It's going to be straight data retrieval . . . no logic programming . . . but I may need a hefty overtime authorization. I want to make up for the wheel spinning we've done."

"For her only. You've cribbed enough on your expenses this month."

"Suits me. I simply want to get this thing finished and return to a normal existence."

"Normal?" the F. O. asked and began a lengthy discussion of normalcy that showed why I, especially, had little if any right to use the word. Or even to think of it for that matter.

31

Q: Will you explain, sir, the difference between an agent and a Projects Officer?

A: Generally speaking, sir, agents administer *things*, while Projects Officers administer *people*.

Minutes of the Hearings,
Subcommittee on National Security Affairs
Volume CCLXVII
Page 92

I touched a button under the dash and the gate to our Mulholland house swung open. It closed smoothly behind me as I swung the Bentley in. Another button opened a garage door.

Strange, I thought. Electronic toys never before worked in the Bentley. Maybe things were beginning to look up.

Harriet met me at the front door with a smile on her face and a mug of coffee in her hand. She said, "Welcome home, Chief."

"Thanks." I smiled wanly at her.

She shoved the mug into my fist and trotted stumpily beside me as I walked to my office. "I straightened things up a bit while you were gone. I didn't see how you'd be able to work in the mess they left in your office, so I took the liberty of having Weaver pick your lock."

"Harriet," I said, "you'll never change." But when I looked at her I realized that she had. She was wearing a bright sweater. Her hair was less severe, almost feminine. Her pinched little expression had loosened to the extent that she no longer looked as though she was peering at the world from a gopher hole.

And there was something else; she smelled differently. I sniffed at her a couple of times and caught a hint of something familiar. White Shoulders? No. Chamade? No, that was Glenda's scent.

"I know it was a little brassy," Harriet said, "but I just didn't want you returning to complete havoc. Try that coffee now. Tell me if you like it."

I stopped and took a sip of the coffee. It was good; as good as the stuff I brewed at home in fact. "It's nifty," I said. "What did you do?"

"Well, the spring water stand is in. And I faked up a req. slip for a coffee grinder. Basset told me where to get the beans; a blend of Java and Vienna roasts." She presented me with a smug little smile. "I think it's worth the extra effort, don't you? Perks up the morale around here."

"Good girl," I said. In the three months I'd known her, it was the first time I had said anything even vaguely pleasant to Harriet.

"I knew you'd approve," she said and started off toward my office again. "Speaking of morale, duck into Weaver's office before you get to work. I nagged at him to tune your garage-opening hardware. You should tell him you noticed it."

"Which one of those doors is Weaver's?"

"Third on the right," she said.

I poked my face into Weaver's office. He was at his desk, surrounded by electronic clutter.

"Thanks," I said.

Weaver nearly launched himself from the desk when I spoke. He looked up with shocked, unseeing eyes and raised a nervous hand to his bald head. I was afraid he would swallow his chewing gum. Weaver had nerves that snapped like brittle rubber bands when he was startled.

"Just wanted to say thanks for the job on my car. First time that one of those damn things has worked in it."

"Oh, yeah, hiya Charley. Glad to do it. Felt I kinda owed you one after you covered for me."

I must have looked blank.

"Prune ranch," Weaver said. His voice rumbled like he was talking from the bottom of a barrel. "Wired it for me."

I remembered then. "How's the little mother?" I asked.

"Doing fine. Caesarean section after all. Six of the cutest little Siamese kits you ever saw. You still got first choice."

"Terrific," I said. I needed a cat like I needed a nervous breakdown. "Anything on that envelope from Miami?"

"Nothing," said Weaver. "No calls, no mail, no nothing."

"Mmmm," I said. "Maybe it was just a travel brochure."

"But I'm staying on it, Chief. I got a blanket request to Gulf States SubSection, Miami Office, for news on any Hungarians they've got running loose."

"Good boy," I said, but it was a useless request, blanket or not. G-S SubSection's specialty was Cuba-sniffing; they wouldn't give a damn about Hungarians—or about Martians landing on the Capitol Dome for that matter.

"Something will come up," Weaver said. "I know a couple of people down there."

"Fine, fine. How about our friends the Russians? I hear they've all gone home."

"All except a trawler off the coast."

I said, "I wonder what they're fishing for."

"Whales," Weaver said sadly. "And they got everyone hopping about it. They're supposed to be protected now."

"The Russians?"

"No, the whales."

185

Weaver had a paternal instinct for all mammaldom. If he could have adopted one of the whales, I was sure to get pick of the litter. "And you're keeping an eye on them?"

"You bet, Chief."

"Do me a favor," I said. "Don't call me 'Chief.' "

"Oh, okay, Chief. Picked it up from . . ."

"I can guess," I said.

Harriet was waiting for me at my office door. I opened it and stepped aside. As she passed through I sniffed at her again.

She said, "Are you catching something?"

"Touch of hay fever," I said.

My office was immaculate and ready for action. As I settled behind the desk I wondered what Basset had done to Harriet while I was gone; put a gun in one of her ears while making guttural noises in the other?

I shuffled the two ash trays, my old shaving mug with its *fasco* of dull pencils and inkless ballpoint pens, and a magnetic cup of paper clips into proper order—King's Indian Defense. "Has Basset checked in yet?"

Harriet materialized a Kleenex and cleared her sinuses into it. "Not yet."

I said, "When he does, put him through immediately."

She nodded.

"How about budget control? Can you tell me how many bodies we have on staff for this project?"

"You, me, Basset and Weaver. That's four."

"Good girl."

"Then there's Grillo at Mammoth, Parsons and Frouchet covering the prune ranch. Harmon and Taub are covering Routenfield's Bel Air house and Given and Warren are on the girl."

I had a quick flash of Given and Warren on the girl and wondered if they were enjoying it half as much as she. "How many bodies total?" I asked.

186

"That makes eleven people on payroll."

"And I'll get a budget report when?"

"Tomorrow, before noon," Harriet said.

"Ahn, one other thing," I said. "Did a Q Clearance dispatch arrive while I was gone? It should have come here directly from Virginia."

"Well, *that's* unlikely," Harriet said. "All Q material comes to us through the F. O.'s office."

"No, this was a Nodis for my eyes only."

"I haven't seen it. But I'll have it on your desk the minute it arrives, Chief."

"Great," I said. I should have been wearing a breechclout and feathers with all the "Chiefing" going on. "Except for Basset, hold my calls, okay? I want to catch up on all this paper work sometime today."

"Wilco," Harriet said, simpering girlishly as she closed the door behind her.

"Wilco?" I said aloud. I dropped two Alka-Seltzer tablets into my mug. When they dissolved I popped a handful of B^{12} into my mouth and washed it down with the effervescent coffee. I stretched comfortably in my chair and tilted it back in order to prop my feet against the desk. Just before going to sleep I remembered where I'd smelled Harriet's odd scent before. It was Old Spice After Shave. Peculiar, I thought drowsily, but it beat hell out of the stale powder odor that used to follow her around.

I had just discovered that Gyula Jakaz was in fact *Reichsleiter* Martin Bormann, and was about to turn him over to a pneumatic young thing from Israeli Intelligence, when the intercom buzzed like an adenoidal bee.

"It's Basset," Harriet said. "Line four."

"So what we've got is murder and maiming," Basset said

187

without any preliminaries. "I told the BH cops I was a Deputy Assistant Attorney General and that we were looking into the phony credit-card angle. Anyway, what they've got is a guy in a coma at USC-County Med Center. It looks like he was clipped on the head with a fence pole, just like the corpse."

"When will he come out of it?"

Basset said, "Maybe never, if he lives."

"That makes sense," I said. "Any leads on why they were messed up?"

"Not one, babe," Basset said. "The BH cops don't even know about the tie in between the two guys and Strauss." I heard a match strike and Basset exhaled loudly in my ear. "This guy—this suspect of theirs—used the name Richard T. Hagopian."

"You run a diversion check with FBI?" I asked.

"Yup. Nothing."

"Like swimming in Jell-O," I said and swiveled to look out my window. The view was pleasant; not like the full-scale war that was being waged outside the F. O.'s office. "So what have you got on the guy?"

Basset said, "The name and a fairly good description. Gray hair, gray mustache, scar on the chin. He looked like a successful exec type who worked out in a gym—very powerful, very fit."

Hohum.

"One funny coincidence," Basset said. "The guy's bungalow was wired."

"Who'd take the time to bother?"

"Us. It was an Agency job."

"What?"

"A real old baby . . . one of those Elradynes we used to use," Basset said. "I remember some talk about our wiring the whole damn hotel when the Cosmonauts stayed there."

"Funny coincidence," I agreed. We were still drawing a blank. I pulled a fresh yellow pad from my top drawer and began doodling as Basset and I wound down our conversation. I said, "That meeting still on?"

"Hell, *I* dunno," Basset said. "Last I heard from Weaver it was."

"No, not the Mammoth meeting; not Routenfield and Jakaz. I meant our meeting."

"Oh, sure," Basset said. "Unless you want it changed, babe."

I said, "No. I'll see you there," and hung up.

On the pad I had scrawled, "Richard T. Hagopian = ?" Under that was, "? = Hungarian liaison?" And under that was, "? = Kovács?"

I punched the intercom button with Harriet's initials on it and said, "Any calls while I was working?"

"Just Glenda," Harriet said. There was a trace of disapproval in her voice, as though we were discussing an unpleasant odor instead of the F. O.'s secretary.

"What did she have on her mind?"

"I'm sure I couldn't say," Harriet said. "She refused to leave a message."

I thanked her and picked up the red phone—our scrambled hot line to downtown.

"Hello, sweet tooth," Glenda said.

I didn't laugh. "You called me. What's up?"

Glenda paused and thought about it, then said, "Yes. Something came in from Buda desk. One of our people got a repro of Tibor Kovács' employee file from Péter Pazmány University."

"Swell," I said. "Did he have tenure?"

"That's very funny," Glenda said. "But as a matter of fact, he did. I'm holding the file for you. It contains a resumé, physical and dental profile, reports from the dean of the school of psychology and blahblahblah—the sort of thing you'd expect. Want to pick it up? Or should I have it delivered?"

I said, "Hang onto it. I'll come by . . . um . . . sometime tomorrow and get it."

"What about this afternoon, Charley-the-spy? I thought we were going to play retrieval games."

"IBM will have to wait." I shot my left hand out and looked at my naked wrist. Shaking my head and digging into the small change pocket of my jacket I found the Waltham and pressed on its stem. The hunting case snapped open and the watch told me that it was time to start for my appointment with Basset.

Glenda said, "What do you have, bad boy? A live one at The Point?"

"Work is what I have," I said. "All play and no work makes Charley a dull boy."

32

Item: 1 Mustang, loaded w/ extras (used) $2,375.00

I was directly behind the blue Mustang when it happened.

An aged Mercedes 300 sprang from the curb and beat itself senseless against the Mustang's right front fender. The Mustang lurched, crippled horse that it was, yawing to a stop.

I slammed my foot against the brake pedal but my reflexes weren't swift enough; the Bentley's heavy front bumper chewed its way into the blue car's sheet metal. Between the two of us, the Mercedes and I created a pile of rubble out of someone's baby-blue dream.

"Jeez, I'm sorry," Basset said to the world in general as he climbed from the Mercedes.

"Not yet you aren't," I said. I had gotten out of my car and was crawling across what was left of the Mustang's trunk; we had wedged the car so thoroughly that it seemed the fastest route from my right-hand driver's door to the other's left-hand driver's door.

"Are you okay?" I asked.

The blonde inside the Mustang looked at me with glassy-eyed disbelief. In a tiny frightened voice she said, "Oh my," and pressed her knuckles against her mouth. "Is it bad?"

Bad wasn't the word for it. "Total wreck," I said.

"Oh my." She began crying silently, pear-shaped tears rolled down her cheeks. "I just got it paid for."

Even with her eyes beginning to swell she was a stunning girl. Her long hair was the color of straw and she had braided it into two thick ropes that she'd coiled over each ear. With her hair and her freshly scrubbed face she might have been a milkmaid.

Since I never carry a handkerchief I couldn't offer her one, but her trembling lip and pained eyes drove me to make a gesture. When I reached through the car's window and patted her head she leaned toward me and pressed her face against my necktie. "There, now," I said. "I'm sure it can all be straightened out."

Beside me Basset said, "It's all my fault. I'll take care of everything. Are you okay?"

"I'm not hurt," she murmured into my chest.

It was a good street for an accident; tree-lined and quiet. No crowd would gather and traffic would not bunch up as we untangled the cars.

"Look," Basset said, "I'm late for an appointment. If we can just exchange drivers' licenses and insurance companies I'll take care of everything."

"Oh my," the girl said again. "I'm going to be late too. I have to be at the dentist."

"No problem. I'll take you," I said.

"Isn't your car wrecked?"

"Chipped some chrome off the bumper, that's all." I turned to Basset. "How about your Mercedes?"

"Dented the fender and cracked a headlight." Basset was going to have to explain that one. He'd borrowed the 300 from a body in Ordnance with the promise that nothing would happen to it. It was supposed to have been a small accident, a fender-bender, but Basset turned it into a production number.

I helped her from the Mustang and stood a little straighter once she was out. Tall girls always improve my posture; she was no more than an inch shorter than I. We all exchanged license and insurance data, spreading our credentials on the sprung hood of her car. Holding her license I asked, "Is this your current address?"

"Yes," she said. "But they spelled my last name wrong. There should be two As."

Mary Louise didn't mention the acute accent over the second A.

"How do you feel?"

"Oooo," she said and made big eyes at me. "Like my mouth is all swollen. Do I look funny?"

"You look beautiful," I said and meant it. I closed the five-year-old copy of *National Geographic* and dropped it on a stack of magazines that littered the table beside me. It hadn't been much use as a time killer; the native women in it were wrapped in floral fabrics. Peeling away from the vinyl couch I said, "That's it for the day? You don't have anything else planned?" I opened the door for her.

"Well, I was going to do some shopping," she said. "But I can't put you out like that. I mean, it's not like you *planned* on bumping into me."

At the elevator I said, "It's not that I feel obligated. I'd like to spend the day with you because I like you." I turned to Mary Louise and smiled. "And that's the simple truth." As though the truth is ever simple.

"Oh," said Mary Louise. Her brows shot up and her eyes became pale-blue saucers.

"It's not a smooth approach, but you'll admit it's original." The elevator doors parted unwillingly, then began closing again before we could step through. I kicked the rubber safety bumper and the doors jumped apart again.

Mary Louise stepped into the elevator and I followed. The

193

doors closed and she touched my hand. "I like you too. Let's spend the day together."

We didn't spend the day. We squandered it.

We went shopping at Cowell's Snow 'n' Sport, but after a few vague glances at ski pants and a parka Mary Louise said, "I have enough clothes to outfit an Alpine rescue team. Let's do something *really* fun."

"Like?"

"What good are ski clothes if you're not skiing? Let's fly to Mammoth."

I smiled and shrugged and did some quick mental calculations. Basset and I had planned our office schedule around the possibility that I might spend a day—and a night—with Mary Louise. We hadn't prepared for a day or more at Mammoth. "Well, uh . . ." I said none too brightly.

"Oh come on. You told me you didn't have anything else planned for the rest of the decade; except to fritter your inheritance. Spend it with me."

"What, my inheritance?"

"No, your time. All of your time. We can have lots of fun." Mary Louise reached out playfully and poked me in the ribs.

I jumped. "Hey, none of that. I'm ticklish."

Mary Louise was a joy to be with; as unpredictable as the weather. She skied superbly, far better than I, and had to scrub off speed to let me keep up with her as we traversed the Cornice. In fact it was Mary Louise who wanted to ski the Cornice, almost pulling me physically to the gondola that carried us to the top of Mammoth Mountain.

The Cornice is an exercise in masochism, a sixty-degree drop

194

for the first hundred feet with moguls cropping up almost every bit of the way. I have seen people lose their forward sideslip on moguls in that first hundred feet and not stop rolling until they plowed up a half mile or so of unpacked snow.

At one point I lost her. We had skied nearly to the base of the mountain and Mary Louise shot over a drop but didn't reappear. I did a quick wedeln series and looked for her: If she had fallen behind the drop I didn't want to follow her over and land on her like a brick. When she didn't show I hammered down my edges and scrubbed to a stop at the point where Mary Louise had disappeared.

The snowball caught me full in the face. I started toppling backward, then overcompensated and tumbled in all directions over the drop. On my first roll the bindings released and I parted company with my skis. The second roll shoved a load of snow down my neck while the third packed the snow somewhere around the small of my back. I landed finally on my butt and tobogganed toward Mary Louise.

She had found a barrier in the snow, a natural fortress, and was crouched behind it sizing me up for her next shot. I caught another snowball square on the nose. Mary Louise had a good arm. And a strong one.

Skittering to a stop I scooped enough snow to make a small hard ball and crouched, waiting for her to appear again. When she did I let fly and caught her in the stomach.

"Wooof," she wheezed. "Not fair. I'm a girl."

I bent to scoop more snow and her snowball whistled harmlessly over my head. "Like hell," I shouted. "You are a pinko leftist agitator." My next snowball was large and soft; I intended to let her have it in her lovely face.

"I'll get you," she said. But when she appeared I got her instead. The snowball mushroomed out from her face and left her standing with a foolish expression on her mouth and an unthrown lump of snow in her hand. "No fair, no fair."

I rushed the fortress and tackled her.

When we stopped rolling I was on top of her and when I kissed her she stopped struggling and started insinuating her fingers into my hair. Our teeth clicked as her tongue explored the interior of my mouth.

"You were really born over there?" I asked. "I don't hear any Magyar in your speech."

We were at Whiskey Creek, a very jammed and boozy kind of place where a folk singer was singing to the folks. The folks ignored him, talking loudly while he sang but applauding wildly at the end of each number.

"I left a long time ago . . . a long long time. Papa took me in as a foster child."

"Papa?"

"Mr. Routenfield."

"Steven Routenfield?"

"Yes."

"Well I'll be damned. I've heard of him. Super-rich as opposed to merely rich."

"That's where we'll be staying tonight." Mary Louise stirred her brandy-laced chocolate with an idle finger. "We have a lodge on Pine Vale Drive."

"Steven Routenfield. I'll be damned."

"You said that."

"I know. It's just . . ." I shrugged and held my open palm above the table ". . . I'm impressed, that's all."

"Impressed?" She smiled and said, "I thought you were rich," in a tone that told me that she knew I wasn't.

"I am. But that's only until the end of next week when my

vacation's over." I unwrapped a cigar and·rolled the tip slowly over a blazing match. The smoke wouldn't be noticed in the Whiskey Creek air. "Actually I just *live* like I'm rich. It's all on the expense account and Uncle Sam flies me around the world for freebees."

"Are you in politics, Charley?"

"Foreign Service. I've just become a dip this year."

"Dip?"

"Diplomat. Or dipsomaniac. It's multiple-choice definition: Take your pick." The cigar was lit and I puffed at it. "It's not bad work, but some of the countries I deal with shouldn't be on the map."

Mary Louise's face clouded. "Don't say that, Charley, not like that, don't say it. That attitude . . . that is how some countries get erased from maps."

I puffed my cigar and watched her Dresden eyes. Mary Louise was going to give me something: She was at the right psychological turning, with tears just around the corner, and she wanted to communicate something to me. Her control was slipping.

I said, "How did you manage the wall? You must have been what, seven when you came over? How did you manage it?"

The lines deepened on her brow. "There's so much I can't remember. It was like . . . like *drowning*. But drowning in violence, and at such a fast pace that nothing clung to my memory; like bits of paper you lick with your tongue and they don't stick to anything."

"But something that cataclysmic," I said. "You don't remember any of it?"

"Funny things happen sometimes," said Mary Louise. "Once in a while I hear someone speak a word or two of Magyar and . . . and . . ."

I reached across the table and traced my fingertips lightly

197

over the back of her hand. "What happens when you hear Magyar?"

"It's funny," she said but her face said it wasn't funny at all. "I hear names of people I must have known. All those poor poor people, I hear names and I see their faces." Mary Louise clutched my hand. "People are always leaving me, Charley; leaving without saying goodbye. And if they ever show up again it's all meaningless . . . it's always too late."

I said, "That's the way of the world, pussycat. Nothing is stable; everything changes. People meet and part every day. And security is a man-made dream, like the philosophers' stone—it just doesn't exist as a fact of nature."

"Oh my God, Charley." Her fingernails dug into the palm of my hand. "Life should be beautiful, not hideous. Let's go to the lodge. Let's be beautiful."

I said, "I am *bête*. I'll follow your lead, *belle*."

"You're no beast, Charley," Mary Louise said. She hadn't gotten acquainted with me yet.

33

Affection, like melancholy, magnifies trifles.

LEIGH HUNT

Routenfield's lodge was opulent beyond reason, or beyond the needs of a ski cabin at any rate. Whoever designed the place for him had done it in basic Louis Quatorze with a hint of Tut-ankh-amen's sarcophagus to give the thing some class.

It was a huge modified A-frame, its exposed ridgepole barely visible thirty or forty feet above us. A gallery circled the main room about fifteen feet up and was punctuated with doors that led to the lodge's bedrooms. A pair of chandeliers hung to the level of the gallery, their gleaming crystal drops refracting and reflecting brilliant pinpoints of light.

Mary Louise and I were stretched before the fireplace, a tremendous, Breton-tiled thing large enough to roast a steer. I nailed my eyes on the ceiling and asked, "What happened to all the people? You ought to be surrounded by ancient retainers."

Mary Louise said, "No. Papa . . . it's very odd. No one's here, no one's in the Bel Air house except some of his business associates. Papa's given everyone a vacation, though he should have someone to look after him."

"Is that a fact?" I said. I breathed carefully. "Is he ill?"

She rolled the question in her mind and counted the rafters with me. "Papa is old," Mary Louise said. "Even for seventy-two, Papa is very old."

199

"How do you mean?" I asked but she stood and walked away from me.

Mary Louise dimmed the chandeliers. She said, "It's like a royal wedding at the Winter Palace with those things. I remember when Papa said he was going to build a cozy little cabin." She rattled her head on the way back to the fireplace. "But this . . . this is incredible, don't you think?"

"Yes," I said. "I think." But not often.

"He built it for me . . . for skiing you know." Mary Louise settled beside me then rolled to her back. "The acoustics are honestly weird in here. You can whisper down here at the fireplace and anyone up there," she pointed vaguely at the balconies, "can hear every syllable." Mary Louise rested her head on my legs. "Papa tries to be thoughtful. And he worries about me in a general way . . . the way he worries about his car." She snuggled her cheek against my thigh. "It's all very very comfortable and very very impersonal."

My right leg was going to sleep. I flexed the muscle slightly but couldn't stop the march of pins and needles that had begun just above my knee. "How come he adopted you?"

"He didn't," said Mary Louise in a distant voice as she lifted her head to sip from her glass of bourbon and warm milk. "The courts wouldn't allow a widower to adopt a six-year-old child . . . this was back in fifty-seven, remember . . . but Papa got some judge to make me a ward of the court. Some judge who owed Papa an election favor; a campaign contribution of some kind. Then the court appointed Papa to be my guardian, so it all came out the same. Except I never got adopted."

"I'll adopt you," I said.

"I'd like that, Charley."

I was unpinning the coiled braids from her ears as we spoke. One braid was completely free, a heavy rope of hair that

200

reached to her elbow. "I wonder why he was so keen to adopt you."

Mary Louise took another sip of bourbon and milk, then settled again on my legs. "I was a symbol, I guess. He'd wanted Eisenhower to invade Hungary and kick out the Russians. When Ike didn't do that, Papa tried to put an ad in the papers about 'The Lily-livered Jew in the White House.' When they turned down his ad, he decided to get his own 'Freedom Fighter'; and that was me."

I held the braid under her nose. "You are Kaiser Wilhelm. You will form alliances with Austro-Hungary."

"No no. I am Catherine the Terrific and I want a package tour down the Volga."

"And I am Peter the Weird, prematurely degenerate," I said, toying with her braided hair. "Will you have me strangled?"

"Never never never," Mary Louise said. "Only choked a very tiny bit."

A knot exploded in the fireplace logs and sent up a shower of sparks to celebrate the event. "You said Routenfield is old even for his years. Has he become geriatric?"

"It comes and goes. Sometimes Papa is lucid for absolutely weeks at a time; and sometimes for only a few hours a day. He's very dear to me, Charley, in spite of his weaknesses and in spite of the fears that make him act so eccentrically."

My right leg was dead and the left was on its way. I stroked Mary Louise's forehead and tried to lean down to kiss her. My lips hovered perhaps an inch above her brow but could get no closer. I said, "I'm not as young as I used to be," and went supine on the floor. "But then, I never was."

Mary Louise sat on my stomach. Her long milkmaid braids dangled to my face as I gazed into her pale eyes. The drinks and the skiing and the heat of the fire had brought a flush of color to her creamy complexion. "You're a funny man, Charley."

"Not always," I said. "Usually I'm a very serious dip." I drank in her laughing face. "You're good for me, Mary Louise. You bring out hidden parts of me I thought were dead." My stomach was dying from the weight of her. I tried to remember what it was like when I was twenty-three.

"I'm glad," she said, stroking my face with gentle fingers. "You're my lovely dip and I want you around for more than a romp in the snow."

"I'll be here," I said. Ignoring the pain in my legs and gut I slowly levered her up and settled her on the floor beside me. Her breasts rose and fell as her breathing quickened. I sat beside Mary Louise, balancing on my hip with a foot flat against the floor, and began working the zipper of her sweater. "I'll be here or wherever you want me to be . . . for as long as you want me to be," I lied.

The sweater was fully open now and I kissed her soft, pale stomach. Mary Louise's breasts were perfectly formed within her bra, jutting up as though she was standing instead of pouring toward either side of her rib cage as they should. I lifted her shoulders from the carpet and pressed my mouth softly to hers while I slipped away the sweater. Her tongue traced quietly across my lips, explored the inside of my mouth and played lovers' games.

When I fumbled blindly with the hooks and eyes of her bra, cursing the jealous lesbian who designed the thing, Mary Louise pulled slightly away from me and said, "Open your eyes, darling. Look at me."

I opened my eyes to see that her face and lips were glowing with excitement.

"I don't want you disappointed," she said, measuring my face with shy eyes.

202

"Not with you," I said. "Not ever." My foot had gone to sleep.

"I mean, I . . . I'm not very large." Mary Louise closed her eyes.

I unhooked it finally and drew the nylon tricot bra away from her. "Lover," I said, "I've seen enough padded bras to recognize them under five layers of sweaters and a trench coat." I dropped the bra and kissed her delicate breasts. They were perfectly formed like young apples.

"I never understood why some men drool over large breasts," I said, "unless it's the 'mother' thing."

The fire had died, leaving dim embers that were smothered by cracked and charcoaled logs. We huddled together for warmth, our bare skin sensitized and glowing.

"You're very gentle," Mary Louise said. "Are you always so gentle, Charley?"

"Sometimes," I said, "sometimes we do things out of . . . out of fondness, not sex." I patted in the clothes that were strewn around us and found my parka. I pulled a cigar from the inside pocket and checked to see that it wasn't broken. "It's rare . . . but sometimes we human bodies do that."

I warmed the cigar to life and drank in her tall form with my eyes. Although her breasts were small, Mary Louise had large hips and thighs. Her ankles didn't turn in neatly from her calves but seemed thick extensions of them. "You are just a joy to look at," I said. "Are there any more at home like you?"

"My sister. She's the pretty one."

"You're the pretty one," I said. I covered my interest behind a cloud of smoke. "Did she come over the wall with you?"

203

"Yes, but they had to separate us," Mary Louise said. "No one wanted the responsibility of two 'Freedom Fighters.' "

I irritated the glowing logs with a poker. They retaliated with fresh tongues of fire that licked back in anger. "What happened to her?" I asked.

"We don't see much of each other." Orange firelight mottled her face and cast mysterious shadows in her eyes. She said, "Nina lives in Miami."

Catherine,
Vacation or not, have to phone D.C. every a.m. at 8 their time—5 ours. (Don't worry, called collect.) Have been ordered to The Hague for 2, 3 days. Didn't want to wake you. Will phone you from there if can get Embassy line. If not, will phone first chance on return.

Peter, the Volga Tour Guide (choke choke)

34

Hagopian sat in a pay toilet at LAX. A Milady's Vanity Now Only $1.49 mirror clung to his neck like a shepherd's crook. His makeup kit rested on his lap and offered him a mob of identities to choose from. He picked a blond wig and wondered if he would have more fun.

He slipped the toup over his gray hair and adjusted it to cover the high forehead. A little fruity, Hagopian thought, but slightly heroic too. The blond hair curled around his ears and neck; it took ten years away from his face.

The blue contact lenses were harder, a real bitch. He cringed at their touch; an ugly feeling against his eyeballs. But the image that looked back at him was good, great in fact. One more detail and there would be no relation between this new character and Hagopian/Richardson.

He removed his teeth, big homely dentures that made him look like a horse, and slipped them into the polyfoam of his makeup kit.

Hagopian settled two new rows of teeth in his mouth and admired himself. Beautiful. The difference always stunned him. He had changed the appearance of his teeth from brown-stained rocks to gleaming white pebbles that reshaped his cheeks and mouth.

Beautiful. Hagopian smiled at himself. Who could recognize me? he wondered. Even with his big pock-scarred shnozz he had become a different person. The nose he could never change. But the rest of it was flawless. Even his olive skin added to the effect; he looked like a guy who'd spent his life at St. Tropez.

Closing and locking the makeup kit he thought, Steven-with-a-V Routenfield—you're next.

The sign above the counter said, RENTAL. It was a nice touch. If they added new items or discontinued old ones they wouldn't have to change the sign: RENTAL said it all.

"You rent things," Hagopian said. He offered the girl behind the counter a view of bright, even teeth.

She said, "Yes sir," and returned his smile. "We're out of big sedans. But there are plenty of Datsuns left . . ."

Hagopian nodded at the cast on her arm and said, "How about snowmobiles? Can I ask you that this season?"

"Let me check," the girl said. She ducked under the counter and walked through an untitled door.

As he waited for her, Hagopian watched a blue and white Piper Apache practicing touch and goes. The plane touched and was gone twice before she returned.

"We've got one," she said. "But you'll have to sign a waiver for it. It belongs to the boss, you see, and he'll get in trouble if you go into any restricted areas."

The Apache touched and went again. "Restricted areas?"

The girl smiled an apology. "Most of the National Forest areas are restricted, and all private property of course."

"I understand." He pulled a Mono County map from his parka and spread it on the counter. "Now this area . . . right around here, see?" He tapped the spot with his finger as though planning a bombing strike. "There're a lot of 'recreation trails' around here. How do I tell the difference between public and private stuff?"

She rested her plastered arm on the counter and pointed to the map with her good hand. "This area . . . here, with the broken-line boundary . . . this is public. Just be careful about the north and east sides of it; that's private land and there are no posted warnings."

"This down here at the south end; is that posted?" Hagopian watched her hands as he spoke. The hand that jutted from the cast had brightly lacquered nails while those on the other hand were bitten to the quick; she'd half conquered a bad habit.

"Oh yes. There's no mistaking that," she said. "That's Mr. Routenfield's property. You can't miss it."

Hagopian nodded. "I won't."

Hagopian crested the hill and snicked off the ignition. The girl had told him not to worry; the snowmobile would start cold. But her life didn't depend on it. He climbed from the thing, lifted its front end and horsed it around until it pointed toward a clear path through the trees. One good shove would get it moving downhill. He could switch on the ignition and start the snowmobile with its own momentum.

Opposite his escape path, over four hundred yards away, there were three A-frames: The target. Hagopian brought them closer with his Zeiss 8 × 20.

A-frame number one would be the main lodge; the place was huge enough to house a theater. A-frame number two would be—Hagopian strained to see through its windows—a guest house? Servants' quarters, maybe. The final A-frame was a sure bet; it could only be the garage. It was unused and un-usable, its big overhead door packed waist high with snow while the back of the place was nearly hidden by a flowing layer of white that extended steeply up the hill.

The yard looked clean—no car tracks or footprints in the light covering of fresh snow.

Hagopian polished the Zeiss with his handkerchief and de-voured the main lodge's window casing. Everything depended on a clear shot at that window. No, there were no curtains or blinds; none that he could see. It was just a fantastic pane of glass that displayed the insides of the lodge like a stage setting. Once Routenfield arrived and they turned on the lights, he'd pick off the old bastard the way he used to nail that crazy mechanical bear at the carny shoot—but Routenfield wouldn't go *ding* and spin around and march to the rear. He would drop dead.

His best shot would be from the garage roof. After he made the hit there would be a hundred-foot wind sprint up to that copse of pines to his right, then the long traversing jog back to the snowmobile.

He wanted a closer look. But not now, not with the sun lighting him and making *him* the target. No, there was still an off chance that someone was in there; he didn't like off chances.

Hagopian folded down the Zeiss, capped the objective and eyepiece lenses and pocketed it. How about that garage for a shelter? he thought. They said the sun disappeared at four-thirty here; it went down behind the mountain and everything turned black, as though a giant switch was thrown. If he could get into the garage he wouldn't freeze his ass off while waiting for Steven-with-a-V Routenfield. The place would be as warm as an igloo.

Before returning to the snowmobile he looked once more at the three A-frames. Routenfield had poured plenty of good green stuff into that place. The guy must have had money he didn't know about. "For all the good it'll do you," he said aloud.

35

The elusiveness of soap, the knottiness of strings, the transitory nature of buttons . . .

> "The Total Depravity of Inanimate Things"
> From *The Atlantic Monthly*, September 1864
> KATHARINE KENT CHILD

Green characters staggered across the 3270's screen like a squad of electronic ants:

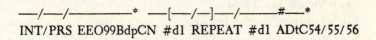

INT/PRS EEO99BdpCN #d1 REPEAT #d1 ADtC54/55/56

Freely translated, the first two programming codes were Glenda's identification and the proper Q clearance verification. The second line said that she wanted information regarding Agency personnel—located in the East European operations, country Hungary, desk Buda—that the request was for numbers of people on staff, REPEAT, numbers on staff— limited to those staff members who were active in the fifty-fourth, fifty-fifth and fifty-sixth years of this century.

"Like that?" Glenda asked.

I nodded. "Let's see how many bodies we dig up."

Glenda studied the screen, clicking her fingernails against it. She said, "I still think we should go back earlier."

"No," I said. "Jakaz didn't appear on any of our reports

---

* Edited, *F. O. SoCal SubSection*

until late fifty-four. I want only those Agency people who were assigned to Buda during Jakaz' active years."

She pressed ENTER. Her fingers had hardly left the console keys when an answering series of green characters flashed on the screen. "Here's your body count," she said.

```
YEAR 1954 . . . NUMBER 162 PAYROLL
YEAR 1955 . . . NUMBER 196 PAYROLL
YEAR 1956 . . . NUMBER 144 PAYROLL
YEAR . . . 3 YEAR TOTAL . . . NUMBER 502
     PAYROLL TOTAL
```

"If you start tomorrow and interview one a day," Glenda said, "you could do them all in two years." She pressed TRANS to capture the data on mag tape. "That's if you take off weekends, national holidays and three weeks vacation."

"Kill the clerks," I said.

Glenda turned to the board again, giving me a view of pink hair that wisped from her head as though she'd backed into a fan. After clearing the board she began programming the secondary criteria. "They're just bodies to you, aren't they?" she asked.

"That's good," I said. "Send it." She did.

```
YEAR 1954 . . . NUMBER 68 PAYROLL
YEAR 1955 . . . NUMBER 62 PAYROLL
YEAR 1956 . . . NUMBER 48 PAYROLL
YEAR . . . 3 YEAR TOTAL . . . NUMBER 178
     PAYROLL TOTAL
```

Clerks outnumbered Projects Officers nearly three to one. But that was fifteen years ago, before the budget increases that doubled our clerical staff.

"Less than a year to interview all of them," Glenda said.

I sucked on my lip and thought about it. Someone was out there; somebody—some body—who knew Gyula Jakaz. "Try AVH contact," I said.

Glenda programmed it. The code vanished into the scrambler. Deep in the intestines of a cinderblock building in Virginia it was translated into electronic impulses and closed a series of synapses. Then the process reversed and spilled its green answer on the screen.

Glenda said, "Same total."

"AVH gets around," I said. "Clear it." I held a match for her Eve then warmed a fresh cigar. It was six o'clock and the traffic on Hope Street was hopeless. Through the window I watched a traffic cop directing sluggish cars like a *premier danseur* in a cattle pen. "Let's punch Jakaz."

Glenda punched him. "I've tried this one before," she said.

"Data regarding our personnel who might have contacted Jakaz? Or just data regarding Jakaz?"

"Data re Jakaz," she said.

"What the hell," I said. "Send." She did. The terminal replied:

> INVALID INQUIRY CODE ENTERED—
> NO ELIGIBLE TASK

"I've tried this one before," she said again.

I said, "So I've heard." No one had ever gotten around to programming him. On the dossier that I'd seen, he was DECEASED in rubber-stamped upper case. But he'd never been considered LIVE in upper echelons. Poor Jakaz.

Glenda's fingers moved briskly over the programming keys and posed a bright green question:

> WHY REMLY AFRAID WOMEN?

211

Before I could stop her the data request was in Virginia and we had an answer:

INVALID INQUIRY CODE ENTERED—
NO ELIGIBLE TASK

"You don't exist either," Glenda said.

"That's half my charm."

"Was your wife just a body?"

"She wasn't 'just' a body. She was a spectacular body." I measured Glenda's slight frame. "But even that was meaningless."

"So why did you marry?"

"It's like jumping out of an airplane," I said. "Everyone should try it once, just to say they've done it."

Traffic clashed on Hope Street. A delivery van and two cars had created a bottleneck. The cop would have to back up a couple of blocks of steaming drivers to untangle it.

"Do you visit your kid?" Glenda asked.

"You're getting personal," I said. "Ask them arrested, detained, held, questioned by AVH."

Glenda typed it out. The answer was immediate.

"That's better," Glenda said. "You'll learn something in less than twenty-one days."

"Routenfield's meeting is almost at our throats," I said. "How many of those twenty-one are still alive?"

Glenda reached for the keyboard. When the answer appeared she said, "Still twenty-one."

"And they say spies are not noted for longevity," I said. "Let's see how many of those bodies were detained at Nyiregy-háza."

"I'd miss him," Glenda said as she programmed the question. "If I had a child, I'd miss him desperately."

212

Curious, I thought. Once aborted, twice maternal—or words to that effect. "It's not that I don't miss the kid," I said. "I don't want to see him grow up."

"You are something else," Glenda said. "Watching them grow up; that's the joy of it."

"So you understand," I said.

"So I understand. That's my excuse. What's yours?"

The terminal said:

```
YEAR 1954 . . . NUMBER 000 PAYROLL
YEAR 1955 . . . NUMBER 000 PAYROLL
YEAR 1956 . . . NUMBER 001 PAYROLL
YEAR . . . 3 YEAR TOTAL . . . NUMBER 001
     PAYROLL TOTAL
```

"That's it," I said. "Get the name, current assignment and the date he was held at Nyiregyháza."

"Drat. There go my new shoes from Robinson's," Glenda said. "I'll have to shop for them at Sears."

"Shoes?"

"I thought we'd get more overtime than this." She punched the data request into her terminal.

"What the hell, stick around until midnight," I said. "I'll initial your overtime slip."

"Too late," Glenda said. "The office is wired."

```
YEAR 1956 . . . MO OCT 20 NOV 1 . . . WALSHING,
DANL F . . . RTRD . . . CHI ILL
```

"Chicago," I said. It could have been worse. I wasn't sure how, but it could have been.

Glenda said, "You know the town?"

"All too well," I said. I'd gone there once on a Student Rad

213

project. Before I left, the F. O. told me, "A bit more slack to the jaw; you are supposed to be a graduate student."

She read my expression and said, "Chicago's just another body to you, isn't it?" I nodded. "You still haven't told me your excuse."

I looked blank.

"Your son. Why don't you want to see him grow up?"

"They make nice pets when they're small," I said. "Trouble is, they become human beings when they mature."

36

It was like walking across a pie. Beneath the thin, brittle crust there was an inch of powder before the snowpack. Hagopian made crisp noises as he moved through the snow one slow step at a time. He liked the feel of it, crunching through and toeing around for the pack. Carrying his blanket-wrapped tools in one hand and an unlighted pen flash in the other, he moved his weight from rear to front foot—carefully—carefully—and tested the powder. Shallow. Good. He completed the step.

He couldn't remember a night this black; not at any six o'clock, he couldn't. It was the altitude and the new moon. Hagopian thought, careful. His foot had sunk up to the ankle. If anyone showed up tonight, it was a print that they might catch in the morning. He brought his foot back and scuffed snow into the depression. Try again, Hagopian thought. Shallow. Fine.

There was nothing but blackness and the crisp sound of his footsteps. He paused to get his bearings. Light from his pen flash cut a thin, sudden hole through the darkness. He was moving too far right; the A-frame garage was over there, ten paces ahead and slightly to the left. Hagopian clicked off the flash and tried a step. Shallow. Good.

At the roof's peak, three feet of which jutted above the snow, Hagopian paused and looked at the main lodge. The place was empty, a looming mass of something that was blacker than the dark night, but still close enough to make out its acute angles. Close enough, in fact, to make an easy hit from the garage roof. Hell—at this distance he could be lethal with nothing more than a pointed stick in his hands.

Hagopian grinned and wondered if his teeth sparkled in the darkness. There was no rush. Getting a nap, that was number one. The other guys were always in a rush, banging around like nervous cattle. Not me, baby, he thought. He needed the sleep. After that he could walk down to the main lodge and give it a look. But first a nap.

Digging his fingers into the snow he felt for the bottom ledge of the window and couldn't find it. Snow had drifted down against this back wall of the garage until only eighteen inches or so of glass was above the freezing stuff. In summer the window must have been beyond reach above his head.

Hagopian peeled the protective sheet from a twelve-by-sixteen piece of contact paper. After smoothing the paper's adhesive side on the window he ran his fingertips across its decorative surface. The stuff had a texture to it. Hagopian ran his fingers across the grain again. Not bad. The stuff really felt like wood: Just the thing for papering the bar in his den.

I'll pick up a couple of rolls when I get home, Hagopian thought as he tapped his knuckles against the contact paper. The glass yielded with a slight crackling sound and he lifted the paper away. It was coated with glass fragments. Warm air drifted up from the gaping window frame.

Rolling the now heavy contact paper into a tube and stuffing it back into his pocket, Hagopian peered through the unglazed casement. Yes; there was a ladder. It leaned into a far corner of the garage. But, *Christ*. His pen flash showed a workbench directly beneath the window. The thing was loaded with tools; it would be like jumping into a punji pit. The dumb bastards. Why couldn't they work at one of the other walls? Any kind of leak in this window and everything down there would rust before the March thaw.

216

This one was going to hurt.

Yet it beat sleeping in the snow; it was either that or choking down a dex, and he didn't trust chemical energy. Get inside where it's warm, he thought. Hell, guys with unions got coffee breaks and lunch hours. Why not him?

Pushing back his left sleeve he began unwinding twenty-five feet of dental floss that was wrapped around his glove cuff. He tied one end to the rope that held his blanket roll of tools and lowered the package onto the workbench below.

Hagopian squeezed feet first through the frame. His gloved hands clutched the sill as he scraped first his knees then his feet back up the wall and squatted vertically against it. Breathe, he thought. His knees were pressed against his chest, his feet just inches below the sill. Inhale—exhale—inhale, now.

Blowing the air from his lungs Hagopian shoved away from the wall and felt a delicious sense of freedom, then fear. It was like jumping from Uncle Mampre's barn roof when he was a kid. His bladder relaxed.

Midair he threw his left arm violently away from his chest and twisted his upper torso. When he felt that he'd done 180 degrees Hagopian threw out his right arm and stopped the turn. Freedom. He was stretched out now, a falling cruciform with knees slightly bent and toes pointing downward. *Christ, where's the floor?*

No, he thought, it's not like the old barn-roof jumps with Uncle's black umbrella. It was more like what they had said in Basic: Time stops when you're trying a ball buster. McNardi the DI told the guys once about Anzio. Going up that little beach was like doing a marathon from Detroit to Des Moines. *Jesus where is the floor?*

When his toes made contact Hagopian relaxed his knees. He jackknifed into a crouch and flexed his legs to absorb the shock. Nice, Hagopian thought. Very nice indeed.

Lighting a True Menthol he inspected his shelter. It was a terrific layout. But these tools—they shouldn't leave stuff like this out to rust. He turned over a box wrench and read, PROTO. Hagopian whistled. Two bucks a wrench, and there were at least fifty box wrenches, sockets and spanners on the bench. A couple of short, fat propane tanks rested on the back of the bench. One of them had a brazing tip screwed onto it.

Hagopian picked up his package and thought, the old bastard oughta fire his chauffeur. He felt his lips drawing back over the neat, even teeth. It didn't matter; when he was done, Routenfield's entire staff would be hitting the unemployment lines.

Hagopian settled on a pile of tarps and fished the M1944/16 SIG-Neuhausen from his parka. He pulled the slide back, jacking out a round, and let it drop. It didn't seem too stiff—his body heat must have kept it loose. He snapped the slide back sixteen more times, until there was a random clutter of seventeen 9 mm Parabellum cartridges in his lap and the piece was finally empty. He refilled the clip and cranked the leftover round into the SIG-Neuhausen's chamber. After pocketing it again he reached for the blanket roll.

Squatting in a lotus position with the tool-littered blanket spread before him, he looked like a strangely blond merchant showing his wares in an Istanbul street market. Besides the two extra clips and a box of Winchester-Western 9 mm ammunition, there were his crossbow and quarrels, a square Eveready 6-volt flash, the makeup kit, a palm sized rangefinder, his collapsible Zeiss 8 × 20 shirt-pocket binocular, and an assortment of candy bars.

This part of the job was best; loosening the M1944/16's action, double checking his tools and getting prepared beyond the logical needs of the work at hand. He rolled up the blanket and tied it.

The cream. The most prepared guy in the business. If only, he thought—if only it wasn't such a fucking mess when you took the bastards out.

When the buzzer woke him Hagopian reached for his Vulcain Cricket and pressed the watch's alarm crown. The noise stopped.

Chewing slowly, making sure that every bite was well mixed with saliva before he swallowed it, he ate a Mr. Goodbar. When the last chocolate-coated peanut disappeared, he ate two Di-Gels and started work.

The aluminum ladder was a perfect fit from workbench to window. Once he was outside Hagopian began his careful step, feel, step until he reached the hard-packed snow around the main lodge.

He'd brought the heavy 6-volt flashlight and the rangefinder with him; the pen flash was wedged into the snow on the garage roof and glowing dimly—a new star, burning oddly below the horizon. At the A-frame's window he focused his rangefinder on the pen light. He saw two lights, one red and one white. Hagopian twisted the finder's scored knob until both lights merged and became one. Using the large square flash he checked the range: Forty-three feet.

The inside of the lodge was something else; a monument to good money and bad taste.

When he'd bought the house in Fielding Hills he couldn't afford a decorator. But after wading through a couple of twenty-five-buck books on period furniture, he didn't need a decorator. His own place was filled with country French reproductions—the good stuff that was being made in Italy. Routenfield's place, though, was filled with the strangest damn collection of French salon pieces, Oriental doodads and Egyptian junk he'd ever seen. Christ, he thought. Routenfield deserved to be shot.

Hagopian focused the rangefinder on a wing chair by the fireplace. Eighteen feet; that made—he added the forty-three to it—sixty-one feet altogether. Beautiful. It was going to be an easy shot with the 9 mm. Noisy, he thought. But this wasn't like Bel Air—there weren't neighboring houses crowding in on the place, and he'd have a good head start from his perch on the garage.

He probed the big flashlight's beam around the room again. Jesus H. Christ in particular. Maybe he should burn the place down after nailing the old man.

37

Account exec for AAAA Chicago-based agency. Must have killer instinct. Prefer European experience. Reply box 438, ad age, 740 N. Rush St. Chi. Ill. 60611

Snow drifted onto Michigan Avenue like soapflakes on dirty laundry. My low-cut, west-coast loafers were filled with slush by the time I turned into the Wrigley Building. In the bar Frank Sinatra's clear, unyielding voice explained that Chicago was his kind of town and I wondered what he was doing in Palm Springs.

Dan Walshing carried his drink from the stand-up bar to my table. He sat across from me and absorbed a Tanquerey martini from a glass that was large enough to breed fish in. His face radiated tremendous health in spite of the fine web of booze veins that flanked his nose. His eyelids had a weird, white cast that contrasted starkly with his tanned face.

"Miami tan," Walshing explained. "It's a status thing this year. You ball up cotton and wad it against your eyes to keep the sun from getting in, see. Very harmful on the eyeballs, sunlight." He absorbed more gin and said, "Gotta have the white orbs or no one knows you can afford Miami."

"I see," I said though I didn't. "About this Gyula Jakaz."

"Hell of a character," Walshing said. "If he was in Chicago right now, I'd hire the son of a bitch. Had a real killer instinct." He stopped a waiter and said, "Where's the meatballs?" then turned to me and said, "I just moved over from Needham to Burnett, see, and I'm putting together my own group; safety in numbers you know."

I peeled off my shoes beneath the table and emptied them on Mr. Wrigley's rug.

The waiter returned with a chafing dish of meatballs and a cup full of plastic toothpicks. We served ourselves a generous helping, spreading them out on cocktail napkins. Walshing stacked his like something from a Civil War monument.

"Never drink on an empty stomach," Walshing said. "Not at three in the P.M." He popped a meatball into his mouth.

"I've only got a couple of hours," I said. "I have to catch a United flight to Toronto."

"Sure, sure," Walshing said. "So this character Jakaz wasn't AVH. I'd gotten interested in him because he traveled a lot from St. Stephen's Boulevard to the AVH compound in Nyiregyháza. You know the place?"

"Intimately," I said.

"This bird kept flapping between the two places and I was curious. What I found out was a laugh, a real horselaugh, see, because the guy was an AVH colonel in Budapest and a KGB captain in Nyiregyháza." Walshing bit into another meatball and looked like an odd species of dog—brown face and white mask—retrieving a ball.

I sipped Schlitz while Walshing gnawed at his hors d'oeuvre. A group of newsmen and a crew from WLS-TV moved languidly onto a light carpet of snow on the Wrigley dock. In the center of the crowd a wet-suited male model carried a surfboard. "Out of their minds," Walshing said. "You surf?"

"Yes."

The model held his board nose down on the dock while two bodies with cornea-withering neckties pointed at a weird protuberance behind the skeg and mouthed unheard words to the newsmen.

Walshing absorbed more iced gin. "So what's the guy doing out there?"

222

"Committing suicide," I said. "So Jakaz was KGB in Nyi-regyháza and AVH in Budapest. So how come?"

"Now this is all rumor, but I got it from a pretty reliable source," he said. "There was this guy at Nyiregyháza who helped me get away from the joint when Nagy emptied it. I was a mess, couldn't think straight for a couple of weeks. This guy helped me get to Budapest and I helped him over the wall to Austria when Nagy caved in."

The model's hands and feet were turning blue. No one had told him that wet suits were available with rubber socks and gloves.

"This guy was an old AVH type, one of the clowns that got purged when Rákosi disappeared Péter Gábor. He wasn't a bad fella; redder'n hell, but not bad."

Walshing offered me another meatball and I held up a de-clining hand. I stripped a cigar and rolled the tip over a flaming match. "So your friend was a 'Freedom Fighter'?"

"Funny description," Walshing said. "Yeah, that's what the newsboys would have called him. He was a good AVH type; Marxist-Leninist-Stalinist but gung ho for Magyar national-ism." He laughed and crinkled his weird, white-lidded eyes. "After I resigned and got into advertising I wanted to set up a tour for the guy; some kind of P.A. shot at all the right-wing clubs. Can you see it? Those joiners thought 'Freedom Fighters' were crypto-capitalists; just a bunch of happy Joes looking to get a fried-chicken franchise in downtown Vesz-prém."

Walshing popped another meatball into his face and ground it with his teeth. "Can you see their faces when the guy starts selling 'em Marx? Old sweet Jesus, I'd give my left nut to catch that show."

"Great joke," I agreed. "So give me the news on Jakaz, okay?"

"Sure. Jakaz was putting together a personnel file on AVH for his boss in Moscow. He had people coming in from all over Hungary to report on their sector personnel; then he sent KGB faces out to every sector to make damn sure no one fudged on his report."

I gagged slightly on a mouthful of smoke.

"You okay?" Walshing asked.

I cleared my throat with some Schlitz. "You mean Jakaz had a complete list . . . of all AVH personnel?"

"You betcha," Walshing said. "All AVH guys, everywhere. More than that, he had a file on every KGB face that had penetrated AVH. A lot of those KGB guys came over the wall posing as 'Freedom Fighters.' That's why the Agency and FBI are keeping dossiers on refugees. Or so I hear, eh?"

"Probably," I said.

We were quiet for a moment. We watched the male model glide across the river on his CO_2-powered board. Strobe units flashed and the TV crew recorded his journey on vid tape.

"I'll tell you the truth," Walshing said. He didn't look at me as he spoke. "I tried to figure some way to get those files. But Jakaz' people burned every damn last thing they had compiled in Nyiregyháza. I never could figure out why."

"I have an idea," I said.

Walshing looked at me then—a hungry, money-eyed look. He had retired from the Agency and ignorance was a virtue. But curiosity drives us all. Walshing finally spoke with a fatalistic edge to his voice, "A million bucks? Two?"

"At least," I said. "If Whitehall was bidding against Bonn it could go to a million." I dragged at the cigar and breathed a screen of smoke between us. "Then you'd get Virginia to make it two or three."

"Lots of money those files were worth," Walshing said.

"Lots," I agreed.

"And old Jakaz bought one at St. Stephen's Boulevard, right?"

"Right."

"All that potential loot and the guy's deader than my virtue."

"Right," I lied again.

We watched the model try to turn his board before smashing into the far bank of the Chicago River. He stuffed his hand into the water and quickly retrieved it, dripping with scum.

"Ah, well," Walshing said, "I'm out of it now. But that's a nice round figure, three million skins."

"Nice and round," I said.

The model plunged his foot into the water. At Wind 'n' Sea, or Rincon, or 22nd Street off Hermosa, the maneuver would have had him eating sand. His foot in the Chicago River, though, turned him gently away from the far bank.

"What's that?" Walshing asked. "Is that what you call 'hanging five'?"

"No way," I said.

"I wonder what he's doing."

"Same thing I am," I said. "Trolling for garbage."

38

Dead men tell no tales.

Spanish Fair, Act IV, Sc. 1
JOHN DRYDEN

Depends on who's translating.

F. BASSET

"Mr. Remly; Mr. Charles Remly, please come to the passenger service counter." The voice reverberated through the terminal. "Mr. Remly, Mr. Charles Remly, please come to the passenger service counter." It sounded as though a female tin can was paging me.

O'Hare Field is the busiest in the country. It's also the fastest exit from Chicago which may account for its popularity. I struggled through a sea of bodies to get to passenger service. The girl behind the counter had a smile on her face and a telephone in her hand. She offered both to me.

"Remly," I said into the phone.

"You sitting down, babe?"

"No, Frank, I am leaning across what may be the most public counter in Chicago and speaking on a phone that very likely has twenty extensions. Anyone with a healthy curiosity and strength enough to lift his instrument could be listening to us."

"Gotcha," Basset said.

"It can't wait till I get back?"

"I've got a Title 23 authorization to dig up a grave," Basset said. "I thought you'd like to know."

226

Basset was in Miami, following up on Mary Louise's sister Nina Paál. Odd, I thought. Nina couldn't be dead; Mary Louise had referred to her in the present tense.

I massaged my eyebrows; it helped ease the pressure that was building. "You're right," I said. "I'd like to know." I smiled at the passenger service girl and mouthed, *What's your phone number?* "How much can you tell me Frank? This line may have ears." The girl raised her left hand and pointed archly at the solitaire on her third finger.

"I'm cool," Basset said. "What I got was this: Mary Louise's older sister in Miami has a much more interesting bank account than Mary Louise. Every month she sends money to this place . . . I thought it was maybe a religious charity, some 'Holy Name' thing. Every month they get eighteen bucks from her. So I check it out, right?"

"Right."

"So it turns out to be fresh flowers money for the Holy Name Cemetery. I check with the cemetery people and learn that Nina made funeral arrangements for some guy back in sixty-five. Funny thing is, she claimed he was her father."

"Funny thing," I agreed, "for an orphan." Good old Basset —one foot in front of the other Basset. It looked as though he'd found time to solve the whereabouts of Dr. Kovács between inspection tours of his parcel of recreational sand. "You sure it's our man?"

"I'll sure as hell find out when we open the box," Basset said. "I brought that employee file with me, the one you picked up from Glenda yesterday. Our forensic guy can do a dental on the stiff and tell if it's our man."

That was it, the end of the project. If Basset was right, Mary Louise still had an acute accent over the final vowel, but her name was Kovács not Paál. And Stosh had been both right and wrong—since he could only hear their voices, he

227

had mistaken Kovács' two daughters for a couple of small boys.

Once we had the reason for Jakaz' existence in Los Angeles there was no need to keep an open file on him. And this had to be the reason—Jakaz was looking for Kovács *and had tracked down Kovács' daughters in order to find the man.* Unfortunately for him, Jakaz didn't have access to bank account records; he couldn't learn about the eighteen dollars that Nina Kovács spent on flowers for her father's grave every month.

I watched the tide of bodies ebb from the terminal to the departure gates as though they had someplace to go. The end of the project, I thought. Everything seemed flat. I wondered if I would look as though I had someplace to go when I walked to my departure gate.

"So now it's over," I said. "There's nothing left but the mop-up."

"Looks like," Basset said.

Pulling together the loose ends of a project is like having sex with your wife; a perfunctory game that is sometimes gratifying but seldom exciting. There are no surprises left; no serendipity.

"When is the meeting in Mammoth?" I asked.

"Day after tomorrow. Usual procedures?"

"Right. Hold all the bodies on standby, don't tell them the target or the purpose; everything is Q Clearance from now on."

"You still going to Toronto?" Basset asked.

If I made the flight I could crib another twenty dollars on my per diem, and the Bentley's wire wheels still needed tuning. But the trip wasn't worth it. "I'd like to find out what our friend the doctor was doing," I said. "But it can wait." There would be more mop-up later—the tedious work of assembling Kovács' significance—but it wasn't the sort of work that couldn't wait. After all, Jakaz was still mobile and we wanted

228

to interdict his freedom of movement. Kovács on the other hand wasn't going anywhere. I said, "I'm tired: I just want to get back to L.A. and pass out."

"See you tomorrow then."

"So long, Frank," I said. "And happy digging."

"G'bye."

I pulled the handset from my ear then quickly returned it. "Frank? Frank?" No use, he was gone. I wanted to ask what he'd done to Harriet that had changed her so. I could find out tomorrow.

When I landed at LAX there were two telegrams waiting for me.

The first said simply, "YES."

The second said, "PARKINSON'S DISEASE."

I drove home and went to sleep with a glass of Christian Brothers in one hand and a Bering in the other. It's a wonder I didn't burn the place to the ground.

39

Better be killed than frightened to death.

Mr. Facey Romford's Hounds
ROBERT SMITH SURTEES

I didn't remember setting the alarm but slapped at it none-theless. The clock's plastic case cracked and it rang again.

I muttered "Good lord," and smashed the thing with my fist. Ugly smelling blue smoke puffed up from the clock as it short-circuited. The bottle of Christian Brothers tipped and fell from my bedside table. Brandy soaked into the carpet.

When the phone rang again I recognized it for what it was. "Hello," I said into the mouthpiece. The hands of the clock had fused at seven-thirty.

"Chief?"

"Wrong number," I said. "This is George Custer."

"We got a rumble on the Jakaz place," said Weaver. "I called Basset first. He lives out in Sylmar . . . he's closest."

"Hold it. Hold on a second. I'll be right with you." I wondered who'd been kicking my head last night. Or was it my stomach? The brothers Christian designed a terrific bottle. Laid on its side the bottle's center of gravity and balance was near its base—no more than half the brandy could spill out. I emptied some into my mouth, slushed it around to rinse out the stale odors and tastes, then swallowed. It may not have been as therapeutic as B^{12} but was closer at hand.

I said, "Okay, let me have it," into the phone.

"Jakaz gets a phone call around seven. Guy on the horn

says, 'I am at the airport.' That's it . . . 'I am at the airport'
. . . and they both hang up. Then there's the usual scraping-
around sounds a guy makes when he's pulling a coat from the
closet, then Jakaz leaves the prune ranch."

I lifted the half-dead Bering from its scorched cradle on my
blanket and checked the night stand for matches. The first
few puffs of the stale cigar were nasty; I rinsed away the taste
with another swallow of Christian Brothers.

Weaver said, "I figure 'That's it for a couple of hours,' and
brew up some coffee. Which reminds me . . . okay if I bring
in a frying pan? I like fried oatmeal on these graveyard shifts."

"Bring in a frying pan," I said. He could have brought in
an asparagus steamer if it made him happy. "So you had a cup
of coffee; so what happened next?"

"I get back to the wire in maybe ten minutes and someone's
in the place. Three different voices, and they're laying for
Jakaz to get back."

I spoke a few terse Anglo Saxon nouns and said, "Which airport was this body calling from?" If it was from LAX we had
a chance of getting the three intruders before Jakaz returned.
But if the call had come from the Palmdale airport, the three
would pluck Jakaz and his visitor while we were still en route
to the place.

"Don't know. Just, 'I am at the airport,' and Jakaz takes
off."

From the prune ranch it could have been one of at least
five different airports; Fox in Lancaster, Intercontinental in
Palmdale, or Van Nuys, or Burbank, or LAX. "Any background
noise? Anything that might sound like LAX or Burbank?"

"Don't think so. I heard a small piston job warming up.
That would make it one of the local ports."

"Or Van Nuys. You have some heavy bodies on the thing?"

Weaver said, "I called downtown. They're on their way
right now."

There is a law of nature that assures us that any disaster capable of happening will happen. KGB had gotten impatient with Jakaz and now they were laying for him. If they got him first, the F. O. would have my skin. Then it struck me: Weaver spoke no Russian beyond *nyet* and *vodka*. "What kind of guys did these voices sound like? Anything distinctive? Any regional accents?"

"Sorry," Weaver said. "I thought I mentioned . . . it was the Limey. That Haring guy."

"That's regional enough," I said.

Basset's Country Squire was parked beside one of our gray vans from downtown. They cast long, knife-edged shadows in the early morning sun. I stopped the Bentley beside them and walked into havoc.

"Hiya, babe." Basset wambled toward me through the rubble. "Some kinda mess, isn't it?"

I said, "What happened? They drive a truck through here?" Anything not nailed down was overturned. It looked like the entire house had been lifted, shaken vigorously, and returned to its foundations. A brown-trousered leg peeked out from beneath the sofa.

"Haring must've forgotten," Basset said. "Jakaz is a pro. Him and his friend tore Beebee's two guys apart at the seams."

"How's Beebee?" I asked.

"Shot in the knee with his own gun," Basset said. "He's going to lose that leg sure as hell." His big face worked itself into an admiring grin. "Jakaz and his buddy took on Beebee and his two guys . . . and Beebee's guys had ordnance."

"What about Beebee's heavies?"

"One's got a smashed squamous temporal . . . that skull bone over the . . ."

"I remember my training," I said.

232

"The other guy swallowed his larynx." Basset pointed at the leg.

"Both *gzzzzchk?*" I said, drawing a finger across my throat.

Basset said, "*Gzzzzchker* than doornails." He jerked his head at the bedroom. "Three of our heavies in there, sitting on Haring and getting your wire out of the phone. You want to go in and say hello?" Basset patted at his suit as though checking to see if it was empty or if he was, indeed, inside it.

"Good-guy-bad-guy?" I asked.

He nodded. "You're the bad guy."

"Thanks."

Basset pulled a rumpled Winston pack from an obscure recess of his jacket. After probing a finger through it and deciding it was empty he crumbled it into a ball and stuffed it back. "Can you spare a cigar?" he said.

I shook my head and said, "I'm the bad guy," and walked to the bedroom.

One of the Agency bodies was peeling the sterile plastic cover from a disposable syringe. He paused and looked up when I entered. "Mr. Remly?"

I nodded.

"Urkowitz," he said. "Mike Urkowitz." The other two Agency types were disassembling and inspecting everything in the room. They went on with their work without glancing up.

"My dear boy," Beebee said. "It's always such a pleasure to see you." His voice was weak, drained of its usual charm. "I only wish the circumstances were more propitious."

Beebee Haring was sprawled on the floor as though he'd been broken in a number of places. His knee was a sanguinary pulp of suit fabric, bone and ligament that seeped thick red liquid into the rug. A tourniquet garroted his lower thigh.

"Hello, Beebee," I said. "That suit is beyond French weaving." Even the jacket was hopeless; shoulder padding puffed out where one sleeve had torn away.

"Occupational hazard," Beebee said. He watched as our man pressed the syringe and brought a drop of fluid to the needle's tip.

"Not if you keep your unusually long nose clean," I said.

Beebee's eyes were riveted on Urkowitz' syringe. He said, "I suppose I've botched things for you." He smiled weakly. "Sorry."

"Botched isn't the word for it, Beebee. You remember my promise in Belgrade?" He nodded. "British Embassy," I said. "They'd like to get their hands on you; around your neck, really."

"I suppose they would." He sighed. "It *has* been one of those decades. It truly has."

Putting a hand on Urkowitz' shoulder I asked, "Morphine?"

"Demerol," he said.

"Hold off for a moment. I want to watch him sweat."

"The guy's about to faint from pain."

I smiled at Beebee but spoke to Urkowitz: "If he does, we'll bring him around with cold water and watch him sweat some more."

"How very thoughtful of you, Charles," Beebee said. "Have you some purpose in mind? Or are you merely relieving the boredom?"

"You get the Demerol when I know who your buyer is, Beebee."

"Surely there are more sympathetic ways of getting information. Haven't you a back room and a supply of rubber hoses?"

"Ha ha," I said. "C'mon, talk to me. You hoped to sell Jakaz' body. Have you got a buyer? Tell me something interesting, Beebee, and you'll get your shot."

"The race has not been decided yet, Charles."

"Maybe so," I said, "but you've been disqualified. What'll you gain by keeping your mouth shut?"

"Were I to answer that, I'll have gained nothing; do you see the logic of it?"

"Okay . . . your way, Beebee," I said and turned to Urkowitz. "Take off the tourniquet."

"You're kidding," the man said.

"Off," I said. "If he's useless to us alive, so what the hell difference will it make if he dies? Take the goddamn thing off his leg." I turned to Beebee and said, "Do you see the logic of it?"

"Your logic is impeccable," Beebee said.

From the doorway Basset said, "Aw, c'mon babe. Maybe he'll give you some poop if you let him have the shot." His voice was jovial, as though we were discussing Beebee's vacation schedule. "Whaddaya say, Beebee? Will you talk to us if you get a shot of pain killer?"

"No games; Frank," I said. "No good-guy-bad-guy, no hustle, no games. I want him to spill his guts *right now*." I stared at Beebee with neither compassion nor distaste; my face was neutral. "His guts or six quarts of blood, he's going to spill something in the next ten minutes."

"I believe you are actually serious," Beebee said.

I didn't answer. I knelt beside him and worked the knot of his tourniquet loose. With the thing off his leg, a gusher of blood poured from the severed femoral artery.

"*Oh my dear God,*" Beebee screamed at the sight of it. "*I'm dying.*"

"You want to say goodbye now?" I asked. "Or shall we wait for the last irrevocable moment."

Beebee's face was a sea of perspiration. Sweat clogged in his fat mustache and dripped from his cheeks into his ears. "I didn't believe . . . I . . . put it back, please Charles . . . put it back."

Urkowitz' face was turning a shade of fine Oxford gray.

Basset looked on curiously, weighing Beebee's fear against the determination in my face.

"Goodbye, Beebee," I said. I stood and walked to the door, the tourniquet dangling from my hand.

"I will tell you . . . please . . . *put it back.*"

Stopping in the doorway I looked back at him. Fear had triggered his adrenals and his heart was working overtime. It pumped blood through the femoral like water from a tap. I said, "No bullshit?"

"The truth. I will tell you."

Tossing the tourniquet to Urkowitz I said, "Okay."

When the thing was retied Beebee said, "I will never look upon you again with the same affection, Charles."

"I'm sorry to hear that," I said. And I was. "Now, who's your buyer? What's he paying? What does he get for his money?"

"KGB . . . do you think I might have that shot of Demerol now? It's becoming quite painful . . ." I shook my head and Beebee continued ". . . KGB are looking for Kovács. Gyula Jakaz is my only lead."

"You keep talking like that," I said, "and we can fertilize half of California. Even if you managed to grab Jakaz, what the hell do you think he could have told you?"

Beebee sucked on his mustache.

"So, KGB wants Kovács," I said.

"Desperately."

"We've already got him, Beebee." I didn't see any reason to tell him that Kovács was dead.

He took it well. "About that Demerol . . ."

"About Gyula Jakaz," I said. "If he knew where Dr. Kovács was, do you think he'd still be hanging around here?"

Beebee pursed his lips as though rehearsing for a long affectionate kiss. "That brings up an interesting point," he said.

236

"Some reliable acquaintances tell me that KGB are preparing to take Mr. Jakaz into their loving arms. Whether or not he had information on Kovács' whereabouts did not seem really germane, you see. For, had they taken Jakaz, I would be left with nothing . . . absolutely nothing. It hardly matters that you have Kovács, *if* you do; without Jakaz in my hands I should be left in the rather awkward position of having to write the entire affair off to experience." Beebee tried to raise a smile and failed. "If nothing else I hoped to sell Gyula Jakaz to KGB."

Pulling a cigar from my jacket I lit it and puffed quietly while watching Beebee's face. I ran curious fingers over my chin; I would have to go back to the apartment and shave when I was done here. A shower and some more Christian Brothers wouldn't hurt either.

"Okay. Let's assume you managed to catch Jakaz. What's the next step? Who do you contact to make the sale?"

It was a hard question for him to answer. If he had a contact within reach of us, we could pick up a potful of KGB bodies and leave Beebee holding the sack for it. He said, "I'd planned to transport him to a convenient spot in Panama and start the bidding in Europe." Beebee tried to shake his head but the effort brought new lines of pain to his face. "I haven't a contact for the sale, not yet."

I said, "You can go to hell for lying too, you know."

"Hell is rather subjective," Beebee said. "It can as well be on earth once you've irritated KGB."

"Yes," I said. "But they don't have you. We do."

Beebee counted the pores on my face.

"Take the damn tourniquet off his leg again, babe." Basset was getting into the spirit of it.

"Nevigelykh," Beebee said. "Yurosha Nevigelykh. Charming fellow, you know."

"No," I lied. "I don't."

"He keeps a dead-letter drop at the Chandler Pavilion of the Music Center. Seat Fifteen-M on the second Thursday of each month." Beebee's face was white. I knew that it would be cool to the touch; he'd lost a lot of blood. "My sources tell me that Nevigelykh is in the market for Jakaz. I hoped to post a note to Gospodin Nevigelykh and set up a sale."

"Give him the shot," I said. "And get him to St. Mallard's."

I walked to the front yard where our cars were growing warm in the sun. As I opened the Bentley's right door Basset lumbered out of the house like a wayward truck. I climbed behind the wheel and waited for him.

He leaned on the door and asked, "Would you have?"

I smiled courteously and tried not to look stupid. "Would I what?"

"Let him bleed?"

I shrugged and turned on the ignition. The engine hummed. "That son of a bitch has put us to the wall. What if we never see Jakaz again?"

"Yeah," Basset said, "well . . ."

I said, "I'm going to have to feed the F. O. the longest line since Scheherazade."

"I know. But would you have let him go the whole length?"

"See you at the Mulholland house," I said. "Tell Harriet I won't be in until maybe two or three this afternoon."

Somewhere around Saugus I remembered about asking what he'd done to Harriet. I wondered if Basset had found her particular tourniquet.

238

40

EXPENSES
Item: One (1) Dixon Ticonderoga 1388
#2⅖₁₀ "medium" pencil   10c

The pencil made a crisp sound as it snapped in the F. O.'s hands.

"Would you care to inspect them?" he asked, offering me the broken yellow stubs.

I shook my head. "I trust you."

"I might be flattered," the F. O. said. "But your trust is worthless coin." His smile was like the first smog-free day of spring. "And you spend it indiscriminately."

"Beebee was terrified, scared witless," I said. "I'm sure he gave me the straight . . ."

"Pay close attention now," the F. O. said. He slipped both halves of the broken pencil into his clenched fist and covered it with a paisley handkerchief from his breast pocket. "This calls for absolute concentration; you must think of a whole, unbroken pencil. Are you thinking?"

"Yes," I said.

He raised a doubtful eyebrow. "No, I can feel it. Still broken. Are you capable of thinking harder?" He reached across the desk with his handkerchief-covered hand. "See if you can pull something whole from this situation."

I held the eraser and drew an unbroken pencil from his fist.

"That's the key to it: You must use your head. With practice you might learn to mend the disasters you create."

239

"I'm getting the picture," I said.

"I wonder." He made a puff of the handkerchief and eased it back into its pocket.

I said, "Look, it's a crapshoot. Everything's a crapshoot. But we've got a few favorable odds."

"Your definition of favorable odds would have you pitted against nothing less than the Sixth Fleet."

"Seriously . . ."

"And you in a rubber raft, armed with rocks."

"Damn it," I said. "I can bring Jakaz in. If the meeting's still on, I'll get him." I bounced a rigid finger on the edge of his desk.

The F. O. looked benign. "Please lower your enthusiasm by a few decibels."

"We're the only ones who know that Jakaz is on the run," I said. "And Beebee's a lot closer to KGB than he says . . . one of his friends in Belgrade spoke Russian as a kneejerk reaction. So Beebee may be their man in Los Angeles; but he's in no position to spill the details. We'll keep him wrapped up until we've taken Jakaz." Ignoring his cool glance I helped myself to one of his Havanas and caressed it with a burning match. "The AVH personnel files are gone, but Virginia will be happy to get Gyula Jakaz and his Hungarian liaison."

"Virginia would as soon get an impacted tooth," he said. "What do you think we will do with this odd lot of people?"

"Control the 'Group of Ten' . . . and maybe crack Ustachi," I said. "What the hell, none of us likes the idea of a private C and D group. Let's see how far Jakaz can be turned; let's see if we can't find some use for his ties with Ustachi. Who knows, we might even be able to get some people into Albania for a change."

"Hmmm," the F. O. said. He pulled at his lip and let it snap back against his teeth. "And you believe you can reach into this fire and remove a chestnut or two?"

240

Looking out his window I said, "Yes. I think so." Lunch-hour traffic honked its way along Hope Street. The F. O. picked up the pencil and rolled it between the palms of his hands. "Next week," he said, watching the pencil, "next week an audit team is arriving from Virginia. That is the first step in closing down SoCal SubSection. Can you appreciate what that means to me?"

I mumbled suitably vague sentiments.

The F. O. said, "Perhaps more to the point; can you appreciate what that means to you?" He snapped the pencil in two, then snapped it again. "There are some things that, once broken, cannot be mended." He dropped the four brittle stubs on his desk. "You among them."

41

Q: The previous witness stated, sir, that your Agency has more
people than jobs to be done.

A: Not at all, sir. We are dangerously understaffed. There is
always an overload of work.

Minutes of the Hearings,
Subcommittee on National Security Affairs
Volume CCCLI
Page 143

The hawks were out. They hunted in random spirals, lifted
by thermals and guided by instinct. It's part of the balance of
nature when they kill. Man's killing, however, is unnatural—
it's murder. I've never fully understood that. But then, I'm not
a student of nature—man's or otherwise. I investigate effects,
not causes.

Turning from the window I pulled out the *Reg.—Zyrian* file
drawer. The chair squeaked as I leaned back and rested my
unshod feet on the files. The day hadn't been a complete bust:
I had gotten as far as Problem 728, "Discovered Check!" in
Learn From the Masters.

1 N—KR6ch!!

With this discovered double check (and Knight fork of
Black's Queen), White offers Black the cruel choice of Mate
in 3 or the loss of *both* Rooks, the pinned Bishop and the
Queen.

As can be seen from the diagram, White's devastating 1 N—KR6ch!! follows a particularly vicious and effective Pawn storm against Black's prematurely castled King. With his ill-developed Knight at K2, and the Bishop at R3, Black is impotent against the violence of . . .

My intercom buzzed.

I said, "I'm tied up, Harriet," into it and released the button.

"It's those books," Harriet squawked from the small oak box on my desk. "Both of them are at the Hollywood Branch."

I poked a finger into Harriet's button. "Terrific. We have a card?"

"Of course," Harriet said. She sniffed into her end and it came out like a vacuum-cleaner endorsement at mine. "I keep a half dozen of them on hand."

With our own L.A. Public Library cards from Documents, we never return the books. It's hell on the city's budget I imagine, but it saves us considerable time.

I said, "Good girl. I like the way you handle your dukes—how'd you like to take on the champ, kid?"

Harriet simpered appreciatively before the box died.

I punched Basset's button. "Tell me something. What did you do to Harriet while I was bumping around Hungaslavia?"

"Yeah, well . . . it was like I said, you don't know how to handle people. It takes a little finesse."

I massaged my forehead, pulling together the skin above my eyebrows until it made a vertical crease that ran into my nose. I had a picture of Basset using finesse. It was superseded by a picture of the F. O. walking across Lake Arrowhead. "So what did you do?"

"So I told her you weren't a Project Officer . . . that the whole thing was a scam to cover your real job."

"Which is?"

"Assassin," Basset said.

"Frank," I said. "Pal." A pressure was building behind my eyes. "We aren't supposed to even think like that, let alone discuss the word. We're in the business of gathering information."

"It convinced Harriet."

I said, "That's not the point."

"Well, look, it worked. And like you say . . ."

"That which works is good," I said. "You'll remember to call me if anything interesting happens?"

"Right-oh."

The box said, "Weaver. Yes sir."

"Anything interesting happen?" I asked.

"Nada," Weaver said. "Nada con nada con carne."

"How about Routenfield; has he landed?"

"Landed all right. Up at Mammoth. But nothing on Jakaz and double nada on the meeting."

I let a bit of ash fall from my cigar. It missed the tray and landed on Problem 753 in the open book on my desk. "How about the girl? Is she anywhere?"

"Home," Weaver said. "One of the guys from our insurance front called her about the Mustang. I just picked it up a couple minutes ago."

I said, "Thanks. Keep me posted."

Problem 753 was too easy: PxP/KN7 mate. I turned to the hawks. They still hadn't scored their lunch. I wondered what Mary Louise had planned for the evening, then remembered that Glenda was coming for dinner. There was tomorrow; but tomorrow was out too. If Jakaz reappeared—and the meeting was still on—I'd be working. I weighed the advisability of

244

making a date for the day after but finally decided that that was somewhere in the dim future. I didn't want to tie myself down too far in advance.

And yet—

"Hello?" I'd forgotten the bright overtones that rang in her voice.

"Hello you," I said into the phone.

"Oh." She was silent as though wondering what to say next. "Oh. Hello Charley."

"Did you get my note? I just got back in town."

Mary Louise said, "Yes. Oh yes. I got your message all right."

"I brought you some tulip bulbs from The Hague," I lied, wondering if any local nurseries carried them.

"Of course."

"I was wondering if you'd be busy . . ."

"I'm kind of busy right now," she said. "I'll call you back sometime."

She would find it hard calling me back; she didn't have my number. Or perhaps she did. I listened to a click and a dial tone and punched Weaver on the intercom.

"Weaver. Yes sir."

"You got an open line on the girl's wire?"

"Right. You just called her."

"No kidding," I said. The hawks were lower now. There was something edible on the sloping hillside just below our house. "What's she doing now?"

"Blowing her nose."

Problem 782 was a ". . . deadly assault against White's timid defensive posture." Black was scooping up pawns and pieces on his ". . . irresistible march to mate . . ." when Basset smiled at me through the door.

"God gave us knuckles for knocking," I said.

"Oh, yeah," Basset said and removed his face. He closed the door, knocked, and opened it again. He smiled at me. "Got him."

"Jakaz?"

He nodded.

I felt my lips pull back and realized that I was carnivorous. "Where?"

"Dunno. Weaver says he called the old guy and confirmed the meeting for tomorrow. It was a person-to-person from a phone booth somewhere here in town."

"And the other body?" I said. "Our friend 'I am at the airport'?"

"He'll be there too. And the girl leaves for Mammoth tonight."

"Call downtown," I said. "Get maybe fifteen bodies. But no details. No place, no target, no time, no travel arrangements, no nothing. Just give 'em a rendezvous at—um—at Sportsman's Lodge in the valley at, say, noon tomorrow."

Basset said, "Gotcha, killer."

"Killer?"

"That which works is good," Basset said. "Right?"

"Not always," I said.

42

"It's the thing Mock Turtle Soup is made from," said the Queen.

Alice's Adventures in Wonderland
LEWIS CARROLL

There are fish-counter displays marked SCAMPI in Los Angeles but they lie. Those fat crustaceans behind the glass are nothing more than hyperthyroid shrimp. Scampi are more closely related to crayfish—Adriatic crayfish. Yugoslavia is on the Adriatic. Cuban cigars were not the only contraband I had smuggled through customs.

"Fascinating," Glenda yawned when I explained scampi to her. "When do we eat?"

"Another half hour," I said. "It takes time for the spumante and scampi juices to render down to a sauce."

Glenda yawned again. "Fascinating."

I nodded and returned to my book, *Cybernetics: Feedback, Conflict and Homeostasis in Bio-Chemical Systems.*

After a while Glenda asked, "Figure out who done it yet?"

I said, "The computer done it," and turned a page. "It says here that our EDP system rates a very bad second for data storage."

"What's first?"

I tapped my head. "The brain, ounces against tons, can store more data bits than any of our present decimal or binary stuff. The problem lies in command retrieval; although you never forget anything you see or hear, you can't always dredge up data on demand . . . you can't get a full subject-coded printout from your mind. For example, the word 'love' . . ."

"Try 'sex' instead," she said.

I pumped a gram of sincerity into my smile and said, "Okay. Sex. You have millions of synaptic responses on the subject, but you can't push a button and recall every input you've had regarding sex."

"What a pity."

"The only advantage to electronic data systems is their push-button capacity for programming, response-coding and retrieval. The mind is a hopeless quagmire in comparison."

Glenda poked an absentminded finger in her glass. "It's good in a way I suppose," she said. "At least those gray little mice who program things in Virginia don't have a threat to their job security."

"Not yet," I said, lifting the other book from my lap. I showed her the spine: *Mnemonic Potentials in Electro-Bio-Chemistry (The Computer as Parachronism.)* "But someone's working on it."

We were sipping Korbel on my living-room balcony. It had been an unusual November day: cool in the morning and heating up around noon as a Santa Ana, that dry desert wind, blew away the smog.

"Can you take a day off tomorrow?" Glenda asked. "I love the beach on warm November days."

I studied her over the rim of my glass and said, "I thought the old man confided in you."

"Not lately. He's nervous as a cat about this transfer thing."

"Keep a secret?" I asked.

Glenda's smile was discreet, mocking herself as much as me. She said, "I've got the Q Clearance to prove it."

"SoCal SubSection might be salvaged," I said.

248

Glenda said, "I'd hold my breath for you, but blue doesn't go well with my hair."

"Basset and I are taking Jakaz tomorrow."

Glenda nearly spilled her drink. "Then you *have* found the files."

I said, "Sound carries around here," and lifted the Korbel bottle from my improvised ice bucket, an oversize chamber pot for which I'd swapped a doorless oil stove.

"More?"

"Always," Glenda said as she extended her glass.

I poured wine for both of us and said, "No," and resettled the bottle in its chamber pot. "No, I'm taking the son of a bitch because we haven't found the files. And never will."

"Lost forever?"

"Kovács is dead," I said. "The files were destroyed. Our man Walshing in Chicago said they were worth millions, literally worth millions."

"Was he thinking of, ahn . . ." Glenda made a pinching gesture with her thumb and forefinger.

I shrugged. "It's a temptation. Korbel is five bucks a fifth. Roederer Cristal sixty-one can go up to forty dollars a bottle. You can drink a lot of Cristal with something like three million dollars. Hell, you could wash your feet in the stuff with that kind of money."

"It's not recommended though," Glenda said. "Gives the wine a peculiar taste."

I laughed tonelessly.

Glenda set fire to the wrong end of one of her Eves and cursed succinctly. After mashing out the smoldering filter she tried again and succeeded in lighting the tobacco. "I'm a little curious about something."

"You are a big curious about everything," I said. "But tell me about this particular something."

"If the files are gone for good, and Kovács is dead, and Gyula Jakaz is quite useless . . ." her smile was sweet enough to send a diabetic into shock ". . . then *how* do you propose to save SoCal SubSection?"

I shaved some cigar ash over the balcony. "I propose to make us the control office for a new Agency branch in Albania . . . a ten-man branch that has some undefined ties with Ustachi."

Reaching across the little ice-cream table she said, "You have been sitting in the sun too long," and felt my forehead. "That 'Xenophon' report that you bought from Beebee . . . didn't it say that KGB had tried to infiltrate the Albanian group?"

"Yes. And failed."

"But you won't."

"No," I said. "I won't fail. Because I won't try to infiltrate the 'Group of Ten.' "

"Hmmmmm," said Glenda, smiling with fifty percent of her face and looking slightly mad with what was left. She rolled her eyes and said, "You're going to infiltrate them, but you aren't going to infiltrate them. I think they're holding a neuropsych room for you at St. Mallards, Charley-the-spy."

"I said *control*. Not infiltrate. And you control a group like this by finding its weak spot."

She stubbed out her cigarette and said, "Which is?"

"Divisive factions," I said. "Jakaz is looking for Kovács, but there's another faction that wants very much to become an operational C and D unit, with maybe a little sabotage thrown in to help relieve the boredom. Right now the Jakaz faction . . . the *chercher* Kovács faction . . . is on top because *they* have the money."

"Routenfield's money," Glenda said.

I nodded. "And once we've interdicted that source of funds, Jakaz will attach himself to us for the same reason that mistletoe attaches itself to certain deciduous trees. He'll depend on us for money . . . and all of this will filter through SoCal SubSection."

"Something like Twenty, yes?"

"Yes."

"There's still Jakaz," said Glenda. "Maybe he won't go along with you."

"It's not just 'still Jakaz,'" I said. "It's the nature of Jakaz. I mean, it's too late for him to start apprenticing as a plumber. Covert intelligence is the only work he knows, and we are his readiest prospect."

I dozed slightly in my chair, Korbel in one hand and the Bering in the other. The books were closed and ignored in my lap. The Santa Ana had made me lethargic; I dreamt the project was behind us—that Glenda and I were sunning ourselves on the beach at Encinada.

"Hmmm?" I said.

Glenda showed me her teeth. "I said, 'Do you think it will work?'"

I opened my mouth to reply. Inside the apartment a stove timer buzzed as though it would tear the place apart if I didn't attend to it immediately. I attended to it immediately. The scampi was ready.

I spread our dinner on the coffee table. The egg yolks I'd blended into the scampi cum spumante juices had thickened for once without lumping. And rich crustacean odors mixed with those of onions, mushrooms, white pepper and sparkling Italian wine. I thought, the French have a lot to learn.

"Here it is," I said. "Code di scampi allo spumante, Peperoni con quanciale and Insalata 'Diva del cinema.'"

Glenda plunged her fork into a scampo, bisected it with her knife and stuffed the larger of the two pieces into her mouth. After chewing and swallowing she shrugged her shoulders.

"Tastes like shrimp to me," she said.

251

43

The crossbow was packed with his other tools because this was going to be a 9 mm job. There was no way he could put a quarrel through that window and hope to waste anyone with it.

One shot, Hagopian thought. One shot and he'd make a run for the snowmobile. It was a shame about the crossbow; maybe he could use it on the next hit. Versatility—that was what made the work interesting. You could use your imagination.

Settling himself on the garage's acutely angled roof he watched the old man in the A-frame beyond. Routenfield was sitting in the large wing chair by the fireplace, sixty-one feet away. "On the nose," Hagopian said. "Sixty-one feet on the nose."

The lodge looked like a large, dim teepee; a sharply angled wedge that stood blackly in the blue night. The A-frame's window cut a bright hole in the night, a crisp rectangle that might have been part of a drive-in movie.

Hagopian held the piece easily in both hands, resting it on the uppermost row of shingles. There wasn't any rush. He'd wait for the old guy to finish drinking his coffee. Hagopian wanted a chest shot and Routenfield was holding a cup and saucer directly in front of his K5–D2 area, that smorgasbord target of heart, lungs, stomach, liver and spleen.

Snow was falling again. It had been another warm day; he'd rested in the woods while Routenfield's entourage emptied the two black Fleetwoods and set up housekeeping. Concealing the broken garage window hadn't been difficult. He'd pressed a fresh sheet of contact paper over it and encouraged a gentle avalanche of slush to cover the thing.

But now the damn stuff was coming down again. A cold snap was freezing the snow that had softened earlier. Maybe he'd take a couple of weeks off after this hit. Detroit was going to be a bitch to go home to—a few weeks in Nassau would help get the cold out of his bones.

Hagopian brought the piece up and balanced Routenfield's middle shirt button on its front sighting nib. The old guy was putting the cup and saucer aside, easing them onto a splashy looking gold and white salon table at his elbow. Lean back and relax now, Hagopian thought. Don't move. Be comfortable.

Not yet.

As Routenfield leaned back another man walked across the room and stood in front of him.

Hagopian lowered the SIG-Neuhausen.

Routenfield talked to the other, slapping a fist into his open palm. "Something bothering you?" Hagopian said. The other turned and called across the room to someone beyond Hagopian's range of vision.

Christ. God fucking *damn* it.

Two guys were carrying an elaborate Chinese screen in front of the window.

Bastards.

As he watched them block off the window with a hinged mural of some moon-faced jerks holding a dragon, he felt a nerve burn like a live coal in his stomach. Hagopian smashed his face into the snow-padded roof and fought to relax his right index finger. Don't shoot; don't make fucking noises, he thought. Don't do it. *Hate.*

Hagopian breathed heavily and rolled to his back. It should have been obvious; the sons of bitches *knew* he was after the old man. What the hell was he thinking about when it all

253

looked so easy? Sure they were going to take some defensive measures. Just because I'm better, he thought, it doesn't make them idiots.

Exhaling loudly and easing his grip on the 9 mm he said, "Give them credit. The minute you think you're dealing with dummies, that's when you retire."

But—now what? How do you get a shot in there? If they were this careful with Routenfield at night, they'd have a ring of guys around him during the day. And even if they didn't, even if the old man was an open target when the sun came up, Hagopian didn't want to make a daylight hit: Getting away would be rough. He had to take out Routenfield during the night.

Okay, Hagopian thought. How? You can't waste the son of a bitch while he's wandering around outside in the sun, so how do you get him to wander around outside in the dark? How do you get him the hell out of that A-frame?

Pet shop. If there was a pet shop in the village, maybe he could drive Steven-with-a-V Routenfield onto the porch.

Hagopian scratched at his blond wig, rubbing the fine net against his hair and pulling at his scalp. Beautiful. Get the old guy onto the porch and use the crossbow. That way they wouldn't know which way to run if they tried to chase him.

But first the pet shop.

254

44

Don't look back. Something might be gaining.

> *How to Stay Young*
> LEROY (SATCHEL) PAIGE

Basset cooled his heels while I ran the mercy mission. Once I got Mary Louise out of the lodge we would move in with fifteen head-pounders from the downtown office and set up a standard "valve" security around the Routenfield compound. Anything from a pedestrian to a flatbed truck could move through our valve into the compound, but nothing would get out unless we gave it leave to do so.

Two black Fleetwoods and a Chevy Vega were parked in front of the place. I pulled the Inter-Agency Motorpool Plymouth in beside them, its tail pipes pointing at the lodge while its headlights peered at the road below. I'm always getting stuck in snow. This afternoon I couldn't afford to.

The lodge was glazed like a wedding cake. Snow had fallen, melted and fallen until there was no hint of wood on its high-peaked roof. The servants' A-frame was a smaller echo; a glistening, icicled shape that looked naked without SEASON'S GREETINGS written in the afternoon sky above it. The front of the garage was an isosceles triangle of sculptured ice while the back was negotiating a merger with slipping snow from the hill that rose above it. Another warm night and they'd need an ax to enter any of the buildings.

"The name's Remly. Is Miss Paál in?" I said to the face that appeared in the door's talk-through panel. The panel closed as mutely as it had opened and the face, which hadn't opened at all, disappeared. It left a wake of suspicion and the smell of anisette. I wondered if Routenfield complained much about the quality of help nowadays.

There were footsteps and the door swung back. Mary Louise had a perplexed look that she offered to me without comment.

"Hello lovely you," I said.

She measured me carefully as though comparing my features to a photograph that had yellowed in her memory.

"Going to ask me in?"

Mary Louise paled slightly under her snowburn. Glancing into the house and back again she spoke to a point some twenty miles beyond my left shoulder: "It's kind of inconvenient now, Charley. Papa's here."

"I see." What I saw was confusion; she was struggling to make a decision and I knew it wouldn't be in my favor. "You ought to let people talk with you on the phone more often," I said.

She was silent for a moment and finally brought her eyes to my face. "I didn't think I would see you again."

"Foreign Service is like that," I said. "I told you it would only be two or three days."

"I didn't think I would see you again," she said again.

On impulse I reached through the door and took her hand. "Let's take a walk," I said and she came toward me, closing the door behind her.

"All my life men have walked away from me," Mary Louise said. "I'm seldom disappointed because I never get my hopes up."

We were sitting on a fallen pine along the firebreak that separated Routenfield's lodge from the main highway. I studied her face but Mary Louise was concentrating on infinity. I couldn't read her.

"Where are you?" I asked.

"Sometimes the world is bright, Charley. And sometimes it is black black black." Burying her face in my parka she said it again. "Black." She was right. Dark clouds staggered down from the north and dimmed the setting sun. "Sometimes I want to tell the world, 'My name is Mary Louise Paál and I feel like crying.' And then I could just stand there and cry." She pulled away from my parka and tried to find something in my face but my emotions were out to lunch. "Do you know what it is to feel like that?"

I watched the first snowflakes fall; a few scouts at first, then armies, then nations. They covered everything, including my unspoken answer.

"You scare me, Charley. You really do. I'm not sure you feel anything."

"Come to L.A. with me," I said. "I have something like a half-hour conference to attend, then we can squander the night searching for my feelings."

"To Los Angeles?"

"I know a great place for dinner. Nice view, cozy atmosphere. We'll have scampi that's out of this world," I said.

Mary Louise said, "I love shrimp."

"Not shrimp . . ." I began, but figured to hell with it and said, "C'mon. The next plane leaves for L.A. in less than an hour."

"Couldn't you stay here? Get a room at a motel . . . ?"

"I have a meeting, lover. I just came up to grab you and take you back to a life of sin, original or otherwise."

"I'd love to, Charley, really, but . . . but I came here to ski and I'd hate to miss all this nice fresh powder."

The smile she painted on her face was as phony as my meeting in Los Angeles. The only meeting I had was with Basset and two van loads of civil servants.

"Tomorrow we might fly to Tahoe," I said. "We could ski Heavenly and take in a show at Harrah's."

Mary Louise slipped from the log and offered me the back of her head. "No Charley, I . . . just no." She began walking away.

It was snowing with a vengeance. Mammoth is like that, clear one moment and punishing the next. As I trudged behind Mary Louise the sudden storm obscured her as though a veil of white antiseptic gauze had fallen between us. The woods quietly disappeared.

I said, "Give it a shot."

"I just . . . I want to ski."

I wondered how she would react to the truth. "Lover," I would say, "fifteen ugly guys that I know only vaguely, and a couple of bodies who work for me—not to mention myself— are going to scoop up Gyula Jakaz, his friend from the old country, and your not-quite-stepfather. Now, if you know what's good for you, you'll disappear for a couple of hours because the work is sometimes messy." What I said, however, was, "Mammoth hasn't cornered the market. It snows in Tahoe."

"Don't press me, Charley. Please."

"Look, it could be fun. I'd like you to come with me because . . . because . . ." I'd trapped myself.

Still walking dismally through the snow she said, "Because you love me, Charley my funny dip?"

"I need you."

"Do you love me?"

"Love is a difficult word."

"Need is sometimes a hollow one," she said. "Alcoholics need liquor. Do you love me?"

258

I patted at the pockets of my ski parka and found a cigar. Damn. No matches.

Mary Louise broke the silence. "That's not much of an answer."

"It wasn't much of a question."

"It's a foolish but very very very simple question," she said. "Look: 'Mary Louise do you love Charley Remly?'" She smiled shyly over her shoulder and said, "Madly."

"Then come with me."

"Charley . . . Charley you've got to know . . . Papa needs me too. He's very agitated; there's been some problem with a business associate and he's surrounded himself with men from his private guard service." That explained the face at the door. "He told me to be prepared to leave in a half hour and not come back until after dinner."

Beautiful. "He's meeting someone?" I nearly said Jakaz.

"Yes. There's something . . . something's not right and Papa's having a conference about it. Later . . . Papa always likes to have a drink and chat with me when he's troubled. He needs me too, Charley. Papa needs me more than you do."

Ahead of us the lodge loomed massive and vague through flurries of snow. "I'll phone you," I lied. "I'll call you tomorrow sometime. Okay?"

Mary Louise said. "You'll call me for sure?"

"For sure," I said. Then I told the truth: "Maybe I'll get in touch with you sooner." I reached out and smoothed my fingertips across her cheek. "I've missed you, Mary Louise."

Her chin wrinkled as she turned and took a hesitant step toward the lodge. She said, "Charley, sometimes I believe . . ."

I didn't learn what she sometimes believed: Mary Louise ran to the lodge and disappeared in it.

When I fell into the Plymouth and started it, a voice in the back seat said, "Just take it down the road a piece, okay?"

I glanced at the glove compartment. "It's not there," he said. "I got two guns . . . yours and mine. So let's go down the road."

We went down the road, I at the wheel and he breathing on my neck. It wasn't anisette; it was Black Jack gum.

45

Cato requested old men not to add the disgrace of wickedness
to old age, which was accompanied with many other evils.

Roman Apothegms: Cato the Elder
PLUTARCH

Errant flakes of snow whispered against the windshield and
died, leaving watery corpses that trickled down the glass and
distorted the scene outside.

We were parked a hundred yards or so up a Forestry Service
road and watching the untrafficked scene on Pine Vale Drive.
Although it was snowing heavily on the street below, the Plymouth was sheltered by a umbrella of pine trees.

"Nice up here in the mountains," Black Jack said. "Y'know?"
I said, "I know."

"What I like is it's quiet up here. I got a place in San Dimas
. . . y'know? Out near Pomona?"

"I know," I said. "Out near Pomona."

"Quiet place when we bought it. Right after the war,
y'know."

"I know," I said. "Spanish American."

"Naw, ranch style. I don't like them phony looking Medi-
terranean places." Every word was punctuated with licorice.

"That's very interesting." I glanced over my shoulder and
looked at the .45 Colt 1911 Government Model in his fist. My
feet were growing crisp under the dash. I hadn't really dressed
for Mammoth. "Mind if I turn on the engine? I'd like to warm
up the heater."

"Naw," Black Jack said. "You don't wanna do that. You oughta wear the right stuff up here. Thermal, y'know."

As I reached for the ignition I wondered how serious he was. Black Jack laid the front part of the .45's action across the base of my skull, breaking the skin and drawing blood. "Naw," he said again, "you don't wanna do that. Attracts attention."

He was right. I didn't want to do it; I was developing a violent headache.

When we heard the sound of tires whining across the freshly powdered road Black Jack said, "Put your hands back here . . . over the back of the seat." I did. "Good. Now reach down to the floorboards." I reached. With his feet on my hands it would have been difficult for me to blow the Plymouth's horn.

The Chevy Vega moved down Pine Vale Drive at an incredible speed. Mary Louise had a cavalier disregard for cautious driving in the snow.

"Now," said the licorice voice from the back seat. "Let's go back to the lodge, okay?"

"Suits me," I said. "You're in the driver's seat."

Black Jack began, "Naw . . ." but thought about it and said, "Yeah. Yeah, I am."

I shifted around in search of an easy slouch on the *Napoleon Troisième* side chair, but Bonaparte's nephew had inspired furniture as uncomfortable as it was ugly.

"We're waiting for the big guy," Black Jack said. He held the huge M1911 Colt with neither familiarity nor contempt. The thing made him nervous.

"I noticed," I said.

Black Jack squirmed in the chair. "You ever see anything like this before?" He finally assumed a rigid posture. He looked catatonic. "Wonder who made this old stuff."

262

"Torquemada," I said.

"I got a coupla those TV recliners for the house. That's real comfort. Wife and I go to sleep in 'em almost ever night. Watching Johnny Carson, y'know."

I nodded and stifled a yawn. I wondered who was on the Student Rad desk and what he was doing for amusement.

The room was furnished in white and gold, the sort of grim ambition you'd expect from film stars whose sudden celebrity exceeded their tastes. The wall raked in to form the A of the A-frame and a dormer window was plunked into the middle of it like an architectural afterthought. There was no phone in the room; Weaver wouldn't be tuned in to this conversation.

The door opened and a face popped through, followed by the rest of him. I had seen Weaver's 35 mm shots of the old man but nothing short of direct, visual confrontation could do him justice. Routenfield looked as though he'd dressed in a storm; and in someone else's clothes at that. His blue gabardine suit bulged at the pockets and bagged at the angular joints of his body. He'd rolled his cuffs twice to show a column of white sock above each black shoe.

Except for the thatch of white hair that bristled up from his head in all directions, he was as pink and hairless as a baby. His sagging face, puddled with age spots, gazed at me without benefit of eyebrows.

Black Jack looked first at me then at the old man. He sucked on his gum. The Colt was clutched nervously in both of his hands and looked as though it had grown in size and weight.

Routenfield pulled a handful of news clippings from a bulging inner pocket of his jacket and stared dully at it. The faded clippings stared dully back. "YUGO MILITIA DE-CENTRALIZED: MANEUVERS IN SLOVENIA," said one of them. Looking up from the wad of newsprint he asked, "Comfortable?" and stuffed the lump of paper back into his pocket.

"Your courtesy is killing me," I said.

263

He pulled his lips across his teeth in a sinister grin. As he studied me his hands had a life apart from the rest of his body. They tugged at his lumpy clothing and scratched urgently at his scalp. After a long silence he said, "Shoe salesman."

"Mother," I responded.

"Mother?"

"Association test," I said. "I always answer 'mother' or 'sex.' It simplifies things."

Routenfield drew back his lips again and poked a thumb into his mouth. I realized he wasn't smiling; his upper plate was loose. When his teeth were firmly settled he said, "I'm a student of human nature. Figure you for a shoe salesman."

I said, "Yes," but he ignored me.

"Doesn't much seem like anyone cares," Routenfield said. The old man's head bobbled vaguely, his white hair undulating like grass in a spring breeze.

When I passed a questioning glance to Black Jack he fielded it with a shrug and an embarrassed smile.

Routenfield jerked absentmindedly at one of the drooping white socks. "Ever been to Hungary?"

"No," I lied.

"Me neither," Routenfield said. "Like to see it sometime, though." He smiled blandly; a simple, childish expression that may have once been charming but now only verified the state of his mind. "They're gonna put a statue of me in the Peter Pan school."

I wasn't sure why Péter Pazmány University would want a statue of Routenfield. They already had one of Copernicus.

Routenfield's eyes focused on nothing and his jaw relaxed.

It was going to be some meeting, I thought. Routenfield was not in one of his more lucid periods. I wondered how much weight he carried in this odd, symbiotic relationship of American enterprise and Hungarian duplicity. More to the point I wondered what the hell he had in mind for me.

"Steve?" The voice was down the hall and getting closer as he called, "Steve?" again.

"In here, Mr. Strauss," Black Jack said loudly.

The body that walked through the door resembled one of those ever-happy male dolls that little girls mate with their lavish, wardrobe dolls. From his twenty-five-dollar haircut to his immaculate *après ski* boots he looked as though he'd been groomed for form—not function. After presenting me a meaningless smile he turned to Black Jack. "How long has Mr. Routenfield been here?"

Before Black Jack could answer I said, "You people are out of your collective minds." I rose from my chair, Black Jack's .45 following my midsection. "I'm getting a reason for all of this . . . this *bullshit* . . . or I'm walking out of here."

"I wouldn't suggest that," Strauss said.

Black Jack extended the .45 in a double-fisted grip and turned his head slightly aside as though preparing to flinch from the noise it would make.

"Fine," I said. "Blow my guts all over the wall. What'll you do with my corpse? Hell, what will you do when FBI and Department of State investigators come around looking for me?"

Strauss' smile seemed riveted in place. "FBI? State Department?"

"Look," I said. "I just came to see Mary Louise . . . and you people are waving guns at me. Why? Who are you?"

"A friend of the family," Strauss said. "Tell me—why would the State Department be interested in you?"

"It's a matter of employee relationships. I am a Foreign Service careerist. And I'm due at a meeting in Los Angeles today."

Smiling at his watch Strauss said, "Little late for a meeting, isn't it?"

"You don't know Foreign Service," I said. "If I miss the conference someone's going to be upset. If I am not back in

The Hague by the day after tomorrow, someone is going to hit the ceiling. And this place is going to be *crawling* with federal investigators." I turned to Black Jack. "Take a shot at me. Short of burning them down, there is no way you'll get my blood off the walls." I grinned. "Y'*know*?"

Strauss said, "You had a gun in the glove compartment of your car . . ."

"Yes," I said. I hadn't wanted to accept the thing, but regulations are regulations and I'd had to check out a weapon from Ordnance for this raid. "I've got a permit for it," I said and handed him the handsome scrap of paper from Documents. "I've also got dip ID." I passed over the dip authorization I'd used to smuggle in the F. O.'s cigars. "And if you'll take a look at my car, I've got government plates on it." I walked to the window and looked down. The Plymouth was gone.

"How about it?" Strauss said to Black Jack.

"Hell, I didn't even notice the license, Mr. Strauss. You told me to check the *inside*."

Strauss said, "Well, that does make us look rather foolish, Mr. Remly. I suppose I owe you an apology."

"Forget it," I said. "You owe me a car. Where is it?"

Although he was still smiling, I could see the microminiature synapses closing in his mind. Somewhere behind his eyes Strauss was weighing the risk of killing me against the danger of setting me free. Suppose I reported the odd gun waving and kidnap business to the FBI? Suppose I brought a host of curious federal investigators down on his head? Suppose . . .

"Look," I said. "You people have some kind of personal problem you're trying to solve here. I don't care what your problem is; I don't even want to hear about it. I have enough trouble getting up in the morning and I don't *need* your problems. So if you'll send your man here," I jerked my head toward Black Jack, "for my car, I'd appreciate it."

I had him. I knew that I had him, but a car growled outside, coughed once and was silent. I looked through the window to see two men walking from a lime-colored Pontiac. Then I knew that I'd lost him: One of the men was Gyula Jakaz.

Basset, I thought, raid this place. In another fifteen minutes the sun would drop like a ball of hot slag behind the mountain and Basset would be literally in the dark.

Strauss walked to the window, smiled down on Jakaz and the other man, then walked to Routenfield. "Steve," he said, "time to go downstairs."

Routenfield wakened slightly, but only slightly: One of his oddly disconnected hands groped in a pants pocket and returned with a hair comb. As Strauss shook him he raked his thumb across the comb's teeth.

Still trying to rouse the old man Strauss turned his iridescent smile on me. "You'll have to stay until we finish some business. I'll have your car brought up in an hour or so."

I returned his smile without speaking. There didn't seem to be much alternative.

Like a tug maneuvering a small, rudderless craft, Strauss gently guided Routenfield from the room.

"Shame about that," Black Jack said once they were gone. "He's a nice old guy, y'know?"

"I know," I said. "Steven Routenfield is the very soul of niceness. Strauss, too."

Black Jack inspected the color of my eyes. Finally he said, "Yeah. A real nice old guy."

My calm exterior was not a façade—even in the worst circumstances hysteria is an exercise in futility. Although I refer to it as a realistic attitude, the F. O. says it's lethargy pure and simple.

"You come up here often?" Black Jack asked.

I massaged my eyebrows. "Whenever I can get away." I thought, what the hell, and asked, "How about you?"

"First time," he said. "Mr. Strauss keeps me on the industrial accounts. That's where the real dough is, y'know. Industrial snooping." He winked. "I could tell you things about bugging offices that would curl your hair. I can wire up a place so tight, the Federal guys couldn't de-bug it."

I reached into my parka and was suddenly looking down the very businesslike hole in the end of his Government Model Colt. The gun's muzzle was large enough to walk into. "Cigar," I assured him, removing my hand slowly with a Bering in it.

"I'll tell you," Black Jack said, "I'm trying to quit the cigarette thing and I sure wish you wouldn't smoke. Every time I smell the stuff my nerves go a little crazy." He reached into his own jacket and tossed me a stick of gum. "Try this instead."

"Tell me something," I said. "What'll you do when Strauss says to let me go?"

"He said he would, didn't he?"

"And if he tells you to blow my head off?"

"Naw, he wouldn't do that."

I worked on the gum and watched him.

Black Jack said, "What the hell'd he want to do that for?" We exchanged stares, chewing like two curious cows who'd just been introduced. I could see the strain on his face as he worked out the answer to his question. With each new thought the strain seemed to lessen and finally Black Jack measured me for a box. If it wasn't getting clearer for him, it was becoming transparent for me.

"Aw, hell, don't worry about it," Black Jack said. "I couldn't shoot a guy in cold blood. They wouldn't ask me to hurt you." I wondered who they would ask. And I wondered if I'd feel more comfortable with Black Jack's .45 in my hand.

"If money talks, maybe you're open for a discussion," I said and reached into my parka again. At last count I had something less than forty dollars; the inside bill in my money clip was a twenty and the others weren't large enough to buy a day's groceries. "How about it?"

"Don't bother," Black Jack said. "I earn plenty, working for Mr. Strauss."

I fingered the bills within my pocket. "Not like I'm talking about," I said. There were six of them. I refolded them with the twenty on the outside and eased the clip back on. "I can give you something over a thousand now, and you name the price you'll want later."

"Forget it, he said."

"Ten thousand? You ever hold ten thousand tax-free dollars in your fist?" I pulled my hand out as though it had been having an affair with the pocket and was reluctant to leave. "How about fifteen, does that sound better?" The money clip landed between us; close enough to Black Jack so he wouldn't have to leave the chair to reach it, yet far enough so he'd have to stretch if he wanted the thing.

"C'mon, take it back," he said. "I don't want your dough."

"There's over a thousand in there," I lied.

"Naw, it's too thin," he said and kept his eyes glued on the twenty that showed.

"One thousand, one hundred and maybe forty dollars."

"Hell, it's a twenty and change."

I said, "What do you keep on the outside—big bills or little ones?"

Black Jack lifted his eyes. I made a face and shrugged. "Okay," I said. I reached for the clip. "Money isn't your interest."

"Lean back." His voice was firm; he'd made his decision. "Fold the hands together and grab your hair."

I did.

Black Jack kept his eyes on my hands and face as he stretched toward the money between us. His concentration level was very good; his eyes never wavered from my hands.

Murder is uglier in theory than in fact. At least that's what I was taught at Unarmed Combat Training in Virginia. When you theorize about murder you have the leisure to reflect on the consequences of the act; it is *just* to deprive another of his life? am I capable of taking it? and whatnot. But, in fact, you don't think of the consequences. You act. You set a goal and achieve it without worrying about methodology; and the training reduces your goal-achievement drives to a course of thoughtless reflexive action. Act. Don't think.

I thought of nothing as he touched the money clip—I simply willed him dead, if such a wish can be simple. While he focused on my hands, my foot snapped into his solar plexus. Black Jack convulsed once before I was on him.

It was a two-handed job. With my left I levered his right fist in at the wrist; the Government Model dropped from his unfolding fingers. With the other I stuffed a handful of his shirt into his mouth. The man wasn't dead—not yet.

He made an ungodly amount of noise, moaning and gagging as I pressed the thumb of my left hand against his external carotid artery and said quietly, "Easy, relax pal." Black Jack writhed miserably beneath my restraining hands. "Don't worry," I said softly, "the pain will go away." His moans filtered up through the shirt and I bore down harder. "Relax, that's right."

When Black Jack went to sleep I debated whether to keep my thumb on the artery.

No, I thought. I haven't the character for it.

46

I never saw so many shocking bad hats in my life.

ARTHUR WELLESLEY, DUKE OF WELLINGTON
(On seeing the first Reformed Parliament)

I had two choices, neither of which seemed particularly inviting.

If I left through the dormer window I would rattle down the steep slope of the roof and drop like a disastrous tumbling act in front of the window below. As much as it might upset me, it would startle the people inside even more.

On the other hand I could stay, praying for Basset's arrival and dreading discovery.

I chose the latter horn of my dilemma and clung to it desperately. As I taped Black Jack with a 200-foot roll of Johnson & Johnson adhesive from the bathroom, I saw that the resolution of one dilemma had created another: Was it wiser to cringe here in the guest bedroom or to see what was happening with Routenfield and his people? Curiosity got the better of me. It always does.

Before opening the door I peered through its keyhole at the balcony on the other side of the lodge. Except for a matched set of Sheraton chairs, a salon mirror and a parson's table, the landing was empty. Carefully easing the door back I poked my head through at carpet-pile level and checked the balcony on my side. Clear. I crawled out.

Mary Louise had said that a whisper would carry from the

271

fireplace to the balcony. She was right. The acoustics were beautiful. Resting belly down on the balcony floor I could hear and see everything that went on at the far side of the room below me.

From where I lay, Routenfield's lodge seemed lifeless. It needed the firelight and glintering chandeliers to breathe some kind of charm into it, and they'd only turned on a couple of lamps near the fireplace. An ugly Chinese screen blocked the picture window.

I looked up at the acute, beamed wedge of the ceiling and realized my insignificance. The place was too big, too supergraphic: The old man had built The Hall of the Mountain King. Nothing short of a basketball squad could have felt comfortable in it.

As it was, only four normally proportioned bodies were clustered around the fireplace below. Strauss must have sent his private security guards outside.

I recognized the speaker; he had climbed out of the lime-colored Pontiac with Jakaz. ". . . could have passed the message to me through the usual channels," he said. If this was the liaison from Hungary, he'd spent most of his time under a sun lamp. You don't get that kind of a tan in Budapest, not in November.

No one spoke. They were waiting for Routenfield.

The old man reached into a bulging pocket, pulled out a rolled sheaf of paper, slapped it twice against his knee and returned it. He said, "Usual channels. Why, hell, money's the only stuff that gets through your 'usual channels' without losing in the translation." He twisted his nose as though wondering if he could screw it more firmly into place. "You ever get my request to hijack one of those Malév airplanes?"

Jakaz and Strauss traded pained expressions. Strauss filtered his through his teeth while keeping a rigid smile on his face. He looked like a salesman closing a deal.

The liaison looked blank. "Hijack?" He turned to Jakaz as though seeking help.

If it wasn't obvious to Routenfield, I doubted that the liaison's relationship to Jakaz was lost on anyone else in the room. "Milos Kay" may have been subservient to the Hungarian liaison, but Gyula Jakaz was still the boss. He nodded to his tanned associate. He looked like he was chopping wood with his sharp nose. "The hijack memorandum," he said. "Certainly you recall it."

"Yes," the liaison said. "And a very fine idea, hijacking an airplane." He made elaborate gestures with a cigarette case and a butane lighter while he thought. "You spoke of money. I must confess that the cost of such a plan was entirely beyond our means."

"He's got a point, Steve," said Strauss with a smile. I wondered if he took injections at the end of the day to relax his face. "They've been doing a pretty good job over there, considering the budget they've got to work with."

Routenfield said, "How about infiltrating AVH? What progress've you got on that?"

The liaison leaned forward in his chair like a figure on a mechanical bank; drop in a penny and he tapped his cigarette over an ashtray. "It will be two weeks before I can bring you up to date on that," he said when he resettled himself in the chair. "These issues can be handled through channels, Mr. Routenfield. Of course I appreciate all that you have done for us, yet I am more valuable to you in Budapest than here in Southern California."

They waited again for the old man to respond. He contemplated his shoe while one of his independent hands clawed at his scalp.

Strauss touched Routenfield's arm. "The reason for the meeting, Steve," he said. His smile was iridescent. "Tell him why you asked him here."

273

Routenfield looked up and was startled to see the others there.

"The reason for the meeting, Steve," Strauss said again.

"Meeting. Yes. I think we should have a meeting with one of Milos' Hungarian people. I keep sinking money into this damn thing, Irwin, and nobody listens to me."

Strauss smiled apologetically from Jakaz to the Hungarian liaison. He massaged his cheeks; they looked fatigued. To Routenfield he said, "Right. We're having the meeting, Steve. This is Istvan. He flew here from Budapest to see you."

"I know that," Routenfield snapped. "Don't teach your gran'ma to suck eggs, dammit."

Strauss rolled his eyes elaborately at Istvan. He wanted the Hungarian to understand what they had to go through with the old man.

"I'm tired of helping you boys with money," Routenfield said. "I'm not your rich uncle that you can keep asking for pocket change without giving something in return. You get me?"

"Yes," said Istvan. "Yes, of course."

"I want some say-so in making policy. Fact is, I want to run the U.S. end of this establishment. Along with Irwin here I can whip things into shape at this end."

Istvan said, "But, Mr. Kay is handling . . ."

"I'll get to him," Routenfield said. "Don't you worry, I'll get to him in a minute." One of his antic fingers bored into his ear and came out again. He inspected it for wax. "Now, here's what I expect from you folks. After we get rid of Milos I expect you to give me a hand with some ideas I've got for operations in the Los Angeles area. Place is crawling with Illuminati and other sorts of Jews. I got some things up my sleeve for 'em."

Gyula Jakaz looked as though he was weighing the situation

274

in his head. He propped his elbows on his knees and tapped the fingers of one hand into the palm of the other. I got the impression that he was balancing Routenfield's amusement credits against a debits column filled with boredom.

"That might be arranged," Istvan said. "What do you think, Milos? Could some of Mr. Routenfield's interesting ideas be implemented here in Southern California?"

Routenfield's open palm landed on the table between them with an impact that rattled the ashtrays. From where I lay on the balcony it sounded like a single round of small arms fire. "Not him, dammit." He stared at the liaison with eyes that were now fully aware. "That man is no longer a part of this conversation. It's you I'm talking to. Not him, you."

"But Mr. Routenfield; Milos Kay is a very . . ." he looked inward for the word ". . . a very *critical* factor in our network. To exclude him from our plans would not be practical."

"You better uncritical him damn fast," Routenfield said. "I just found out . . . that conniving Hungarian son of a bitch is trying to kill me."

Istvan didn't get it at first. He began, "Of course, it is very difficult to ignore Milos. Without him our Southern California . . ."

A jackass bray of laughter rang through the room as Jakaz reacted to Routenfield's words. He'd finally reached the totals column and the incongruity of the situation seemed its most obvious asset.

"Of course, of course," he said. He turned to Istvan and said, "Hear him through. I am trying to kill Steven Routenfield; let him tell you why."

"You damn well are," Routenfield said. "I got proof."

Strauss said, "My God, Steve. What are you talking about?"

"Don't think I'm such an old fool I don't listen to you behind doors once in a while. I know about this fella you been

275

trying to catch. And I pretty well got it figured out who hired him."

"Incredible," Istvan said.

Strauss glanced covertly at Routenfield. The old man was facing away from him. Strauss turned quickly to Jakaz and offered him a reassuring shake of his head. Jakaz grinned his reply. He seemed to be enjoying himself.

Istvan was right. The idea was incredible. Jakaz had no reason to want the old man dead; Routenfield was considerably more than just a goose—he was an assembly line of golden eggs.

"Strauss's got the man up there . . . the one's going to kill me." Routenfield pointed directly at me and the other three looked up. I melted into the carpet, wondering if any of my fifteen excess pounds showed. Black Jack's .45 seemed suddenly ridiculous in my hand; I was a four-point favorite to lose. "Bring him down," he said to Strauss. "Let's have a look at him."

Strauss was fighting to keep up his smile. He said, "Look Steve, that man up there isn't the one we're looking for. Even if he were, why would *Milos* have hired him?"

"Bring him the hell down and ask him," said Routenfield impatiently. "Hell, I know he's there. I just talked to him. Tried to tell me he's a shoe salesman."

They hadn't seen me. Still, I didn't breathe. I'd found another dilemma, this one even more interesting than the first: If I moved I would be seen and if I didn't move I would be seen. While I searched desperately for a third alternative Jakaz said, "It doesn't matter, I confess all."

Strauss looked from Jakaz to Routenfield. "Sit down, relax," Jakaz said. He looked at his watch again. He'd seen the show and he didn't have time for encores.

Istvan hadn't gotten the joke yet. He swiveled his head from Strauss to Jakaz to Routenfield. He said, "But why?" His face

276

was a puzzle of unanswerable questions. "Why would he plan such a thing?"

Although they watched Routenfield, Routenfield was watching an idea that none of them could see. His left hand trembled as though it was eager to rummage through his loose and oddly bulging suit.

Strauss touched his knee and said, "Steve?"

"Jewish," Routenfield said quietly.

Istvan said, "Jewish?"

"I said *jealous*," Routenfield said. "The man's afraid of the organization I've put together. He knows that we can initiate projects here . . . right here in Southern California . . . that he would never think of. Milos Kay is jealous of my group; that's why he wants me dead. Why, good Lord, man, I have ideas for those Freedom Fighters that would shake Hungary loose in a matter of months."

Loose from what? I thought. Those of his "Freedom Fighters" that hadn't been expatriated—to Canada, to the States, to Austria and, the saddest of the lot, something over two hundred thousand to Mother Russia's euthanasic bosom—were more inclined to return their empty bottles for the fifty filler deposit than to fill them with gasoline.

"Just you take your Illuminati," Routenfield said. His twitching hand found a target in the soft underside of his knee. "You ever get our report on Illuminati?"

Istvan snapped his head from Routenfield to Jakaz and back. "Yes," he said. "Of course."

"Jews. It's worldwide." The old man's lips moved up and down, mouthing unsaid words. He was leaving us again. He said, "Kikes," and stared through Istvan.

Strauss was like a teeter to Routenfield's totter. As his employer's mind began to wander, he said, "Let's get down to business. How much more did you intend to ask for?"

"Twenty," Jakaz said.

"Annually?"

"Quarterly." He pulled a package of Player's Navy Cut from his jacket, tapped a cigarette on his thumbnail and waited for Istvan to produce the gold lighter. "Our costs have gone up at least eighty thousand a year."

Strauss thought about it, rolling the money around in his mind until his eyes glinted with the thought of it. "That's a lot of money," he said. "It's going to be a hard figure to sell him."

"He will buy it," Jakaz said. He puffed on the cigarette without inhaling; his face was obscured by the smoke. "We've given him the Hungarian liaison to look at . . ."

Strauss interrupted him. "What the hell could that've cost you?" He turned to Istvan. "Even first class it's what . . . no more than four hundred dollars round trip from Miami?"

Jakaz leaned forward in his chair to rap Strauss on the knee. "I am discussing overall expenses. It will cost money to bring a new contact for Los Angeles." He smiled without humor. "I am being shot by Istvan, yes? Then you will explain to the old man that my—ahm—superiors found me guilty, and a new face will replace mine. That is just one expense. Inflation and the increasing difficulties we encounter in Europe add even more. Your dollars are not as well respected as once they were."

"Even so," Strauss said. "Eighty thousand." And he shook his head.

"And let us say a twelve-percent commission for you, instead of the ten you have been receiving." Jakaz read Strauss' face and quickly added, "Twelve percent on this eighty thousand, not on the total budget."

That explained his safe deposit boxes bulging with cash.

"I'll try," Strauss said without confidence. "You'll have to cover me though. Get those reports in on time, and for Christ's sake make them lively. We're going to need a lot of flak and fireworks to keep his mind off of the local projects he wants to initiate."

Jakaz spun his cigarette into the fireplace where it made a modest burst of sparks. "Good. I will have a new man contact you within the week; ten days at most." He glanced toward my perch on the balcony. "I am curious; who *do* you have up there?"

"Don't worry," Strauss said. "It's the wrong man. He doesn't seem bright enough to be a professional killer. But the killer's real enough; some guy in Detroit phoned us and sold us the information for twenty thousand dollars. When we tried to grab the hit man he killed one of our freelance men and put another in the hospital." For a second he removed his smile in reverence for the dead. He restored it before speaking. "What I can't figure is, who'd want Steve dead?"

"I have an idea," Jakaz said. He looked coolly at the dozing old man. "I have an idea who . . . and why."

Strauss said, "Care to tell me?"

Jakaz shook his head.

Istvan became articulate enough to utter two syllables: "The farm."

"Don't worry about it," Strauss said. "I'll have the old man's broker list it for rent."

"It becomes more complex than that," Jakaz said. "We created a mess before leaving it yesterday. You may have to remove some casualties."

Strauss' eyebrows moved toward his hairline.

"It has nothing to do with our business together. It is a separate matter that I am involved in."

"You should have told me earlier."

Jakaz said, "Yes." He rose and smiled down on Strauss. "We are a confusion of undelivered messages, you and I. The pur-

279

pose of this ridiculous meeting should have been explained to me in advance."

"I thought I could sidetrack him," Strauss said. "If you'll keep those reports coming . . . keep his mind occupied on what's happening in Hungary, Yugoslavia and where ever else you're operating . . . it won't happen again." He tried to lay a reassuring hand on the other's shoulder. Jakaz flinched beneath the touch and brushed away Strauss' hand.

Istvan joined them as they walked to the door. Jakaz hesitated with his hand on the knob. He spoke casually but the question was weighted. "Mary Louise, is she well?"

"Oh sure," Strauss said. "She's never any problem; always in great spirits."

"Give her my regards," Jakaz said.

"I sure will," Strauss said and they were gone, out the door and out of my grasp unless Basset had set up the security net.

When Strauss called his men in from the porch I edged away from my vantage point to the guest room where Black Jack curled on the floor and moved his lips silently behind the tape. I locked the door and wedged one of the Napoleon Troisième chairs beneath its knob. Time and luck were the two things I most needed and seemed least likely to get. If action led to disaster, so did indecision.

I looked down at the parking area where dim light spilled from the porch. I could see a corner of the garage and all three of the cars parked below.

Jakaz flicked on his headlights and backed the lime Pontiac in a half circle then started slowly toward the main road. If he got away—if Basset hadn't set up the security net—it wasn't probable that we would see him soon whether I escaped or not. I leveled the .45 on his car. A contraction of my finger would keep him in the yard, perhaps long enough for Basset to arrive. It would also attract attention. I lowered the pistol.

Gyula Jakaz was gone.

280

And I felt like an idiot, closing my hand on empty air where there should have been game.

I sat on the edge of the bed and massaged my temples. The ones I had were not the ones I wanted; and even then, I didn't have *them*. I glanced at my watch: Six-fifteen.

At six twenty-eight someone tried the doorknob. A voice said, "Michael?" He rattled the latch once and shouted, "Mr. Strauss, something's wrong in here."

I returned to the window and wondered whether to jump now or later. Basset, I thought, show your homely face.

"Michael," the voice shouted. "Open the damn door."

When Michael didn't open the door, they began filling the room with pepper gas. I staggered to the bathroom to turn on the shower—and hope the humidity would suspend the stuff and keep it from my skin and lungs. It didn't.

47

The skier stood in the copse of pines, shifting from one foot to the other and hugging himself for warmth. If he had remained motionless—if he'd settled with his back against a tree—Hagopian might not have noticed him. As it was he rocked back and forth like an indecisive bear.

Hagopian was interested in the man. Although he was nattily dressed in ski togs, he held an ugly High Standard Model 10 Police Auto shotgun in his gloved hand.

Hagopian moved silently behind the skier, his hands spread as though inviting an embrace. In the darkness even he couldn't see the three-foot length of dental floss that separated his hands.

Quietly, softly, hardly daring to breathe, Hagopian lifted both clubbed fists above the skier. He brought them down with the hope of driving the guy's shoulders into his knees; it was the best way to assure follow through. The impact paralyzed the man's brachial plexus, the two networks of cervical and upper dorsal nerves that controlled everything from his shoulders to his fingers.

When the shotgun dropped from the skier's numb hands Hagopian snapped his fists back and shot a knee into the other's lumbar vertebrae. The man went limp. Maybe he's wasted, Hagopian thought as he held him up by the dental floss around his throat. A shot like that usually finished a guy; but better safe than sorry. He strained on the dental floss and maintained the pressure until his arms were sore.

It had stopped snowing. The occasional flakes that drifted before his face told him he woudn't have to worry about windage; there was no wind tonight.

He was lying on the sharply peaked garage roof, the crossbow in his hands. Next to him was his insurance; the 9 mm rested on a clean handkerchief. With a crossbow you never got more than one shot—the SIG-Neuhausen carried seventeen.

From his vantage he could see every available window of the main A-frame. There were windows on the far side but they'd been snowed in. The only item of interest on that side of the lodge was a second-story protuberance that housed the central heating unit. Hagopian felt his lips pull back; he'd already taken care of that.

The bomb should go off in no more than an hour. An hour at the latest. It was a shame he couldn't have taken a couple of days to build a timing device for the thing, but the heat activation should blow it off pretty soon. Although he couldn't see the central heating unit, he'd know when the thing went off.

Hagopian counted the scales once more on the Chinese dragon in Routenfield's window. He knew there were a hundred and thirty-eight scales on that baroque lizard but wondered if there was a slower way of counting them. Maybe if he took them in horizontal rows instead of totaling them up one panel at a time.

There was a shout inside the house. Another voice yelled, "What is it?" "Gas leak," came the reply.

Now, Hagopian thought as he leveled the crossbow. This one was going to be nice, a very calm hit and a leisurely retreat to the snowmobile. The adrenalin jobs—the times that he operated on sheer hatred—those were bad for the system.

They made his heart work overtime. And he'd read somewhere that the stress enlarged the liver, kidneys and suprarenal capsules to a nearly fatal degree. No, this was going to be nice. A nice quiet piece of work.

The first guy came out like a badly thrown stick, tilting forward as he ran and tripping off the end of the porch. He landed on his right ear in the snow. Hagopian ignored him as he scrambled toward the closer of the two Fleetwoods.

Another came tumbling out and dove into the black Cadillac's open door. "Hey, Murph. Hey. You up there?" He was shouting at the copse of pines behind Hagopian.

"Yeah," Hagopian said quietly. "Yeah, Murph's up there. But he's not taking any calls."

Now. This was the time.

Two men staggered out supporting Routenfield between them. The old man shuffled his feet and turned his head from one of the guys to the other.

As they worked their way down the broad redwood stairs Hagopian had a beautiful view of Routenfield's K5-D2 area. He squeezed the crossbow's trigger and watched as the old man stumbled and . . .

Bastard!

One of the bastards helping Routenfield reached down to support the old guy and caught the quarrel in his shoulder.

Hate.

Hagopian smashed down the bow and grabbed for the SIG-Neuhausen and thought, lousy damn kids' toys—I should have stuck with the piece all along. But by the time he'd swiveled the thing around, lining up the two guys and Routenfield, they were in the back seat of the car and closing its door.

Screw you, he thought. He squeezed off two quick shots at the old man's head through the rear window. Nothing. Two large frosted ovals appeared where his shots had caromed off the transparent surface. The rear window was a poly-carbon sandwich of armored glass.

Jesus, what now? Hagopian's hand shook. What the hell now—chase them?

Three more guys ran from the house, moving low and trying to zigzag through the snow like soldiers in a mined field.

Made a decision, he thought; decide now. The rear Fleetwood was pulling awkwardly around the other, easing between it and the second A-frame and taking a piece of taillight as it passed. Hagopian thought, don't be stupid. Don't make any more mistakes tonight; let them get away. Be cool for Christ's sake. The last three were nearly at the parked Cadillac. Don't do it, he thought; but a spasm hit him—hate—and he squeezed off three snapshots.

Ignoring the crossbow Hagopian scrambled over the peak of the garage roof and tobogganed toward the three corpses below.

Although he'd dropped easily, Hagopian tucked and rolled when his feet touched the hardpack. Someone was shooting at him from the departing Fleetwood. He landed on his stomach and returned their fire, snapping six more 9 mm slugs at the wildly accelerating car. Armored glass or not, he must have gotten something: the huge Cadillac stalled and slewed into the servants' lodge like a stunned whale. It teetered up on its far wheels, exposing its undercarriage.

Hagopian ran in a crouch to the first body. Nothing. It was empty-handed. At the second body a key ring lay just inches away from its rigid fingers.

The occupied Fleetwood was still bouncing on its springs when Hagopian slammed into the driver's seat of the second car. Both cars' starters turned over in a harmonic whine.

"Start," Hagopian screamed at the dashboard. "God damn it start." Oblivious to the Cadillac's lush black leather interior he glanced at the rearview. The other car was still some twenty feet behind him, stalled and sputtering, its two right-hand doors touching the flat back wall of the servants' A-frame. The men inside were below the level of the windows. One guy fired a round at him from the partially opened rear door, but the thing only made a frosted line up his back window.

When the engine turned over he jammed the shift lever into reverse and pressed the accelerator to its limit. The Fleetwood coughed once, hesitated, then leaped backward, its rear wheels squalling as they spun through the snow. Hagopian lay flat on the seat; what he didn't need was a whiplash when he smashed into the other car.

The noise of it was staggering: There was a multiple crash as he hit the other car, the other bounced off the A-frame, and the two Fleetwoods collided again. After the bang and rip of sheet metal, frame members and glass subsided he heard a single human cry. Leaving it in reverse, Hagopian eased his foot off the accelerator and peered through the rear window. There was nothing to be seen; the car's trunk lid had sprung and was covering his view.

Insurance, he thought. Get 'em again for insurance.

Hagopian moved the shift level down to DRIVE-1 and pulled the heavy Fleetwood to its original parking spot. Someone was still alive back there, moaning in the other car. Not for long, he thought as he brought the lever back up to reverse and slammed his foot onto the accelerator again.

This time the noise was simpler; the glass was already gone and there was no secondary bang of the other car bashing into the A-frame. Still, it was a satisfying noise. Really satisfying, he thought and started laughing. Jesus Christ this was beautiful. Hagopian tried closing his mouth against the laughter that bubbled up, but continued sputtering through his noise.

One more time, he thought. But not for insurance. No one

—oh Mother of God *no one*—was alive in that thing. One more time because—because, well, Jesus, this was a wild experience. He'd never done anything like it before.

He pulled forward. Fighting down the laughter he shot backwards again and rammed the other car. When his rear bumper chewed its way into the wreck Hagopian heard a *snap* beneath the hood. Something ground in the transmission and the engine died; it had finally broken loose from its mounts.

Still laughing he wiped the tears from his cheeks. The jolly, snow-frosted scene was blurred and wavering. Hagopian pulled up his eyelids one at a time and winked out the blue contact lenses. But *Christ* that was funny. Jesus what a laugh.

He stepped from the ruined Cadillac. What was left of the other car he could have carried off in a couple of grocery bags. Even the A-frame had buckled where the combined weight of the two cars had rammed it.

Hagopian moved toward the black four-door coffin as though he was walking on eggs. None could be alive in there, but still . . .

He peered carefully into the car.

Oh sweet Mary, merciful Mother of Christ. Pray for me.

For the first time since he'd been in the business he couldn't control the involuntary reflexes of his diaphragm and abdominal muscles. When they contracted, the cardiac sphincter of his stomach relaxed and Hagopian poured warm vomit down the left rear door of the car. He turned his head aside and spat to clear the rotten taste from his mouth. He'd never seen anything like that before: Crushed skulls dripping gray cerebral matter, pink ragged ends of shattered bones that had penetrated muscles and clothing to stand like flagpoles that flew limp banners of ligament and viscera; and all that fucking blood. It was as though someone had flocked the inside of the Cadillac with thick red ooze.

He'd been right. None could be alive in there.

Hagopian scooped a fistful of gasoline tainted snow and rubbed it into his face. Get out, he thought. Get out of the fucking business, get out of the fucking state, get out of fucking here.

As he jogged up the hill he heard a voice behind him shout, "Routenfield! Strauss!" He drove into the snow, rolled once, and lay in a perfect prone; the 9 mm in both hands, legs spread for stability and his elbows jammed into the cold powder.

"Routenfield," the voice shouted, "Strauss! Are you okay?"

Some clown in an upstairs window was leaning out and yelling foolishly at the carnage below.

How could he have stayed in there? Hagopian wondered. Once the bomb went off you'd have to be nuts to stay in the lodge. But this one had. And now he was balanced on the front nib of Hagopian's SIG-Neuhausen like the dot of an "i."

No. No more, he thought. I want to go home.

Hagopian lowered the piece, rose and jogged wearily toward the snowmobile.

48

How shall we praise the magnificence of the dead . . .

Tetélestai
CONRAD AIKEN

I sat on the porch with Black Jack to my left and a bottle of Steven Routenfield's grand armagnac to my right and three lifeless bodies in the yard in front of me. The smell of pepper still clung to my clothes.

Basset finally arrived with a flourish of white rooster tails that whipped up behind the two government-gray vans. Weapons bristled from their windows like hockey sticks. At the sight of them skidding to a stop in the frozen yard I emptied more of the armagnac and rubbed the back of my neck.

"Where the hell were you?" Basset asked as he spilled from the forward van. Stepping casually over one of the corpses he said, "Where the hell's Jakaz?"

"You tell me," I said.

"He didn't come out of the valve," Basset said. He walked awkwardly around the three bodies and inspected them with his toe. An AR-18S dangled from his hand. "The Pontiac went *in*, but it sure as hell didn't come *out*." He waved the carbine's muzzle in a line from the drive to a spot somewhere behind me as though Jakaz had driven into Routenfield's lodge and left an oil stain on the carpet.

I said, "It went back out. It had to."

"Couldn't have," Basset said. "We had both ends of the road blocked and there was no way around us. All the Forestry

289

Service roads dead-end in the woods. We covered the only way out."

"Yes," I said. "Of course. How much traffic went through your valve?"

"It looks like—" he shifted the AR-18S to the crook of his arm and pulled a rumpled piece of lined yellow note paper from his jacket "—like just short of three dozen. Everything that went in came out again."

"Except the lime-colored Pontiac."

"Well, yeah." Basset looked around the yard and focused at last on the two crippled Cadillacs that formed a T against the servants' A-frame. "Jeez," he said. "What's that?"

"Not much," I said and watched while fifteen of our people climbed stiffly from the vans and stood around them like chicks around a couple of mother hens. They were waiting for directions.

Basset walked toward the Fleetwoods with the sort of heavy gait reserved for innocents and process servers. He looked inside and said, "You did a hell of a job, babe."

"Weaver?" I said. Weaver stepped from the group around the closer van. "Get rid of these bodies, will you? Drag them around to the far side of the servants' lodge." When he'd gotten three men working on it I said, "They ditched my Plymouth somewhere down the road. Take a few people and see if you can find it."

"Right," Weaver said.

"And, Weaver?"

He paused.

I jerked my head toward Black Jack. "Take this guy with you."

"Sure," he said. "St. Mallard's?"

"No. Let him pay his own medical bill; take him to the nearest bus stop and dump him."

290

Black Jack stared at me with saucer eyes. He tried to speak but couldn't. The blow to his solar plexus had fouled his motor responses.

"Just get him out of here," I said. "I suppose we could nail him as an accessory to kidnapping, but it's not likely that the F. O. would let me press charges." I shook my head at Black Jack. "Keep your nose clean. Forget what you saw here, or . . ." I clutched my throat and rolled my eyes up.

He nodded until his head threatened to come loose.

"You talk about what happened tonight and you'll get nothing but trouble. We don't exist. This place doesn't exist. You don't exist. You weren't here today. You spent the whole time in your TV recliner, right?"

"A hell of a job," Basset said again as he walked back to the porch.

"Find my car," I said to Weaver. Then to Basset I said, "You stay."

"I dunno what you're so hacked about," Basset said.

He'd scrounged a fresh bottle of brandy and we had finished half of it. Although Weaver had returned my gray Plymouth before leaving for L.A., Basset and I still sat on the porch steps. I didn't want to wait in the car; it would have been too comfortable.

I said, "It's nothing Frank. Forget it."

"Okay," Basset said.

"Nothing at all," I said and massaged my eyebrows. "We lost Jakaz . . . Routenfield's dead . . . we're sure to lose SoCal SubSection . . . and if you think this place looks like a charnel house, wait until the F. O. gets us on the carpet tomorrow."

He said, "Oh." Along with the brandy, Basset had found a

full carton of Pall Mall Golds and was determined to chain-smoke all two hundred of them. "You sure she'll come back tonight?"

I inclined my head. "She said she would."

We puffed quietly, Basset on his cigarette and I on my cigar. Finally he said, "You smell funny; like pepper gas."

"Cat repellent," I said. "That guy . . . the body who wiped out the bodies in the yard and in the Fleetwood . . . that guy hung five pressurized cans of cat repellent in the central heating system with a wire coat hanger. When the stuff went off I thought I'd choke to death."

Basset said, "It sure smells lousy."

"Don't tell me. I'm inside my clothes and a hell of a lot closer to it."

Basset lit a fresh cigarette with the butt of the old one. "So what'd you find out?" he said.

"Nothing. I found out that the guy who wasted Routenfield was hired by the dissidents in Jakaz' group in Tirana."

"The guy tell you that?"

"The process of elimination told me that," I said. "Ask yourself why anyone would have wanted the old man dead."

Basset sucked on his Pall Mall and filled the night with smoke. He said, "Well, um . . ."

"Put it this way: What was Routenfield doing? And why would anyone want to stop him from doing it?"

"Well, sure, he was giving a lot of dough to Jakaz."

"Which made Jakaz powerful in Tirana," I said.

"I'll be go to hell," Basset said. "So this other faction hired a hired killer."

"Nicely put," I said.

"I didn't think those guys even existed anymore."

"They exist. Not many, but they're out there."

"We going to track him down?"

I shaved a piece of ash from my cigar and watched it tumble

into the snow. It hissed, then formed a little gray ring. "What for? So, we catch him. So what? He hasn't broken any federal laws . . ."

"Murder," Basset interrupted.

". . . and if he had, we wouldn't have the power to arrest him anyway," I finished.

"Murder," Basset said again. "We could turn him over to FBI."

"That's part of the California code," I said. "According to federal law there's nothing wrong with murder. Hell, the most the FBI could nail him with is violation of the Civil Rights Act."

"You're kidding."

"I'm not. He deprived Routenfield, Strauss and six others of their constitutionally guaranteed civil rights and life, liberty and the pursuit of happiness," I said. "It sounds nutty, but that's the way the law works. And unless the F. O. tells us to give some assistance to the Attorney General in Sacramento, we don't even worry about it."

Basset plugged his mouth with the armagnac bottle and tilted it up. Bubbles surged up in the bottle as he drank.

"This whole thing has become a farce," I said. "A farce or a tragedy, I'm not sure which." Before he could empty it I took the bottle from Basset's huge hand and eased my nerves with a swallow of the stuff. "Routenfield just wanted people to listen to him. He'd always been an administrator in the business world, and the role of silent partner was one he couldn't live with."

"You betcha," Basset said, looking pointedly at the two Cadillacs.

I said, "He wanted this meeting with Jakaz' supposed superior so he could make policy and implement some of his bizarre ideas. And he had a few lulus when it came to political theories."

"What was he; one of those 'the Chinese Army is massing in Tijuana' people?"

"Something like that. He was the sort of body who'd believe almost any story that was told to him . . . as long as it was what he wanted to hear." I drank again and passed the brandy to Basset. "Jakaz was feeding him one hell of a line—one hell of a piece of fiction."

Basset said, "You mean there isn't any 'Group of Ten' in Tirana?"

"I'm sure there is," I said. "But they aren't operational in sabotage, subversion and covert hanky-panky. Not yet at any rate. If they were, Strauss wouldn't have told Jakaz to . . . ahn . . . I think he said, 'Put a lot of flak and fireworks into your reports.' Whatever it was, I got the feeling that Jakaz was culling his stuff from the East European press."

"Yeah," Basset said. "So that's why the other guys in Tirana wanted to cut off Jakaz' water . . . so they could become a real C and D unit?"

I nodded. "They've succeeded."

Mary Louise didn't arrive until after ten o'clock. Her little Chevy Vega pulled into the frozen yard, sniffed once at the two ruined Fleetwoods, then crawled to the porch steps and peered at Basset and me with bright headlights.

Shielding my eyes from the glare I tried to give her a calm, reassuring smile. But Mary Louise wasn't having any. In her haste she left both the engine and headlights on as she jumped from the car and ran to me.

"Charley, oh my God Charley, what's happened here?" Her face had gone white and her nostrils flared with shock.

"Turn off the car," I said to Basset. Then, to Mary Louise, "You'd better come over here and sit down."

She watched Basset as he wambled to her car. "I recognize that man. Wasn't he with you when . . . ?" She swiveled her face mechanically from me to the Cadillacs and back again. "Where's Papa?" Her voice began a hysterical ascent from speech to scream as she said, "Where *is* he, Charley?" Mary Louise took a step up and called to the house, *"PAPA? Mr. Strauss?"*

I rose and caught her before she could run into the lodge. "Let's sit down and talk about it, lover." I tried to pat her shoulder but she grabbed my wrist and stared at me with frightening intensity.

Basset had turned off the Vega. We could hear his heavy footsteps as he crunched toward us through the snow.

"Sit," I said again and forced her down. It took every last pound of my weight to do it; Mary Louise was a big girl.

Glancing at Basset then at me she said, "Who *is* he, Charley? Who are you? What is this about?"

"It's about lying," I said. "And it's about time we told each other the truth. Like, why your father came here."

"He comes here every winter," she said.

"No, not Steven Routenfield, pussycat. Your *father*. Tibor Kovács." She stared at me as though I had run a knife into her stomach. "Why did he come here in sixty-three? Why'd he go to Miami in sixty-four?"

"Oh, Charley." Her face quivered with terror.

"Why, Mary Louise?" I wondered how far I'd have to push before getting an answer. "C'mon, level with me. We dug him up from the Holy Name Cemetery just two days ago."

When her fist flew at me I lifted a defensive arm. Basset caught her from behind before she could strike again. "Give me some answers," I said coolly. "Why did your father come to the States? Was he here all the time?"

Basset said, "You'd better tell us, Miss Kovács."

Two tributaries of tears coursed down her cheeks and pooled beneath her nose. "He came here to *die*," she screamed. "My father wanted to die in *peace* . . . he wanted to see Nina and me, and die away from the horror that he'd faced over there."

"Did he bring anything with him?" Basset asked. "Any files? Anything like that?"

Mary Louise said, "Oh my dear sweet lord, you're with them. You're one of Milos Kay's people."

"No . . ." I began.

"What are you after? What is it that all of you people want?"

"Listen to me," I said. "I'm not one of Milos Kay's people. I'm one of the people who're going to nail Milos Kay. Tell me who Istvan is."

"Who?"

"Istvan, a man from Miami. I gather he's watching your sister Nina, and I want to know who he is."

"No," she sobbed. "No no. That's what we ran from."

"Milos Kay is what you ran from," I said. "This man Istvan is what you ran from. Help me find them, Mary Louise."

"No. No no no." She looked as though she was trying to stuff both fists into her mouth at the same time. "Charley, you lied to me."

I shrugged. "You lied to the world, lover. Lying is something we do, we human bodies. Maybe we can make a fresh start . . . if you'll tell me who Istvan is."

Mary Louise's nose was running. "Can't I trust anyone?" she sobbed at the trees. Then facing skyward, "*Not anyone?*"

"You can trust me," I said. "At least you can trust me more than you could have trusted your father . . . and certainly more than you could have trusted Steven Routenfield."

"Could have?" She looked at the two Cadillacs with fresh understanding. Without warning Mary Louise stood and Basset, who'd been hovering over her and pinning her arms, fell backward.

As she ran toward the cars I said, "Don't," but she was nearly there before I could rise from the steps. We were not unprepared. Basset pulled a syringe of Demerol from his jacket while we jogged after her.

Mary Louise looked into the pinned car. Before she fainted her scream cut like a razor through the fabric of the night.

49

Q: You have commented on the pressures of your work, sir. It seems to me that the average man would break down were he faced with the Herculean problems you treat so lightly.
A: Ahn . . . yes. Yes, sir.

Minutes of the Hearings,
Subcommittee on National Security Affairs
Volume CDIV
Page 4

Two squad cars were parked fender to fender in the dark, their black-enameled steel and polished chrome smiling Cheshirelike while red lights blinked in their rear windows like angry, bloodshot eyes behind Brobdingnagian spectacles.

At the sight of them I turned to Basset and said, "Where did you set up your valve?"

Basset thought about it. "About a half mile down the road," he said.

"Did you check that Forestry Service road?" I pointed at the squad cars beside it.

"Hell no, babe. Those things don't go anywhere."

I nodded skeptically. "You have any impressive looking federal ID?" I asked.

"Weaver had some nifty FBN credentials for the raid," Basset said. He tapped a finger on the TEMP light that glowed on the dash. It stayed on in spite of him.

I said, "I mean right here, right now. What've you got that looks good?"

"I've got a whole bunch of stuff," Basset said. He guided the Plymouth's wheel with his knees while he dug into his pockets with both hands. "How about USDA?" Offering me a card he said, "Meat inspector."

"Keep digging," I said. We crawled slowly toward the winking red lights. Through the windshield I could see the choreography of disaster; frantically waving cops, white jacketed attendants closing the back door of an ambulance with the sort of insouciance that let you know their cargo was in no particular hurry, and finally the tow-truck crew carelessly dragging a lime-green Pontiac from the Forestry road onto the main highway.

Basset said, "That's all the federal stuff I've got. How about Sacramento?"

"Okay. What is it?"

"Deputy Assistant Attorney General, State of California, Great Seal thereof affixed."

Taking the ID from him I struck a match to read the name and jammed it into my pocket. I glanced at the back seat. Mary Louise slept quietly in a Demerol dream. I pulled the blanket over her face and opened the door. "When you get to the amusement zone, pull in *beyond* the far CHP car," I said as I stepped out.

After a curt glance at me the sergeant returned his attention to the sparse but creeping traffic. "Back in the car, buddy." He didn't miss a beat with his impressive arm gestures. "This ain't the movies." I expected the cars at which he waved to respond with a crescendo of arythmic sound.

Without speaking I held Basset's card in his face. He read it.

"I'm sorry, Mr. Waxman. We get a lot of . . ."

"Forget it," I said. "The bodies in that Pontiac, are they banged up much?"

299

"We only found one occupant, sir."

"Dead?"

He nodded. "No identification; just a John Doe with a healthy tan."

That would be Istvan. "How did it happen?"

"Forced off the road, sir. Here, you can see the tire tracks." He flashed his huge Kel-Lite on the converging marks. "The forcing vehicle exited the road at a merging speed with the subject vehicle, then slowed and collided with the subject vehicle's left front fender and headlight. After the subject vehicle turned into the service road, the other vehicle stopped for a period of no less than five minutes, but not much longer than ten."

"How can you tell?"

"Two indications," he said. "First, the vehicle left four distinct tire spots where it was parked. Second, they left the engine on; it blew a lot of heat into the snow and melted it. See, right there."

"I see." I was beginning to see too much. "Any witnesses on the other car?"

"Yes sir. The subject vehicle." He motioned me to follow him to the tow truck. "We've got paint scrapings all over this left-front area." He shocked the Pontiac's damaged fender with his Kel-Lite and I squatted to look at it. "White paint . . . cheap stuff, I'd say, like one of those thirty-buck jobs. But we can't tell until it goes through the lab in Sacramento."

"Terrific," I said and looked up at him. "Thanks for your time."

At the car again I said, "Open the door, Frank." Basset stared at me, his face a question mark of confusion. I said it again, "Open the God-damned door." My hands were clutched and I couldn't get them loose.

Once inside I pressed my trembling hands against my stom-

300

ach and said, "Have you got any more Demerol?" I'd become uncontrollably rigid and was vibrating in the seat like a badly tuned motor. "I think I'm cracking up."

"Oh hell babe, not you . . ." Basset began, then looked at me and said, "You look rotten." He smashed open the glove box and pulled out the first-aid kit he'd taken from the van. There were enough disposable syringes in it to addict half of California. Basset emptied one of them into me.

"Jakaz is gone," I said.

"You mean dead?"

"Gone. The other one's dead. Somebody kidnapped Jakaz. Some body."

"Who?" Basset shook his head in disbelief. "KGB?"

"Couldn't have been," I said. "They couldn't have known. What we've got is an entirely new bunch. Not KGB. Not Beebee Haring's people, if any. And probably not the 'Group of Ten' dissidents."

"Jeez, the F. O.'s gonna love that." He started the Plymouth and pulled into the slowly moving line of traffic. A horn blared. Basset raised his left fist, middle finger extended, and pumped it twice at the honker.

I said, "Right now I don't give much of a damn what he loves or hates or even feels mildly affectionate toward." The drug was beginning to penetrate the motor area of my brain. The shaking had stopped and I felt a slight euphoria. "You should have seen the inside of that car, pal. Blood all over, like that Fleetwood back at Routenfield's lodge."

"Look, don't think about it," Basset said. "Try to get some Zs, babe."

"Jakaz is gone," I said. "He slipped through our fingers like money."

"Well, we've still got the girl."

"Yes," I said. I thought about her all the way to St. Mallard's, not sure what we should do with her now that we had her. After dropping Mary Louise off at the hospital I was still awake, though groggy, and wondering if she did love me madly.

Before I finally went to sleep Basset said, "I've been thinking."

"Congratulations," I said.

"We shoulda grabbed another bottle of Routenfield's booze before we left," he said.

50

weight . . . 187

fortune . . . You are soon to begin a long and pleasant vacation

"You are familiar with our counterinsurgent training base in Bosque Mojado?" the F. O. said.

"No," I lied.

The F. O.'s office was depressing. It was filled with people who were bent on stripping it bare. Glenda helped the F. O. wrap his more valuable memorabilia in yesterday's news while three large bodies carried away heavy things in their blunt fingers. Basset tried to look useful. I leaned against a wall. The chairs had gone first.

Even with the furniture disappearing the place seemed confining.

"Par'me," said one of the large bodies as he and another shuffled out with the tuxedo sofa.

"You will enjoy it," the F. O. said. It was an order, not a casual observation. "They've solved much of the insect problem. And you'll be inoculated until you resemble a pincushion; so there is little chance of malaria or trypanosomiasis." He stabbed me with a miserable look and said, "More's the pity."

"Try a pan o' what?" Basset asked. He reached for a Crown Derby ashtray and a sheet of newspaper.

"Don't touch that!" the F. O. said.

"Sleeping sickness," Glenda said.

Basset dropped the newspaper.

"Not that, damn it. That!"

Basset replaced the ashtray.

"You'll miss skiing at first, but you will get over it soon enough I should think. There's quite a bit in the rain forest to occupy your mind, such as it is."

I watched Glenda's thin little hands as they swaddled the F. O.'s humidor in the Sunday funnies.

The F. O. said, "The discomforts will seem trivial compared to your sense of accomplishment as you train fine young people in the art of jungle combat. I almost envy you."

"Jeez." Basset couldn't decide what to do with his hands. He warmed them under his armpits at first but the sweat was pouring through his seersucker jacket. He pulled them out and wiped them on his pants. "Look, seriously," he said. "My wife'll kill me if we get relocated. I mean, we've got payments on the house . . . things like that." He stuffed his hands in his pockets and jingled coins and keys until the F. O. stared him into silence. Basset's hands finally grappled with each other behind his back. They looked like two hams at a choir fund lottery.

"Oh, she'll be happy enough," the F. O. said. "God knows, she won't get bored. There's no electricity in the jungle. No washing machines, no hair driers, no toasters."

In Basset's eyes I could see his wife, up to her thighs in a stream, beating soiled laundry with a rock. He said, "C'mon, seriously. You're kidding us, right?" The juice had drained from him.

"I cannot think of a time when I've been more serious. You two have plunged a knife into my career. Did you think to ask how my wife feels? Certainly not. I am pushing fifty," the F. O. said, neglecting to mention that he wasn't pushing fifty but clinging desperately to it while kicking at sixty. "I am too old to become a faceless nit in Virginia whose most taxing de-

304

cision is whether to keep his paper clips in a drawer or in a cup on top of his desk. *Of course I'm serious.*" He smiled dangerously. "I only regret that there is no worse place to send you."

The last cardboard carton was packed. There was nothing left to remove from the room but that and the F. O.'s desk. Glenda scrawled cryptic figures on the carton just above ALMADEN MOUNTAIN RED CLARET. She copied the carton's code number on a yellow legal-sized pad that listed the physical condition of everything they had packed.

It was all very neat and efficient, the death of the F. O.'s career. Not at all like the haphazard carnage of yesterday.

The three movers listened intently to Glenda's ballpoint as it oozed across the paper. They had not looked at any of us while hauling away the F. O.'s life, but kept their toes in the carpet and their embarrassment to themselves.

Basset couldn't stand the silence. "Look, what are we . . . infallible? You want us to do a water-walking number for you? I mean, Beebee was on ice; he couldn't have told anyone that Jakaz was loose. How could we know that someone else was after Jakaz? What the hell, babe, we gave you Dr. Kovács' remains. And we found out why everyone was after Jakaz' and Kovács' files. What do you want from us?"

"Blood," the F. O. said. "And you are not to address me as 'babe.' I am not at all interested in your paternal fantasies." He pulled a thin gold pen from his pocket and initialed the sheets in Glenda's notepad. He nodded to the movers. They walked out with the desk, the last carton and what was left of the F. O.'s status within the Agency.

"Had you bumbled something less . . ." he searched for the words ". . . less sensitive, less delicate than this project, I would cover for you and think nothing of it. But as things stand . . ." The F. O. turned his back to us and stared down at Hope Street. The smog seemed more fascinating than Basset or I.

Glenda mouthed a silent, "Tonight?" with an exaggerated, almost antic stretching of her lips. When I nodded she blew me an equally silent kiss.

"As things stand," the F. O. told the window, "I am throwing both of you to the wolves. Your expense accounts are being audited and you'll end up owing the Agency at least three months' pay. You . . ." he spun to jab a neatly manicured finger at Basset ". . . you are going to return every penny of kickbacks you've gotten from the rental of that house on Mulholland." He turned the finger on me like a divining rod. "You've been unusually silent. Is there something on your mind, or did you drink yourself to sleep as usual last night?"

The envelope I drew from my jacket and handed to him was straining its thinly glued seams.

The F. O. said, "What's this?"

"My resignation."

His eyes narrowed and his mouth became a crescent that pulled down at both corners. "You will resign from the Agency when I *tell* you to resign. Not one second before and not a breath later." The F. O. held my envelope between his thumb and forefinger like something he'd scraped from his shoe.

"What you're holding is my past. You'll never get your hands on my future again."

"Don't be an idiot," the F. O. said. "Take this thing back."

I made a theatrical gesture of spading my fingers into my pants pockets.

The F. O. looked at the envelope. Then he looked at me. "Don't be an idiot," he said again. "What do you expect me to do with this thing."

I said, "If the fit isn't exactly right, you might get some help from your proctologist," and walked out.

As usual nobody laughed.

51

The busy bee has no time for sorrow.

Proverbs of Hell
WILLIAM BLAKE

North of Malibu and just above Point Dume, Pacific Coast Highway curves as gently as the arched back of a yawning girl. On summer weekends you can hardly reach the place; traffic is a solid, indigestible knot from Sunset Beach to Silver Strand. But on a cool midwinter night you would have the road to yourself.

I turned the Bentley left toward the ocean, leaving the highway and driving down a private road that was surfaced with pitted asphalt. We were stopped by a chain-link gate to which a large sign was wired. In the glare of my headlights the sign warned us of a number of local and county ordinances that we would violate if we trespassed.

I shook a key from the envelope that Basset had given me and pointed at a lock post that peered at Glenda through the left-hand window. She turned the key in the lock and the electric gate swung grudgingly open. I drove through.

"There it is," I said.

Basset's wife's father had bought the private cove in '33. The beach was supposed to be public up to the high-tide line, but the only way you could get to it was through the gate—palisades of sheer rock embraced the three-acre parcel and kept strangers away as effectively as a pack of angry dogs. There was an asphalt parking strip above the high-water mark. A planked walkway led to the boat slip. Basset's father-in-law had never built a house on the land—not even a summer place. His wife's sinus condition was aggravated by salt air.

"I'll buy it," Glenda said.

"Half a million," I said.

She nodded, her pink hair floating around her head like unclear thoughts. "You buy it. Too rich for my blood."

I killed the engine and the Pacific's rhythmic sounds came in through the Bentley's open windows. "I'd like to," I said. "But I'm not even sure if I'll get two-weeks-severance-in-lieu-of-vacation pay."

"Oh, Charley." Glenda put her small hand on my knee and I kicked the underside of the dashboard.

"I'm ticklish," I said and pulled her hand away.

Basset's wife's father's boat was an impressive sport fisherman with a flying bridge above and not much stability below. Glenda started turning green in less than five minutes. Like blue, as she'd said when she declined to hold her breath, it didn't go well with her hair.

"I think I'm going to upchuck," she said.

I pointed her toward the lee rail and steadied our course on southwest by south. I checked my watch again: Ten thirty-four. At ten thirty-nine I would bring the boat around to south-southeast and start scanning the bow for running lights.

Glenda turned her pale face to me and said, "you sure this is the way to Catalina?" Even her freckles had disappeared.

"It's the scenic route," I said and gestured at a monotonous vista of whitecaps that looked like meringues in a dimly lit restaurant.

She said, "Ha, ha," and rinsed the bad taste from her mouth

with a swallow of Korbel straight from the bottle. "You've been very cool about this whole affair."

"It's a job," I said. "Not a religion."

"You're really really serious?"

"Maybe maybe."

"What will you do? Get into private investigations?"

I patted my pockets for a cigar, then realized that I couldn't light it in this wind and keep on course. "It's a hard decision. I'm too old to apprentice for honest work yet I'm sick of inspecting people's dirty laundry. Maybe I'll go back to Stanford, get my doctorate and a teaching credential. It's a less punishing field, student riots and all."

Glenda made a wry face. "What would you teach, snooping?" She snuggled next to me and insinuated her fingers under my jacket and into my shirt. She pulled at the hair on my chest. "I suppose you could always give cooking classes."

"Languages," I said. "My Slavonics and Urgics are still pretty good, though I'll need some work on Sorbian."

"Hohum," Glenda said, "to quote a former Project Officer I once knew."

"Not yet," I said. "Not quite yet."

"You're speaking in tongues already," Glenda said. "Not yet what?"

"I'm not a former Project Officer yet. I promised the little man that I'd clean up one detail before my resignation becomes official."

Glenda said, "Sometimes I don't understand you at all."

"If you ever do," I said, "please tell me. Then I'll be the second to know."

"Why are you doing it? What do you owe them?"

"It's a little detail on this Jakaz thing. I want it out of my hair."

"You are a funny man, Charles Remington Remly, if that

309

is still your name. Besides your incredible rudeness to the boss this morning, you haven't shown much reaction to leaving. You aren't bothered at all?"

"Certainly I'm bothered," I said. "I'm bothered about where the money's going to come from until I land another job. I'm bothered about the ominous noises in my rear end." Glenda raised a provocative eyebrow. "The *Bentley's* rear end," I said. "I think the spider gear is shot and there's no money for that, either. But as I said, the Agency isn't a religion."

"And that's all that matters to you, the money?"

"Why, hell," I said, "this whole affair has been about money. The F. O. put the screws on us because Virginia was cutting off the money for regional SubSections. Beebee wanted the Jakaz files for the money that they represented. Routenfield's man Strauss was raking ten percent off the top. Jakaz wanted to find Kovács and get back the personnel files for their power value, which is another way of saying money value. And for all we know, it *was* the money value he was interested in. Then there's me; I did maybe a little more hopping around than was absolutely necessary because I needed the extra per diem money to pour into the Bentley. Basset . . . sweet Jesus . . . it's no wonder that he and his wife don't have any kids. Basset doesn't have any energy left for that kind of thing because money is his *sole* source of amusement."

I glanced at my watch, waited exactly twenty seconds and brought the compass needle around to south-southeast.

"Well," Glenda said, "it's not your sole source of amusement, thank you very much."

I said, "Now, now," and pulled her hand from my shirt. "Don't mess with the chef, not yet." I scanned the darkness off our bow.

Glenda pointed. "There're some lights ahead."

It was a Coast Guard cutter—a WPB. In most cases Transportation is jealous about the use of its equipment, but the F. O. had a backlog of favors due from their Secretary and he'd had our Secretary call just a few of the notes. If he'd wanted, the F. O. could have requisitioned an armada.

A thirty-two-foot Chris was secured to the cutter.

"Just one quick stop," I said, "and we can get under way for Avalon."

52

EXPENSES

Item: 1 set wrist & ankle manacles Cat. #3408 $64.89

Nearly six feet of dark-blue wool separated Lieutenant Colonel Yurosha Nevigelykh's chin from the deck. The face above the chin was slightly pained and the body beneath it was as supple as a diplomat's tongue. In fact he had moved easily in dip circles until the Agency blew his U.N. cover and State pulled his visa.

A blond CPO was covering him warily with his eyes when Glenda and I clattered down the ladder into the well-scrubbed wardroom. Two sailors flanked the CPO, threatening Nevigelykh with M-16s that were only slightly more lethal than the young petty officer's glance.

The CPO turned and saluted as we entered. I responded with a nod and said, "This is it? One body?"

He glanced nervously at Nevigelykh and said, "We've got five more manacled aft. Your man's getting Polaroids and prints on them."

Glenda was turning green again. I could hardly blame her. My own stomach explored the walls of my abdomen as it searched for the exit. The eighty-two-foot WPB was designed for cruising and pursuit, not for lying to. It wallowed drunkenly against its hook in the channel current.

I said, "Did they get mug shots of this one?"

"Yes sir. Mugs and prints both. The big guy did him first."

I smiled. We wanted the Russian to be humiliated; it was part of the plan. Getting his fingerprints and a handful of color pictures was just the beginning. "How are ya, Yuri?" I said.

"Big guy?" Glenda asked.

Nevigelykh nodded stiffly at me.

"Yes, ma'am," the CPO said. "Mr. Beagle from your office."

I peeled a cigar and somehow got it lit without losing my toehold on the deck. Nevigelykh watched with a trace of amusement when I nearly gagged on the first puff and smothered the thing in an ashtray. Even more than I resented his assurance, I envied his sea legs. My own were as effective as Silly Putty.

Nevigelykh materialized a pack of Sputniks from his pea jacket and shook out a cigarette. After screwing it into his face he set fire to it. When Basset lumbered in, pushing Jakaz ahead of him, Yurosha Nevigelykh hardly noticed. He focused on a point between Glenda and me, and didn't look at Jakaz who was dripping manacle chains from his hands and feet.

Basset shoved Jakaz next to the colonel. Carrying a second set of manacles, he walked around the wardroom table to stand beside me. He looked glum. "The rest of 'em are just a bunch of Russian sailor boys." He bobbed his head in apology to the CPO. "No offense, okay?"

"You'll have to leave," I said to the CPO. "This requires clearance up to Q level."

The two sailors were disappointed. They seldom had live people at whom to point their M-16s. "Aye aye, sir," the chief said. The last man out closed the hatch with a clang and secured it.

Once they were gone I turned to Yurosha and said, "You've got ink on your fingers, Yuri." He dragged on his cigarette without glancing at his hands. Beside him Jakaz maintained a noncommittal expression. "I thought of merely delivering a cordial note to your mail drop at the Music Center," I said. "But the F. O. suggested that I take Gyula Jakaz away from you and give you the message in person."

Glenda said, "I'm going up for some air."

Before she could turn toward the hatch I put a gentle hand on her elbow and said, "This won't take more than a couple of minutes." To Nevigelykh I said, "We have personnel files, Yuri. And they're really something, let me tell you—over eighty-five thousand names and perhaps thirty pages per entry."

"I have never truly appreciated American humor," he said calmly.

Jakaz, though, wasn't sure how to react. He'd been after those files for a long miserable time.

I shrugged. Glenda and Basset were turning *verde nauseado* and my own face was feeling clammy. Only Yurosha seemed cool as he puffed at his Sputnik. My objective was to press him into losing his temper. I didn't seem to be achieving my goal.

I said, "I've got a warped sense of humor. I wanted to see your face when you heard that we have the files. I thought there might be some amusement value—maybe I was wrong."

He still didn't believe me.

I tried again, speaking slowly as though to a child: "It's a fact. We've got the name of every AVH employee in the world, current as of nineteen fifty-six, and of every KGB face that came over the wall that year posing as a . . . you'll forgive me . . . a 'Freedom Fighter.' "

"Bluff," Yurosha said. "You have taken Jakaz back. Do not waste your breath on ill-considered jokes."

I shrugged again; I would get a cramp in my shoulders if I kept it up. "When we start hauling in your faces next week, you'll have more than ink on your fingers."

The hatch wheel squeaked and the CPO flew down the

ladder and landed with a bang on the deck. "That Russian whaler's starting to move. It's closing on us at eleven knots."

"How fast will this thing go?"

"Twenty-seven knots," he said.

"Towing the Chris and the sportfisher?"

"Um . . . yes sir . . . maybe closer to twenty-three."

"Give us a shout if they get too close. We'll make for territorial water and finish up there."

"Aye aye, sir," the CPO said and went back up the ladder.

"About these files, now," I said. "The first thing you have to understand . . ."

"Enough!" Nevigelykh boomed. "I understand that you are wasting my time."

Good, I thought. He was reacting. "Don't flatter yourself," I said easily, pressing for his soft spot. "You're a nice enough guy, Yuri, but let's face it . . ." I let the words hang between us like a smirch on his mental capacity.

Basset shifted nervously and Glenda touched my arm. I smiled at them and said, "I realize everyone's in something of a rush so I'll keep it brief." Turning my smile on the colonel I said, "But you really ought to hear the whole story."

Yurosha opened his mouth to speak but I held up a self-deprecating hand. "No," I said. "No, don't thank me. I'm glad to do it for you, Yuri."

Leveling a finger at Jakaz I said, "You were the only man in Nyiregyháza who had access to all of the AVH personnel files. And you realized that the man who could carry those files out of Hungary could use them for money or power . . . or, the best of all possible worlds, both. But you faced a problem; the one thing that made the files valuable also made them impossible to steal. They were almost too comprehensive. I mean, what the hell, with more than eighty-five thousand personnel entries and maybe five hundred entries on KGB faces—at

315

thirty pages per entry—you'd end up with over two-and-a-half million pieces of paper. Maybe even three."

Nevigelykh puffed on his Sputnik like an automated smog machine. When he spoke, his words were formed in clouds of smoke: "I am not going to become irritated with you, young man."

"Does it make you feel noble?" I asked, but he didn't respond. "Okay, the next question was, How do you get nearly three million pieces of paper out of what is essentially a police state?" I looked from Nevigelykh to Jakaz. Although they remained expressionless I knew they were irritated by my reiteration of the obvious. "Any answers to that one?"

"You are making yourself a fool," the colonel said.

"Even microfilm wouldn't do it," I said with a smile. "It was just too much physical stuff to try to smuggle, three million frames of data. So, what's the one thing no one can search at the borders?" I looked at Nevigelykh and spread a thick layer of sincerity across my face. "C'mon, Yuri. I heard you were pretty good at these games."

"I am quickly losing patience with you . . ." he began.

"Can't answer? I'll give you a hint." I tapped my forehead. "The mind, Yuri, the mind. Gyula Jakaz found a mnemonics whiz at Péter Pazmány University; a body named Tibor Kovács." I paused and rubbed the back of my neck. Yurosha was right; it was a sophomoric performance. Sophomoric but effective.

"At any rate, I'm sure we all know about that—about how Dr. Kovács programmed between two and a half and three million pieces of paper into two human minds. It was the perfect filing system, and the subjects never knew they'd been programmed. Those two AVH bodies . . ." I snapped my fingers and said, "I almost forgot. Do you know how many words that represented? Over one and a half *billion*." They

316

didn't look impressed. "Boggles the imagination, doesn't it?"

"Charley," Glenda said, "I really don't feel well." She didn't look well either.

"I'll make it fast, lover," I said. "I think they'll want to know what happened to the two AVH 'filing cabinets.'"

Jakaz leaned forward slightly, his manacled hands turning white at the knuckles.

I said, "Kovács let them go. Somewhere in Austria he simply turned them loose."

"No!" Jakaz said. "No, they were priceless."

I smiled solicitously. "That's a very relative word, 'priceless.' It all depends on your perspective."

"Impossible," Jakaz said. "He would never release them."

"Very possible," I said. "He let them go for the same reason he came to see his two daughters here in the States: Tibor Kovács had Parkinson's disease. Where he was quickly going, the money and the power were useless to him."

By now Basset was leaning on the wardroom table.

"I suppose that's it," I said. "I hope you'll forgive me for dominating the conversation." Then to Basset I said, "Why don't you have the sailors put that extra set of manacles on Yuri before you return him to his boat."

"Jeez," Basset said. "I dunno how the F. O.'d go for it. I had to check these cuffs out personally—they'll deduct it from my pay if I lose 'em."

"I'll give you the money if they do," I said. "It'll be worth it, imagining the stupid expression on Yuri's face when he boards the trawler, all chained up like Marley's ghost."

I helped Glenda up the ladder and paused with a hand on the hatch. "I've neglected to explain about our copies of those files," I said to Nevigelykh.

I tried to sound even more like an idiot than I may in fact be, because no one—especially not Yurosha Nevigelykh—likes

317

to hear the truth from his inferiors. "What do you usually do with important documents? I mean, besides the usual protection of fireproof safes and whatnot."

He didn't answer. He was smashing the cigarette like a poisonous insect beneath his heel.

"You make duplicates," I said. "No matter how sensitive the stuff is, you make duplicates if the files are really important."

Jakaz began to get it even before I spoke. His face was developing a fine screen of horizontal lines. "You and Istvan were sitting on the duplicate files all the time," I told him. "Kovács programmed his daughters for insurance."

Jakaz exploded silently. He looked apoplectic; his eyes bulged and sweat bathed his face. Yurosha took it with a much calmer attitude. He turned gray.

"Nina and Mary Louise are in a private hospital we maintain," I said, "and they are talking to us from a deep, deep sleep. Narcohypnotics put the information in, narcohypnotics is getting the information out."

I turned to Glenda. She looked awful, as though the world had caught up with her and stuck in her throat. I said, "Let's get out of here."

"Take me home, Charley," Glenda said. "Get me away from all this damn water."

"Yes." I opened the hatch and followed her out.

53

Nothing except a battle lost can be half so melancholy as a battle won.

ARTHUR WELLESLEY, DUKE OF WELLINGTON
(In a dispatch, 1815)

Except for saying, "That was quite a show," Glenda was silent as I brought the sportfisher back to Basset's father-in-law's cove. She said it again as we threw our overnighters into the Bentley: "That was quite a show."

I didn't respond. I didn't think she expected me to. At the top of the private drive I turned left.

"South is the other way, Magellan," Glenda said.

I said, "I know," shifted from second to third and settled into the Bentley's plush old leather for security. When I shifted to fourth I let my hand linger a while on the gear lever's mahogany knob and wondered whether it was pleasure I found in the car or escape.

"Where are you going, Charley-the-spy?"

"One more stop," I said. "The F. O. has a quarantine house up near Point Mugu."

She clicked a fingernail against an incisor. "Someone going into protective quarantine?"

I nodded.

When she said, "PSE?" I nodded again.

"And where to after that?"

"On a therapeutic drunk," I said. "I've got a lot to forget."

"Taking me with you? I could use a little amnesia."

I shook my head and gripped the wheel with more pressure than it really needed. "No way."

In the dim glow of the instrument lights I saw a tear crawl sadly down her cheek and stop just short of her lips. Glenda licked it away absentmindedly. She fumbled in her purse for a Kleenex. "Stop the car, Charley?"

"No way," I said again.

"Please stop the car." Her voice bounced around in an upper register, looking for a high soprano note it wasn't sure of. "I'm going to be sick."

I shifted down to third to take a slight bend in the road.

Glenda touched my arm and pleaded, "I'm going to be sick. Don't make me throw up on my new pantsuit and your upholstery."

She had a point. I down shifted to second and eased into an emergency parking cutout. Before I could kill the ignition Glenda was out of the door and becoming violently ill on Pacific Coast Highway. She made keening noises like a dying animal. I set the brake and climbed after her.

I held her head in my hands and tried to wipe the sweat from her forehead. Glenda retched again but nothing came.

"Did you have to do it like that?" she asked. "All that show of packing up the F. O.'s office . . . your resignation . . . parading me in front of Yuri while you humiliated him?"

I smoothed her tears away with a gentle finger. Glenda had lost her sardonic look.

She said, "It was cruel, Charley. Sadistic."

"Pragmatic," I said. "I didn't want you to warn him, and I had to humiliate him. Had to. Now Yurosha thinks you've turned your coat again to meet the changing wind. If he's insinuated anyone else into the Agency, he's going to be nervous about their reliability. We want him nervous."

320

Glenda said, "And now I'm going into quarantine." She shook her head. "When Yuri doesn't hear from me, he'll be sure I've gone over."

"Absolutely sure."

"Oh, Charley. Don't you know how dangerous that could be for me?"

"I know," I said.

A set of headlights came at us from the north. We made a bizarre couple; Glenda squatting on her haunches, a Kleenex in one little fist, and me kneeling beside her as though we were sharing secrets. I looked down from the headlights and blinked. But I wasn't too blind to see her fist arcing toward my eyes. It was the white flash of tissue that warned me.

I rolled away from her, jerking my head back at the same moment. Thank God for reflexes, I thought as she caught my cheekbone and the wing of my nose. Glenda had palmed a nail file in the Kleenex. The thing had opened up my face and I felt a warm ooze of blood beneath the sting of the cuts. "Knock that off," I shouted as I reached for her hand.

Glenda didn't knock it off. She had something else in mind.

I was off balance and leaning toward her and she did exactly the right thing, depending on your point of view. She grabbed my wrist and rolled aside, pulling me in the direction I'd been moving. I sprawled flat in the gravel.

Glenda's nail file buried itself in the back of my left hand. That was when I started to scream; when the thing came through my palm between the second and third metacarpal bones and bent on the crushed rock. When she tried to pull the file out—and it wouldn't come because it had formed an L beneath my hand—I went slightly berserk.

My hand was useless but my feet were still good; I kicked viciously at her face. I felt the sphenoid sinus crush under the bridge of Glenda's thin nose.

It wasn't enough.

I had rolled to my back. My left hand was on fire. I pinched it with my right as though I could somehow shut off the nerve ends. Glenda was suddenly above me and I wondered how the hell she got there.

Glenda's odd, large foot was coming down in sickening slow motion. I could see the sole pattern on her deck shoe. It was herringbone. Her foot was just above my knee and moving for my testicles. As I brought my leg around I wondered who was screaming in that clear soprano. It couldn't be Glenda, I thought. Her voice cracked on the high notes. I caught her foot with my knee and she went down like a bowling pin, feet flying up as she brought her hands around to absorb the fall.

I tried to speak and couldn't. I realized the scream was coming from my lungs. I finally rasped at her, "You've blown it. Don't make it worse."

Glenda was scrambling to her feet. "It's not over yet." There was a weird glint in her eyes. She wasn't thinking. Desperation had driven away her reason. "I can get out."

It was like trying to lift a house when I stood. Glenda said, "I'll kill you Charley," in a pleading voice but I kept moving cautiously toward her. I couldn't do much with both hands clutched together. In the effort of separating them and trying to make a fist with the right I nearly fainted.

Glenda backed a step at a time to the car. I followed. "I'll kill you," she said. "I can do it, Charley. I can."

I took another step toward her and Glenda became a flash of feinting hands that dazzled me. Her first blow was a straight-forward thrust of rigid fingers at my eyes. I parried with my crippled left hand—there are no words to describe the pain as her fingers jogged the nail file between my metacarpals—and tried to follow through with an elbow into her throat. Glenda spun away from me in a complete circle, bringing her other hand around in a second feint at my kidney. She was good at this sort of thing; they'd taught her more than typing and Gregg at the school in *Arkhangelsk*.

She was good enough to use my second parry against me and tilt me forward like a slowly falling tree. When her deck shoe connected it felt as though my kneecap was trying to circumnavigate my leg.

We were beside the Bentley's open left-hand passenger door; I sprawling in the gravel and Glenda clambering into the car, as though it was the last exit from hell and she couldn't wait for a reservation. She locked the door behind her.

Glenda was going to have a hard time starting the Bentley; that would give me one last chance at her. I hoped she hadn't watched me fiddle with the choke—three notches out and a half turn to the right to lock it in place—or pump once on the accelerator before jabbing at the starter button. One way or the other she would either starve or flood the engine.

I held good thoughts and started crawling under the car. It was like pulling myself across broken glass. My left side was useless; the hand impaled with her nail file and the knee making lumps where there should be none. At least the Bentley's eighteen-inch wheels gave me a comfortable clearance to scratch and hump and moan my way to the driver's side. Looking up I noticed the grease nipples were dry; the car needed a lube.

Headlights glinted across the oil-soaked surface of Pacific Coast Highway and flashed away, leaving me a view of receding tail lights.

I heard the throttle linkage click a half dozen times. Gas fumes assaulted my nose; she had flooded it.

The right running board was within reach and I reached for it, drawing myself from under the car with one hand while Glenda kept a finger on the starter button. It sounded as

323

though she was grinding a mountain of coffee. Pumping impatiently on the accelerator she managed to drown the engine beyond all hope.

I levered my right foot beneath me and lunged for the door handle. *Success.* The door swung open as I fell back, dangling from the handle like a subway-strap commuter. Glenda stared at me foolishly, one hand on the starter and the other clutching the wheel. She had a red goatee of blood from her broken nose.

I tried to speak. Nothing came out. I tried again. "It won't start. You flooded it."

The battery was dying under her finger. You could hear it in the declining whine of the starter.

Glenda released the button and leaned away from me. Here comes that damn foot again, I thought.

She shouldn't have tried it.

English machinery of the '30s had certain inherent discomforts; right-hand drive was not the least of them. The Bentley's floor-mounted shift and brake levers weren't in the center of the car but to the driver's right. They separated Glenda from the outside world. The nickel-plated levers were also a hindrance for her kicking foot. Her deck shoe deflected off the shift and smashed against my shoulder instead of my face. I brought my mouth down and seized the canvas and foul-tasting rubber between my teeth.

Glenda punched her foot up and down and nearly succeeded in rattling my teeth loose.

It was going to be a gamble but I didn't have much choice. Releasing the door handle I brought my right hand down against her shin as I fell, wedging it between the gear and brake levers. The blow carried the full weight of my body. I felt her tibia crack just below the knee; Glenda had brittle bones.

324

"*Charley*," she screamed.

Glenda made one attempt to extricate herself from the trap of shift and brake levers.

She shouldn't have tried that, either.

She grasped the nickel-plated pincer grip on the brake, releasing it before she fell back.

The Bentley began rolling away from me.

"Charley, get me out," Glenda said with an edge of desperation. Her oddly twisted leg dangled from the car like a piece of limp string.

"Yes," I said.

The Bentley was rolling away from me. I grabbed the front bumper.

"Charley please, please Charley. Get me out of here." The excitement in her voice was almost sexual. "Charley I'm frightened."

The car was rolling backward now, dragging me and going the wrong way in the northbound lanes and moving diagonally toward a four-by-sixteen-inch island of concerete that was meant to discourage head-on confrontations between cars traveling north and south.

Given a good left hand I might have made a grab for the lip of the fender and pulled myself toward the door. But Glenda had given me a very bad left hand indeed. Maybe the divider will stop us, I thought.

It didn't.

The Bentley went over it like a juggernaut and picked up momentum in the southbound lanes.

"Charley, please."

I said, "The brake pedal. Can you reach the brake?"

"I've tried," she said. "Every time I move it's like dying."

"You'll know what dying's like if you don't reach it," I said. "Try harder."

Glenda, the Bentley and I were off the highway now, rolling across a broad graveled parking strip. I couldn't remember if there was a guard rail at the far edge of it.

Even if she could reach the brake pedal with her hand she'd never find the leverage to press hard enough. The Bentley weighed over forty-three hundred pounds and its ancient hydraulic system called for a leg of steel.

Glenda said, "Oh Charley, I don't want to die," and I couldn't think of any reasonable alternative as the left rear tire dropped over the edge of the palisade. Dust boiled up as the differential scraped along the gravel. No, I thought, no there isn't a guard rail.

The right rear wheel joined its mate and the car slowed but didn't stop.

I shouted, "Glenda I'm sorry."

As the Bentley teetered back it lifted me up from the gravel. I let go of the bumper. Northbound headlights illuminated every greasy detail of the undercarriage.

Glenda shouted, "You're sorry," and didn't stop screaming until the Bentley slammed against the first outcropping of the palisade below.

54

My life is a series of mishaps,   6 1-2
    Of trains that ignore their rails;
Of messages from Garcia,
    That get screwed up in the mails.
                Collected Noncents
                Roy Hayes

When they did the job on my knee they used a local anes-
thetic and asked if I would like a mirror set up overhead; that
way I could watch as they worked. No thank you, I would not.

The F. O. had a better head for that sort of thing and made
cheery conversation until the OR nurse told him to leave the
operating theater. He waited for me outside the doors.

When they wheeled me out the gurney's casters made small
whirring sounds beneath the F. O.'s voice. "Our leaders are a
fascinating lot," he was saying, "especially when it comes to
secretaries whom they hire directly through Virginia and foist
on various SubSections."

I assumed he was talking about Harriet. "So I've got a new
secretary," I said.

"Not at all," he said. His face violated the airspace between
my drowsy eyes and the ugly neon lights that flashed into and
out of my line of sight on the ceiling. He blessed me with a
smile and said, "I am discussing the Q level security review
they sent on Glenda. According to Virginia she is . . . she
was . . . as virtuous as Caesar's wife."

327

"Calpurnia slept around," I said.

The F. O.'s bright little face hove into view again and flashed a pink line of gum between teeth and upper lip; he wanted to let me know that he had caught the humor of it. He said, "If only they hadn't pulled the tail off of Jakaz. That was their mistake, getting out from underfoot and assuming that she would keep tabs on your progress once they released you from Nyiregyháza."

"It was more than that," I said. "They could have double-teamed him and triple-teamed me and I still would have been suspicious." A half dozen neon tubes passed above before I spoke again. "It was more than that. It was Glenda. She tipped it that first night at The Point."

"Ahh," the F. O. said as we turned a corner in the gleaming white hall. He sounded like he was having his throat examined.

"I'm not the sort that women chase. I mean, let's face it . . . I'm not the sort who's often recognized—even by women who've known me."

"I assume you mean that in the biblical sense," he said.

"Ha ha," I said. We were in the elevator now; one of those tremendous hospital jobs in which you could get up a handball game. "That night I got to know enough about her . . ."

"Ahem," said the F. O.

"Besides in the biblical sense," I said. "I learned enough about her to realize she'd been whipped by life. Glenda was as bitter as grappa wine; she remembered all the sour parts of growing up, but little of the good."

The elevator doors opened and I was wheeled out.

"That's the worst sort to hire, of course," he said. "They are easily turned. No, this business calls for a more pliable and complaisant type."

I said, "Like yourself, I assume."

The F. O. said, "I said 'complaisant,' not 'complacent.'"

328

He dropped back while the two orderlies negotiated a complex bend in the hall. When he caught up he said, "She had one odd and very blank spot in the clearance review—a six-month vacation in Helsinki; time enough to be recruited and sent to school in Archangel."

"One thing they neglected to teach her," I said. "Don't get greedy." I touched the bandages on my face and wondered if there would be a scar. "Only four people knew about our raid on the Routenfield lodge in Mammoth. It had to be one of the four who tipped Nevigelykh so he could pick up the Jakaz on the way out."

"I'm flattered that you suspected neither Basset nor me," the F. O. said. We were quiet for a moment. Then he said, "Yes. Yes, she was greedy to a fault."

As a topic of conversation Glenda was wearing thin. "About Harriet, now," I said. "When do I get my new secretary; the one with the large breasts?"

"Ahh," the F. O. said again. Then he said, "Umm." I understood him all too well. He said, "You see . . ." and let it trail off.

"So much for that," I said as they wheeled me into my windowless room. As gentle as they tried to be, sweat broke out on my forehead when they lifted me from the stretcher and settled me between the sheets of my bed. "I've just figured it out," I said to the white-jacketed orderlies. They both looked at me with patient eyes. They were used to postoperatives' nonsense talk. "Hospitals have ugly light fixtures because the doctors never get wheeled around flat on their backs."

"Yes sir," they said in counterpoint with each other and left me alone with the F. O.

"In the last twenty-four hours or so, we've collected a surprising number of people," he said. "The sisters Kovács have been very useful—very informative. It's scattered to be sure,

329

but we've cracked a number of AVH and KGB cells here and in the East European sphere."

"Congratulations," I said.

"I've even considered your mad killer."

"He's not mine," I said. "We've never been introduced."

Wandering around the room, the F. O. found a large spot of dust on the doorjamb molding and an unsanitary wad of chewing gum beneath the visitors' chair. "I've considered tracking the man down," he said.

I said, "Why bother?"

"Unlike you, I enjoy my work."

"Yes. You want to find out everything about everybody."

He asked, "Is that unreasonable?" and I couldn't answer.

We watched each other with the kind of dull-witted wariness that hospital patients share with hospital visitors. An artery throbbed in my shattered knee and I said, "How's Beebee? Did they save his leg?"

The F. O. shook his head and ran a finger across one thigh. "Prosthetic," he said. "We're paying for the artificial leg and keeping him around for a time. There might be some use for him."

"I thought he was promised to the British Embassy."

He smiled again. "All the more reason he'll be happy to work for us."

"Did I ever tell you I like your style?" I asked. "You'll use everyone around you to achieve your goals."

"Certainly," the F. O. said. "Haven't you?"

Again I couldn't answer. After all, there was Mary Louise. "How's Mary Louise?" I asked.

"Here at St. Mallard's," the F. O. said as though I'd asked him where she was. "Down in the neuropsych wing, purging her memory of the personnel files."

"I know. How is she?"

The F. O. said, "Doing nicely," but didn't look at me as he

330

spoke. Without a window the room had no view, so he focused on a large, funereal spray of get-well flowers that Basset, Weaver and Harriet had sent.

I asked, "How's Mary Louise?" again as though he hadn't answered.

"I told you, doing . . ."

"You smell," I said. "I'm down wind of you, so stop shoveling that stuff. How's Mary Louise?"

The F. O. lifted the cigar case from that secret pocket of his and opened it. He offered me a Tony and Cleo and I accepted. It was impossible to light the thing properly with only one hand so I jammed it in my teeth and set fire to it with the match he held in his neatly manicured fingers.

"She's doing very well," the F. O. said. "A bit hysterical, still, but very well indeed, considering . . ." He warmed his own cigar to life then puffed gingerly on it as though it might be loaded with *plastique*. "I've got something for you." He handed me a plain white envelope that had MARY LOUISE scrawled across the front in my semilegible hand.

I took the envelope from him and turned it over. It looked simon pure, but the F. O. could easily have had it opened and resealed without a hint that it had been raped. After all, that was our business—prying into things.

"One of these days I'm going to kick you in the ass," I said. "You or Basset. I asked him to deliver this to Mary Louise . . . not to you."

"He did," the F. O. said. Then he did something that surprised me: He reached out and patted my shoulder as though trying to comfort me.

"I see," I said. With a casual motion I dropped the envelope into my bedside wastebasket. I began counting the holes in the acoustical tile overhead.

"Basset said she . . . she mentioned something about you and Jakaz being in the same . . . umm . . . business; that

331

sort of thing. He said she was not overjoyed by the thought."
He tried to smile but it was as phony as a religious relic in
Tijuana. "She'll come around, I'm sure she will. It's the de-
conditioning that they're putting her through. That is enough
to rattle even the most stoic of us."

"Yeah," I said. "Sure. Now tell me the good news." I tipped
some cigar ash into a water pitcher; there were no ashtrays. I
supposed they didn't want postoperatives to smoke.

The F. O. pulled at his nose. Good news was like British
coins to him; confusing and alien. He seldom traded in the
stuff and it took a few moments before he could think of any.
"Ah, yes," he said finally. "Petropavlovsk Kamchatski!"

"Is a port on the Kamchatka peninsula famous for its trawler
and whaling fleets," I said. "Also for its electronic maintenance
and repair factory since, as the world knows, Russian trawler-
men are inordinately fond of their little transistor radios.
Among other things," I added.

"Yes," the F. O. said. "Among other things." He shaved a
bit of cigar ash into my flowers. "They are holding a warrant
for Lieutenant Colonel Yurosha Nevigelykh's detention at the
port master's office in Petropavlovsk-Kamchatski." He smiled.
"I thought you'd like to know."

"I'm not all that vindictive," I said and the F. O. spent five
minutes telling me exactly how vindictive I was.

"We've got the funding," he said when he ran out of adjec-
tives and expletives. "NoWest SubSection has been merged
with Great Plains, but SoCal remains as autonomous as it has
ever been."

Which was pretty damn autonomous, the way the F. O.
ran it.

"I even managed to ring Virginia's cash register in your be-
half," he said.

I held out a shaking hand, palm facing heavenward, and
said, "I'll believe it when I see it, right there."

"You mistake my meaning. It is one of your irritating habits, though I'm sure it makes you feel a bit more individual." The F. O. snaked a chair around with his foot. When he sat he was neither taller nor shorter than when he was standing. "I've gotten funding for you to open an Affairs Desk at that Mulholland house of yours. You are the first to know, and don't you dare tell Basset until I've negotiated the purchase of the house. There is still the matter of his kickbacks on our lease payments. I do not intend to buy the place, only to learn that the firm of Basset & Father-in-Law was the seller."

Peering at the F. O. through drowsy eyes I said, "So we have the money. How did you get so much? Have you already turned Jakaz?"

"One might raise Lazarus, but Gyula Jakaz will never be turned." Stuffing the Tony in his face and lifting one of the flowers from my get-well spray he began dismembering the flower one petal at a time and inspecting each petal as though it might be guarding secrets from him. Intent on his work he said, "Your performance of last night was a show stopper. Not only did you break Yurosha Nevigelykh—you put Gyula Jakaz into a paralytic and apoplectic coma: The man had a massive stroke."

"The Group of Ten goes operational, then," I said. "Without Jakaz we can't control them." I fought to keep my eyelids up. "Will they be a pain in the butt?"

"Crudely put," the F. O. said, "but true. Yes, I imagine they'll pose a problem. It's a shame we can't simply eliminate the entire group." He gathered his brows in a sad line that peaked above his nose. "Unfortunately we're not in that business."

My eyelids were growing heavy, verrrry heavvvvvy as the hypnotists say. The F. O.'s features swam in a bouillabaisse of flowers and neon fixtures and perforated acoustical tile.

He said, "About your car; I have some favors due from

333

I-AMp. The Bentley will be better than new when you get out of here."

"No," I said. "Sell it. Scrap it. Get rid of it."

"You say that now," the F. O. said. "Once you've seen it . . ."

"I don't even want to see the pink slip," I said. "Have someone in Documents forge my name on the pink and get the hell rid of it. That car is . . . that car is . . ." But I never told him what the car was. I drifted into a fat marshmallow of sleep in which I watched a bell-bottomed leg, with a deck shoe attached, jutting between the running board and right-hand door of a nineteen thirty-two Mann Egerton 3.5 Bentley Sport Saloon. It was uncomfortable to watch because leg, shoe, Bentley and all were arcing in a graceless back half gainer over the edge of the palisade.

They tell me I cried in my sleep.

55

Flight 483 touched down at MIA like a pregnant swan. It lurched to the international terminal where most of its sun-tanned cargo would transfer to other airlines for stateside destinations.

When Sertashian entered the Customs lounge a human net of silent, somber-faced men crowded around him, graded him from the other passengers and fished him toward an unmarked door beyond the inspection area.

"What the hell is this?" he asked. They'd worked it beautifully, very professionally, without disturbing any of the other travelers. It had happened so quickly that his heart still pumped at its normal rate. "What d'ya want from me?" There was nothing they could nail him with. His baggage was clean; not a stick of contraband in it. So what did they want him for?

"In here please." The man spoke quietly. His voice oiled a passage through the open door.

Sertashian looked at the man, at the wall of unyielding bodies around him, and walked through the door. There didn't seem to be much choice.

The room was really something; windowless, totally unfurnished and paved with an unbelievably ugly pink-and-gray mottled linoleum. The door closed softly behind him—none of the others followed him in. He kept his face neutral as he studied the three guys who'd had him delivered to this bureaucratic purgatory.

The one in the wheelchair looked as though he'd barely lived through a car wreck. His left hand was in a cast, his left foot was propped almost parallel with his hip while his knee bulged like a melon. A fresh scar traveled vividly from the corner of his jaw to the wing of his nose.

Standing behind the wheelchair was a regular moose of a guy who presented Sertashian with a simpleminded leer.

It was the third man—the fat guy—who spoke first. "We're so delighted to meet you," he said. "Delighted indeed." The words whistled oddly through his mustache. Leaning heavily on his cane, the man limped toward him with a rolling, leg-snapping gait. He thrust out a plump hand and said, "How did you like Nassau? One hopes you tried the broiled sunfish at *Au Sel et Poivre*."

Without thinking he returned the other's handshake. "Okay, we're cordial," he said. "I'd like to see a lawyer."

The guy in the wheelchair peeled a cigar and roasted its tip with a kitchen match. Without looking up from the flame he said, "We have a proposal that should interest you, Mr. Hagopian."

Christ. Something started burning in his duodenum. Don't think, he thought. Breathe slow. "Sorry," he said. "The name's Sertashian." *You miserable bastards,* he added silently. "John Sertashian."

"Yes," the guy said and blew out his match with the word. "Sticks and stones may break your bones, but names will surely kill you." He puffed at the cigar. "We saw how you handled yourself as Hagopian. While you're working for us, your operational name is Hagopian." He picked a small piece of tobacco from his lip and studied it. He finally looked up and said, "Now, about the proposal. Ahn . . . there are eight bodies in a feisty little country just below and beside Yugoslavia . . ."

"Jesus, you're *kidding*," Sertashian blurted. "*Eight guys?*"

"My dear Hagopian," the fat one said, "for a man of your talent . . ." and let the words trail off.

"I'm not talking to you bastards. I want to see a lawyer."

The big one leered again and said, "What the hell, babe. I want to see a naked broad . . . but you're all we've got."

The guy in the wheelchair closed his eyes, slowly shook his head and began rubbing his eyebrows as though he was suffering from a case of terminal frustration.

GLOSSARY

AVH   *Államvédelmi Hatóság:* Hungarian State Security Office. By '53, Péter Gábor (who was to AVH what Lavrenti Beria was to the then *Ministerstvo Gosudarstvennoy Bezopasnosti* [MGB], the Soviet Ministry of State Security) had compiled files on nearly every adult in Hungary. It is not surprising that, although Péter was purged in '54, the earliest and most virulent attack of the '56 upheaval was against AVH headquarters.

Abwehrableitung   Third Reich espionage, counterespionage and sabotage service generally referred to as the *Abwehr* or simply *ABW.*

Bosque Mojado   (see Counterinsurgent Training)

C and D   Cloak and dagger.

Counterinsurgent Training   Officially we are not involved in guerrilla training of extra-nationals at bases like Bosque Mojado. Yet unofficially—if we don't help, who will?

DAAD   Defense Accounting and Auditing Division of the General Accounting Office (GAO). Whenever DAAD tries to audit the Agency, we rubber-stamp CONFIDENTIAL on our books. DAAD then assigns CONFIDENTIAL-cleared accountants to the job and we escalate to a CLASSIFIED stamp —and so forth up to Q. Beyond Q, of course, we cannot reveal the names of the higher secrecy levels that we stamp on the books unless DAAD's accountants have been cleared for those levels. And DAAD never knows what levels of clearance are required because they cannot be told the names. As frustrating as the game may be for DAAD, it is only slightly entertaining for us: We know in advance who will win. (See Q)

DDI   Deputy Director—Intelligence. Over the years, the agency's internal power has moved from the DDP (Deputy Director—Plans, who heads the dirty tricks [covert operations] end of the business) to the DDI, whose people sift and interpret facts.

As a result we spend a lot less time zapping spooks and a lot more time analyzing the political repercussions of say, the United Nations' experimental earwig abatement program in Costa Rica.

DIVERSION CHECK   Although we have the highest regard for law enforcement agencies (N.B. The Agency has nothing to do with law enforcement.), we never ask them for information because we do not necessarily believe that the interests of national security are served when *they* know about our projects. As a result we often run a diversion check, requesting information from one law enforcement agency in the name of another. Our wires to these agencies can be opened on short notice; we overhear the answer from the responding bureau or department. (The agencies involved, however, tend to become confused when they get answers to unasked questions.)

FBN   Federal Bureau of Narcotics and Dangerous Drugs.

"FACE"   A double agent, a Projects Officer posing as an agent, or a general fraud. The term is an abbreviation of "two-faced" and has an elastic definition within the business.

FT. MEADE, MARYLAND   Headquarters of the National Security Agency's National Cryptologic Command, the code making, code breaking and international electronic surveillance arm of our intelligence establishment. NSA employs 20,000 or so bodies at the NCC and has the largest, most complex computer system known to man.

I-AM$_p$ Inter-Agency Motor Pool.

KOS   *Kontra Obaveshtajne Sluzhba*, Yugoslav Counterintelligence Service.

M.I.5   U.K. Counterintelligence—the people who, among other things, blew the cover of every *Abwehrableitung* (q.v.) agent in Britain during the hot war. (See "TWENTY")

M.I.6   (See SIS)

M.I.8   U.K. Signals Intelligence Service. (M.I.8C is the cryptographic division of M.I.8—something like our own National Cryptologic Command at Ft. Meade, but with hardly a fiftieth of the computer hardware.)

NAGY, IMRE   The apolitical politician who led Hungary during its thirteen cathartic days; October 23 to November 5, 1956. Nagy confused our political analysts at the Agency by saying, "Every man must have a compass and mine is Russia," one day—and emptying the AVH prisons the next.

NODIS "No Distribution"—a new wrinkle developed by State. Documents marked "Eyes Only" are put into distribution patterns that have been know to include *The New York Times* editorial offices. "Nodis" papers escape even the F. O.'s eyes.

PETÖFI CIRCLE A literary group that punctuated its ideas on intellectual freedom with wine bottles full of gelatinous gasoline.

PSE To call the Psychological Stress Evaluator (PSE) a "lie detector" is like referring to the first moon walk as a "field trip." The thing is fully portable—custom-fitted in a Samsonite briefcase—and gives the lie to liars by analyzing inaudible, stress-related frequency modulations of the human voice.

PROTECTIVE QUARANTINE Since the Agency is not a law enforcement agency, and has no right to arrest or detain individuals, we sometimes quarantine subjects for their own benefit.

Q A level of secrecy, of which there are five (that I can name). From least to most sensitive they are: 1, Confidential; 2, Classified; 3, Secret; 4, Top Secret; 5, Q. (There are three higher levels of secrecy that I know of, but I cannot name them for you since you must be *cleared to those levels before you can hear the words that identify them.* Most work at these upper three levels is done within sealed vaults [often within a sealed vault *within* a sealed vault] within sealed buildings that are in Q clearance compounds that are inside of Top Secret compounds.)

RÁKOSI, MÁTYÁS Hungary's Stalinesque head of state from 1949 to 1956. Shortly after Khrushchev's "cult of personality" chat in February of '56, Rákosi was called to Moscow for a scolding from the First Secretary. On his return to Budapest he said, "That idiot in the Kremlin will be purged before I will." He was wrong.

RANKOVIĆ, ALEKSANDAR Former head of KOS (q.v.) and UBDA (Yugoslav State Security Police). Ranković was "retired" in 1966 at a party plenum and has lived since then in a villa near Dubrovnik on the Adriatic.

SIS   U.K. Secret Intelligence Service, though the F. O., like a lot of old-timers in the business, still referred to it by its wartime designation: M.I.$_6$.

St. Mallard's   A not-quite-affectionate term for the nameless, private hospital that the Agency maintains at its old training center near Monterey. The slur derives from a value judgment of the quacks who practice there.

Secrecy   (See DAAD, Nodis and Q)

Title 19   Authorization to investigate bank accounts and safe deposit boxes without approval or knowledge of the account holder. Any bank employee who informs the depositor of such investigation is subject to no more than three years in prison or $10,000 fine or both.

"Twenty"   The Roman numeral for twenty is XX—the Double Cross System created by Section B.$_1$A of M.I.$_5$. (See Abwehrableitung and M.I.$_5$)

Ustachi   Croat terrorist group. Ustachi sided with the Nazis during the hot war—are currently willing to form alliances with any anti-Tito group that will have them.

Z–2   Affectionate term for Ministry of Internal Security, Poland. (There are other, less affectionate terms for the Ministry. Few of them are printable.)

My genuine thanks to the following people for their editorial and research assistance:

Mr. Michael Korda, Editor-in-Chief, Simon and Schuster, for discovering me in the woods

Mrs. Phyllis Grann, Senior Editor, Simon and Schuster, for holding my hand and leading me out of the woods

Dr. H. Stanley Cowell, Chief of Medicine, Glendale Community Hospital

Mr. H. Kyle Given III, Administrative Editor, *Motor Trend* Magazine

Mr. Allan D. Bell, Jr., President, Dektor Counterintelligence and Security, Inc.

Mssrs. George and James Barnes, Principals, Barnes Investigation Agency

Mr. Joe O'Connor, Principal, Brass Rail Gun Shop

Mr. Jerry Pierce, Finance Counselor

Mr. ———*, Field Officer, SoCal SubSection

Mr. Branko Wohlfahrt, Master Gunsmith

Mr. Ben Hartman, Linguist

* Edited, *F. O. SoCal SubSection*